CHANGE FOR THE BETTER

CHANGE FOR THE BETTER

MENOPAUSAL SUPERHEROES - BOOK 5

SAMANTHA BRYANT

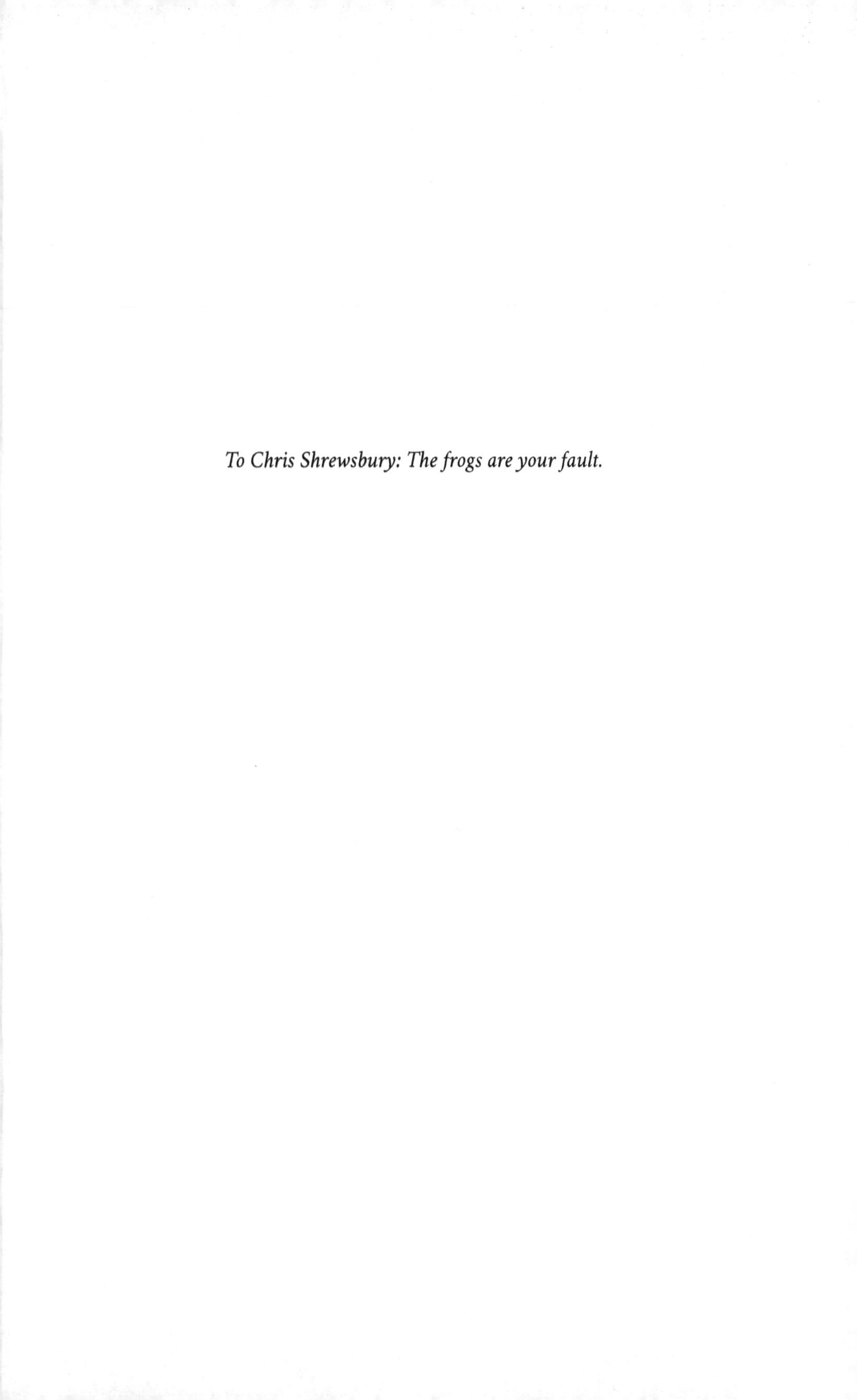

To Chris Shrewsbury: The frogs are your fault.

TUESDAY

NEVER TAKE A LIZARD TO A FROG ORGY

Patricia put her claws on her hips and glared out at the pond. "Oh look, a frog orgy."

Leonel gasped, glancing back at the grounds crew to make sure none of them had heard. "Patricia!"

Patricia couldn't roll her eyes when she was transformed into her Lizard Woman form, so she settled for blinking them sideways, a move that always made Leonel shudder. Bad enough they'd been sent out to the countryside to deal with a strange disturbance. Worse, she'd been partnered with Leonel when she was in no mood to put up with his prudery.

That the disturbance was a preponderance of frogs made the situation even more ridiculous. What did the Unusual Cases Unit expect a bullet-proof lizard woman and Springfield's strongest citizen to do about this? They should have called Animal Control instead or left it to the science geeks. Where was a good terrorist threat at City Hall when you needed one?

Ignoring Leonel's approbation, Patricia squatted and stared more closely at the frolicking amphibians. There was a desperation to their endeavors, but as far as she knew, that was usual for frogs during the last hurrah of mating season. The extra appendages, though? Definitely not ordinary.

Grabbing a stick near the bank of the pond, she reached into the algae-thick muck, lifted one of the little critters out, and ferried it to shore. The frog—or maybe it was a toad, Patricia never learned the difference—clung to the stick, one long leg dangling toward the water. When she set the stick down, the frog remained lodged on it, the entire creature expanding and contracting as if breathing were a full body effort.

With all the stealth of a drunken moose, Leonel made his way to her side and squatted beside her. Surprisingly, the frog didn't flee. Maybe it could tell that Leonel, for all his bulk, was a huge bleeding heart. For a long moment, the two heroes stared at the offending amphibian.

It was a regular-sized frog. Patricia could have held it in her human-sized hand without difficulty. Not that she would. Despite her own affinity for reptiles and amphibians since her transformation into the Lizard Woman, she bore them no affection. Like small children and couples who baby talk one another in public, Patricia simply did not see the appeal. Slimy little bug-eyed creatures that leapt higher than they had any right to. Disgusting.

She twirled the collection net in her hand. "Are they supposed to be that color?" she asked Leonel. Leonel had kids and grandkids. He'd probably dealt with frogs before. Kids liked gross things.

Leonel peered down, then sighed and pulled a pair of glasses out of a side pocket in his costume and slipped them on over his sun-shaped mask. Leonel appeared younger and more virile since his acquisition of super strength, and the gender changes that came with it, but his middle-aged eyesight remained unchanged. Even with the glasses on, he still squinted. Patricia reminded herself to give him the number of the office that did her LASIK surgery.

After taking a good, long look at the frog, Leonel finally answered. "Yeah, they're usually kind of mud and grass colored like this. Helps them hide in the shallows." Leonel tilted the stick, eliciting an angry little croak from the frog. "But, they do not generally have so many legs." He rotated the stick so they could see the back end of the frog, where the stub of a triangular, alligator-like tail protruded. "Nor tails."

The frog must have tired of their investigation, because at that point, it leapt off the stick and made a break for the pond. Patricia dropped her collection net over it, waylaying the creature's escape to the murky waters. After a couple of feeble jumps, it accepted its fate and crouched in the mud, glaring with yellow-eyed malevolence.

Standing, she scanned the pond for any signs of danger. It wasn't large, maybe twenty feet or so across, roughly circular in shape. Not particularly scenic, unless you liked mud and weeds. It looked natural, rather than man-made. Tall grasses grew around the edges, and while a light greenish scum collected near the banks where the water was more stagnant, the center water remained clear and reflected the bright sunlight overhead. The shore writhed with hundreds of frogs crawling over each other.

An Indiana girl by birth, Patricia had spent time beside a pond before, usually with high school friends and an illicit collection of alcohol cadged from the refrigerators and liquor cabinets of their parents. Hardly a naturalist by inclination, she did know that frogs could be noisy during spawning. The sound here was unnerving in its volume and intensity, somewhere between highway buzz and a helicopter landing. Surely, that wasn't normal.

She was starting to glean why the UCU had been called in. This was definitely an "unusual case." Though she still had questions for Sally Ann about the duty assignment. Surely the science geeks could have handled this?

Patricia considered the unhappy thought that she'd drawn this particular short straw as punishment for disobeying orders at the nightclub shootout last weekend. She didn't know what Sally Ann's problem was—they'd captured the group, and no one had gotten shot. Well, no one except Patricia. But Patricia was bulletproof, so it didn't count. She could only hope that Sally Ann would be satisfied with one boring, muddy mission to make her point.

Leonel remained squatting next to the frog Patricia had netted. He gestured for Patricia to join him, and she complied, knees creaking as she settled into a wide squat on her taloned feet.

"There's something weird about its tongue too." Leonel pointed at the offending appendage.

Patricia wrinkled her nose. To think, she could be out to dinner with Suzie and her parents right now, instead of squatting in the mud examining frogs with Leonel. As if in answer, an image of Suzie's sour-faced mother popped into Patricia's mind and she shuddered. That woman always looked like she smelled something terrible when she looked at Patricia.

On second thought, getting this call had been the better part of the deal. She could skip this round of passive aggressive comments and barely disguised age insults and stay on Suzie's good side, since missing dinner hadn't been her idea. Mud washed off more easily than vitriol.

She refocused her attention on the captured frog and waited. It took a little while, staring into the bulging yellow eyes, but finally, the creature's long pink tongue shot out, making short work of an insect trapped with it in the netting.

Patricia snorted. "I thought I was the city mouse between us, Leonel. That's how their tongues work."

"Wait," he said.

It didn't take long. The frog's mouth opened and his fat pink tongue protruded between its slimy lips, resting there, ready for more insects. As the two heroes watched, a blue pulse ran through the flesh, illuminating the frog from within. Something sparked, arcing in front of its face.

"Damn." She frowned at Leonel. "Did you get some footage for the lab nerds?"

Leonel nodded. "Weird, right?"

Patricia shrugged, affecting boredom, though internally she, too, found the whole thing eerie and strange. "What's weird to us these days? I say it's just another day that ends in 'Y'."

Leonel pulled out one of the specimen containers and shook the frog into it. The creature didn't resist much. "We should gather a few more and check out the surrounding area. Make sure it's safe for the lab guys."

Patricia tried to follow her colleague but found resistance. She had sunk to the ankles in soft, gooey mud. As she freed herself, grimacing at the nasty thickness between her talons, she heard Leonel cry out but didn't look up. "What is it?" she asked.

Feet freed, she stepped onto more solid turf up the bank a bit and turned around. She was alone. No sign of Leonel where he'd been standing seconds before. Just a specimen container laying on its side in the muck, beside the equipment bag.

"Fuerte?" she called out, remembering to use his code name in case they weren't as alone as she'd thought. Patricia didn't bother with the whole codename thing for herself. Privacy was an illusion in the first place. But then, she didn't have children to protect.

The only response was a fresh surge of frog noise, the already-loud chirping and grunting, now becoming a cacophony of clicks and gurgles, coalescing into one flow, as if a single gigantic frog sang out with one disturbingly throaty voice. Reflexively, Patricia thickened her scales, armor-plating rising on her head and shoulders.

A splash drew her attention toward the water, where Leonel stood thigh deep, grabbing at his chest and biceps, flinging frog after frog to the side, doing his best not to hurt the creatures. For each frog he flung, eight more leapt from the water and he staggered around making ridiculous squeaking noises of distress. He must have waded out to bag another specimen and gotten overrun with aggressive green jumpers.

Before Patricia could decide whether she ought to laugh at her friend or help him, Leonel stumbled over something unseen beneath the surface of the pond, fell backward, and disappeared from view.

Cursing, Patricia flung the supply bag further up the bank, then trudged into the water, moving as fast as her bulk and the sludge in the pond bottom would allow. Frogs vaulted into the air shrieking amphibian outrage, but they bounced off her scales ineffectually, sliding back into the pond. A few unluckier creatures impaled themselves on her spikes. Patricia barely noticed them, concentrating instead on locating Leonel in the water.

The pond was deeper than it appeared from the shore, and Patricia was standing in chest-high water by the time she reached the spot where she'd last seen Fuerte. With a clenched jaw, she took a deep breath and dropped beneath the dank water. Leonel owed her big time for this one.

Beneath the surface, the pond was teeming with blue streaks of frogs and black and green flickers of fish. Patricia gave in to her reptilian nature and her vision changed, revealing all in infrared heat signatures. *There!* A Leonel-shaped red blob lay a couple of feet ahead of her, surrounded by small yellow and green blobs darting around with incredible speed.

She lunged, grasping for him, and wrapped her claw around a muscular calf. Tugging him toward her, she found an arm. Unceremoniously, she spun, pulling Fuerte free. Twirling around, she stood, bringing both of them out of the water. After retracting some of her spikes, she flung him over her shoulder, his head dangling down her back and trudged back to shore. Behind her, the water roiled and she felt the impacts as frogs hurled themselves at her again and again.

She ignored them, worried by Leonel's stillness. Had he sucked in pond water when he slipped? Or hit his head?

When the two were almost back to shore, the man began coughing and gagging. Patricia breathed out a sigh of relief, even while she tried not to think about him vomiting pond sludge down her back.

Back on dry land, she carried Leonel some distance up the bank before laying him down under a tree. He immediately rolled onto all fours and threw up.

Patricia looked away from his misery, her gaze taking in the innocuous-seeming pond, the surface now undisturbed and the frog song reduced to the chirping croaks one might hear on any sunny day. If she didn't know better, she'd think there was nothing wrong.

When Leonel finished gagging, Patricia turned her attention back to her companion. Even soaking wet and sick, the man was disgustingly handsome. It was one of the most annoying things about him. Mud slick hair clung to well-shaped cheekbones and called attention to Leonel's lantern jaw with the perfect amount of five o'clock shadow. No wonder so many fans called his name when they made public appearances.

Patricia glanced down at herself. Lizard Woman or not, she knew she resembled a drowned cat more than an apex predator after her foray into the pond. And before that, she'd looked like something out of a nightmare.

"You all right?" she asked, voice raspy as it always became when she was fully transformed.

Leonel wiped his mouth with the back of his hand, a move which only succeeded in smearing the mud and pond scum into a new pattern on his golden-brown skin. He fell back onto his butt, leaning against the tree. Whatever he mumbled was in Spanish, but Patricia didn't need the words to understand that he was upset. She would be too.

Patricia searched for the supply bag she had tossed out of the way, found it entangled in a bush, pulled it free, and transformed one of her arms to its pale and freckled human form so she could operate the zipper. Back at Leonel's side, she tossed him a white towel, which he turned greenish-brown by rubbing it over his face, hands, and head. She handed him a water bottle, and he rinsed and spat three times before taking a long swallow.

Patricia attempted a little levity. "So, do I get to tell Suzie that the mighty Fuerte was taken down by an army of frogs?"

He didn't laugh. He grimaced, tight-jawed and squinty eyed. "I slipped and sucked in half the pond," he said between coughs, already defensive. He glared at Patricia. "And those weren't ordinary frogs."

Patricia sighed, hearing the teary note in Leonel's voice that meant she had hurt his feelings once again. The man was so damned sensitive sometimes.

She softened her tone. "Of course they weren't." She held out her hand, the one she'd transformed to human shape, and when Leonel grasped it, tugged him to his feet.

He grunted. *"Dios mío,* but that was disgusting." He pulled at his clothes, holding the sodden material gingerly with his fingers.

"Come on, pretty boy." Patricia gestured at the frogs skewered on the spikes on her shoulders. "We should bag these up and take them to the lab boys and pick up that live sample you jarred."

He spit again, rubbing his ears with the remaining clean corner of the towel. "Better call it in too. Parks and Rec needs to close access to the pond, maybe the whole park."

Patricia pulled the phone out of the supply bag. "Which park is this again?"

Leonel gaped at her. "Weren't you listening during the briefing?"

Patricia growled, and Leonel spread his hands. "All right, it's Old Homestead Park."

Patricia held the phone without dialing it. "Wait. Old Homestead?"

Leonel was dumping the water over his face, still trying to clean the mud from his ears.

Pointing at the rooftops visible through the trees on the far side of the pond, Patricia said, "So, that's your neighborhood over there, right?"

Looking annoyed, Leonel squinted at her. "And?"

Patricia didn't speak, just stared at Leonel for a long, quiet moment until realization dawned on his face.

"Dr. Liu." The two words were a curse in his mouth. Patricia knew how he felt. Of course. It had to be her.

HOME IS WHERE LEONEL'S HEART IS

Leonel tried to slip into the house, but the door thudded in its frame. He must have pushed it too hard again. Ever since the weird spike in his powers last year, he had to be more careful about his strength.

The emerald shard he now wore helped—he'd stopped breaking everything he touched—but he still overdid it occasionally in the day-to-day things. He was grateful to Walter for the discovery that carrying a bit of irradiated emerald helped him keep control.

At the sound of the thud, his husband David came out of the bedroom, rubbing sleep from his eyes. "I didn't think you were coming home for lunch today, *mi amor*. Do you want—" He stopped short, taking in the sight of Leonel, dripping with mud. "*Qué pasó?*"

Pulling off his boots and dropping them on the mat, Leonel frowned. "I'll tell you later. Can you get me a couple of towels? I'm ruining the floor."

David obeyed, running off into the hall. Leonel peeled his slimy shirt over his head, dropped it next to the boots, then began working on the pants. The snap at the waist was slick, and he almost ripped the fabric trying to undo the fastening. He forced himself to slow down, blowing out a long, slow, calming breath that shook a little.

Why was he so upset? It was just mud.

David returned with the towels, and Leonel gave him a grateful smile, rubbing one over his head and down his chest. "*Ay, guácala.*" He grimaced at the brown smear on the pink towel. That would leave a stain if he didn't get it in the laundry soon. "*Lo siento*," he apologized. "I'll clean this up after I clean myself up."

David wrinkled his nose. "What did you get into? You smell terrible."

"I ended up at the bottom of the pond at Old Homestead." Leonel shuddered again, finally succeeding in shedding his pants and adding them to the pile on the rug. He used the other towel to wipe down his feet and legs, hoping to minimize the amount of mud he tracked from there to the bathroom.

Maybe he should have gone to the office to clean up instead, so someone else would have the responsibility of washing the towels and mopping the floor. If he were honest with himself, though, Leonel was too embarrassed to face his colleagues looking such a mess. He hoped that Patricia would be kind and not use his clumsiness as an amusing story. He dreaded the idea of showing up for the debriefing, only to find a room full of smirking faces and sarcastic jokes.

The shower felt amazing. There was nothing like washing off grime to make a person feel brand new. David remodeled the bathroom after Leonel's transformation, setting a second shower head higher up so Leonel could let the water flow over his entire body without having to duck. They'd splurged on an expensive setup that amplified the water pressure, enjoying the fruits of Leonel's hefty new paycheck. Hero work was dangerous, but it paid well. It tripled their family income.

Leonel lingered in the luxurious new shower until he emptied the water heater, reluctantly turning it off when the temperature dropped from tepid to cold.

When he emerged from the bathroom, a billow of steam followed him out. He snagged his soft pink bathrobe from its hook outside the bath-room door and enveloped himself in its luxurious softness. The robe had been his Christmas gift from David, the last Christmas he'd been a woman. Luckily, the expansive robe still covered Leonel in his new body. He hugged himself, rubbing the soft material against his arms. It was the robe equivalent of a hug.

The matching slippers had been passed on to one of their daughters, too small for his feet after the change. Leonel slipped his feet into the new ones he'd received for his birthday. They weren't as attractive, with their manly blue plaid pattern, but they were cozy and Leonel wiggled his toes into the fleece lining.

He padded into the kitchen and found that David had left him a cup of tea on the table, a small saucer placed atop the mug to keep the contents warm. Uncovering it, he added a little milk and sugar and carried it with him to the window. He stood staring out at the backyard as he sipped.

The vista blurred before his eyes, and Leonel wiped his eyes on the generous lapels of the bathrobe. He needed to let it go. Anyone might have slipped on the muddy floor of the pond. It was just one of those dumb accidents that could happen to anyone. His brain knew that, even if his heart was unconvinced.

He told himself that if the same thing happened to Sally Ann, she would have come up laughing and told the story herself over drinks that evening. Why couldn't he let go of the hot waves of shame and embarrassment and shrug it off like she could?

Reaching above the window, he straightened a piece of art hanging there, a frame painting by the youngest of their grandchildren. In it, he'd painted himself kicking a soccer ball. In the corner, two figures watched him play, big smiles on their round faces. David, and himself, when he'd still been Abuela Linda.

Leonel could tell which blobby person was him because of the pink apron and the tray of cookies she was holding. A few years ago, he'd thought that would be his life forever. But how long had it been now since he'd stayed home and made cookies for Carlos? Working at the UCU seemed like a dream when the offer came, a chance to make a difference in the lives of thousands, to have a lasting effect on a larger world.

But looking back on what he'd accomplished so far, it didn't feel like much. He struggled with so much of his training, and the incident today wasn't the first time he'd ended up injured or in the way; causing problems instead of solving them. Could it be that he wasn't made for the hero business after all?

Lost in thought, Leonel didn't hear it when David re-entered the room, so he gasped in surprise when he felt himself embraced from behind. "Feeling better?" David asked.

Leonel turned around, wrapping his arms around his husband, grateful he was still there. When he'd signed on for better or for worse, when they'd both been young, foolish, and deeply in love, neither of them could have anticipated an unexpected gender change and a dangerous new career in the public eye. They'd had some rough patches, making this transition together, but their connection survived, even strengthened in some ways.

"What's the matter, *mi vida?*"

David was gazing searchingly into his face, and Leonel couldn't hold back the dam of frustrated doubt any longer. A sob escaped him. He fled to the living room and threw himself into the corner of the sofa, hiccupping and whimpering. Embarrassment spiraled until he was crying because he was angry with himself for crying.

When he was finally able to staunch the flow of tears, he found David sitting in the armchair, his dark brown eyes soft with such kindness and love that Leonel nearly fell into another wave of weeping. But he must have been cried out at last, because all that came out was a sigh.

David handed over the box of tissues and moved the wastebasket closer, then went into the kitchen. Leonel mopped his face and blew his nose several times, sucking in long slow breaths that grew a little less shaky on each exhalation. By the time David reappeared, holding a new cup of tea, Leonel was calm.

When the cup was empty, David took it and moved it to the end table, then seated himself in the other corner of the sofa and reached for Leonel's hand. David rubbed his thumb over Leonel's palm, the familiar roughness of his hands soothing. "It's been a long time since you had a good cry," David said.

"I guess so."

David laid a hand on Leonel's cheek. "Did it help?"

"Yes, I think it did."

"Do you want to tell me about it?"

Leonel considered. Once upon a time, he might have wanted that, but not now. It was enough that David was there. Rehashing the embarrassment would only get him started again.

"No. I don't think I do. Is that okay?"

"*Claro.* But I am here, if you change your mind."

"Are you working today?"

David shook his head.

Leonel picked up his phone and sent a text, then tossed the device back down onto the couch. "There. Now neither am I."

"*Cuna de lobos?*"

Brightening at the thought of an afternoon with his husband and his favorite telenovela, Leonel leaned over and kissed David with a loud smack. "Yes! You find the disks. I'll go make the popcorn."

FLYGIRL AND THE JUNIOR
LEAGUE

Across town, at the public library, a stalwart stone and marble edifice built during Andrew Carnegie's philanthropic fervor and one of the architectural gems of Springfield, Jessica Roark held court as Flygirl.

The "Breakfast with a Hero" event was hosted by the city's Junior League, an influential organization of women united by a desire to improve the community. The Springfield chapter attracted some of the richest and most impressive women who called the small Southern city home.

Jessica appreciated the flattering invitation. The women of the Junior League included more "tickets to opera" people than the "fist fight in the street" sorts, but then again, Flygirl's public image emphasized acrobatic feats over violence.

It would have been more surprising if they had invited Patricia. Jessica suppressed a giggle at the image of Patricia, fully transformed into the Lizard Woman, speaking to this crowd of businesswomen and professionals. Wouldn't they be surprised if they knew what kind of life she lived before working with the UCU. In fact, as a leading businesswoman of the city, she might have been invited to join if she played nicer with others.

Outfitted in her pale blue and white unitard, cowl firmly in place with its red-haired wig dangling beneath, Jessica felt out of place among all the coordinated suits and dresses. But she and the Junior League women had in common a passion for women's health, and she'd been pleased to speak about the importance of the Springfield Women's Hospital in the state.

The PR department approved Jessica's sharing of her own cancer survivor story, so long as she was careful to leave the details vague and not endanger all the work they'd put into keeping her identity secret. By the end of her talk, Flygirl had the entire room dabbing at their eyes.

"I wouldn't be here today if not for the care I received at Springfield Women's Hospital. I owe them my life. I couldn't be more pleased to help you raise funds to support this most worthy of causes."

Halfway through the sumptuous repast of Eggs Benedict, fresh strawberries somehow obtained in September, and a variety of tarts, pastries, and other sweets, the room went quiet. Jessica jerked to attention, heart racing in anticipation of a fight, until she saw everyone was focused on a slender woman dressed all in white, crossing the long hall tailed by two men in black suits.

Mrs. Cafry, the First Lady of the state.

As the woman approached, Flygirl stood, prompting Mrs. Cafry to speak, her honeyed drawl disarming. "Oh, please don't let me interrupt your meal. I couldn't pass up the opportunity to see you again in person and thank you once more for saving my life."

The president of the Junior League vacated the place of honor at Jessica's right hand, and Mrs. Cafry arranged herself in the chair with grace and dignity, ignoring the murmur of conversation welling up around them. Flygirl sat back down, accepting another cup of coffee from the waiter who hurried up with a new cup for the First Lady.

She might need the extra caffeine. The controversial Unusual Cases Unit needed political alliances on both sides of the aisle—conservatives and liberals alike. She'd need to be warm enough, but not too warm, or it would look like the UCU was taking sides. The Director would not be pleased. She guessed the governor's wife's presence had not been prearranged, or her team would have warned her.

The two women sat in silence for a moment and the event photographer took a few discreet shots, then backed off to a respectful distance. Jessica was the first to breach the quiet. "I'm so glad to see you looking so well, Mrs. Cafry."

"Francine, please."

Flygirl smiled beneath her cowl. "All right, Francine. We'll have to stick with 'Flygirl' for me please. My first name is a state secret, you know."

Mrs. Cafry's smile revealed the deep lines in her face. She was still much thinner than was healthy for a woman of her height and frame. But she managed to attend this event and walk in under her own power.

Jessica remembered well how weak and depleted chemo and her surgery left her during her own battle with ovarian cancer, not to mention the hormonal impact and the emotional toll. Mrs. Cafry's presence here so soon after her experimental treatment spoke volumes for its efficacy.

"Did Flygirl tell you the dramatic story of my rescue?" Mrs. Cafry asked the group, her eyes shining.

A flutter of denials twittered across the group, and Jessica could feel the focus of the room shift, all ears now tuned in to this moment. Mrs. Cafry turned to the gathered women and recounted the story of Evelyn Mueller, the woman who tried to take her hostage in order to force the hospital to try an experimental cancer treatment on her wife.

The effusiveness of her praise had Flygirl blushing under her mask. To deflect a little of the attention, she spoke up. "And it was only coincidence Fuerte and I were at the hospital that day, as one of our stops on our Good Will Tour."

At the mention of Fuerte, a gurgle of appreciative sighs swept across the table. Jessica suppressed a smile. Leonel was certainly a heartthrob, and his kind heart only made him more attractive to those lucky enough to know him in person.

Confined to her bed, Mrs. Cafry didn't see Fuerte's work that day, but he had been instrumental in evacuating the building and saved hundreds of lives by keeping the structure standing through sheer physical strength. Cell phone footage racked up millions of views on social media. Flygirl gave a glowing report, making certain her colleague received his fair share of the acclaim.

When it was time to go, the library director came in to thank Flygirl for attending and shared that they'd blown their fundraising goals through the roof. "Speaking of which…" The woman gestured toward the domed ceiling, where an escaped bouquet of balloons roosted. "Any chance you could help us out, Flygirl?"

With unnecessary flourish, Jessica spun into the air and zoomed to the dome, gathering up the balloons and delivering them to the librarian with a deep bow, all captured by the gleeful event photographer. "Easiest rescue of the day," Flygirl said as the room erupted in applause.

Jessica stood shaking hands and taking pictures for twenty more minutes, until at last the room was quiet and empty. She flew back to her seat to down the last of her glass of water and found a beautiful mono-grammed envelope sitting in her place.

She broke the seal and pulled out scented paper of the palest pink. A spidery script invited her to come by the governor's mansion on Friday for a private discussion. It seemed innocent enough, but trepidation raised the hairs on the back of her neck, prickling under the wig. She tucked the letter into the bag she'd brought with her, and after thanking the librarians one more time for hosting her, she vaulted out the front door and into the sky, making a show of her exit.

TIME FOR LOVE, AGENT ROGERS

Agent Sally Ann Rogers rested on her side, head dangling off the edge of the mattress. One leg lay across Darrin's torso and he gripped her calf with his still-sticky fingers, kneading the muscles with his long, strong fingers.

"Is there any part of you that isn't toned?" he asked.

She drew her leg back, fluidly spinning her body around to plant a kiss where his ear met his neck. She hopped to the floor, bare feet gripping the rug, and flexed for a moment before winking at her reporter-boyfriend over her shoulder. "I could say the same of you."

Leaving him on the bed, she made her way to the bathroom and turned on the shower. She eyed the bottles on the shelves, all scented with manly themes like cedar, sea salt, and bourbon. She picked one up and sniffed it. Lovely. No wonder he always smelled so good. She turned the bottle around to check the brand name and nearly dropped it when she read the price sticker. *Damn.* He'd better smell good for that kind of money.

Sally Ann could afford good bath products herself these days, but she kept the frugal habits of her days on the police force. As she stepped into the luxurious shower in Darrin's bathroom, sighing with pleasure as she shifted the strength of the stream to further soften her already relaxed muscles, she thought it might be time to upgrade.

After her shower, Sally Ann treated herself to some of the thick body butter in a jar by the sink. There was something to be said for dating a man who took care of himself. With products like these, no wonder his skin shone like it did, dark and vibrant. No ashy elbows on this guy.

Some might call Darrin vain, but he was a television reporter, so looking good was part of the game, just like staying fit and strong was part of hers. Sally Ann wasn't about to complain, even if he was unnervingly good-looking.

Back in her training clothes, body-hugging black pants and a lightweight yellow tank top, she made her way to the kitchen. They'd spent most of her lunch break enjoying other kinds of nourishment, so Sally Ann would have to hurry if she was going to eat at all. She stepped through the doorway with her usual hurried goodbye ready on her lips, and stopped short.

The kitchen smelled amazing. Darrin stood in the middle, naked except for a pair of bright blue boxer-briefs that fit him well enough to make Sally Ann want to take them back off him. But sexier than that, the man was lifting a beautiful panini sandwich off the grill. She watched in silence as he wrapped it in parchment paper and slid it into a brown paper bag.

He bowed as he handed it to her. "Will Mademoiselle need a bottle of water with her luncheon?"

Sally Ann reopened the bag to stick her nose inside and savor the scent.

Darrin slipped a bottle of water into her hand and laid his forehead against hers. "You'd better go, or we'll both get fired."

Sally Ann was still grinning when she took off her helmet back in the parking garage, her Harley secured in its usual spot. She stepped into the elevator and pulled out the sandwich, tearing the paper and stuffing it into her mouth, warm and delicious. She groaned with pleasure as a hand shoved itself between the doors, stopping them from closing.

Jessica Roark stepped in, already laughing. "Um, should I leave you alone with your sandwich?"

Sally Ann smiled around her food. Jessica had been standoffish lately, and it was nice to be teased by her again. She wasn't sure what the tension might be between them, or if maybe Jessica was upset about something else altogether and she hadn't been able to figure out how to broach it.

Sally Ann joined the Department for the action, but her work involved as much touchy-feely shit as punching and leaping. She wasn't quite comfortable with it yet.

Opting to continue the banter, she said, "No time for lunch during my lunch break today."

Jessica's bright blue eyes opened wider. "That good, huh?"

Sally Ann took another bite and moaned with pleasure. "Oh yeah," she said, her mouth still full. "He made the food too." She held it up for Jessica to admire. Bacon and turkey, with mayonnaise and dijon mustard, some kind of fancy cheese, and thin slices of tart apple. She thought it might be the best sandwich she'd ever eaten.

Jessica's lips folded in amusement. "A keeper?"

"Maybe." Sally Ann tried to sound neutral, but her heart made a weird little flip in her chest at the thought. She'd never made room for romance in her life. Sure, she'd had the occasional fling, but that had been about physical need rather than emotional connection. She wasn't sure how she felt about the shift.

As the two colleagues rode the three floors to the main floor of the Department, housed beneath the bank covering the underground facility, they fell silent. Sally Ann poked at her feelings for Darrin, trying to figure out what she wanted.

Darrin was not only smart and sexy, but he could cook too. She loved what he did to her body and could lean into what he did to her heart, if she let herself.

She might have to keep this one in her life…even if his career made that complicated. Darrin worked for WPRK's *Springfield City News*, as the newest reporter on staff, and he'd already made a splash in Springfield. When they went out together, he was almost always recognized, and Sally Ann had become adept at fading into the background when fans approached him.

It would be a difficult balance, dating the reporter on the superhero beat while heading up the Unusual Cases Unit for the Department. So far, they'd found a balance. Helping each other without using one another. Operating with complete candor would be key. But some secrets needed keeping, and secrets at the core could tear a relationship apart before it even got started.

She found herself feeling jealous of Jessica. She had recently married Walter Peeples, the head of science at the Department. No need for secrets between them. That had to make things easier. And now that

Patricia and Suzie were an item, they shared the inside track on the UCU. Even Leonel, whose husband was a civilian, shared most of his secrets with David.

Sally Ann swallowed her last bite with a little bit less pleasure, the sandwich's flavor tinged with the bitter edge of doubt and worry. She upended the bottle of water and drained it in a single go, then tapped Jessica on the shoulder as the elevator doors opened. "See you in the gym, Flygirl."

It would be good to move for a while. Too much thinking was ruining her appetite.

CATCHES AND ULTERIOR MOTIVES

Ouch! Dude! I get it." Mary Braeburn threw up a hand in front of her face, as if the Director's psychic missiles could be blocked by flesh like too bright sunlight. "You really *really* want me to like your idea. How about you let me find out what it is first?"

The Director lowered his head, inhaled and exhaled three times, and the force of his psychic power dulled to a level Mary could manage.

Mary dropped her hand. "That's better." She peered around at the office. Something was different, but she wasn't sure what it was. The big picture window was the same, as was the giant wooden desk and cool-looking but uncomfortable office furniture. Still not able to identify what had changed, she perched on the edge of his desk, crossing one booted foot over the other and tossing her scarf around her neck. "All right, let's hear it."

The Director templed his fingers in front of his face but didn't quite manage to hide the manic smile. Mary squinted and concentrated, breaking through the mental projection of young Jimmy Stewart to the true face of Steven, the man they all knew as "the Director." The gleam in his eye gave her pause.

"What would you say to releasing your mother?"

Mary almost fell off the desk but steadied herself with one hand. "I'd ask you to roll again for sanity," she said. "We've just gotten her back on track after the power surge last spring. What makes you think she's safe to set loose on the public?"

The Director's face fell, and Jimmy Stewart flickered in and out of focus. Mary drummed her fingers on the shiny surface of the desk while she waited for him to quiet his mental manipulations and talk straight with her. He'd come a long way since they'd first met, and part of why he valued Mary's participation as a consultant to the UCU was her ability to resist mental manipulations—even his own. But using his powers to skew decisions in his favor and make people like and admire him was as natural to the man as breathing air. He had to concentrate on *not* influencing emotions and perspective.

Mary imagined him as a child. He'd hinted that his mother, at least, had been able to resist his charms, but what a terror he must have been at school.

"I met with the mayor today. She's still concerned people are afraid of us. Jessica and Leonel are great with the public, but Patricia..."

Mary shot a look at the wall behind the desk. Ah! New framed publicity stills of the front-facing UCU agents hung there. Jessica hovering midair, holding a flawless pose; Leonel holding up the front bumper of a truck and smiling sheepishly at the camera; and Patricia...was she smiling? Mary didn't know who had thought it was a good idea to have the Lizard Woman of Springfield smile. It only made her more terrifying.

"Okay, so you try some more publicity campaigns, like the Good Will Tour from a year or two back? How would releasing my mother help?"

He spread his hands out, emphasizing each syllable like it was a head-line: "Rehabilitation."

Mary hopped off the desk and walked over to the windows. The view of Springfield was spectacular, with the sun hitting its apex and reflecting off all the glass and metal of the tall buildings surrounding them. After a moment or two, the Director came and stood beside her.

"Last spring, during the Power Surge, the people of this city became aware for the first time how many powered individuals lived among them. Some were excited by the prospect, but many were terrified. The mayor's office has been inundated with calls demanding everything from exile to incarceration for these so-called dangerous people."

"So you want to paint the UCU as a rehab center for wayward mutants?"

The Director laughed. "Something like that."

"And you think my mom would make a good poster child?" Mary thought back to the last time her mother had been out in public: the fire-fight in the park, her laser-like focus on vengeance. Dr. Liu had been lucky to survive, saved once again by her own ingenuity: the fire-retardant gel she bathed herself and her clothing in kept her from ending up the crispy victim of Mary's mother's vengeance, but being covered in sticky goo hadn't kept the UCU from capturing the scientist and taking her into custody.

The Director's voice rose a notch to a salesman's excited pitch. "They still run footage of Helen's run of destruction across our city. If we could show we took that dangerous wild woman and turned her back into a responsible citizen…"

"But we haven't done that, Steven."

He smiled. "That's where you come in."

Mary barked a bitter little laugh. "You think I can get my mother to cooperate with this? She's barely spoken to me since I helped you bring her back in."

The Director touched something on his watch and a whirring sound caught Mary's attention. She spun to see a TV pushing out of a panel in the wall. A series of still photographs taken during her visits with her mother ran on a slow slide show. He tapped his watch again, freeze-framing one that showed Helen smiling at Mary.

"You guys look cozy right here," he said.

Mary shook her head. She'd suspected their visits were being recorded but hoped she was wrong. "Do you know what I said that made her smile?"

He frowned, a furrow appearing in his forehead.

"I told her that I'd heard that Cindy Liu almost died trying to escape."

The Director was saved from having to respond by a rap on the door. "Come in," he called.

Jessica peeked around the door frame. "Suzie said you wanted to see me?" Seeing Mary, she crossed the room in a bound to give the young woman a hug. "Mary! I haven't seen you since the wedding. How are you?"

Mary pushed her way back out of the hug, in no mood for polite banalities. "I'm fine," she said, in a flat voice that brought a puzzled expression onto Jessica's face. Mary softened. "It's all right." She hooked a thumb at the Director. "He's got another wild hair, and I'm not happy about it."

"Oh yeah?" Jessica turned a curious expression on the Director. Mary watched her, wondering if something was wrong. Jessica's enthusiasm at seeing her felt a little false, and there were hints of dark circles under her eyes.

The Director cleared his throat. "Can you stick around for a minute, Mary? We should talk about this some more."

Mary grunted her assent and flopped down onto the stiff sofa, pulling out her phone to give the other two the illusion of privacy for their conversation.

The Director turned up the wattage on his positive vibes, making Mary wince like he'd shined a bright light into her brain. Jessica gave no sign of feeling it.

"I wanted to congratulate you. We've already received several calls. You made quite an impression of some of our city's most influential women. And the photographs!" He did a chef's kiss gesture, which seemed ridiculous to Mary. She wondered how Jessica saw him—if the gesture seemed more natural in her view of the chameleon they all worked for. Did he resemble Jimmy Stewart for her, too?

Jessica shifted her feet, demurring. "You can thank the head librarian. I don't think losing that bouquet of balloons was an accident. She knows how to make sure good publicity happens." She stopped and stared at the carpet between her feet for a long moment.

Watching, Mary felt like there was something Jessica decided not to say. She studied the Director, who didn't seem to have picked up on the significant pause. Mary would have to find time to talk to Jessica soon. Something was off about her.

Jessica cleared her throat. "Speaking of handling things, there were protesters out front of the library."

Mary stopped pretending she wasn't eavesdropping. Protesters? She pulled up a newsfeed on her phone, scanning through the afternoon's coverage while she waited for her turn to talk to the Director.

The Director grimaced. "They're getting more vocal. A big group?"

Jessica fingered her necklace. The sunlight from the office windows glinted on the emerald's mottled surface, lighting a flaw within the stone, so that it glowed a hypnotic yellow.

"No. Maybe seven or eight people. Standing there with signs, though of course I don't know what they did while I was inside." Without letting go of the stone, Jessica glanced over at the clock on the wall.

"I've got a training session with Sally Ann in a few minutes. Was there anything else?"

The Director shot a look at Mary, who pressed her lips together in renewed disapproval. If he was proposing what she suspected he had in mind, it would not go over well.

Catching her signal, he sighed. "Not right now."

"I'd better go. Mary, can I take you to lunch tomorrow? There's something I want to ask you about."

Mary was surprised but agreed readily. "I'm coming in to visit Mom anyway. I'll find you in the cafeteria, if that works."

Jessica waved from the door, but she didn't look back. As soon as the door closed behind her, Mary turned her attention back to the Director. Someone had to talk some sense into the man, and once again that role fell to her. She rubbed her hands on her thighs, like she was going to lift something heavy, and got to her feet.

"Sounds like we need to talk," she said.

JESSICA'S MOTHER IS WORRIED...
AGAIN

Jessica slid the heavy oaken door closed. It was late, and a school night as well. She didn't want to wake the boys. The hinge squeaked, a small, high-pitched whine like a puppy.

"He tried to wait up for you, but I made him go to bed."

Jessica jumped several feet into the air then lowered herself to the ground. "Jesus, Mom. You scared me."

From the corner chair of the living room—the one they called the command chair because you could see into the hall and the kitchen, as well as the bottom of the stairs—Eva Roark lifted her wine glass in apology.

Jessica hung up her jacket and keys then pulled her wig and cowl off. Joining Eva in the living room, she grabbed a glass and held it out to her mother to fill. "Why are you still up?"

The wine poured in three glugs, filling the glass past the halfway mark before Eva pulled back her hand. "I don't sleep as much as I used to, and I was worried."

Jessica took the first sip, checking her phone. Her texts showed as sent. "Didn't you guys get my messages?"

Eva turned the glass in her hand so it caught the dim light of the lamp and glowed golden. "Yes, we got them. I think your husband even believed you."

Jessica narrowed her eyes. "What do you mean?"

Exasperation made Eva's voice louder, or maybe it was the wine. "Please, Jessica. I'm your mother."

Face hardening into stiff lines, Jessica squeezed her words through a tight smile. "I was on patrol."

"I'm sure you were." Eva leaned forward, hands resting on the knees of her soft pink slacks. "If by 'on patrol' we mean flying around in the dark to avoid a hard conversation at home."

Jessica set down her glass and stood up. "I'm tired, Mom. Can we talk about this tomorrow?"

"No. I think we'd better talk now."

Surprised, Jessica sat back down, curling her legs into the chair with her. "All right then. Shoot."

"You're different."

Jessica laughed. "Of course I'm different, Mom. It's been a hell of a few years around here. We're all different."

Eva nodded, but her eyes remained unconvinced. "Yes, we've been through a lot together, but there's something else going on. Something with you alone. It's not like you to keep secrets, not from me, and certainly not from Walter."

Jessica stood. "I'm not keeping any secrets."

Her mother looked up at her. "Aren't you? Where are your emeralds?"

Jessica's hand flew to her chest, her thumb landing on the hard lump at the center of her bra–the secret pocket where she kept a piece of emerald when she was flying. "Close to my heart, as always."

"Not that one." Eva set her empty glass on the table. "The rest of your stash."

"My stash? You make it sound like I'm on drugs."

Eva blinked and swallowed hard. She reached out a hand, and Jessica took it. When her mother tugged on the fingers, Jessica seated herself on the arm of the chair. Her mom seemed lost in the oversized chair, one slender leg dangling over the other. Jessica noticed how she could feel all the delicate bones in Eva's hand.

Pushing a strand of blond hair out of Jessica's face, Eva sighed. "I'm going to worry. It's my job, you know."

Jessica squinted toward the stairs, thinking about her boys sleeping up there under their Fuerte-patterned sheets, dreaming about their upcoming taekwondo tournament. "I know. It's the same for me with the boys."

"It doesn't stop just because they grow up."

Tears welled in Jessica's eyes, and Eva gasped in surprise. Jessica was surprised too. Roark women didn't cry. Cool, calm, and collected was the family motto, and teary scenes were beneath them. Even when fighting cancer, Jessica only cried when she was alone. Angry with herself, Jessica flung the tears off her cheeks with a flick of her wrist. Self-pitying nonsense.

"Jess." Eva's voice was soft, and when Jessica raised her chin, she saw answering tears glistening in her mother's eyes. Eva grasped Jessica's hand in both of hers and pulled her close. Jessica let herself slide off the arm of the chair and into her mother's arms, then laid there while her mother traced gentle circles on her back, letting Jessica's tears run into her neck. They were useless tears, but it felt good to let them out.

They sat that way for several minutes, until Jessica finally slid off her mother's lap and onto the floor. After she mopped her face with some tissues, she turned back to her mom, who was still eyeing her with concern. "Mom, your sweater!" The shoulder of the pink top suffered black smears of eyeliner and mascara, which gave Jessica a hint what her face showed.

Eva pulled the shoulder out where she could see it, then let it slide back into place. "It's only a sweater, Jess. It'll come clean, or I'll buy another one. It doesn't matter." She leaned in to lift Jessica's chin, staring directly into her eyes. "You, on the other hand, matter more than anything in my world and I can't let you ruin what you've built."

"Ruin?"

"Walter isn't stupid."

Jessica laughed. "Hardly. Mensa came calling before he counted his age in double digits."

Eva didn't join in the laughter. "That's not what I mean."

"I know."

"You know I've got your back. I always have, from your gymnastics career, through the modeling fiasco, and the painful auditions for acting. I only ever wanted you to have what you wanted. Whatever that was."

She let go of Jessica's chin and finished her wine. "When you married Nathan, even though I thought it was a bad idea, I supported you. Some mistakes a woman has to make for herself before she can learn. When you divorced him, I supported you in that too. When you joined the UCU, I swallowed my fears and took my place in your corner, like I always have."

"I hear a but coming."

"You definitely do. The emeralds are doing something to you, and you need to get away from them."

Jessica rolled back onto her feet, stalking to the kitchen with the wine glasses. She leaned her hot hands on the cool, smooth marble countertop. If only she could cool the heat in her head as easily.

Eva had followed and now stood leaning against the doorway, her pale nearly-white-blond hair illuminated by the custom, recessed lighting behind her. She crossed her arms over her chest, but she looked more concerned than angry. Jessica almost broke into a fresh wave of tears at the sight of it. Instead, she let her anger out.

"This is ridiculous." She picked up a glass and slammed it on the counter, putting a chip in the foot.

Eva came over and mirrored her daughter's stance. She traced the swirls in the marble with one well-manicured finger, ignoring the shard of glass. "Where do you think your anger comes from?"

Jessica shrugged.

"Is it stress?"

"Not exactly."

Eva raised an eyebrow.

"Things have been a little weird at the UCU. Sally Ann keeps watching me, like she's waiting for something. And Leonel is always asking if I'm okay."

"Sounds like I'm not the only one who feels like something is off with you. When did it start, do you think?"

Jessica thought. A few months ago, all she'd been able to think about was her wedding, and she'd been as excited as any bride. Then, there'd been the mission to the Midwest to pick up Patricia and rescue Patricia's mother, the forced proximity with Dr. Liu, and the problem with power spikes.

"Maybe last spring?"

"Wasn't that when everyone was having power spikes? When Walter figured out that the emeralds could help?"

There was something about the way her mother said "emeralds." Like she was talking about something dirty or shameful. Jessica felt herself grow cold, defensive. "They're just rocks, Mom."

That eyebrow arch again. Jessica wanted to scratch it off her mother's face.

"If they're just rocks, why do you hoard them? Why does your face take on that fierceness whenever someone mentions them?"

"I need them. They help me fly."

"Do they? How long has it been since you tried flying without them? Walter says the team can't find any physical connection, that your improvement in control probably came from confidence at first, and then from practice."

"They also said they didn't see any harm in me carrying them, if I want to."

"Of course, they'd say that—they need you to perform, and that matters more to the UCU than your health or wellbeing. But *I* see the harm. Look how angry you are right now, just because I asked you about them."

Eva took a big breath. "Imagine how you'd feel if I told you I'd found your stash in the attic and thrown it away."

"You did what?!" Jessica rose from the floor and hovered in midair, fists clenched at her side. Her arms quivered with rage.

Eva raised a hand to her mouth and backed away, shaking her head.

Jessica flew across the counter, knocking her mother back against the wall. It was only when Eva grimaced and touched a trembling hand to the back of her head that Jessica realized what she was doing. Back on the floor in a flash, she grasped her mother by the forearms and led her to a kitchen stool. "Did I hurt you?"

"A little," Eva said. "I'll be all right." She let out a wobbly breath. "I didn't do anything to your emeralds, Jess. It was hypothetical."

Jessica couldn't find a bump on her mother's skull, but her gut still burned with guilt. What was *wrong* with her? Even if her mother had thrown out her emerald collection, it wouldn't have justified hurting her. Of course, Eva wanted to help. That's all she'd ever tried to do.

"I don't know what's wrong with me, Mom."

Eva wrapped her slender arms around her daughter. "We'll get you some help, Jess. We'll make it through this just like we've made it through everything: together."

WEDNESDAY

SUZIE GRAYSON, CATCHING
FLIES WITH HONEY

Suzie let herself into Cindy Liu's cell and stood in the doorway for a moment. The small room was dim and smelled of sweat and a distinctly adolescent funk. She supposed it was better than the bleach and urine smell of the domiciles of some women Liu's age, but it was hardly potpourri.

"What do you want?" Cindy, lying sideways on the bunk in her cell, head dangling upside down and feet propped against the wall, made no attempt to hide her contempt. Her dark hair had been cropped shorter since the last time Suzie had seen her, and it stuck up on one side like feathers.

Suzie bumped the cell door closed with her hip and gave a wide smile as if she was greeting her best friend. "Can't a girl just stop by to say hello?"

Cindy's scowl deepened, an expression Suzie found profoundly amusing, especially when viewed upside down. She didn't let her delight show on her face, not even when Cindy actually growled aloud. A petty part of her enjoyed making Dr. Liu squirm, a small act of vengeance for what the woman did to Patricia, Jessica, and Leonel. Suzie took no small pride in the role she played in landing Cindy in this cell. Not bad for a woman with no superpowers. Once in a while, when she felt shunted aside in this superhero life, she reminded herself that it was accountants that took down Al Capone.

"Does that mean you don't want the tea?" Suzie set the tray down on the small table, removing the lid and letting the aromatic steam waft into the small room.

Cindy groaned dramatically, then rolled over, landing on her feet with a grace that had not been suggested by the awkward sprawl of limbs on the bed. She walked backward until she bumped the chair, then dropped into the seat and inhaled deeply before pouring herself a cup, all without sparing a glance in Suzie's direction. "This doesn't mean that I'll help you," she said. "But I'm not passing up an opportunity for decent tea."

Suzie examined her fingernails, rubbing at a small flaw in the manicure of the middle finger of her left hand, saying nothing. Leaning against the wall, and crossing one ankle over the other, she expanded her examination to all of her fingers, as if she had nothing but time. Liu needed to remember who was in charge here.

After a minute or so of silence, Cindy broke and barked at her. "Out with it, already. What does Walter want this time?"

Suzie laid a hand on her chest in mock offense. "Do you mean Dr. Peeples?"

Cindy blew out an exasperated breath, and a sheaf of shiny black hair, greasy with need of washing, lifted off her deceptively youthful cheek. The streaks of silver that had appeared last spring were still there, sprinkled among the black hairs like strips of tinsel. Cindy spat her words from between clenched teeth. "You know I'm old enough to be his mother, but sure. What does 'Dr. Peeples' want?"

Suzie crossed over to the bed, smoothing the rumpled bedspread and sitting primly on the edge. "Oh, we'd just like you to clean up another one of your messes."

"My messes? What kind of mess am I supposed to have made?" Cindy lifted the small stoneware cup and gestured at the stark ten by ten room. "I've been here."

Suzie amped up the saccharine in her voice, while letting her eyes go hard and cold. "Oh, you made this mess a few years back. Around the same time that you illegally experimented on women all over Springfield. You remember?"

Cindy rolled her eyes, as if she really were the teenager she appeared to be. But of all the people at the Department, Suzie never forgot who she was dealing with. Like a venomous snake, Cindy was awaiting her moment to strike. Suzie planned to be there when she did, garden hoe in hand.

Another sigh. "Don't you get tired of trying to pin every strange thing that happens in this city on me?"

Suzie tilted her head and blinked slowly. Maybe she was pushing it too far, but she carried a hot coal of hatred for this woman in her heart for everything she'd done to hurt Patricia. It felt good to torment her.

Besides, it was working.

Cindy continued to drink the tea without further comment, but she couldn't stop herself from stealing glances at Suzie, who sat on the bed in silence, one leg now crossed over the other, flexing her foot so that her high heel slid part way off and then back on again, with a satisfying little *thwack.*

As the frequency of the glances increased, Suzie knew she had her hooked. Despite all the protestation, Cindy Liu was desperate for a challenge. Boredom was anathema to a woman like her, and it had been several months since the tedious research of analyzing bloodwork and settling on how much exposure to irradiated emeralds was necessary to keep all the Liu-vians who experienced power spikes last spring in check.

Liu couldn't even claim the kudos for the discovery that the emeralds were key. That was all Walter.

The infamous Dr. Liu fixated on Jessica's status as a cancer survivor, certain that explained why, of all the Liu-vians, only Jessica had not experienced dangerous spikes and fluctuations in her power. She ignored all evidence to the contrary and had lost reputation among the science staff for her stubborn refusal to consider other options. She'd been relegated to grunt work, running analysis and examining blood work like an intern.

Suzie gave her some credit for swallowing her pride and helping the team, but not too much acknowledgement. She was the root cause of all the problems in the first place, and it was mere good fortune that some Liu-vians found ways to utilize their newfound abilities to help others. Well, good fortune, a well-funded secret organization, and the support of friends and family like her.

Many others suffered and struggled for basic control that allowed them to continue living ordinary lives. All because they'd sought relief from the discomforts of menopause and had the misfortune to pick up products developed by Dr. Liu.

When Suzie thwacked her shoe back against her heel for the seventy-fifth time, Cindy snapped. "Fine! Tell me what he wants."

Suzie stood up, pulled her phone from her suit jacket pocket and tapped on the screen. A couple of seconds later, a faint ping sounded from the tablet computer sitting on the small shelf above the bed. Cindy leapt to her feet, avid interest flooding her countenance with a reddish hue.

"I can see you're anxious to get to work, so I'll leave you to it," Suzie said.

Cindy scowled and crossed her arms over her narrow chest, though Suzie didn't miss the glance she shot back to the tablet. "Do you act like this with Patricia?"

The remark was intended to hurt, to remind Suzie that Dr. Liu had been there on the mission last spring and knew about Patricia and Suzie's relationship. Suzie shrugged. "There's no need. She's not a manipulative liar with a history of using people for selfish ends, then painting it as an important scientific discovery."

Cindy's mouth dropped open and Suzie slipped through the door. She half-expected to hear the teapot crash against the door behind her. When she didn't, she scanned her card to open the observation camera. Cindy sat cross legged on the bed, brown furrowed in concentration, already immersed in the information on the screen.

Suzie pumped her fist in the air. "Too easy," she said. She almost skipped down the hall, already imagining how she'd tell the tale to Patricia over dinner.

Three corridors and one elevator later, she was knocking on the doorframe in Walter's office. He dropped the paperwork he had been studying and stood up, waving her in. "How did it go?"

"She was putty in my hands." Suzie took the chair he indicated.

"So, she'll do it?"

"She was elbows deep in the data almost before I closed the door behind me." Suzie picked up a pen on Walter's desk and twirled it in her fingers. "I'm not sure you need her. After all, she isn't the one who figured things out last time."

Walter's discovery that shards of the emeralds that made the base of Dr. Liu's formulas and products could be used to stabilize some of the unusual side effects had literally saved lives, but, of course, it hadn't made the evening news. In fact, it was important that the general public never learn about it at all.

Still, she well knew it was nice to get a little recognition and credit from time to time. She could let him know his genius mattered, even if the rest of the team didn't remember to tell him.

Walter looked down, but not before Suzie spotted the pleased little smile lifting his lips.

Lab results, like well-managed meetings and perfectly allocated resources, weren't flashy. It was easy for people to take the efforts of support staff like Suzie and Walter for granted, which made for a kind of camaraderie among them.

Well, that, and the fact that both loved one of the heroes. Patricia and Jessica weren't much alike, but both of them were scary powerful in their own ways. It wasn't always easy, being the ordinary one in the relationship.

Walter shuffled the papers on his desk around again, and Suzie spotted the label "H60" at the top of one of the documents. Suzie had helped develop the cataloging tags and knew that Helen Braeburn was H60. She also knew Mary visited the office just the day before, and the conversation between her and the Director had gotten a little heated, though Suzie couldn't hear it all. Her curiosity was piqued.

"What are you working on?" she asked, pointing at the files. Maybe she could get Walter to fill in some of the gaps the Director's secretive manner left in her understanding.

"This? Oh, more data crunching, checking stability for some of our guests who went through power surges last spring, making sure we're giving them what they need to keep things under control."

Suzie's fingers itched to pick up the files and organize the data for him, making nice, neat charts that clarified what was going on. "And are we?"

Walter frowned at the pile of papers. "I guess that depends on how you define stability." He met Suzie's gaze, eyes clear and unblinking. He understood what she was really asking. "But, yes, the mutations are under control."

A quick nod acknowledged the reassurance that Patricia would be fine. It had been terrifying last year, when Patricia lost control over her transformations and had been unable to shift back from her more saurian form. Suzie felt helpless, and that wasn't something she tolerated. Walter, more than anyone else, understood that.

Suzie stood up and walked over to a shelf near the window. She bent to lean closer to the gem specimens, lined up in their carefully labeled containers. Walter had collected a lot of data, including where the emerald sample originated and how it came into UCU hands, what exposures and interactions were known, as well as the usual geological statistics about hardness, luster, grain size, and so on.

An entire team spent years analyzing samples, trying to understand the properties of these emeralds and their effects on some people who were exposed to them, but there was so much left to learn. Suzie picked up the sample nearest the window and held it up to the light. She knew it had to be reflection and refraction, but the sample seemed to glow from within, the flaws in the shard of emerald fooling the eye into perceiving movement.

While she shared her life with a woman who sometimes broke out in scales and spikes, she still found it hard to believe that these tiny pieces of rock were responsible. Something so small to have upturned all their lives. They were beautiful.

Holding the sample to the light and shifting it in her hand, she asked, "Do you ever wonder why them?"

Walter blinked. "Why who?"

"Why Patricia? Why Jessica? Why any of them?" She set the sample back in its place on the shelf and came back over to the desk. "I mean, we've all been exposed to these rocks, but we're still ordinary."

Walter shook his head. "There's nothing ordinary about you, Suzie."

She crossed her eyes at him but felt a warm flush of pleasure at the compliment. "Sure, but I can't fly."

Walter's gaze shot to the framed photo of his wife on his desk. "Sometimes I wish she'd keep her feet on the ground a little more often."

Suzie leaned on the desk and picked up the photograph. She'd seen it before. Walter snapped it at the beach on their first weekend away together, the one he'd come back glowing from.

She remembered how the entire organization pulled for Walter and Jessica to get together. Leonel in particular celebrated Jessica and Walter finding love. Suzie had been a little jealous of the attention and support, even though it was her idea to keep her relationship with Patricia on the down-low.

In the photo, Jessica sat on the sand, toes half buried, and smiled at the camera, her blond hair hanging loose around her face, wind tousled. A greenish flare shining through Jessica's mesh coverup caught Suzie's attention.

All the other times she'd seen this photo, she assumed it was a light leak or a reflection, but she now realized it must be the shard of emerald that Jessica always wore, even in her civilian life, a habit that saved her from the weird power spikes and fluctuations that affected all the other Liu-vians.

"I haven't seen much of her recently." Suzie put the photo back in its place on Walter's desk.

He frowned. "Me either."

When Suzie shot him a surprised look, he spread his hands. "I shouldn't complain. I knew what I was getting into, marrying a super-hero. It's just—she's been working evenings and nights a lot. We've been a little 'two ships passing' since we got back from our honeymoon."

Suzie considered that. She hadn't been following scheduling as closely of late, as she'd been concentrating on updating the systems for resource allocation and tracking. So far as she knew, there was no particular need for Jessica to work nights, though. There wasn't an upswing in criminal activity, or anything special going on that Jessica's flight ability was especially useful for.

"Hmmmm. I'll look into it. Maybe I can get her shifts changed to align better with yours."

Bright hope lit Walter's eyes. "Could you do that?"

Laughing, Suzie slid off the desk and back onto her feet. "There's nothing I can't do, if I put my mind to it, Walter. You should know that by now."

JESSICA, FLYING WITHOUT A NET

All right, Flygirl. When you're ready."

Jessica looked at the team lined up at different points in her flight path. Each scientist held a different piece of equipment, ready to measure every aspect of her flight: velocity, altitude, climb, descent, drag, stability, lift. Other sensors attached to her flesh would track her vital signs.

Tucking into a crouch, Jessica counted down. Three-two-one. And she was in the air, speeding faster than her worries, a feeling of power surging through her. All too soon, she landed on the other side of the hangar. Someone applauded. No matter how many times she abandoned the ground and threw herself through the air, it thrilled and amazed anyone watching.

Jessica wasn't immune from the thrill herself. She promised the team three runs with gemstones and three without, and the repetition of the drill reminded her of her days in competitive gymnastics. She was already promising herself some free flight around Springfield afterward to make up for the restraint, noone analyzing her flight, just the wind and the open sky.

"Now, without the emeralds, please."

The voice in the headset was business-like, without emotion, but Jessica still rankled as if she'd been verbally abused.

She bit back the resentment and smiled. "Of course." Lifting the cord from her neck, Jessica deposited the emerald shard onto a small tray placed for that purpose. A young woman dropped a lid over the stone, as if it were a room service meal, the little mental *ting* striking a nerve that made Jessica's teeth hurt.

Jessica's anxiety rose. She didn't like being without her emeralds, even short term. She always kept at least a small piece on her person, slipped into the lining of her bra, or worn as a necklace. Without it, she felt naked, exposed, and vulnerable, like her safety net had been removed.

But they'd had this test on the books for weeks, and after the fight with her mother last night, she owed to herself to find out to what degree she needed the emeralds for flight stability and speed. She wanted to show her mother and herself that the emeralds had no ill effects on her.

The gymnasium was a safe place to try. If the worst happened and she lost control and floated without volition, she'd end up in the rafters and a nice person in a cherry picker would pull her back down. There was no danger.

The rational part of her brain understood all of that, but somewhere within her, monstrous claws scraped at her intestines, nasty twisting panic trying to climb up her spine. She squelched the urge to knock over the young woman with her emeralds under a lid and flee the room. It took several deep breaths to bring herself under control. She wondered how that would show up in the data.

Crouching again, Jessica counted down and relinquished her hold on the earth. She didn't cheat, though of course she could have dragged her metaphorical feet, ensuring that her flight from one end of the hangar to the other took a little longer or was a little more ragged around the edges.

It was tempting to skew the experiment, walk away with evidence that the emeralds improved her performance, but part of her wanted to know the truth. She could keep the emeralds after all, as a good luck charm, or because she wanted them. It would be good to know she didn't *need* them.

Focusing, she imagined someone on the other end of the path in need of rescue and made a beeline, straight, true, and fast. She stuck the landing.

Twice more and the young woman with the lidded tray was at her side, unconsciously bowing a little as she presented the gem to its owner. "Thank you, Flygirl."

"Of course." Jessica forced herself to move casually as she retrieved the gems, slid the necklace back in place, and walked out of the room, keeping her gait steady and even, like it had been no big deal at all.

~

WALTER WASN'T among the testing crew today. That made sense. As head of the sciences branch of the Department, he had a lot to manage. But it was strange to look out among the lab coats scurrying about the room and not find her husband.

As she moved through the busy subterranean halls of the Department, she relived their first meeting, when she had not yet developed control over her powers, and he was teaching her to use air canisters to influence her direction and speed. Right from the outset, he'd been patient and kind. No wonder she'd fallen for him.

But things shifted between them after the mission to Ohio last year. She found herself pulling back from him, avoiding long conversations that went too deep. She didn't even know why that was. He hadn't done anything wrong, but he should have asked her before borrowing from her stash of emeralds.

That was silly. She'd been several states away, in the middle of a mission, and Leonel and the other Liu-vians had been in immediate danger. Ridiculous to object under those circumstances.

Maybe it was baggage from her first marriage getting in the way.

She hadn't been able to be herself with Nathan. His expectations didn't leave much room for mistakes and imperfections. Even through her cancer treatments, she'd kept a brave face for him, protecting him from the worst of her symptoms and the emotional rollercoaster of it all.

And when Dr. Liu's tea brought on this whole new set of problems in the form of the power of flight, he convinced himself he'd hit his head too hard and had been seeing things. She'd let him, which must have meant she didn't think their marriage was worth fighting for either. It had to mean something that her primary emotion upon receiving divorce papers was relief.

But Walter was different. He'd known about her from the start, and he had no problem with any of it. It didn't matter that she couldn't cook, that she already had kids and couldn't have more, that she'd be fighting crime in midair and giving interviews on the news. They were building a good life together. The boys loved him, and so did she.

Jessica turned on her heel in the middle of the hall, changing direction to head for Walter's office and nearly plowed into one of the research assistants who had been walking a little too closely behind her. She gripped his elbows to stop him from falling. "I'm so sorry! I just remembered something and moved without looking first. Are you all right?"

The young man turned scarlet. "Yes, ma'am, um, Flygirl. It's no problem at all." He gripped his tablet computer tight to his chest, swerved around her and hurried on down the hall.

It was sweet, the way some of the staff got nervous around her, like she was a celebrity. Funny when you considered that unlike all of them, who were top of their field and trained for this, she'd had some bad luck with some tea and ended up here. Her skills were flashier, but they were the ones who figured it all out.

Shaking her head, she ducked down the third hallway on the left and followed the maze of rooms around until she ended up at Walter's office. Tapping on the doorframe, she stepped into the cluttered office, then stopped to let her eyes adjust.

"Jessica!" Walter popped out from behind a shelf, a jar in his hands and a grin on his face. He put the jar back in its place and hurried to her side. "What a nice surprise!"

He kissed her, and for a moment, Jessica let herself melt into it, appreciating the warmth of his hands at her waist and the gentle pressure of his lips on hers.

"I missed you at breakfast," he said, after they'd stepped apart. "I'd forgotten you'd be in early. How did the testing go?"

Jessica shrugged, running a finger along the jars of emeralds, letting it bump against each one and feeling the answering pulse within her. "I'm sure we'll see the data soon, but I think it was a success. My flight didn't feel any different without the gems."

"That's great news!"

Walter's enthusiasm jarred her nerves and Jessica spun away from him to hide her face, feigning interest in some of the other things lining the shelves in her husband's office.

He reached for her arm, giving it a gentle squeeze. "It'll feel good, won't it? To be able to leave the emeralds behind? Knowing that they're a support you no longer need?"

Acid bubbled in Jessica's guts, but she forced herself to smile and nod. He didn't understand. He *couldn't* understand. There was no point in trying to explain.

She did need the emeralds. It wasn't about whether she could fly without them, but about whether she wanted to. Walter pulled her in for another embrace and she let him, but her heart wasn't in it. She was already miles away, streaking across the open blue sky of her mind.

HELEN GETS AN OFFER SHE
CAN'T REFUSE

Helen blinked at her keeper, Brayan-the-orderly. "I'm sorry. I must be losing my hearing. Can you say that again?"

The broad-shouldered Black man looked back down at the tablet in his hand, clicked a couple of items, then turned it around for Helen to see. Same as always: three meals, an exercise session, a therapy session, her medication breakdown. But there it was in black and white. After lunch and before her scheduled visit with Mary. Fire-wielding practice.

"I don't understand."

"Hey, I don't make the rules around here, I do what they tell me. And today, they tell me to take you to a fireproof room at 1:30 p.m. and watch while you burn things down for an hour."

Helen leaned back in her chair, thinking. What did they have in mind? Ever since Mary had brought her here, they'd worked to suppress her ability to wield fire. For the first few months, she'd been unconscious more often than she'd been awake. And every time, she'd lit a fire, no matter how small, she'd been punished.

A few months ago, she'd started setting fires in her sleep. They'd been so intense she couldn't control them. Even when she was awake, she struggled. She'd thought it was because of the medications the UCU used on her, but Mary later told her that all the Liu-vians had experienced power surges. Some kind of mutation. Another "gift" from Dr. Liu—the thought brought a feeling of heat into her fingertips, but she pushed out a hard breath and cooled them to a normal temperature.

She fingered the sliver of emerald she wore around her neck. They'd all been given them, and it made a world of difference. She was back in control of her powers, for what good it did her. While she'd been granted some small freedoms in the months since, rewards for her cooperation with the doctors and keepers, she hadn't been permitted to do as much as reheat her coffee using her abilities, at least not if they caught her.

Now, after all that, they were going to let her cut loose again? Let her free her inner flame? She fought against the giddiness rising with her. All these months, it had been like a part of her was missing. She'd desperately missed the crescendo rising within her. The very thought had her heart beating faster. But the UCU wouldn't change their minds without a reason.

She needed to know what they were after. She turned back to her keeper, waving a fork with a chunk of pancake on the end at him. "You know, Brayan, I don't think I'm interested. Thanks anyway."

Brayan's eyes widened. "You're kidding me. All these months, you've done nothing but talk about fire and flame and now that you've got the chance to get your freak on again, you're going to turn it down?"

Helen swallowed her bite of pancake, which seemed to have grown thick in her throat. She could almost feel the tickle of flames in her palms, though she hadn't summoned any. Doing that here in the cafeteria had landed her long hours alone in a fireproof chamber more than once in her confinement here. She knew better.

"Did they say why?"

Brayan peered into her face, his eyes taking in every muscle twitch. Helen cocked an eyebrow at him, eliciting a smile from her keeper. He'd been with her longer than anyone else they'd assigned. Under other circumstances, they might even be friends.

Leaning into his elbows, so his face remained close to hers, Brayan said, "Officially, I don't know anything it doesn't say right here." He pointed at the tablet.

A gleeful energy flared in Helen's chest. "But unofficially?"

"There has been talk," he said.

Helen speared another syrup-soggy square of pancake and shoved it in her mouth to stop herself from flinging all her questions at Brayan. He'd tell her what he would, and he'd tell her more if she didn't interrupt.

Brayan looked around. Helen spared a glance at the dining hall and couldn't see anyone paying attention to the two of them. The other tables were all occupied by other so-called patients of the hospital wing and their keepers. UCU employees in dark blue scrubs, and inmates, like her, in yellow.

Another morning, Helen might have expressed some curiosity about some of the others, like the Hispanic boy who was rotating a fork two feet above the table without touching it, or the lady whose every gesture was accompanied by small sparks of electricity. Brayan usually refused to answer her questions, but he wasn't a very good liar, and she'd learned a thing or two about the other denizens during her stay, by paying attention to what he didn't deny.

But all her curiosity focused with laser intensity on one thing right now: what Brayan would say next.

Satisfied that no one would overhear their conversation, Brayan told her about the rumor circulating through the staff about a new program for the freaks under their care. "Most of y'all are here voluntarily."

Helen snorted and Brayan shook his finger at her. "Even you, Hot Stuff. You signed the paperwork."

She shrugged. "It seemed like a good idea at the time." They'd offered her a choice between jail time and voluntary commitment to the care of the UCU. Most days she thought she'd made the right choice. Sometimes, she would even admit they'd helped her here. Mary hadn't been completely wrong to worry about her anger and loss of control. Not that she'd admit it out loud.

Brayan shook his head. "Anyway, the story is the big guy wants to demonstrate our benevolent mission of rehabilitating dangerous people into contributing citizens. My guess is you're under consideration."

Gobsmacked, Helen dropped her fork back onto her plate, the clatter drawing the angry eye of more than one of her fellow diners. "You think they might let me go?"

"I can't say for sure; but think about it. You were all over the news a few years back. That footage of you from the Urgent Care? The fight in the park?"

Brayan showed her the clips, along with the conspiracy theory videos positing her role in the Old Homestead house fire and the firefight on campus. Officially, those had been a lab accident and a disgruntled kid with a flamethrower, but the conspiracy theorists weren't that far off from the truth.

She'd assumed they'd thrown away the key when they locked her in here, that she'd spend the rest of her days in concrete cells with only the occasional visit from her daughter Mary to break up the monotony. Sometimes she thought she deserved it, but it didn't make it any easier to take.

What would she do if they let her out of here? She didn't think she could go back to selling real estate to millennials. But they were hardly likely to welcome her among the other super-agents. Patricia the Lizard Woman of Springfield would never agree to work beside the woman who'd tried to kill her, reformed or not.

So, what would she do? Join the circus? Become a welder? Join the fire department? It's not like there were want ads for people who could produce fire from their own bodies.

Helen's mind spun, images of mundane life circling around rings of fire. She lost track of what Brayan was saying, her imagination rolling out possibility after possibility.

This changed things. She needed to talk to Mary.

LEONEL'S IMPOSTER SYNDROME

Leonel dropped onto the locker room bench and let his head fall into his hands. The morning had been one misstep after another. First, he'd broken another heavy bag. What was this, number five or number six? They probably had a special budget item for "Leonel broke it" at this point.

He hadn't even been punching it, merely trying to hang it for a new trainee who was too short to reach, but he'd yanked a little too hard on the hook and the whole thing fell out of the ceiling, covering them both in plaster dust.

The young woman laughed and made the usual joke about not knowing his own strength, which made him feel worse. After all the work Walter had done to stabilize the spike in his strength a few months earlier, he ought to have figured this out. It was ridiculous that he kept breaking things like a clumsy fool.

He'd finished last on the obstacle course once again. Mike, the agent running the training and one of Leonel's mentors within the Department, tried to make him feel better, reminding him that most of the agents were fifteen or twenty years younger than he was, but Leonel didn't find that comforting or reassuring. It made him feel old and out of place.

True, he had managed every obstacle without slip or need for a second attempt but coming into an empty locker room afterward emphasized how slow he was compared to the others. A tortoise among hares. Hares who were all already in the cafeteria tossing around jokes with a vocabulary that Leonel would only half understand. No hurry to join them.

Moving toward the showers, Leonel prayed that he'd perform better in the strategy sessions after lunch. In his heart though, he harbored serious doubt about that too. So many of the other agents came from security work or transferred from the police force. Others came from a military background.

While they'd been building up a repertoire of combat skills, Leonel had been organizing Girl Scout events and baking for the PTSO fundraiser. He felt chronically behind. If he didn't have super strength, would the UCU even want him? Was he cut out for this?

As the hot water ran over his skin, Leonel's mind wandered to the incident at the pond the day before. He'd been useless, requiring rescue and ending up covered in disgusting muck. He could imagine Patricia describing it to Suzie in excruciating detail, and the capable young woman shaking her head in sympathy, suppressing a desire to laugh out of kindness.

Dried and dressed, Leonel made his way to the cafeteria. There was still a half hour left in their break. He ought to be able to grab a sandwich.

The cafeteria was pulsing with excited chatter when he walked in. He paused inside the doorway to look around. Spotting Jessica, his mood lifted. He started in her direction but stopped when he saw that she was in deep conversation with Mary.

He'd been missing Jessica lately. They'd joined the UCU together, and, for Jessica, it had been as natural as breathing. She was the master of the press conference as well as an asset in the field. Leonel, on the other hand, felt like a clumsy buffoon in both settings, tongue-tied or useless. He'd gotten himself shot and had to be rescued as many times as he'd been of help, and he hated the spotlight.

Sometimes he missed being able to blend in and have eyes bounce over him in a crowd, like when he'd been a woman, but between his notoriety and the size of his new body, he was hard to ignore these days. The attention was flattering, but it also made him uncomfortable. Thank goodness for the mask he wore in the field, or it would be even worse.

Sighing, he looked toward Jessica's table again. She'd been a little distant since she got back from her honeymoon. Leonel supposed that was natural—her focus was on her husband and her family, where it should be. But it still stung, and he wondered if he had offended her in some way. Their families used to get together regularly, and it had been weeks now since he'd seen her except in passing.

Not sure of his welcome, Leonel went to the cold case and picked up a sandwich and a bottle of water. When he turned around at the cash register, the short trainee—Jameela—from the broken heavy bag that morning was standing next to him. "Mr. Alvarez, can I ask you something?"

"Leonel," he corrected. Then, a little nervously, "Of course."

"How do you do it?"

"Do what?"

"Balance all this." She gestured back at the table where the rest of their cohort still sat. "The training, the classes, the work itself, and a family."

Leonel laughed—funny that she would ask him of all people about that. But he stopped when he looked into the young woman's face and saw she was in earnest. "I hear you talking about your children and grandchildren all the time, and your family sounds so close, and I'm worried about finding a balance like that in my life."

He gestured toward the door to the outside. "You want to go outside and talk for a minute?"

She glanced back at the group of young agents at the table then followed him to the door.

It was much quieter outside. A few people sat at the umbrella tables on the enclosed patio. A light breeze shifted some dried leaves across the tile with a comforting rasp. Jameela whistled. "This is lovely! I had no idea this was here."

Leonel raised a finger to his lips. "Don't tell too many people. It'll ruin it if they start coming too." He'd sought out all the quiet corners in the facility. Sometimes it helped to step out into the sun for a moment and breathe the air.

"Absolutely," she agreed, admiring a large vase with vining purple and green plants drifting down its sides before plopping into the chair beside it.

Leonel shoved a bite of sandwich in his mouth, then realized he should have asked his question first. Holding a hand over his chewing, he said, "Tell me about your situation. How old are you? What are you trying to manage?"

For the next few minutes, the agent laid out the parameters of her life. She was very young, only twenty-eight, having come to the UCU from a brief stint with police work. Similar to Sally Ann, she'd become disillusioned after being asked to cover up something. She didn't give any details, but he could tell from the tightness around her eyes when she talked about it that it gave her pain. He should get Sally Ann to reach out to her. She'd be a good mentor for Jameela.

Like so many of the UCU agents, Jameela was recruited by the Director just when she'd gotten to her breaking point. She had nearly turned in her resignation letter every day that week but worried about giving up the benefits and regular paycheck. Her husband fell in and out of employment, and their little family—they had twin boys, now two years old—relied on her as the breadwinner.

Leonel leaned back in his chair, letting his gaze follow the patterns of light and leaf shadow on the umbrella above their heads. "This is demanding work. There's no way around it. But you can have boundaries. It's important that you do."

He considered for a moment, unable to decide how to continue. His own history was more complicated than hers, including an unplanned gender change along the way and a rocky patch in what had seemed a rock-solid marriage. Even now he harbored doubts about the balance of his new career alongside his family.

"My husband did not take it well when I came to work for the UCU," he said.

Jameela's eyebrows shot up, but she made no other comment on her discovery that Leonel had a husband. It wasn't a secret, but most people assumed Leonel was married to a woman, and he didn't bother to correct them unless it came up.

"I stayed home with our children for most of our marriage," he said. "That's part of what has made this challenging for us—it's not only that the work is dangerous, it's the shift in me having outside work at all. There are so many things I used to handle on my own that became shared responsibilities. Our spheres are no longer so separate." He drained the last of the water in his bottle. "What does your husband do?"

"He works from home. He's a web designer for a big west coast company. We were lucky to be able to get him a flexible position that leaves him able to take care of our boys."

"Is he satisfied in that role? It's important that you both have a chance to do work that leaves you feeling valued and stretched in good ways."

Jameela shifted a little uneasily. "I'm not sure. He loves the work, but I think he misses the camaraderie of the office. He used to work for a local start-up, and he and the other designers would hang out all the time."

"Look. Everyone's marriage is different, so you should do what works for you, but I'll tell you that it's important to talk through these things, openly and honestly, before resentments can build." He took a deep breath. "I almost lost David a couple of years ago. I'd gotten shot on a mission, and David was so angry at me for putting myself in danger. But this work matters to me, and I refused to give it up."

Leonel was startled by the rush of heat in his heart when he spoke the words. Images of grateful faces and smiling children rushed across his brain, reminding him how many people he'd been able to help in his years at the UCU, how much the work mattered.

"Did he come to terms with it?" Jameela sounded breathless.

"Mostly. There are still tense moments here and there, and I know he worries a lot, but in the end, we love each other and we want each other to be fulfilled and happy. It can be difficult, making that happen for both of you at the same time, and it's a scale that has to be balanced and re-balanced, over and over again as things change."

Jameela looked thoughtful. "Thank you so much Mr. Alvarez. You've given me a lot to think about."

"Leonel, please." He offered his hand for a shake. "And thank you! You've reminded me why I keep doing this, even when it's hard."

JESSICA WANTS TO GET
SOME INK

Jessica slipped into the busy cafeteria and looked around for Mary. If anyone could help her with this, it would be Mary Braeburn.

The room was busy as always, full of blue jump-suited agents, lab coat wearing techs and medical personnel, and lots of other people Jessica didn't recognize. They all recognized her, though, and a ripple of whispered conversation grew into cacophony.

At last she spotted Mary, sitting in a quiet corner, half-hidden by a large potted plant. If not for the girl's dreadlocks, Jessica might not even have noticed her in the crowd. Maybe the noon hour hadn't been the smartest time to plan a meetup to talk about something private, but she'd jumped at the chance to put her plans into action.

Plastering a bright smile on her face, Jessica leapt across the room in a long bound. She'd promised not to fly inside the facility, except in the testing and gymnasium facilities, but a jump slightly disconnected from gravity wasn't the same thing as flying. Besides, she might as well give her fans in the Department something to talk about—they *lived* for that stuff.

"Mary!" She called out as she landed beside the table.

Startled, Mary almost knocked over her drink, but she steadied it with a quick hand. Jessica gave her a tight hug across the shoulders, ignoring the stiff surprise she met with, then sat down in the other chair. Breathing out slowly, she counseled herself to rein it in, before she freaked the younger woman out.

The confrontation with her mother the night before left Jessica shaken. She'd lain awake most of the night, having slipped into bed beside her quietly snoring husband, and pretended to be asleep when he got up to get ready for work in the morning to put off the inevitable discussion with him a little bit longer. A couple of hours ago, Walter had expressed such relief at the idea that she didn't "need" the emeralds for flight.

The thought that she might be separated from the emeralds flashed like a warning red light under her every moment. Her mother and her husband both wanted to take them away from her, and she couldn't let that happen.

Underslept, she'd indulged in a triple shot latte on her way to this lunch date, and it wasn't mixing well with her agitation. If she didn't watch it, they'd have to literally peel her off the ceiling.

Mary played with her straw, pulling it out and mashing it back down in to find the remaining rivulets of soda in the cup now mostly full of ice. The straw rasped through the plastic lid on the cup like a seal honking. The sound irritated Jessica enough that it was difficult to keep herself from smacking the cup out of Mary's hands.

Clenching her hands in her lap, she put on her best press conference wooing smile. "Thanks so much for meeting me. I hope I didn't keep you waiting long."

Mary seemed nervous—her gaze darting around the people at the other tables, but she returned Jessica's smile with open curiosity. "No problem. What can I help you with?"

Jessica noticed that the cafeteria at the Department was not the wisest place she could have chosen for this conversation. The "freaks" of the UCU were celebrities within the Department, and Jessica's appearance in the cafeteria attracted many curious eyes. She wanted to keep it casual, but they were bound to be overheard here and she didn't want this to get back to Walter, not until she was ready.

"Do you want to get out of here? Go something a little quieter?"

Obvious relief spread over Mary's face. "Absolutely. Got anywhere in mind?"

A FEW MINUTES LATER, the two women were settled at a table at a farm-to-table bistro a few blocks away. They must have known Mary there, because the two of them didn't have to wait long before they were ushered to a table in a back corner. Soon after, they were drinking house-made cream sodas.

"This is a neat little place. I don't think I've ever been here."

"A friend of mine owns it."

Jessica looked around at the mismatched tables and variety of lighting fixtures. One wall was plastered in posters for musical acts and another featured a few paintings of city lights reflected in the river.

It felt like the kind of place she might have frequented as an undergraduate, and Jessica wondered when she'd stopped seeking out this homey, comfortable sort of charm and the artsy crowd that tended to go with it. She guessed it was a part of herself she'd set aside when she'd married Nathan and bought into his glossy dream of wealth and popularity. Now she still had the house, but no longer the heart for that kind of life.

"I like it. I'll have to bring Walter and the boys. I think they'd love it."

Mary smiled, but her gaze was assessing, unsettling in its focus.

Jessica suppressed a shudder, feeling as if the girl could see straight through her, shining a light on the hidden corners of her heart. She blurted out, "So, I want to get a tattoo."

Mary blinked, surprised. "You do?"

Jessica nodded emphatically, making her short blond hair bounce. "Something special." She looked into Mary's eyes, forcing herself not to look away even though she felt like her eyeball was twitching. "It's my cancer-versary."

Mary sat back in her chair. They were interrupted by the arrival of their food, then Mary picked up her fork. Twirling it in her hand, she asked, "How long has it been?"

"Five years." Jessica knew her smile was a little tight, but she hoped Mary would interpret that as something to do with her fight against cancer, instead of her desire to have her story believed. She wasn't lying. She just wasn't giving all of her reasons.

"Major milestone. Congratulations!"

Jessica relaxed a little. Maybe this would go okay after all. "Thank you. So much has changed for me since then."

It certainly had. Jessica was not quite ten years older than Mary, not yet forty, she'd been through a lot. She'd divorced, remarried, started a new career, and learned to fly all in the last five years, as well as surviving being burned. Her fingers reached reflexively for the emerald necklace that hung between her breasts. The small hunk of rock made all the difference. She *wouldn't* be separated from it.

Mary's gaze bounced down to the fingers worrying the stone, a thoughtful expression on her face. Noticing, Jessica let it go and leaned forward, bringing her face nearer to Mary's.

"Anyway, I want to do something special. But the truth is I don't know the first thing about tattoos. Can you tell me about yours?"

Mary laughed. "Sure."

The next half hour was a show and tell of Mary's body-art, interrupted occasionally by the waitress. Mary pulled up a sleeve, lifted her hair, dragged up a pant-leg, and narrated the story of each piercing and tattoo.

Jessica listened avidly, *ooh*-ing and *ah*-ing over each reveal, waiting for the right moment to ask what she really wanted to ask.

At last, it came. When Mary was pulling her sleeve back into place after displaying her sleeve tattoo, the neck of her t-shirt slid to the side, revealing three star-shaped dermal piercings along her collarbone.

Jessica gripped Mary's hand, tight enough to hurt, then made herself relax her fingers, puffing out a breath to force her body back into the chair she'd begun to float above. Her eyes wide and round, she pointed, "What about those?"

Mary tugged the t-shirt further aside, stretching her neck back so Jessica could see more clearly.

Jessica's eyes grew brighter as she leaned in for a better look. "So beautiful!" Her hand drifted out to touch the embedded gems, but, at the last minute, she realized how invasive that would be and let her hand drop to the table. "Did it hurt?"

Mary shrugged. "I mean, it all hurts, in varying degrees, but if you go somewhere good and follow the care instructions, there's no reason to expect trouble."

"What's that called?" Jessica pulled out her phone and opened the notes app, texting finger poised. She'd already googled it, but there was no need to tell Mary that. She would play student and hope Mary's enthusiasm would keep her from asking any of the wrong questions.

Mary gamely gave a short lecture on dermal implants and tattoos and fielded questions about care, durability, healing, and whether the two might be combined, while Jessica took dutiful notes. Another half hour went by and the lunch crowd that had filled the restaurant dwindled to just the two of them.

The waitress told them to ask at the bar if they needed anything and

Mary blushed, realizing how long she'd been talking. "And thank you for attending my Ted Talk," she quipped. "I'm sure that's more than you ever wanted to know."

"This is perfect," Jessica gushed. Her voice became quiet and serious. "I have some stones that are special to me. Can you use your own stones?" This was the crux of the matter. The whole plan was no good unless she could embed the emeralds in her flesh, make them permanently a part of her no one could take away.

An odd expression clouded Mary's face. "Zeph could do that."
"Zeph?"

"Z-E-P-H, short for Zephyr. His place is over on Third." She paused while Jessica wrote down the address, pretending not to notice the hesitation that crept into Mary's tone.

Mary pulled back her hair on the right side of her head so Jessica could see her ear. A small lotus flower nestled in the upper curve, lying so perfectly in the flesh it almost seemed like it grew there. "I found the glass on the beach in Mexico and Zeph made it into this piece for me. He's quite an artist, and his partner Callah did my sleeve tattoo."

"That's beautiful! Do you think they'd do something for me, maybe something more like your stars—something that can always be a part of me?"

"I can call him if you'd like, let him know you'll be coming his way."
"Would you? That would be wonderful!"

PATRICIA, PASTA, AND APOLOGIES

S he was knee deep in the data before I left!" Suzie went silent, having finished her story.

PATRICIA FLICKED the bits of pasta around on her plate, staring out the window. The evening had turned rainy, and the lights from the cars made atmospheric smears of colors in the glass on the restaurant window.

"Patty Jean O'Neill!"

Shocked by the shouting of her childhood name, Patricia flung the bit of gnocchi on her fork, flattening it against the window. She looked across the table and was instantly sorry she had. Suzie's arms were crossed, and she was leaning menacingly across the table.

"Have you heard a word I've said?"

Dropping the fork into the half-eaten meal, Patricia picked up the napkin and wiped her face and fingers, then let it fall over the plate, disguising how little she'd eaten. "I'm sorry. I guess I'm distracted."

Suzie peered at the window, wiping away the flung pasta with her napkin. "By traffic?"

Annoyance pitched Suzie's voice higher than usual, and the diners at the next table gaped at the sharpness in her tone. Patricia met their gaze with her best "not your business" glare. She suppressed the temptation to transform her face as she did so and give them a fright.

Clearly, she had missed something. She tried to run it back in her mind. Something about "eating out of my hand" and "elbows deep in the research"?

Patricia let her attention wander, and Suzie must have moved on from small talk to something of more importance, something she expected Patricia to have a response to or an opinion about. But she hadn't been listening, and she had no idea what she'd missed.

Burning under the heat of Suzie's glare, Patricia knew better than to say any of that out loud. "Maybe I'm tired."

Suzie's eyes narrowed, skepticism roiling in the air between them with an almost palpable stench. She raised a hand to attract the attention of the waiter and turned a winning smile on him when he arrived at their table. "Can we get some boxes, please? I don't have much of an appetite."

"Certainly. Will it be one check or two?" The waiter's gaze flicked between the two of them.

"One, thanks," Patricia said.

After he walked away, she tried to deflect Suzie's anger with a bit of humor. "He thinks I'm your mother."

"Nonsense. My mother listens to me when I talk."

Patricia knew she'd screwed up, but she didn't have the first idea how to make things better. It had been a long time since she'd had someone in her life she truly cared about losing, so she didn't have a lot of practice in making apologies.

Now Suzie was looking everywhere but at her, as if the faux terracotta tile and still life of fruit were works of great art that required all of her attention. When the waiter came back with the boxes, Suzie didn't even uncross her arms and Patricia shrugged sheepishly at him as she handed him her card. She boxed up her food then reached across the table for Suzie's.

Suzie grabbed the plate. "I'm perfectly capable of boxing my own dinner!"

Patricia relinquished her hold on the plate, nearly flinging ravioli onto Suzie's pale blue silk blouse in the process. Nodules rising on her neck cued Patricia to rein in her temper before she made an entirely different kind of scene in the restaurant. She breathed in and pushed out the breath slowly before she spoke, but the words still came out as more of a growl forced between clenched teeth.

"What do you want me to do here, Suzie?"

Suzie didn't answer, keeping her focus on shoveling the ravioli out of her wide flat bowl into the cardboard container. Her hand shook a little. The consternation was so unlike her usually imperturbable girlfriend that Patricia felt shaken herself.

She pressed her hands flat against the table, pulling in the nails when she noticed they were trying to curve into talons. She swallowed hard before the next words—words seldom heard from her lips. "I'm sorry."

Suzie stood up, tossing her napkin onto a spill of red sauce on the tablecloth. She didn't meet Patricia's gaze. "Make your own way home, will you?" Her voice was light, business-like. She might have been speaking to a stranger rather than her girlfriend of many months.

Patricia swallowed the lump in her throat, nodding her agreement, but it didn't matter. Suzie turned away without waiting for an answer and stalked out of the restaurant.

The waiter returned with a bag, and Patricia slipped the boxes of pasta into the plastic sack. She tipped generously, as if that could somehow make up for the embarrassment, and left.

~

OUT ON THE STREET, she stood for a long moment watching cars drive by. What the hell happened? Suzie's red roadster was gone from the parking place where they'd left it and not visible in the block or two Patricia could see.

She could call for a ride, but Patricia thought a walk might clear her head, so she turned toward the bank that served as cover for the Department's underground offices where she'd left her car and set off at a good clip. It was only a mile or so, and it was still early. She didn't sleep much these days anyway.

At six feet tall, Patricia was accustomed to shortening her stride most of the time, especially when walking with Suzie, who wasn't far over five feet and tended to wear heels that further impeded her walking speed. She'd walked two blocks before she realized there was no reason to hold back.

The next two blocks were almost a blur. If she'd been dressed for it, she might have broken into a jog, but she had changed into a pantsuit for the dinner date, and it didn't move with her well enough for more athletic endeavors. Maybe she could build up enough speed to outrun her thoughts—her guilt about hurting Suzie with her inattention.

A wind swept up from the river, the moist air rife with a rotten, sewage-like scent the city officials swore was not a sign of pollution, but of "natural minerals and vegetable matter in our city's waterways." Today, it smelled like regret to Patricia and went well with the bile in her throat. Avoiding the maudlin turn of her thoughts, she picked up her pace and cut over into a less familiar block, one without a direct path to the river.

The air felt cleaner as soon as Patricia turned the corner and traffic lightened, allowing her to hear tinny music muted by the buildings between her and the bar or concert venue responsible. She paused to unbutton her jacket and froze when she heard a shoe scrape the pavement behind her.

Her alter ego, anxious for an excuse to punch something, urged her to unleash her Lizard Woman. But it was just as likely that the person coming up behind her was a fellow citizen of Springfield making their way home, so she reined in her impulse to transform and kept walking. No need to cause trouble, though she wouldn't be disappointed if trouble found her.

The next block opened onto the park at the city center. A homeless man, draped in a blanket despite the temperate night, sat on a bench across the street, and Patricia made for him, plopping down beside him. He startled and pulled into himself.

Patricia watched the block she'd left in silence until a young man wearing a band t-shirt and walking with the mild stumble of a person who has enjoyed one more drink than they probably should have stepped into the light. He didn't even glance in her direction.

Bummed to learn there would be no reason for a fight, Patricia lifted the bag of still-warm leftovers onto the bench and addressed the homeless guy. "You hungry? This is from Luigi's."

The man's eyes widened. "You don't want it?" His voice was a little raspy, but younger than Patricia would have guessed from his hunched over position.

She grimaced at the plastic bag resting between them. "Naw. It tastes like the fight with my girlfriend to me now."

The man laughed. "Yeah, that'll do it."

Patricia stood up, leaving the food. "Enjoy it, man. Someone should."

"I will, thanks."

He called after her when she was a few steps away. "Florist on the other side of the park is open late. You know, if you need an apology bouquet."

She saluted and continued in the direction he indicated. Suzie had never walked out on one of their arguments before. Should she get some flowers? Take them over to Suzie's? She pictured herself showing up at the door with a bunch of daisies in her hands and wrinkled her nose at the pathetic aura of it all.

Maybe it would be better to give her space. Or maybe failing to call or show up would make things worse. She had no idea what to do, and no one to ask.

Once, she might have asked Cindy. Cindy would have made fun of her, but the two of them would have cooked up a reconciliation plan over a bottle of wine. Something that stayed on the safe side of humiliation, but the dramatic side of romance. But Cindy could no longer be called a friend. Damn, but Patricia missed her sometimes.

Walking toward the giant acorn that marked the center of the park, Patricia pulled out her phone and let her thumb flick through the list of contacts. Her mom would tell her to do whatever it took to get "that wonderful girl" to take her back. Sally Ann would make uncomfortable noises until she faked a bad connection and hung up. She wasn't going to bother Jessica, the newlywed. Leonel was probably still wallowing in embarrassment after his trip to the bottom of the pond, and half the time they ended up pissing each other off when they tried to be there for each other.

She scanned the list twice before clicking the screen to black and putting the phone back in her pocket. All those people in her phone and no one she could talk to about this. She looked back in the direction of the bench where she'd left the homeless guy and the expensive pasta.

Maybe flowers weren't such a bad idea after all.

SUZIE WILL NOT BE IGNORED

Suzie stood inside her studio apartment, arms wrapped around herself, watching her doorstep through a gap in the blackout curtains. No way was she opening the door. She was still fuming. In fact, her whole body felt shaky with rage. She couldn't remember the last time she'd been this angry.

Patricia had taken her time getting there. Suzie checked her phone. Two hours since she'd left the restaurant. No phone calls. No texts. Nothing. Had Patricia even cared that she'd left?

No. That wasn't fair.

She abandoned Patricia at the restaurant without a ride, after all. And it wasn't like she made a habit of running out on their conversations. This was new territory for them both.

Patricia must have walked back to the office, several blocks away, to get her car before she came here. Knowing Patricia, she walked even further than that—the woman was a real believer in physical activity to deal with tough emotions. She'd probably walked the city twice over. If she'd worn better shoes, she would have run. If not for her favorite pants suit, she might have transformed and run lizard-footed through the streets.

But she had shown up.

After a stop at a florist?

Suzie flicked the panel aside to check what she'd seen. Yes, Patricia was holding a bouquet. Asiatic lilies from the look of it. She knocked again, calling out Suzie's name, her voice a little raw and ragged.

A flicker of guilt twitched across Suzie's chest, like something hot dragged across her skin. Then her anger returned, blazing hot. What did *she* have to feel guilty about? Patricia was the one who hadn't been listening. All she'd done was refuse to tolerate being ignored.

She'd listened to Patricia talk about the weird frogs at the pond ad nauseum, but when it was her turn to talk, Patricia had zoned out, like nothing she said mattered. Like she wasn't important enough to pay attention to. And if she were honest, it wasn't the first time. It had been happening more and more.

Suzie was proud of the way she'd gotten Dr. Liu on board with the frog problem, and usually the two of them liked to dissect and discuss everything about that woman—analyzing and strategizing together. Suzie loved it when they dug into a problem, their minds in sync, building on what the other one said. Moments like that were the highlight of their relationship for Suzie, maybe even better than the sex.

Patricia's mind was as stunning as the woman herself. The questions she asked. So incisive, cutting straight to the heart of the matter and digging out the core.

But Patricia didn't ask any questions. From the blank expression on her face, it was clear that she didn't even know what Suzie had been talking about, and that left Suzie feeling like a fool.

Her mom often hinted that Patricia wasn't right for her, but Suzie had never believed it. "Age is just a number, Mom. Patricia gets me. She understands me like no one else ever has." Tears built up in her eyes and Suzie wiped them angrily, turning away from the pathetic sight of Patricia on the doorstep, flowers in hand.

There wasn't much room to get away from the door in her tiny studio apartment. She spent so little time here of late, sleeping over in Patricia's palatial condo most of the time, that it seemed unimportant to upgrade from the place she'd rented when she moved to Springfield and didn't have a real salary. Right now, though, the walls felt like they were closing in on her. She wanted out, but she didn't want to talk to Patricia. Not yet.

Effectively trapped in her room by an apology bouquet, Suzie began to pace. Even that was unsatisfying. There was only room to move about four steps in any direction before she hit an obstacle and had to turn around. She spent more time turning around than pacing and her head swam. Patricia was saying something through the door, but Suzie's angry pulse filled her head until she couldn't make out the words.

Giving up on pacing, she tugged her suitcase out from under her bed and threw it on top. When she popped it open, she found it was still partially packed from the August beach trip with Patricia. She tossed the coverups and sandals across the room, ignoring the sand they trailed across the floor, and shoved the images of cocktails and dance floors in happier days down in her mind.

Moving faster now, she flung open drawers and thrust her hand into the closet, hurling random items into the suitcase. When nothing else would fit, she slammed it shut, clicking the latches and lowering it to the floor. Grabbing the handle, she rolled it across the floor, growling when the wheels got mired in the throw rug and yanking the suitcase into the air, wrenching her elbow in the process and swearing in frustration.

She had her hand on the doorknob before she remembered Patricia might be standing on the other side of the door. Jumping back as if the chunk of metal hand burned her palm, she stood, hand at her chest, listening. The knocking stopped sometime during her frenzied packing, and all she could hear was the hum of the HVAC system whirring and some traffic noise from the other side of the parking lot.

Had Patricia gone?

She stepped to the window, flicking the curtain to the side again so she could peek at the doorstep. Patricia was gone, but the lilies were still there, laying like an offering on the doormat. Pink stargazer lilies inter-mixed with white ones like a traditional Valentine's box, wrapped up in paper, their petals turned up expectantly, curling like fingers.

Suzie stooped to pick them up on her way to her car and tossed them into the passenger seat beside her.

Hands on the steering wheel, she sat for a long moment. Then she pulled up her phone, sent a text to the Director and another to her mother. She ignored all the other notifications, turned off the phone, threw it in the glovebox, put the car in reverse, and squealed out of the parking lot.

THURSDAY

RAY-GUNS, AND DINOSAURS, AND SALLY ANN, OH MY!

The earpiece crackled once more before a high-pitched tone made Sally Ann pull the device out to protect her hearing. She glared at the little chunk of plastic in her hand. Technology. So useful when it worked, and such a complication when it didn't. Whatever Fuerte had been trying to tell her was lost now. She'd have to hope things were going according to plan.

Gesturing "follow me" at the agents squatting with her in the emergency stairwell, Sally Ann jogged up the three flights as soundlessly as she could manage, given the tactical gear. The crepe-soled boots helped. She paused outside the door that led into the service corridor behind the main exhibit hall, leaning against the door to listen. Nothing.

At least there was no gunfire or screaming. She could still hope they'd come through this mission with minimal damage.

The Springfield Museum of Natural History wasn't generally a hotbed of crime on a Thursday morning, and personal property protection wasn't usually the purview of the Unusual Cases Unit, but they'd gotten the call about an hour ago about an attempted theft turned into a hostage situation.

Normally, Sally Ann would have let the mundane authorities handle it —no super strength or flight required to deal with a couple of would-be thieves—but the Director couldn't pass up the opportunity for some good press, so here they were. There were kids involved, a second-grade field trip group. Saving kids was always good optics.

To be fair, there were indications that the special brand of UCU expertise might be needed—these weren't ordinary thieves. These guys brandished an impressive array of technology, including some gadgets one doesn't just pick up on the streets. Sally Ann rubbed the pocket where she stowed her now-useless earpiece, considering whether the interference might have been intentional.

The question on her mind right now was what these men wanted. It wasn't like you could hock relics from a museum on the local black market. If simple thievery of valuable objects was the goal, there were better targets with more salable items. Jewelry stores, pawn shops, sporting goods stores, electronic stores. Heck, even a bank—though it would be a mistake to choose the one the UCU used for cover. Why a natural history museum?

Something about the call bothered her. She couldn't explain it, but she had a feeling in the pit of her stomach she knew better than to ignore. She'd keep her eyes open—the right, the left, and the inner one that sometimes saw things others could not.

Opening the door just wide enough for entry, she slid through, sliding low in case any danger awaited her on the other side. Finding an empty hallway, she tapped on the door to cue the other agents to follow. The two agents filled the narrow corridor, standing side by side—bulky men made bulkier by their equipment. She knew them both to be capable fighters if not exactly original thinkers. Sometimes it was good to work with people who would take orders and do their best to follow them.

Double-checking the schematic on her handheld, Sally Ann set off for the main exhibit hall. Her map indicated they could enter behind the scenes through an employees-only access point. That should let them get into the room and get eyes on the scene before the hostiles knew they were there.

The door clicked louder than she would have liked when she pushed it open, but the sound didn't attract any immediate attention. She could hear voices now and focused on what she could make out. A kid was crying. A female voice was making soothing, cooing noises. A male voice rose in volume, irritation clear in the staccato patterns of his words, until "Shut that kid up!" came across clearly.

The three agents moved toward the voices.

"You don't want to do this." Fuerte's sonorous baritone stopped Sally

Ann and her companions. It sounded so close, as if he were in the corridor with them.

They were in another narrow hallway, one wall of which bowed outward. Sally Ann tried to picture the exhibit hall in her mind, recalling the security footage and images she'd received in her briefing. This wall was little more than molded plastic, painted to suggest a cave wall and make visitors feel more like they were among dinosaurs. They might be mere inches from Fuerte, Patricia, the hostages, and the would-be thieves, or they might be on the other side of the hall.

"There's no reason anyone has to get hurt." Fuerte continued.

Sally Ann signaled the other agents to stay out of sight. She herself moved forward, crouching low. She maneuvered herself into position to see into the wider room at knee level. Fuerte's boots came into view, with Patricia's terrifying taloned feet beyond him. She couldn't see the gunmen, but she knew by the position of Fuerte's feet that they must be against the other wall, near the glass cases of funerary artifacts. But where were the hostages? How many were still in the room?

Sliding forward, Sally Ann wriggled a little further out of her hiding place. She wished Flygirl were there. Her ability to fly into the rafters and hover out of sight was invaluable in surveillance situations.

But Jessica Roark said she liked night-flying, and what Jessica liked, she generally got. Since Flygirl was the golden girl of the media, the Director was happy to let her take her pick of assignments, even if her colleagues could have used her support at other times of day.

But that was a battle for another day. Today's battle existed a few feet further into the room, between the model Tyrannosaurus Rex and the gunmen.

Sally Ann could view another slice of the room by peering under the cart that served as a desk for museum employees. The group of kids huddled against the wall, a teacher and two chaperones poised in front of them, bodies spread out to protect their charges. Six other civilians crouched on the floor a little apart from them: a young mom—or maybe a nanny with her charges, one pulled into each hip, a pair of college kids wearing Springfield College hoodies and gripping each other's hands, and a middle-aged Hispanic man holding a bloody handkerchief to his brow.

The blood worried Sally Ann. It showed a willingness to hurt innocents. She wriggled back into the darkness. She'd just pulled out her phone to share position information with the other two agents when all hell broke loose.

Fuerte yelled something incoherent. A loud collision shook the floor. Then gunfire echoed. Muffled screams erupted. Broken chunks of plexiglass skittered across the tile.

Ignoring her plan to enter stealthily, Sally Ann burst into the room in time to see Patricia skid backward, her talons tracing a long scar into the patterned flooring. One of the gunmen was on the floor, Fuerte crouched beside him.

The other trained his weapon on the Lizard Woman—a strange gun with a large round barrel and blue lights running in coils. Was this what had pushed Patricia back? Patricia squatted in a runner's stance, one arm clutching her ribs. If this weapon could get through Patricia's armor, it deserved a little respectful attention.

"Get the hostages out of here." Sally Ann pushed the two agents toward the cowering crowd. Reaching behind her back, she pulled her baton out of its holster and clicked the button to open it to a full-length bo staff. Swirling it, she circled, placing herself between the gunman who was still standing and the hostages.

He was a large man, 250 pounds or more of muscle. Other than his size, there was nothing striking about him. White guy, late twenties or early thirties, patchy facial hair, wearing lab goggles. Were the goggles for disguise or protection? A quick review of her mental "most wanted" list didn't find a match for him. A new player in town maybe.

Grinning at her, he held up the weird gun in his hands. Sally Ann had already noted the unusual size of the barrel and the sci-fi design. "Looks like somebody brought a stick to a gunfight," the man said, posing like a fool.

Without breaking her focus on the gunman, she spoke. "Fuerte, you got that guy, right?"

"Affirmative."

The man on the floor groaned, and Sally Ann knew Fuerte had tightened his grip. She tossed him a pair of handcuffs off her belt. A quick scan of the room revealed a broken display case housing dinosaur bones. She sent a silent prayer that nothing took damage.

The still-standing gunman shifted his stance, glancing at his partner on the ground, then to Sally Ann, then back to Patricia. His mouth tightened and he gripped the gun tighter, spreading his legs into a stronger stance. No surrender, then. A stand-your-ground sort of man. That was all right by her. She hadn't hit anyone yet today.

Holding her hands out to her sides, Sally Ann rolled the bo staff in her fingers like it was a plaything. Behind her, she heard the shuffle of the other agents getting the hostages out of the room. The gunman made no move to stop them, a realization that made Sally Ann hesitate. What kind of end game did he intend if he was letting them take his negotiation leverage without a struggle? Did he think he could shoot his way out of this and escape?

The gunman stiffened and the hairs on the back of Sally Ann's head stood up in anticipation. What alerted him? She spared a glance for Fuerte and the man on the floor, then risked turning her head to check on Patricia. The Lizard Woman was back on her feet. As Sally Ann watched, Patricia flexed, pushing out the final stage of her transformation, a bony protuberance widening around her head and her entire body expanding in bulk.

Before Sally Ann could react, Patricia lowered her head and charged, running full bore at the gunman. The floor shook and display items rattled on the walls. The gunman's eyes grew wide and he raised his weapon, screaming wordlessly as he fired at the Lizard Woman. A whoosh sounded, and Patricia's right shoulder flung back for a moment, but she kept her feet and barely slowed.

The man fumbled with his weapon, and a high-pitched whine bounced off the ceilings, like a battery charging. Before he could do anything else, Patricia was on him. When she collided with the man, they flew back together several feet, a tangle of scales and metal.

"Shit!" Sally Ann sprang into action, scrambling to intercede before Patricia ripped the man's arms off. "Patricia! Stand down!"

Patricia gripped the man by one bicep and lifted him into the air, tearing the gun from his grip with her other claw. Grinning, she grabbed the barrel of the weapon and squeezed.

"Patricia! No!"

Sally Ann's yell came too late.

When the barrel folded in Patricia's taloned grip, it was like the air became solid. Sally Ann was thrust back and landed gasping on the ground, her chest screaming from the impact. Patricia was flung several feet into the air, dropping the gunman she'd held like an unwanted toy. The plates in her head struck the skeletal Pteranodon hanging above them, setting it spinning before Patricia herself crashed to the floor, cracking the tile.

Sally Ann forced herself to her knees, sucking in what air she could and trying to clear her blurry vision. Her ears rang. The Pteranodon rocked and reeled. First one, then another pinioning wire broke from the ceiling, leaving the Pteranodon unsupported on one wing. Even though Sally Ann still heard a roar in her ears more than the actual sounds of the room, she could see the crack forming in the ceiling. How heavy was that thing?

She crawled forward, fighting for balance, and grabbed the gunman from where he lay on the floor, dragging him toward the exit. Across the room, she saw a double image of Fuerte carrying the cuffed suspect after her. "Over here," she yelled, pointing at the emergency exit door with her arm and hoping Fuerte could hear her.

When Fuerte caught up to her, he grabbed the second man, easily carrying both, one tucked under each arm like a pair of unruly toddlers. He settled them against the wall and turned back. Sally Ann's vision came in and out of focus. She sat next to the suspects and groaned. She likely had a concussion, but she'd have to worry about that later. "Patricia," she said.

Whether Fuerte heard her or not, she didn't know, but he jogged across the floor toward Patricia's inert form huddled on the floor. Above him, the pteranodon jerked away from the ceiling, the wires holding the other wing snapping. Sally Ann yelled. "Look out!" And then there was dust everywhere, reducing her to a coughing fit.

When the dust cleared, Fuerte knelt on the floor, like Atlas under a globe, a pteranodon resting on his shoulders. Sally Ann had time to laugh to herself about the Lizard Woman nearly getting squashed by a dinosaur before she lost consciousness.

JESSICA'S PRECIOUS

Jessica stood outside the tattoo and piercing parlor examining her reflection in the window. She had already walked by five times without getting up the nerve to go inside. Her experience came from television and movies, and that impression left her nervous.

An innocuous-looking place, the tattoo shop was not markedly different from the shops on either side—a wine bar and a bookstore. She expected a blinking neon sign and the smell of marijuana in the air, but the logo on the window was a simple set of lines suggesting a breeze with the word "Zephyr" above it in a flowing calligraphy script. It seemed more like an art gallery than anything seedy.

The only thing Jessica had pierced were her ears, done at a shopping mall when she was six or seven years old. Her mother raged at her father for letting her do it. She'd never considered a tattoo, a belly button ring, or anything.

She rubbed one of the gray pearls in her ears. They'd been a wedding gift from Walter's sister, simple and elegant. Though, just now, they struck her as a bit old fashioned and stodgy. Jessica was sure she wasn't cool enough for this place.

Pulling her purse more firmly onto her shoulder, she shook off her doubts and pushed open the door. A set of tinkling chimes rattled as she stepped into the shop, then settled into a more musical pattern. She thought she smelled cookies, which seemed odd until she spotted the essential oil diffuser—vanilla.

A young woman with her hair shaved on one side and worn in a fluffy pink cascade down the other cheek walked toward her. A name tag on her chest read "Callah." "Good afternoon. Welcome to Zephyr. How can I help you?"

This must be the tattoo artist Mary recommended. Jessica tried not to stare at the little silver ring hanging from the bottom of Callah's nose. "I'm here to see Zeph, if he's free?"

Surprise raised the woman's eyebrows, calling attention to the small spikes at the corner of the left one, but her tone remained professional. "Sure, I can see if he's available. Are you here for a consultation?"

"Yes, actually. Tell him Mary Braeburn recommended him to me."

A wide grin lit the Callah's face. "Mary! I haven't seen her in ages. How is she?"

"She's doing well." Jessica hoped Callah didn't ask too many questions. She couldn't explain her connection to Mary as a work colleague if this was a friend who might know more details of Mary's life. Luckily her curiosity remained focused on Mary.

"Is she still with that guy? Jorge?"

Jessica frowned, remembering a conversation with Leonel at her wedding reception. Ever the matchmaker, he'd been lamenting that the girl couldn't settle down in a romance.

"Well, kind of? You know how Mary is about romance."

Callah sighed. "All too well." The obvious longing in her voice startled Jessica. Mary must have made another conquest in this woman. After a moment, Callah shrugged, then turned away, calling back over her shoulder. "You can have a look around or sit down over there by the windows. I'll go find Zeph for you."

Alone in the salon, Jessica walked up to one of the display cases. It held a bunch of tiny barbells and rings in every color imaginable. Another showcased a set of plastic ears, each with a different size ring in a distended earlobe. Mary wore something like that, with a sky-blue disk in it.

Jessica wandered over to the seating area and settled on a sofa that resembled a set of lips. A bright green binder on the table caught her eye, and she flipped through the photographs of tattoos and piercings. She paused on a picture of a woman's throat, with a bright blue gem in the dip of the clavicle. She read the description below: "Microdermal piercing with custom jewelry."

That's what she wanted. Mary had been surprised when Jessica asked her for advice but became enthusiastic as Jessica asked for details about Mary's tattoos and piercings. The work in the portfolio impressed her.

If anyone could help her, Zeph was the guy. And after her fight with her mother the other night, it felt even more important to make her connection to the emeralds permanent, irrevocable, as much a part of her as her own eyebrows.

While she flipped through the photos, Zeph slipped into the room, moving quietly despite the heft of his boots and stopping on the other side of the table. A burly man of some forty or fifty years with an astonishing mustache shaped into curls on his cheeks, Zeph dressed like her father on the weekends, wearing a flannel shirt that had seen better days over stained blue jeans. Jessica leapt to her feet, leaving the binder on the lip-shaped sofa.

She held out a hand. "Thanks so much for talking with me. I'm Jessica."

Zeph grabbed her fingers and held them, looking into her face a little too long for comfort. "I'm Zeph. Any friend of Mary's."

He hooked a thumb to indicate an unlabeled door near the window. "Come on back. Let's talk about what you want."

He led her into a cozy office with natural light streaming through a skylight in the center of the room. After settling her into a yellow armchair with a tall back and talking her into a cup of tea, Zeph settled into his seat, a massive leather desk chair that creaked when he leaned it back to rest a booted foot on the desk. He held a sketchpad on his thigh and sketched as he asked her questions.

Jessica had settled on the story that she wanted body-art to celebrate her cancer survival. She'd inherited the emeralds, she told him, from her grandmother and they meant a lot to her, so she wanted them incorporated.

"I was thinking of a microdermal. Mary said you could make custom jewelry. I loved the lotus you made for her."

"May I see the stones?"

Jessica shifted her purse from the floor to her knees and pulled out a little velvet bag from within. She shook the shards and pieces into her hand, holding them for a moment before making herself let them slide out of her grasp and onto the desk. Zeph swung a lamp arm around so the pieces were spotlit and poked at them with his finger.

Jessica gripped the arm of the chair, feeling agitated by his handling of the stones even though that was why she'd brought them.

Shifting his gaze from the stones, he asked. "Where are you thinking?"

"That's a little tricky. I maintain an active lifestyle, and I work at a bank, which means I need to choose somewhere hidden by most clothing, but won't be knocked off or cause me injury if I'm sparring at the gym."

Zeph looked her over, gesturing at his own body to indicate his shoulder, back, and chest.

"Not the back. I want to be able to touch the stones." Jessica rested a hand at her chest, where she imagined she could feel the warmth of the stones sewn into her bra. "They comfort me."

He pursed his lips, making his waxed mustache waggle. "How about the navel? Or the hip?"

"Maybe the hip." That would be appropriate in a way, making a truth of her lie about commemorating her survival of ovarian cancer, by decorating her abdomen.

He turned back to his sketchpad for a moment, his pencil flowing over the paper, then flipped it back around to show her. He'd sketched a butterfly, with the familiar cancer ribbon as the body. The elaborate wings resembled mandalas, and he'd put a little star in each section of wing. He pointed at them with his eraser. "We could do microdermal pieces integral to the wings, so the gems work together with the tattoo."

"May I?"

He nodded, so Jessica took the sketchpad and examined the sketch. The more she looked, the more she liked the idea. Ribbon for cancer. Wings for her flight, which had at first been as uncontrolled as a butterfly. And the gems, always a part of her.

Dropping his feet to the floor, he leaned across the desk and poked through the gems on the table. He found four round pieces of nearly the same size and set them apart from the others. He pointed at some of the sharp edges. "I'd need to smooth these down to keep them from catching on your clothing, but otherwise, I wouldn't need to do much to change the stones themselves. If you leave them with me, I could have the jewelry by next week."

He spun his chair and pulled a leatherbound book out of a drawer in the table behind the desk. He flipped through the pages. "Callah has an opening in about two weeks if you want to get the tattoo started."

Jessica's mouth went dry. She hadn't dared hope it would happen so quickly, and at the same time two weeks seemed an eternity to wait.

"She's good, and patient. This is your first tattoo, right?"

Jessica bit her lip. "Can I bring someone?"

"Of course! A lot of people like to have a friend with them."

She imagined Leonel coming with her, holding her hand and making bad jokes when it hurt. "Let's do it. What time?"

Zeph stepped to the door and called out, "Callah!"

The heavy sound of boots announced her approach. "Were you right?"

Zeph swung his fingers over his head, snapping them dramatically. "Nailed it."

Jessica looked back and forth between the two of them. "Nailed what?"

"It's a sort of game we play, guessing what kind of work a new customer is going to ask for. My bet was on a piercing, probably the navel."

"You were close," Zeph said, taking his sketch pad back from Jessica and spinning it across the desk.

Callah whistled. "Lovely."

Together, they laid out a plan. Even though Callah and Zeph advised against it, she insisted on getting the tattoo and the dermal done at the same time, and for some extra cash, they'd open early for her on Tuesday —a mere five days away.

Jessica left the shop, feeling so giddy she had to fight to keep her feet on the ground. Soon the gems would be a part of her, permanently.

PATRICIA'S GUILTY CONSCIENCE

Patricia sat in the hall outside Sally Ann's room in the medical wing at the UCU, head in her hands, waiting. She wasn't sure if she was waiting to make sure Sally Ann was all right or waiting to be fired. But she knew she couldn't go home until the hammer fell, whatever the hammer turned out to be. And she hated waiting.

Doctors and nurses cycled through all afternoon and evening. Few of them spared a glance in her direction. The only person to sit down and talk with her had been Walter, and he was kinder than she deserved. He'd tried to make light of the situation.

"It's not even her first concussion this year. She'll be fine."

But it was the first one Patricia had caused.

When she was in Lizard Woman form, her skull was literally thick, but that was no excuse. She'd never been a good team player and was proving that again and again. Ever since she'd stepped into the hero's life, she'd done nothing but hurt people. She got Leonel shot. She failed to keep Jessica from getting burned. And now, she'd put Sally Ann in the hospital.

She checked her phone again, but Suzie had not responded to her messages. When Patricia showed up on her doorstep with the bouquet of flowers after their disastrous dinner date, Suzie didn't even open the door. Patricia stood there for long minutes before she left the Asiatic lilies on the doormat, spilling crumbles of yellow pollen over the "Welcome" like ashes.

Ashes, just like she was making of her life.

Self-pity washed over her and the sensation made her angry. When did she become such a sap? Patricia stood and stared down the hallway in both directions, trying to decide which way to go, fists clenched at her sides.

Down the hall, she could hear the echoes of laughter. The night staff had time on their hands tonight. Leonel was discharged within minutes, with reassurances that the partial deafness was short term. Patricia didn't know where the two gunmen were confined and right now, she didn't care. So it was only Sally Ann and some longer-care patients on the ward tonight.

She could go home, but she didn't want to be there either, not with Suzie still avoiding talking to her. The condo was way too quiet. What she needed was someone to talk to—a distraction. With one last guilty look back at the door that sheltered Sally Ann, she pushed her shoulders down and stalked to the elevators.

The doors opened, and Patricia stepped into the opening without registering that the elevator was occupied.

"Patricia! Just the woman I wanted to talk to." A politician's smile spread across the Director's face.

Patricia stepped aside to let him leave the elevator, thrusting a hand in front of the door to keep it from closing. "Maybe tomorrow."

The Director frowned. "I don't think so. Now is better."

Her brain fogged for a moment, and Patricia felt her resolve melt. It was hard to say no to the Director. Before she'd quite decided to do so, she found herself following him down the hallway, back the way she had come. He didn't say anything along the way, and Patricia couldn't glean anything from his expression so she followed in silence.

He rapped on Sally Ann's door before opening it. The room was dim, which made sense for a concussion patient. The lamp and floor lighting glowed red, which made the room feel like a horror movie but did seem to be easier on the eyes than the traditional fluorescent lights lighting the hallways. Automatically, Patricia transformed her eyes to take advantage of the greater night vision that came with her Lizard Woman form.

Sally Ann's bed was tilted, and her eyes were closed, but she opened them when they entered. Normally, she put off a larger-than-life aura that made it easy to forget she wasn't much over five foot tall, but Sally Ann looked tiny in the hospital bed. Patricia took some reassurance from the lack of tubes and wires. She must not be too badly off if they were letting her rest without much monitoring.

"How are we doing, Agent Rogers?" The Director sat on the edge of the bed, and Patricia took up a position at the foot.

Sally Ann peered at each of them in turn. "My head still hurts, but the ringing in my ears is gone. Did the docs say I could go home?"

The Director shook his head. "Not yet. I think they'll want to keep you overnight, just to be sure. I have some news though, if you're up to hear it. Patricia, you'll want to hear this too."

"Go for it. It would be good to have something to think about. The doctors won't let me have my phone or any television, and I've done all the sleeping I can do for now." As she spoke, Sally Ann grappled with the remote control and brought the bed to a more upright position. "Did you get anything out of our gunmen? I've got a weird feeling about this one. It doesn't make any sense."

"You're right about that. It seems our friends were intended as a distraction."

Patricia snapped her gaze away from Sally Ann to focus on the Director. "A distraction from what?"

The Director pulled out a photograph from a leather folder he'd held tucked under his arm and laid it on Sally Ann's lap. Patricia circled the bed so she could see it too. A man lay sprawled on the floor of a lab, and the room was in disarray—papers on the floor and all the cabinet doors hanging open. Someone had ransacked the place searching for something.

Sally Ann squinted at the photograph. "Who's the victim?"

"Dr. Reed. He's a herpetologist at the museum. His lab is in the basement level."

Sally Ann passed the photograph to Patricia without turning her head. Patricia wasn't sure if that was a desire not to look at her or more an unwillingness to move her head too much.

"Herpetologist. They study what?"

"Reptiles and amphibians," Patricia answered.

Sally Ann snorted, then gasped from the pain it caused her. "Since when are you a science nerd?"

Patricia stretched out a hand, transforming the fingers into talons as she did so. "I've developed a personal interest in the field in recent years."

"Right, the frogs from the pond. The mutated ones." Sally Ann reached up and Patricia gave her back the photograph. "So, this is who we sent the samples to."

The Director nodded. "All the samples were taken, along with his notes. Dr. Reed walked into the room and found a man digging through the cabinets. Then someone hit him on the head."

Sally Ann squinted at the photograph. "Did Reed get a good look at them?"

"His description wasn't very helpful, but the security footage was." He pulled out another photograph.

Sally Ann drew in a sharp breath. "Damn it."

"I thought you might feel that way."

Patricia took her turn with the photograph. Daniel Price, the latest meat sack for Cindy Liu's body-hopping horror of a father, stood looking almost straight into the camera, like he wanted them to know it was him.

Seeing him raised nodules on Patricia's neck and she had to close her eyes and calm herself to avoid ruining her jacket with her shoulder spikes. She'd not forgotten their last run-in, and felt the scales run up her cheeks as she contemplated violent revenge for his attempts on her and her mother.

Sally Ann was more business-like. "Daniel's still looking damn good for a dead guy. Who's the other one?" The other man in the picture was not fully in view, but he was a large man, bald, with a bulbous nose and no neck to speak of.

"Nobody. At least nobody we've got in our databases. Same with the gunmen. It looks like Mr. Price has found some new staff."

Sally Ann made a sound that was very nearly a growl. "I told you we should have taken him in. It was a mistake to leave him there in Indiana."

Patricia agreed. That decision was the subject of more than one late-night speculation with Suzie—they were both sure the Director had made some kind of deal and that his end of the bargain was to let Daniel Price remain free, in spite of all his crimes. The question remained as to what he'd gotten or been promised in return.

She opened her mouth to say as much, but the Director spread his hands, and the words seemed to drift away before she could speak them. A brief feeling of dizziness overtook her, and she gripped the side rail of the bed to steady herself. When the moment passed, she found Sally Ann squinting at her as though in pain despite the dim lighting, but the agent turned back to the Director without saying anything.

"That's neither here nor there." The Director's voice was all sugared indulgence. "What matters now is figuring out what he's up to, and stopping him."

"Quieter." Sally Ann said, rubbing her temples before she asked, "What did you get out of the gunmen we brought in?"

Patricia tried to catch the Director's eye, but he avoided meeting her gaze, looking a little guilty. "Maybe you should rest now," she said to Sally Ann. "We can talk about this tomorrow, when you're feeling better."

Pushing a button on the remote, Sally Ann moved the bed a few degrees nearer horizontal. "You're probably right. I hate it, but it hurts to think. You should send Suzie in to talk to Liu again. See if she's figured out anything about the frogs herself yet, and if she can shed any light on what dear old daddy might be up to."

"Ms. Grayson has taken leave for a few days." The Director's tone went cold and disapproving. "Something about needing to see her mother." He waved a dismissive hand.

Patricia was grateful for the dim lighting as shame lit her cheeks. She hadn't known Suzie left town. If she'd gone home to her mother, who already hated Patricia, things were even worse than she'd imagined.

Sally Ann cursed softly. "That's bad timing. No one else can get through to Liu like she can."

"I could." Patricia could hardly believe the words as they came out of her mouth.

The Director smirked. "That's exactly what I was thinking."

Sally Ann finished lowering the bed and turned up on her side, weariness evident in the tightness around her mouth and eyes. "Don't kill her, Patricia. We might still need her."

HELEN AND MARY, IN THIS TOGETHER

Mary glowered at her mother across the small table. "Come on, do you think you're the only one who wants to burn it all down?"

Helen raised a small globe of fire in her left hand and set it spinning like a tiny planet aflame. "Some of us can actually do it, you know."

If Mary rolled her eyes any harder, they might have fallen out. "Just because we can, doesn't mean we should."

A desire to needle her self-righteous daughter proved more than Helen could resist. She arched an eyebrow, no longer bothering to hide her smirk. "Since when do you care about 'should'?"

Pushing back from her table hard enough that her chair flipped onto its back and rattled against the tile, Mary bellowed her rage. The wordless scream of frustration echoed in the tiny room.

Brayan-the-orderly appeared at the door so fast he smacked his head on the glass observation window trying to grab the door handle.

Quickly extinguishing her fireball, Helen wiggled her fingers at the man, shrugging and pointing at her daughter. "It's okay," she mouthed.

Brayan scowled, rubbing his forehead. He pointed at his dark brown eyes and then at her, his face devoid of mirth. Helen laid a hand on her chest and opened her eyes wide to indicate her innocence. It didn't get Brayan to move on, but at least he stayed on his side of the door, arms crossed over his broad chest, watching.

Mary remained facing the opposite wall, bouncing one foot into the pliable surface, leaving small dents in the fire-retardant material they covered the room in. Turning, Helen watched her, knowing from years of experience that it was better to let Mary calm herself for a while before trying to talk to her. The girl's shoulders were so tightly hunched she practically wore them as earrings and remorse overtook Helen's feeling of spite.

Mary and she were so much alike sometimes: headstrong, stubborn to the point of intractable, and so very, *very* sure they were right. No one knew how to get under your skin like someone who used to be there, and Mary was good at pushing Helen's buttons. But Helen was the mother here and it was high time she behaved like it, even if it meant she ate some humble pie.

"I'm sorry," she said.

Mary spun around to face her, face dark with her frustration, suspicion narrowing her eyes. "Yeah? What for?"

Helen sighed. Knowing she deserved this didn't make it any easier. "I'm taking things out on you, and that isn't fair."

Helen gestured at the long-resented white room, ugly, institutional. The thing that kept her safe all these months, even from herself.

"Everything you did — turning me in, cutting a deal with the Director — you did to help me. I know that."

Surprise dropped Mary's jaw and Helen laughed—the girl didn't know everything after all. "Oh, I'm still pissed off. Don't you doubt that for a second. But I also understand the position I put you in. I really was a danger to myself and others, especially you."

"Mom...I–"

Helen raised a finger, the tip aflame like a birthday candle, cutting her daughter off before she embarrassed both of them by letting the warble in her voice break into actual tears.

"They're offering me a chance to prove myself, and you're scared I'm going to blow it, that I won't contain my temper." Helen stretched the small flame out until it was a slender reed of fire, a foot or so long. She willed it to spiral around itself, snaking into a coil that rested on the fire-proof table, rotating.

Mary's eyes followed the ring of fire, her face a mixture of awe and tight-jawed anxiety. But she picked up the chair and put it back in place.

Helen straightened the ring and pushed it back with two fingers until it extinguished when her index fingers met, a slender thread of black smoke dissipating into the air. The two women watched it until it disappeared, then looked into each other's eyes. Mary had her father's eyes, Helen noticed again with a twinge, long eyelashes and all.

Her ex-husband could see through her, too—and it pissed her off just as much as it did when it came from Mary. But daughters weren't like husbands—daughters were for life. And she needed Mary, not only in this moment, but in a broader sense.

"Sit down, Contrary Mary," she said.

Mary didn't smile at the use of her childhood nickname, but she didn't object either. She slid into the chair and rested her elbows on the table focusing those dark-and-judging eyes full bore on Helen.

Calmly, Helen laid out the situation as it had been presented to her. For now, she would continue to reside at the UCU, checking in and out and constantly monitored. It was sort of like house arrest, but not at her own house. She'd be assigned a mentor, sort of a case manager.

"Did they tell you who?"

Helen shook her head. "Not yet." She continued explaining. "The Director wants to make me part of the team, the hero squad or whatever they call it. Big press conference to announce it and everything." She swallowed hard, imagining confronting the same people who helped capture and put her away and asking to be accepted as one of them now. "What do you think I should do?"

"Are you asking my advice?" Mary's eyebrows were raised so high they almost disappeared into her hair.

Helen shifted in her chair but held her daughter's gaze. "I am."

"And you'll take it?"

"I think I'm going to have to hear it before I can answer that. But I will listen. I know you have my best interest at heart, as well as watching out for all the fools out there. And you know a lot more about what the UCU has in mind. They wouldn't do this out of the kindness of their own hearts—they want something. And I need to know what it is before I can decide if it's a fair trade."

"That's...very reasonable."

"No reason to sound so surprised about it."

A shadow of a smile playing around Mary's mouth. "No reason?"

"Okay, okay. Maybe you have some reasons. But I am serious. You're the only person who can help me with this."

Mary walked over to the door and opened it, leaning her head out and exchanging a few words with Brayan who hadn't moved from his post during their conversation.

She came back and sat down then stared up at the camera in the ceiling. Helen turned to see what she was looking at and saw the moment when the blinking red light turned off. Staring at her daughter with wide eyes, she said, "Connections, huh?"

Mary blew on her fingernails and wiped her folded fingers against her sweater, then splayed her fingers. "I know a guy." Then she leaned across the table and started talking.

"This is all about optics."

Helen tilted her head to one side, wondering what the hell eyesight had to do with anything.

"Appearances. PR."

Now *that* Helen understood. "So, they want me to make the UCU look good and, in exchange, I get my freedom back?"

"That's what he claims."

The hairs on the back of Helen's neck stood up. "'Claims' is not a word that fills me with warm fuzzies."

"It shouldn't." Mary stood and walked around the small room, pacing a circle around the table before turning and retracing her steps.

Helen watched, waiting.

"The thing is—I don't know what he's up to—not yet. But I can feel it all the same." Mary shook her hands in front of her, like there was something on them she was trying to fling off. "It's there, underneath everything, this oily feeling."

Helen frowned. She didn't like the sound of this. "You have good instincts, Mary. You should trust them."

Mary's eyes widened. "Mom, it was my instincts that told me to bring you back here, even after I worked so hard to get you out."

"And you were right both times." Helen turned her chair so she could see her daughter's face. "Your instincts told you I had been abducted, so you came to rescue me, which was more than I deserved."

Mary started to object, but Helen raised a hand, letting flames envelope it for a moment before she extinguished them in a closed fist. "You didn't know what was going on with me—there was no way you could have. You thought the mother you'd known all your life was locked up by some kind of secret organization. But really, they'd captured a dangerous woman who intended harm."

Mary sank back into her chair. "Was it the pills?"

Helen shrugged. "Yes? No? Maybe? I mean, the Surge Protector caused this." She formed a little ring of fire and set it to rolling around her index finger. "But the pills didn't make me throw fireballs at people." She spun the little ring of fire, watching it and thinking, then flung it into the air, letting it dissipate to smoke.

"That time…it's hard to explain. Your father was gone, and with him, most of my friends because they had been *our* friends and people didn't want to be put in a position where they'd have to take sides. Work had become a teeth-gritting experience, where people barely out of high school spoke condescendingly to me and assumed I didn't know even the most basic things about the business I'd been in for fifteen years. And I was forced to take it because I needed the money."

She leaned back in her chair, pushing the hair out of her face, and made herself look Mary in the eyes. "My daughter and I couldn't talk to each other without devolving into yelling matches. My cat died. Nothing was good."

Mary reached across the table and took Helen's hand. Helen squeezed it. "Then the fire came. Dr. Liu found me. She was so excited about what I could do, talked about how amazing I was, pushed me to find my limits. I hadn't felt so important—so *seen*—in years." Tears welled up in her eyes, and Helen shoved the heels of her hands into the sockets. "It was a kind of mania, like I couldn't see the wider picture because it felt so damn good."

After wiping her wet hands on the table, she asked, "Mary, what if it's the fire that does it? What if I let myself use my fire again and it takes me over? What then?"

Mary pulled her mother toward her, pressing their foreheads together. "We're not going to let that happen."

"What if it's not up to us?"

"We'll figure it out," Mary said. "Together."

LEONEL'S WORK-LIFE BALANCE

eonel looked up when the kitchen door swung open. Their eldest
daughter swept into the room, dropping her purse in one of the
chairs and picking up her niece from where the youngster had sat playing
with blocks at David's feet. "Oof! You're getting so big, Nani. Such a little
gordita, just like your mami."

Even when her sister wasn't there, slender and svelte Lupita liked to
remind everyone the family beauty Viviana had been a chubby baby.
Leonel kept slicing the jicama for the salad and didn't comment, a gentle
cluck of the tongue the only sign of his displeasure.

"Hi Tata!" Lupita leaned in to kiss David on the cheek. David put
down his magazine and stood to give his daughter a quick hug.

She plopped the toddler back down on the floor and came over to the
stove where Leonel was working. She reached for the pot lid, and Leonel
smacked her fingers with a dish towel. "They're not ready yet."

Lupita kissed her fingers and shook them in the air. "No need for
violence, Mami. They just smell so good."

Leonel smiled. "It's been a while since we've had all of you for dinner,
so I wanted to spoil you."

"Okay, okay. I'll wait." Drifting back over to the table, Lupita sat down
at the table with David, stretching out her feet so Nani could play with
the bows on the toes of her shoes. "I miss when mine were little like this.
Carlitos is almost seven already, and the girls will be ten this summer."

Leonel picked up a plate and carried it over to the table, then whipped off the covering towel with a flourish to reveal a stack of biscochitos. Lupita snatched one up and groaned with pleasure as she took a bite. "You *are* spoiling us tonight."

"Well, I miss when mine were little, too, you know. But some things never change—cookies always make you happy."

With a little cry, Nani reached for David's knee and pulled herself up to standing, then clambered into his lap. He gave her a boost, and she immediately dove for the plate of cookies. Lupita rescued the plate and broke off part of her own cookie to share, showering the tablecloth with cinnamon and sugar. They all knew better than to let the little one eat a whole cookie by herself—she'd be bouncing off the walls for hours.

"When are Carlos and the kids coming?" David asked, bouncing Nani up and down, and turning her so she saw the toys on the floor instead of the plate with the rest of the cookies.

Lupita checked her phone. "Should be any minute now. He was picking the girls up from dance class, then coming straight here."

As if on cue, the door opened again. Carlitos came running in and flung his arms around Leonel's waist. He was getting so big. His head nestled well above Leonel's belly button now. "Abuelita! I saw you on TV tonight!"

Leonel widened his eyes and feigned surprise. "Was I on TV today?" He squinted up at the rafters, pretending to look for a camera. "Did you see me making tamales?"

Carlitos whispered, like he hadn't already shouted a moment earlier. "No! Not here! At the museum, with your mask on—but I knew it was you."

The twins came in with their father, setting their dance bags by the back door before sliding in for hugs of their own. "Everyone was talking about it at dance class," they said, speaking over each other. "Did you really catch a dinosaur?"

Leonel posed with his arms in the air like he was holding something big. "I did." He spun around in a circle, making his apron flare around him. "The hardest part was figuring out where to set it down."

Lupita gasped and passed her phone around to show everyone the photograph she'd found. It was a little grainy, pulled from the security footage at the museum, but there he was, wearing his golden sun mask and the red shirt, kneeling in the middle of the room, holding a skeletal pteranodon above his head. Patricia lay at his feet.

When they passed the phone to Leonel, he scrolled to see the headline: "Fight at the Museum Threatens Beloved Fossil." He frowned. The Director wasn't going to like that take on things. Without reading the rest, he handed his daughter back the phone.

"Enough about my work. How are things at the law office, Lupita?"

Lupita was still talking about all the inter-office drama when her sisters arrived.

"There's my angel-girl! Nani!"

Nani toddled over to be swept into her mother's arms, and Leonel thought his heart might swell right out of his chest with pride and happiness.

When he'd first faced the unexpected gender change and development of super strength just a few short years ago, he'd been sure it would mean the end of his family. But here they all were, crowded into his kitchen, happy and laughing together. He reached out a hand to squeeze David's fingers, and when their eyes met, he knew David felt the same. He squeezed Leonel's hand, then raised it to his lips and planted a kiss on the knuckles, eliciting groans and giggles from the grandchildren.

"Everyone get washed up! It's time to eat!"

By the time the last grandchild was packed into a car, Leonel was yawning with exhaustion. David stood next to him in the driveway, one hand around his waist, waving and blowing kisses as the blue minivan moved down their street. Leonel rested his head against David's, savoring the quiet moment.

"It was good to have them all here tonight." David stretched up to plant a kiss on the side of Leonel's neck.

"It had been too long," Leonel agreed. He leaned forward, peering down the now-empty street. Tree shadows stretched long in the lamplight and the air felt crisp. "Let's walk a little." He patted his stomach. "I ate too much."

David patted his considerably softer belly. "Me too, and not all of us have superhero metabolism."

"You know I wouldn't change you for anything."

The two linked hands and meandered down the street at a leisurely stroll. It had taken them a long time to learn to walk together again after Leonel's transformation. When he'd been Linda, he had been quite a bit shorter, and sometimes Leonel still set a pace like he needed to scramble to keep up with taller companions. Now, he was the one who needed to remember to shorten his stride for others. Doing so made him weave a little as he walked, and his body bumped gently against his husband's.

"You are quiet tonight, *mi amor*. What's on your mind?" David's dark brown eyes were hard to read by streetlamp light, but the concern in his voice made Leonel's heart flutter a bit.

"I don't know. Just sorting things out, I guess."

"Work stuff?"

Leonel nodded. "Work stuff."

David nudged him in the ribs with their joined hands. "It's okay to talk to me about it, you know. You always used to listen to me when I needed to vent about work."

It was true. But somehow, this felt different. Taking on this dangerous line of work had been a point of contention—it almost cost them their marriage. Leonel wasn't sure he should admit to David that it wasn't all sunshine and roses, that sometimes he wished he had not opted to take on such a public and absorbing line of work at the age when most people their age were slowing down.

"I think I just want everything, you know? I want to be here making tamales for my family and to be out there, making a difference." He gestured at the distant city lights, visible over the trees at the end of the block.

David grunted. "I know I haven't always supported you in your work."

Leonel demurred, and David went on. "I knew how much it mattered to you, but I fought you on the changes it would mean for our lives."

The two of them arrived at the halfway point between their house and the park that abutted their neighborhood, where an intricately carved wood and iron bench sat beneath a stately magnolia tree. David sat down and Leonel joined him.

Across the street was the old Liu house, still marked off with sagging caution tape. The part that had suffered the most fire damage was in the back, so from the front it looked unwanted rather than half-destroyed, the porch listing to one side and the garden overgrown. Leonel let his gaze wander the scene, waiting to see if his husband would say anything more.

"And then you got shot."

David leaned forward, and Leonel spread a hand to rub his back.

David softened into the touch. "I thought we had lost you forever, and I was so angry at you for putting yourself at risk."

"I remember." An icy spike stabbed Leonel's heart at the memory.

David turned to gaze into Leonel's face. "I still feel that way sometimes. Why should my wife be the one who has to catch dinosaurs when they fall from the ceiling? Or pull trucks back onto the bridge? Or hold the building together while the workers evacuate?"

Because I can. The thought sat on Leonel's tongue, but he held it, knowing this was his time to listen, not to speak.

"But the truth is—you were always at risk. We all are, every day. There are no guarantees that just because you are careful, you are safe." He reached up and pushed a lock of hair back from Leonel's forehead. "You were always holding the world together and saving us all. I just didn't see it back then."

He took Leonel's hand again and pressed his lips into the palm, then folded the fingers around it—a gesture as old as their romance, something he'd first done when Leonel had been a shy sixteen-year-old-girl flattered by the attentions of the worldly nineteen-year-old man who'd already started making his own living and moved into his own apartment.

Leonel frowned. "Sometimes I have doubts about the path I have chosen."

Laughing, David shook his head. "Of course you do. That's the way of things. There is no perfect road, *mi amor*. They all have potholes. Do you think I didn't sometimes wish I could work fewer hours and spend more time with our daughters?"

Leonel stretched an arm across the back of the bench and David snuggled under it. They looked up at the night sky over the Liu house, easy in the quiet. Finally, Leonel laughed.

"What's so funny?" David's voice was drowsy.

"It's just…I was jealous of you then, for getting out in the world having a career while I was at home with the kids. And I'm jealous of you now, for getting to stay home and spend time with the grandkids."

"Well, my life has always been amazing. I can see why you'd be jealous." David got to his feet and reached out a hand to pull Leonel up, a comical prospect given the difference in their strength. Leonel took the help anyway; glad they were in this together.

SUZIE GOES HOME TO MAMA

Suzie let her head loll back in the chair while the pedicurist worked on her feet. It had been too long since she'd given in to pampering like this. She rolled her neck, frowning at the popping sounds at the extremities of the turn. As the pedicurist moved to work on the other foot, she let her head fall to one side.

Opening her eyes, she found her mother staring at her, her dark brown eyes boring into her like lasers.

"Suzie, you know it's always good to have you home, but when are you planning to tell me what's going on?"

Groaning, Suzie shifted in her chair to sit more upright. She smiled apologetically at the pedicurist for disrupting her work and pulled the towel off her head. Her blond mop was plastered to her forehead and scalp, so she ran her hands through it, making it stand up in awkward waves like a sort of halo.

When she'd gotten in her car Wednesday night, she knew she had to get out of Springfield, or more specifically, away from Patricia. So she'd come home, because it was the one place she could still go that wasn't intertwined with her girlfriend. Suzie arrived late enough that the housekeeper opened the door in her bathrobe.

She didn't come downstairs until lunchtime, unheard of in her parents' house. It was telling that her mother let her lay abed so long. She must have been worried.

Her mother reached across and swatted at her elbow, the chairs too far apart for proper contact. "Sweetie, you know you can tell me anything."

Suzie grimaced. "I know, Mom. I'm not sure there's anything to tell."

"Is it that job of yours? You know you could do better, sweetheart."

"It's not that."

Her mom didn't know what Suzie did, of course. She thought Suzie was managing the office at a bank. And she did work at a bank, or at least in the same building as the bank the UCU used as cover. She didn't know Suzie was working with superheroes, saving the city on a regular basis. She certainly didn't know Suzie had gone into the field and into the line of fire more than once.

"I love my work," she said.

"So, if it's not work, what is it, honey?" Eloise Grayson *nee* Russo picked out a nice coral paint that would glow against her sun-kissed skin and handed the bottle to the tech. "This one please."

Suzie often wished she'd gotten her mother's skin, but she took after her father's side of the family, pasty New Englanders who traced their origins to boats of pilgrims, proud of that history as if it meant something more than an inability to fit in back in England. Patricia often joked about finding the one person in all of Springfield even paler than herself. "If all else fails, we could take off our shirts and blind them with our skin!"

When Suzie didn't offer an answer, her mother pursed her lips. "I can't help you if you won't tell me what's wrong, darling."

What was wrong? That was the question. She wasn't sure she could explain it herself.

"It's my girlfriend," she finally admitted.

"Ah, Patricia." Her mother said Patricia's name like it tasted bad in her mouth.

The pedicurist looked up, pushing her dark bangs off her forehead with the back of her hand, and meeting Suzie's gaze for a moment before returning to her tools, her expression as neutral as ever. Suzie guessed gossip must be one of the perks of the job.

A svelte man dressed in a tailored suit appeared at Suzie's elbow, bowing and holding out a tray with a glass of lemon-infused water. Thanking him, she accepted the beverage.

He moved over to her mother, who smiled as she accepted her drink. "Sergio, I don't know if you've met my daughter, Suzie?"

"Your daughter?" The man's face spread in theatrical surprise. "But surely this is your sister, Miss Eloise."

Predictably, her mother brightened at the trite compliment, one Sergio offered to every middle-aged woman in the shop, Suzie was certain. She managed not to roll her eyes at the banter. If it made her mother happy, what was the harm?

"Suzie is visiting for a few days." Eloise leaned toward him and stage whispered. "Romance troubles."

Sergio ducked his head and shook his head, tsking. "Ah. The heart wants what it wants." He paused, and the look in his eyes was surprisingly tender. "Even when it hurts."

Tears stung in Suzie's eyes. She took a long swallow from her drink to disguise her discomfort. Did she really want to talk about this? Some part of her did. Why else would she have showed up on her parents' doorstep? But there was so much her mother didn't know, some of which she *couldn't* know. It was hard to have a heart-to-heart when you had to hold back.

She closed her eyes and took three slow breaths, swallowing the tears before they fell. When she opened her eyes, her mother hadn't moved, her gaze still focused on her daughter's face. She opened her eyes wider, sculpted eyebrows disappearing into the towel turban on her head, a silent demand that her daughter fill her in.

"I don't know where to start," Suzie said.

"You and your girlfriend fought. What about?"

That was the question. "It's hard to say."

"Honey." Eloise laid a hand over Suzie's, flattening her fingers against the arm rest. "You've got to give me something to go on, here. Did she cheat on you? Steal from you? Hit you?"

Suzie rolled her eyes. "No, Ma. Nothing so dramatic. We're not soap opera characters."

Eloise squinted at her. "So, what was it?"

"She doesn't listen to me."

"Ah." Eloise wrapped her arms around herself, running her hands down her upper arms as if she felt a chill. "That is hard to take."

Suzie's brow furrowed. Was her mother saying her father didn't listen to her? "What do you mean?"

Eloise raised her shoulders. "It happens to all of us, you know. Even the best of partners can't be there for you every single time, in every single moment. When it works, you're there for each other when it really matters."

Suzie understood the truth in her mother's words, but her heart still rebelled. When she thought about the moment in the restaurant with Patricia, anger built like a wave under her skin. She'd been so excited to share her success, to show off her skill to the woman who appreciated her most, and Patricia had zoned out.

She opened her mouth to speak, then closed it again, unable to decide what to say. The whole time, her mother studied her face like she might be asked to draw it afterward.

"Let me ask this. Was it just the once? Or is this a pattern?" Eloise turned her head and watched the trickle of water spilling down the decorative fountain for a moment. "Be honest. If this is happening a lot, it's a bad sign. But, if it was just the once, you might need to ask yourself if you're overreacting."

Heat rushed to Suzie's face. How many times had her mother accused her of overreacting across her life? "Everything's always the end of the world with you, Suzette Marie." The refrain of her childhood.

The worst part was her mother wasn't wrong. Maybe she wasn't right either, but Suzie lost more than one friend in her life because of her rigidity, her refusal to let things slide.

It was why her college girlfriend broke up with her. Her parting shot had hit home. "I'm not perfect, Suze. No one is. And I'm not willing to kill myself trying to be good enough for you."

She thought of it as having high standards. And she was fair about it—she held herself to high standards, too, maybe even higher than the ones she held for the people around her. It was part of what drew her to Patricia in the first place: her hard-nosed, unrelenting stance; her persistence and strength. It felt like a view through a portal into her own future, having gone where ambition and hard work could take her.

Patricia had been her hero, and through Patricia and the UCU, Suzie got a taste of heroism herself, an opportunity to make a difference, something she'd been reaching for all her life. What they did mattered, both in the moment and in the wider sense. She'd hadn't realized how much mattering mattered to her until she'd signed on, and now she couldn't imagine returning to a world where her bottom line was about profit margins instead of lives saved.

Did she expect too much of Patricia? Was she unwilling to let her be human as well as heroic? From the very beginning, Patricia had dragged her heels about the whole superhero thing. It was Suzie's idea to save the beauty queen at the mall, even if it was Patricia's bulletproof flesh and intimidating physique that made it possible. Suzie didn't like admitting it, but she realized she'd probably been using Patricia to fulfill her own aspirations.

She'd been flattered when Patricia joined the UCU, knowing Patricia had chosen the path, at least in part, because Suzie had signed on. That was a level of faith and trust she hadn't found often enough in her life, where people were all too willing to write her off as another pretty little blonde hired for her looks or assume she'd gotten her position through family connections.

Patricia never underestimated her. When she was with Patricia, she felt seen, valued, appreciated. She thrived on the assumption of strength and competence. Not only thrived, she depended on it.

She replayed the restaurant scene in her head. Patricia told her about Leonel, and her worries about how hard he had taken his trip into the mud. Then she'd gone quiet, staring out the window. Suzie jumped in with her own story about her triumph over Dr. Liu, already anticipating the praise and admiration she'd receive, the way the two of them would laugh together.

When it hadn't come, it was as if the rug had been pulled out from under her. She'd lost her temper. But was it Patricia's fault? Or was she frustrated by a general lack of recognition at work and taking it out on Patricia?

Suzie groaned. "Damn it, Mom. You're right."

Her mother looked back from the fountain. She'd kept her gaze on her nails while her daughter ruminated, but now her dark brown eyes met Suzie's blue ones, the corners folding into lines like shooting stars. "I've been known to be right from time to time. I've learned a few things in my life."

"And I can't believe you defended Patricia."

Eloise scrunched up her face. "There's no need to tell her, you know. I still don't think she's good enough for you, but I also know no one is. If she's what your heart wants, she's what you should have."

SALLY ANN SPIRALS

Sally Ann didn't handle boredom well. An entire day in the hospital thanks to her concussion made her manic with restlessness. She couldn't even distract herself with cheesy movies or social media, since screen time made the pain in her head blossom afresh.

She'd tried podcasts, but she couldn't stay focused with nothing else to do at the same time. Generally, she listened while she cleaned up or worked out or something. Music was even worse. It made her want to move, and moving too much made her eyeball twitch in its socket and her vision go white.

The medical staff checked on her often and saw to her every need, but they couldn't linger by her bedside and entertain her. They had work to do after all.

So did she, damn it! But it would have to wait. Dr. Sugg's healing accelerant helped with the external bruising, but it couldn't do much for her scrambled noggin. Even the ever-optimistic Walter Peeples said, "These things take time."

She'd refrained from throwing her pillow at him but only because her head weighed two tons at the moment.

Even though it made her head hurt, the visit with the Director and Patricia had been the highlight of the past twenty-four hours. She wondered if they'd gotten anywhere with Dr. Liu, and if there were any updates about the gunmen. The Director probably thought he was doing her a favor, letting her rest undisturbed. But this much rest was disturbing in and of itself.

She fumbled with the remote for a moment, intending to call the nurse and see if she could take a bath, just for something to do, when a light knock came at the door.

"Come in." She'd spoken too loudly and rubbed her temples to soothe the spike of pain.

The door opened, and a bouquet of yellow daisies appeared in the opening, followed by the handsome face of Darrin Berger. Even the wrinkled brow of worry couldn't detract from his fine features, and she raised her arms to beckon him to her side.

"Hey, baby," he whispered, bending to brush her forehead with the lightest of kisses. "I hear you got caught without a helmet."

"Well, I wasn't expecting people to start throwing dinosaurs." Sally Ann rolled onto her side as Darrin settled into the visitor's chair, so she could see him without moving. She suppressed a groan from shifting position.

He laid the bouquet on the table and leaned forward, slender fingers interlaced between his knees. His voice was low and soft, like he'd already guessed she was noise-sensitive and adjusted for her. "How are you, though? I tried flirting with the nurses, but they wouldn't tell me much."

Impressive that the nurses could resist his charms. Even a little out of focus in poor light, the man was gorgeous. "Concussion. I'm still having light sensitivity and headaches."

He scooted to the edge of his chair, lowering his already quiet voice to a near whisper. "Should I go? If you need rest…"

"No!" Sally Ann laid a hand on her head where bright white light flared when she'd called out. She tried again more quietly. "No. Please stay, if you've got the time. I'm dying of boredom."

Darrin scooted back in his chair. "For you? I've always got time."

She smiled. They both knew it wasn't always true, no more for her than for him. If a big story broke, or an unusual crime happened, their plans would be cut short. In a way, it was nice because it was both of them. Darrin did truly understand the demands of her work. Still, it was sweet of him to say it, and she believed he meant it, at least emotionally.

"I can't read or anything. Tell me what's happening out there today."

Darrin straightened, tightened his tie, and thrust his shoulders back and down into newscaster mode, keeping his voice at a quieter volume than he'd have used on air. "It's a fine day in Springfield, despite the onset of fall. It's a perfect fifty-two degrees, with no rain and only the lightest of breezes. The skies are clear, except for the occasional flash of blue spandex as our very own Flygirl soars across the city."

Sally Ann adjusted her pillow, bunching it under her neck.

"Rumors abound as the infamous Director of the UCU has scheduled a big announcement this Monday afternoon. What does he have in mind?"

One of Sally Ann's eyebrows went up. "Monday?"

Darrin's brow wrinkled. "That's what I'm told. There's no information about what the man intends to announce. I'm guessing you don't know either?"

There was an eagerness in his tone, but Sally Ann knew he wouldn't push her to share details if they needed to be secret. Good thing too. She didn't know anything. "I'm in the dark on this one." She gestured at the dimly lit room. "Literally."

"He's giving you time to recover."

"He" was, of course, the Director and even though Darrin's words painted a positive picture, Sally Ann could feel the disapproving vibrations coming off of him even with her eyes closed. She didn't know if it was love, her psychic abilities, or that they'd had this conversation more than once in the past few months.

A wave of nausea burbled her guts, and she curled her body into more of a ball, unsure whether it was the stress or the concussion that made her writhe.

Darrin had every reason to mistrust Steven, the man he knew as "the Director," as did most of the city. After the way the Director messed around with his memory last year, Sally Ann couldn't defend him. She'd read Steven the riot act over that stunt.

But she still tried to give her boss the benefit of the doubt; to assume he did bad things for good reasons. Sometimes the work required that. But the man was becoming more and more secretive, and that worried her. She wasn't sure what she could or should do about it yet.

But Darrin wasn't the person she should talk to about all that. His work as a reporter meant there were things she couldn't tell him. Mostly, they just avoided talking about the Director, but she knew they'd eventually have to confront the subject, and there would be big changes coming whichever way the discussion went. She hoped she'd be ready when the moment came.

Ignoring the long pause she'd left in the conversation, Sally Ann said, "Make sure you line up a good camera crew. I'm sure there will be one helluva dog and pony show."

"Spandex and capes?" He rubbed his hands together like he'd been offered a treat.

"No capes." She opened one eye. "Edna says so."

"Edna?" He looked confused.

"Don't tell me you haven't seen *The Incredibles*."

He pressed his lips into a closed-mouth smile and pantomimed locking them closed.

Sally Ann blinked at him. "As soon as I can handle screen time again, we'll have to remedy that. How can you be my Lois Lane if you're not up on all your superhero lore?"

He reached out and caught her fingers, holding them tightly as he sputtered. "Your Lois Lane?"

Suppressing the laugh lest it move her head too much, she squeezed his fingers back. "Reporter dating a superhero. Sound familiar?"

"Does that mean you'll fly me around the city later on?"

"I do have the keys to the Dact."

Darrin's eyes got big. He would love a chance to see the inside of their fancy jet. The Pterodactyl, or Dact for short, had gotten a real outing on the rescue mission to Indiana and Ohio last year. Darrin was still annoyed that he didn't get any good footage of it in action.

Not for the first time, Sally Ann thought it was too bad Agent Gabe Driver didn't talk. The two of them could geek out together over the "cool toys" part of hero life. And Gabe could use a friend outside of work, she thought. Couldn't they all?

Maybe she would try to get Darrin that ride. She could sell the idea to the Director as a great PR opportunity, as long as Darrin signed an NDA restricting what he could reveal. The toys were the best part.

Rolling onto her back, she asked, "Have you heard anything about the gunmen at the museum this morning? Did we learn who they were?"

"Yeah...about that..."

Sally Ann didn't like the sound of this, but she stayed on her back, hand over her eyes, waiting.

Darrin cleared his throat. "There's something fishy about this whole thing. I can't find out where the suspects were taken. It's like they just disappeared. And it's suspicious as hell that Dr. Reed was attacked in his lab at the same time."

Darrin went silent and Patricia knew he was waiting for her to enlighten him, if she could. "Not on the record, yet, all right?"

He nodded. "Understood."

Sally Ann took a deep breath, then let it out in three shaky exhales, waiting for the sparks behind her eyes to settle. She whispered, "We think the attack at the museum was a distraction to cover up the attack on the lab."

"What would anyone want from the lab in the Natural History Museum?"

"Frogs."

"Frogs?" She could hear the confusion in his voice. Darrin had to be wondering if this was her concussion talking.

She considered how much to say. She'd been given no gag orders, and the Director relied on her judgment about what to tell the press. "Frogs that escaped Dr. Liu's laboratory last spring and took up residence in the pond at Old Homestead. Weird-ass frogs."

Darrin made a small thoughtful sound. "Okay. So this is still on the down-low, but can I look into the frogs, gathering info for the eventual story?"

That seemed reasonable. Darrin could have stumbled into the story on his own, just checking on why Old Homestead Park was closed. "Should be okay. Tell me what you find out? I can't do my own research from here, and the medical team says it'll be a few more days."

He agreed.

"Hey," she whispered, after a few moments of silence, wondering at her own stupidity in not noticing up till then. "How did you get in here anyway?"

"I got a call from the UCU. Someone named Richard? He told me you'd been injured and arranged for a car to pick me up and bring me here. I had to wear a blindfold and everything."

"Richard?"

"Uh-huh. Skinny White guy, kind of prissy?"

Sally Ann remembered that Suzie was out of town. Richard must be filling in for her. But Richard making the call meant Darrin and Sally Ann were more of a known quantity than she realized. The Director knew. And if he'd had Darrin brought here, he wanted something. Did she just play into his hands again?

She'd have to think about that later. Her mind was spinning. Or maybe that was vertigo from the concussion. She flopped out a hand, and Darrin squeezed her fingers. "I'm glad they called you."

"Me too." He rubbed her knuckles with his thumb.

He was gone when she woke up, morning light glimmering around the window shades, the memory of his touch lingering on her skin.

FRIDAY

PATRICIA AND CINDY, FRENEMIES

This was a bad idea. Patricia had hardly spoken to Cindy since the UCU captured and imprisoned her. Thinking about her once-best-friend and all the levels of betrayal made the back of her tongue burn with acid.

There had been the one time, when Cindy tried to escape by making herself invisible and Patricia tracked her, saving her life in the process. But that didn't stem from love or even friendship—if anything, her motivation to help came from spite. She'd wanted Cindy to stay right where she was, under the thumb of the UCU. Contained. Punished. Safe.

But here she was standing outside Cindy's door, sent by the Director to talk to everyone's favorite mad scientist. It was her own damned fault —she volunteered. She still wasn't sure why she'd done it. It pulled like a compulsion—like she *had* to. They'd been talking in Sally Ann's recovery room and it popped out. "I could," she'd said, like an idiot.

The Director's smile hit a level of smug satisfaction the Cheshire Cat would have found intimidating. "That's exactly what I was thinking." And in a blink, her long stretch of keeping her distance from Cindy Liu came to an end.

Sally Ann insisted the conversation wait until morning. The Director didn't want to wait, but he admitted it would go better after Patricia had a shower, a meal, and a good long rest. She'd managed two of those, but the third eluded her. The bed stretched overlarge and empty without Suzie's blond curls spilling over the other pillow. Every time she'd rolled over, she'd checked her phone, just in case. Every time she'd wanted to smack herself for being so pathetic.

Her coffee went tepid while she'd stood there thinking, so Patricia dropped her cup in the waste can, pushed back her shoulders, punched in the temporary access code she'd been given, and entered the room. Time to face the music.

The room was smaller than she'd expected. The bathroom in her condo was probably bigger. A bed, a fold-down table with a chair, and a toilet partitioned from the rest of the space by a short wall that made the room seem smaller yet. Staying there must be like living on a boat. One thing out of place and you'd trip trying to walk.

Of course, Cindy hadn't been allowed personal possessions, so there wasn't much to clutter the space. Not like her house—stacked with books, papers, and forgotten teacups. Here, Cindy herself was the messiest thing in the room—sprawled on the bed, head dangling down in the few inches between the mattress and the wall. She hadn't moved when Patricia entered, so Patricia cleared her throat.

Cindy popped up, smacking her head on the wall in the process. Her grimace of pain melted into a wide-eyed expression of surprise as she registered who was standing there. "Patricia? What the hell are you doing here?"

Patricia grabbed the chair and dropped into it. "It's good to see you too."

Rubbing her head where a reddish spot would eventually turn into a bump, Cindy folded her slender legs around each other, and Patricia flashed to their college days, when they'd stayed up all night talking about everything under the sun and a few things beyond it. Cindy looked younger than when they met, thanks to her experiments. She'd gotten the hip flexibility to go with the young face too.

"Why didn't you run?" Patricia was surprised to hear the question come out of her mouth. That wasn't what she'd intended to say.

Cindy stared at her, unblinking.

Patricia went on. "You had the chance, in Ohio, last year. You'd gotten the hard drive and the emeralds, incapacitated your father. You could have slipped out a window and walked off into the night. Instead, you came back upstairs and sought us out."

"It wouldn't have been worth it." Cindy sighed. "I'd still have been in Ohio."

A laugh escaped Patricia before she could suppress it. All these years and she couldn't be sure when Cindy was joking and when she was blunt. Either way, it was funny. She missed that.

Without rising from her seat, Patricia stretched out an arm. Her fingertips grazed the wall. "Ohio has more room than you've got now."

Cindy moved her arms in a dramatic arc. "I could be bounded in a nutshell and count myself a queen of infinite space."

Patricia stood and took the two steps to the door. She laid a hand on the knob. She should go. She was flooded with memories of the summer Cindy helped her get through her Shakespeare class, sparking a tradition of going to see at least one play together a year. Every year until five years ago, when their worlds turned upside down, when everything Patricia thought she knew about their friendship was called into question.

Five minutes in the room and Cindy was already getting to her. This was definitely a bad idea. She turned the knob.

"Wait." Cindy's voice trembled.

Suspicions raised, Patricia glanced back over the shoulder. Was this more manipulation? "Yes?" She pushed the door closed again.

"You didn't just come to see me in my cage."

"No, but I can see this was a mistake."

Cindy untangled her legs and scooted off the bed. She crossed to the chair Patricia had vacated, gripping the plastic back tightly enough to whiten her knuckles. "Just because it's a mistake doesn't mean it won't be a good time." Another reminder of their history and all the mistakes they'd made on purpose together in the name of adventure.

Patricia turned around and leaned against the door, tucking her hands into her pockets. For a few long seconds, the two old friends watched each other. Patricia tried to keep her face placid, but under the surface, confusing emotions swirled like winds that might become a tornado. She'd missed Cindy as much as she'd hated her these last few years.

Cindy chewed on her lip and started to fidget, the portrait of a guilty woman. Patricia found it painful to watch and fought the desire to reassure her old friend. *Damn it.* If this was a manipulation, it was working. She'd avoided contact all this time for exactly this reason. What was she doing here? The Director had been out of his mind sending her.

Blowing out a breath that pushed her hair off her forehead, Patricia broke the silence. "They want me to ask you about the frogs."

"The frogs?" Confusion clouded Cindy's face. "From the pond? The ones the blonde asked me about?"

"Those are the ones." Patricia shuddered a little, remembering removing the frog bodies from her spikes after her trip into the pond to pull Leonel out. Disgusting little things. She punched down the twinge that came with the mention of "the blonde."

"What about them?"

"You tell me. Why would someone want them?"

Cocking her head to one side, Cindy indicated the chair. "Maybe you should tell me what's going on."

Still feeling wary, Patricia picked the chair and swung it around, so its back rested against the door. Catching on that Patricia wanted some space between them, Cindy retreated to her bed and sat on the edge of it, hands primly folded on her lap. Her feet didn't reach the floor, but then again, they wouldn't have when she'd looked her age either. They'd always been an odd pair, Patricia towering nearly a foot taller than her friend.

"The samples were sent to the Natural History Museum for analysis."

"Good idea. Dr. Reed is well respected, and for good reason. Very thorough. Did he offer anything helpful?"

"He didn't get the chance. He's in the hospital right now. Someone broke into the lab yesterday afternoon—taking the samples and his preliminary notes. They hit him over the head when he walked in on them."

"Is he all right?"

Patricia narrowed her eyes. What was she up to? Cindy wasn't famous for her empathy. A few short years ago, she'd literally shot Patricia in the back to find out if she was bulletproof—and that's when they'd been friends. But she'd sounded concerned about Dr. Reed.

Picking up on the skepticism emanating from Patricia, Cindy sniffed and folded her arms across her chest. "I'm not a monster, you know. I never wanted anyone to get hurt."

"That might be true. But you didn't care if we did. That's not much better."

"It's not that simple." Cindy waved her hands in exasperation, passion making her voice strident. "I was racing against time—the answers were life and death."

Patricia could believe that. Cindy's own life had been at risk, since she'd experimented on herself too. If she hadn't figured out how to stop her age regression process, she might well have eventually become an infant, maybe even died. Self-interest was a powerful motivator, even for people who weren't narcissistic mad geniuses.

"I feel bad about the things I did." Cindy wrapped her arms around herself, pulling the scrubs she wore tight around her narrow frame. Her chin shot up in familiar defiance. "I was having impulse control problems, going through puberty again."

"Right. So, your defense is that hormones made you do it?" Patricia felt her mouth compress into a disapproving line, and her consternation broke through in her voice, which became louder and more strident. "You kidnapped Jessica—you kidnapped me! You had Helen trying to kill all of us."

"I know it's no excuse."

Cindy took a deep breath and lowered her voice. "Taking Jessica was an act of desperation, and after that I was on the run, trying to survive. There wasn't time to think, let alone reflect. I never—it was my father's idea to kidnap you—not mine."

"And now?"

"One thing I have plenty of is time to reflect." She paused, her gaze sinking to take in the floor in front of Patricia's feet. "I have a lot to make up for."

Was that a kind of apology? Or something approaching one? Patricia's head swam and she rubbed her temples, not sure how to feel about what she was hearing. She decided to steer this conversation back to why she was there. "Well, what did your reflections tell you about the frogs?"

Stretching across the bed, Cindy reached into the space she'd been dangling her head into when Patricia arrived and came back up with a notebook. "What do you know about mutation?"

Patricia transformed her eyes and hands, then stroked her cheek beside her yellow eyes with a black talon. "I have some experience with it."

Cindy waved her hand. "Yes, yes. But what do you understand about how it *works*?"

Shrugging, Patricia leaned back in her chair and turned her eyes and skin back to their normal appearance. She might as well get comfortable —a deluge of information was coming.

Sure enough, once Cindy started talking, she picked up speed like a rock rolling down a mountainside. She sketched out structural formulas and gestured at them emphatically with a pencil. Her explanation rolled through evolution, natural genetic variants, DNA, enzymes, alleles, chromosomes, and dozens of other concepts Patricia understood less well.

Patricia's concentration wandered in and out as Cindy lectured on. Finally, when she stopped to take a breath, Patricia spoke. "And this connects to the frogs, how?"

Cindy threw her head back in frustration. "I don't know why I bother to explain these things to you."

Patricia folded her hands in her lap, waiting.

"Last year, all of the people affected by my products—"

"Liu-vians."

"What?"

"Liu-vians. That's what they call us."

Cindy sputtered. "That's—that's." She paused. "That's kind of wonderful, actually." She grinned, and Patricia's heart clenched a little tighter in her chest.

Her voice breathy, Cindy went on. "Last year, the Liu-vians experienced a spike, an escalation of their mutations."

"You think?" Patricia brought out her head plates, enjoying the way Cindy's eyes widened before she got her face under control.

After a long pause, Cindy managed to pull her gaze back down to Patricia's eyes, set her jaw in determination, and continue. "Frogs have a much shorter lifespan. Some as short as four years. So, these frogs are likely the offspring of the original frogs that escaped from my lab during the fire." Cindy's lips twisted into a scowl as she mentioned the fire.

Patricia tipped her head to the side, waiting for the punchline.

"You can be so dense, Patricia. Don't you see?"

"I guess I don't."

"It's not the frogs themselves. It's what their presence indicates. This shows that the mutations are being passed down. They can be inherited. That's huge!" Cindy's voice got louder as she spoke, her arms spread wide at the end.

Patricia had heard this tone before, right before Cindy fell down a research hole. She didn't have time for that right now. "So that's why he wants the research."

"He?"

"The thief. He went to a lot of trouble, too, staging a distraction that evacuated the museum and kept us focused elsewhere."

Cindy shot Patricia a suspicious look—the narrowing of the eyes showed she knew Patricia was holding something back. "The thief?"

Patricia considered. The Director wanted Cindy to weigh in. "No one understands Daniel Price and his work better than she does," he'd said. And it was true. Cindy's insight and knowledge had been essential in Ohio last year, when Cindy's father kidnapped Patricia's mother in hopes of finding the key to all the fantastical transformations Cindy's works had wrought.

She should be grateful for Cindy's assistance—they'd gotten her mother back after all. But the blame for the whole thing rested with Cindy. If she hadn't been so reckless in her experiments, so many things would not have happened. The whole of the past five years would have taken a very different trajectory indeed.

The rub was that some of what happened were good things—like falling in love, repairing family connections, and even hero life itself. But just because Patricia, Jessica, and Leonel had made silk purses out of sow's ears didn't mean they hadn't been handed pig parts in the first place.

So Patricia held back on telling Cindy the mysterious data thief was her father. She hesitated, unable to quell the swarm of doubts assaulting her like wasps whose nest has been dislodged. Was the potential good worth the potential harm?

Cindy stared at her, waiting for an answer.

Patricia shifted uncomfortably. If she didn't do it, the Director would send someone else—someone who might give away too much. At least this way, she could control things. "You might want to sit down."

"No one ever says that unless the news is bad, Patricia. I'm not a child, regardless of appearances. I'm older than you. Just tell me."

"It's your father."

"Shit." Cindy sat down.

Patricia wasn't sure what to do, and she hated feeling uncertain. She waited.

After a few moments of silence, Cindy made a fist and slammed it on the mattress, knocking her binder onto the floor. "They should have taken him in when they had the chance."

They were in agreement on that one. The Director's decision not to bring in Price caused a shift in Patricia's willingness to trust his judgment. And she wasn't the only one. That was a discussion for another day.

Cindy flopped backward on the bed, gesticulating at the ceiling like she was conducting an orchestra. Patricia knew Cindy was visualizing pieces of information, moving them around on a kind of whiteboard of the brain. She waited.

She didn't have to wait long. Cindy popped up, rolling smoothly onto her feet. She held up three fingers, counting down her questions. "First—how did he know about the frogs at all, let alone where we'd sent our data and samples for analysis? Second—who is he working with now? Third—where has he gone?"

A chill ran up Patricia's spine. Did they have a mole?

LEONEL, THE RIGHT MAN FOR THE JOB

Leonel didn't know why the Director wanted to see him, so he entered the office quietly, his expression guarded. Despite a few years' experience with the man, Leonel had not learned to read him well and had no idea if he was about to be praised, called on the carpet, or given an assignment.

At first, the Director didn't seem to notice his entry. He sat at his desk, clicking through images on a large screen hanging on the wall. From the selection, Leonel thought he was choosing new promotional images. He caught a quick glimpse of Patricia holding up a taloned hand and of Jessica floating above the water tower at the edge of town.

As the door clicked closed, the Director stopped on an image from the news—the same one that had Leonel's daughters tittering at dinner the night before. It showed Leonel, dressed as Fuerte in his flashy red shirt and golden mask, holding the skeletal pteranodon above his head. Leonel suspected the Director of manipulating the image. The whole scene looked cleaner than it was—and Patricia had been removed from the picture entirely. All the heroism, without any of the connected destruction.

"Nice work at the museum," the Director said.

"Thank you, sir. Have you identified the gunmen yet? They had some unusual weapons."

The Director waved his hand. "Yes, sonic weaponry. Showy. I can see why the press is interested. But it's not very efficient, is it? Not…sleek."

Leonel blinked. Why would that matter? "They still did a lot of damage. Our Sally Ann is still in the hospital."

"I'm not worried about Agent Rogers."

Leonel drew in a sharp breath and the Director shifted focus, turning bright eyes on him. He didn't break eye contact as he stood and walked around to the front of the desk. A wave of warmth washed over Leonel, something almost like love.

The Director smiled. His teeth were perfect. "She's tougher than any of us. In some ways, she's stronger than even you."

Reassured, Leonel found himself nodding his head in agreement. Sally Ann would be fine. He didn't need to worry about that.

A firm hand clapped on Leonel's shoulder. "But that's not why I asked you to come in. I've got a proposition for you." The Director gestured at a couple of armchairs.

"A proposition?" That seemed like an odd way to phrase it. It made Leonel think of pyramid schemes and other shady deals. He sank into the chair the Director indicated, feeling pensive.

The Director sat in the other chair and crossed his legs, then steepled his fingers in front of his mouth and nose, tapping the two index fingers together. He took a long moment to gather himself before he leaned forward, focusing intently on Leonel's face in a way that made his head feel strange. "It's time I brought you in on my little scheme," he said.

A desire to help bubbled up in Leonel. Of course he would support the scheme. The Director had excellent ideas. Leonel was filled with a desire to impress the man. "What can I do for you, sir?"

"That's the spirit!"

The Director pulled the remote control out of his pocket and aimed it at the monitor. He clicked through a few images of Helen Braeburn, some of which Leonel had seen before and some he hadn't. There were stills from the news and images from security cameras, as well as her professional real estate agent photograph, and a more recent one where she wore the blue scrubs the patients and prisoners of the Department were given.

"You remember Helen Braeburn, of course."

Leonel chewed his lip. "Yes, sir." The memories weren't good. They came wrapped in stress, anxiety, and guilt.

The Director raised an eyebrow. "Have you heard anything yet about our rehabilitation program?" When Leonel didn't respond, he went on. "The UCU has been able to help quite a few people in our short history, aiding them in gaining control over their unusual abilities so they can live normal lives."

The Director stood and walked over to the windows, shoving his hands into his pockets and staring out at the city. Leonel twisted in his chair to keep the man in view.

"We'd like to expand the program, taking some of the tougher cases and showing Springfield how we've helped them become productive citizens, perhaps even become heroes like you."

Leonel felt a little sick to his stomach. "I'm not sure I understand, sir."

Returning to his seat, the Director patted Leonel on the knee. "You're a calming influence, Leonel. Time and time again, you've shown an ability to talk people down, to help them make better choices." He paused. "I'd like to partner you with Helen Braeburn. I want to bring her into the UCU, and I want you to show her the ropes."

Surprise silenced Leonel for a long moment. Then his brain started spinning. The Director believed in him and gave him a chance to use his strength for good. The UCU saw him through a gunshot wound and found a way to help when his powers spun out of control. He owed the organization and its leader so much.

But surely it wasn't wise to release Helen Braeburn. Not long ago, she'd been hurling fireballs in the street, not caring who got hurt in the process. Leonel didn't know much about what she'd been doing while the UCU had her in custody, but he doubted she could have done a complete about-face in such a short time.

Leonel cleared his throat. "I'm not sure I'm the right person for this job, sir."

The Director's eyes narrowed for a moment before his face settled into his usual affable expression. "Why would you say that?"

Leonel ran a hand through his hair and tugged on the ends of the strands, a nervous habit he had never been able to break. He stared out the window rather than at the man across from him. "I'm the one who threw her against the wall, back at the college. She must hate me."

The Director laughed, a warm, buttery chuckle that reminded Leonel of his father. Odd in such a young man. The Director still didn't look a day over twenty-five to him, slight and nimble as a boy.

Leonel swiveled his head to face the man, confusion clouding his face. Did he think this was a joke?

"That's what I love about you, Leonel. You care so much." The Director stood, walked to his desk and leaned against the front of it, his hands in the pockets of his suit jacket making the lapels gap and showing the colorful suspenders he wore beneath. "Plenty of men in your position would have no compunction about actions taken in the heat of battle. But you never forget the little guy."

Leonel blushed and shifted in his seat. It sounded like compliments but burned like criticism. He didn't like the tug in his gut. Gazing into the Director's eyes—so clear and blue, like a summer sky—Leonel's doubts diminished, relegated to a dusty, unexamined corner of his mind. Of course, the Director meant it as a compliment. Of course.

The Director smiled broadly. "Don't forget you saved lives by stopping Helen that day. That's what heroes do."

"Maybe." Leonel still didn't feel like his actions had been heroic. Justifiable? Maybe. But heroic?

"No maybe about it." The Director stood, gesticulating with his hands as he spoke. "Helen wasn't pulling her punches. Well, fireballs." The Director winked. "She intended to burn the campus and everyone on it."

Leonel thought about that day. Had it really been as the Director described? It was hard to be sure, four years later, to separate what parts of his memory of the fight were real and which were the exaggerations that played out in his nightmares. It all happened so fast. All he wanted to do was stop her—to make sure no one got hurt.

The Director's voice went on, but it seemed soft and far away. "You did the right thing."

Had he? More often, Leonel believed he had failed. Jessica was gravely injured, and Helen ended up broken and unconscious. He and Patricia had a falling out in the aftermath. His entire career with the UCU had been fraught. Injuries, mistakes, the effect on his family. There was a lot more to regret than take pride in, in his thinking.

"That's why you're the man for this job, Leonel."

Leonel snapped back to attention. "Sir?"

"Your empathy. Helen will open up to you. I'm sure of it. You can be a role model for her, helping her find her way as an ally instead of an enemy."

Listening, Leonel found himself nodding along, even though a small voice in his head wanted to push back, to ask some of the questions that left him unsettled. It was hard to hold on to the questions when he was sitting here in the Director's office. In the face of his positive assurance, Leonel's reservations became slippery, like mossy stones.

Before he knew it, he was standing in the hallway again, committed to mentor Helen Braeburn.

JESSICA AND THE FIRST LADY

Jessica, wearing her Flygirl costume, perched at the edge of a voluminous easy chair, feet firmly planted on the elaborate rug at her feet. She felt ridiculous, sitting in the well-appointed living room in tights and a mask, like she'd come to a school dance in pajamas when everyone else wore tuxedos and ball gowns.

Mrs. Cafry sat still, hands folded in her lap, legs tucked to one side, one ankle resting on the other at a geometrically perfect angle. Well-coiffed and poised, she might have been posing for her First Lady portrait. She thanked the maid who brought them the tea tray but sat in silence, watching until the door closed behind the woman. Only then did she turn her gaze to Flygirl.

"May I offer you some tea?" Mrs. Cafry's voice was so modulated, it seemed guarded.

They were alone now. What was she worried about? Flygirl leaned forward. "Perhaps later." She looked back at the door. It was closed, but she lowered her voice all the same. "After you've told me what this is about."

"Of course. I have been rather mysterious, haven't I?" She shifted in her chair, tucking her graceful ankles against the other chair leg, one hand fluttering to land briefly on her chest, her elbow, and the arm of the chair before rejoining the other clasped in the creases of her light green dress. She huffed a nervous little laugh. "It's hard to know where to begin."

"May I offer you some tea?" Flygirl gestured at the teapot, a lilt of humor in her voice, aiming to elicit confidence.

Mrs. Cafry laughed for real that time. "I doubt more caffeine would help." She stood up and circled her chair, standing behind it, golden light through the long windows making her green dress glow like one of Jessica's emeralds.

"Would you mind if we walk while we talk?" she said.

Jessica stood. "Not in the least."

The governor's wife led the way, surprising Jessica by opening a door that she'd assumed was a closet but instead led to a narrow hallway. It made sense there would be servant's passages in a house this old and grand, but she was surprised the First Lady of the state would utilize them to traverse her own home.

Jessica followed in silence, curiosity building. The hallway came to a head and Mrs. Cafry turned left, went down some stairs, and opened another door. The two women exited into a beautiful garden. As soon as they stepped out into the open air, Mrs. Cafry relaxed.

Once outside in the lovely setting, Jessica found tension rolling out of her too. She breathed in deeply. "I should spend more time in gardens."

A wide smile spread across the First Lady's face. "One of the perks of office. I love gardens, but I have a black thumb. But since Jim was elected, I've had the privilege of long conversations with talented gardeners who surround me with beauty. Let me show you the best part."

Mrs. Cafry led the way around the corner of the house toward a giant willow tree. Stopping beside the tree, she stretched out an arm and held back some of the dangling fronds like a curtain, beckoning to her guest with the other hand. Jessica walked through the opening the other woman created. Behind her, Mrs. Cafry let the greenery fall and the two of them were in a cone of lush green. "I told Felipe I sometimes wished I could sit in a tree like I did when I was a kid and he created this hideaway for me."

Under the tree was an old-fashioned yard swing with floral cushions. At Mrs. Cafry's invitation, Jessica joined her on it and the two of them let their heads lean back, so they faced upward into the leaves and the patch of blue sky above.

"My boys would love it in here. They'd make it into a secret hideout." Jessica said.

"How old are they?"

Jessica gulped, realizing her gaffe too late. Secrecy was hard work sometimes, exhausting even. She flashed a quick, apologetic smile. "I'd better not say. I'd be in trouble with the folks working so hard to protect my privacy already for even telling you I have children."

The First Lady pressed her lips together into a thin line. "I understand. I won't press, and I won't tell anyone else. It can just be between us."

Jangled now, Jessica's relaxed mood faded. She wasn't sure what the game was yet but felt she'd already given something away. "So do you want to tell me what's on your mind, Mrs. Cafry?"

"Francine, please."

"Okay, Francine." The professional smile Jessica kept on her face when dealing with the public as Flygirl became stiff and frozen. She folded her arms over her chest, pressing on the nub of emerald she could feel through the cloth of her costume. The motion pushed the gemstone against the bare flesh beneath and a relaxing warmth spread through Jessica.

"I'm sorry. I don't mean to waste your time. It's such an awkward topic to raise."

Jessica tried to channel her patience, opting for humor again. "Well, we've already established I'm a mother. I know all about awkward questions."

Mrs. Cafry laughed. "Yes, children do ask some tough ones, don't they?" Her laughter trailed off into silence, and she folded and unfolded her hands several times before she went on. "You'd think I'd be good at asking difficult questions after all this time in politics, but I can't figure out a way into this one, so I'll be blunt, and hope you'll feel you can be honest with me. I don't know anyone else I can ask."

Jessica nodded once, waiting.

"How do you feel about the Director?"

Surprise and relief flooded Jessica's brain. As usual, all the ways she'd imagined the conversation could go were worse than the truth. She'd worried the First Lady was going to ask her for some kind of favor, rope her into a political committee or some volunteer work. She'd speculated that the woman was experiencing strange side effects from her cancer treatment and wanted help managing the power of flight. She'd even thought that, perhaps, Mrs. Cafry had somehow learned about the emeralds and the role they played in helping the Liu-vians control their powers. That last bit caused more than a little panic, even if her rational mind understood how unlikely it was.

Jessica felt her body settle back against the cushion, finding gravity again now that her anxiety was relieved. She shrugged. "Well, he's my boss."

"I know." Francine's face seemed longer, and her soft brown eyes grew sorrowful.

"What do you expect me to say?"

Francine turned her body so she faced Jessica, their knees nearly touching in the middle of the swing. "I know this puts you in an awkward position, Flygirl, and I assure you I would never name you as my source, but I need to know if the Director is trustworthy."

Stalling, Jessica pressed back. "Why?"

"My husband is considering partnering with the UCU for law enforcement and rescue support for the entire state."

This was the first Jessica had heard of plans to take the UCU broader than the city of Springfield. The thought was exciting and daunting at the same time. A confusing rush of emotions ran through her like a shot. Did Walter know? If so, why hadn't he told her? Then again, *when* would he have told her? She'd been avoiding lengthy alone time with him almost since they returned from their honeymoon.

Francine tucked one ankle under her knee so she could lean closer. "I have faith in the agents of the UCU. You saved my life as surely as the doctors did."

Jessica spread her hands, ready to deflect the compliment, but Francine went on.

"Don't tell me it was just your job. No one does this kind of work for the paycheck alone. It takes a special person to put themselves in danger for the sake of others. You and Fuerte deserve all the accolades laid at your feet."

Her face heating up under her mask, Jessica shrugged, the closest she could come to acknowledging the praise. "You support our work, then."

Francine's hands fluttered in the air. "The work, yes. But my question isn't about the work—it's about the man in charge."

An image of the Director flashed in Jessica's mind—his smarmy smile and salt-and-pepper hair. A feeling of goodwill rose in her. Behind her mask, she narrowed her eyes at the governor's wife. "It sounds like you have doubts."

"I can't explain it. I get a strange feeling about him. Like something isn't what it looks like. This will sound strange coming from a politician's wife, but something about him raises my hackles. He seems manipulative in ways I don't understand."

Jessica let her head fall back against the cushion, watching the clouds float through the patches of sky she could see between the dangling fronds of the willow tree. She wished she were up there, flying over Springfield in the quiet.

Several answers came to her lips, but Jessica swallowed them. She didn't want to play politics today. Finally, she decided to take a chance and say what she thought. "The truth is I don't know if the Director is worthy of our trust. He can be phony, and I don't always appreciate his sense of humor. Sometimes, I feel like something is a little off about him too."

Slippery, she thought but didn't say aloud. *Sly.* She held up a hand when it looked like Francine might interrupt, continuing her thought.

"What I do know is that he has put together a team of amazing and dedicated people who care about using their skills for good and making a difference in the world. He personally recruited many of the agents and staff, and I can and do trust those people with my life."

She paused, gathering her thoughts. "I can tell you he has come through with resources and support for us when it mattered, and he has never asked me to do anything that contradicts my own conscience."

A deep breath, her conviction growing. "So, yes, for what it's worth, when the chips are down, I think he can be trusted."

Francine reached out and squeezed Jessica's hand, her long fingernails biting lightly into the flesh of her palm. "Thank you."

HELEN CAN'T BEAT 'EM…BUT CAN SHE JOIN THEM?

Helen pulled the yellow tunic down over her hips. It had a tendency to ride up, but it was better than the prison-hospital pajamas they'd kept her in the past couple of years. Subtler than the costume she made for herself, when she was calling herself "Flamethrower" and running with Cindy Liu. Classier.

She sniffed it—it didn't smell of borax, though she'd been assured her new uniform was fireproof enough to stand up to her powers. She raised a flame in one hand, a small one—not enough to set off the sprinkler system—and held it against the sleeve. It didn't catch or even grow warm. She pinched the material between her fingers and it snapped back into place. Whatever her new costume was made of was quality stuff.

"Are they really okay with this?" She turned to check out her backside in the mirror, frowning over her shoulder at the expanse of her hips in the red leggings. The flame patterning down the sides of the legs flickered as she moved. She wiggled her leg back and forth to watch it shift.

Mary laughed at her mother's impromptu cha-cha. "Would you be?"

Closing her eyes, Helen tried to imagine herself in the same position. She'd never been the forgiving sort herself—and that's what landed her in the custody of the UCU. If she'd been able to let Cindy Liu go and just move on with her life instead of letting a desire for vengeance take over, she might have lived a very different life these last three years.

She poked at the little coal of hatred in her heart, the secret fire she'd fanned, promising herself that someday she'd make Cindy pay for abandoning her. The coal flared, but not as high as it once had. Maybe it would be the same for the others. Maybe time had given them some perspective as well and they could give her a chance to show them she meant no harm.

Mary gripped her arm. "Hey, it's going to be all right. We'll make sure of it." She sounded so sure, but then again, self-doubt had never been Mary's problem. She got that from her mother, Helen thought ruefully.

This time Helen didn't jerk away. Instead, she rested her fingers on top of her daughter's hand, pressing them into the fleshy part of her arm. Spinning away, she wiped the tears out of her eyes. There was no reason to get maudlin. She'd win them over, with time. Real second chances were rare, and she wasn't going to waste this one.

"Okay. Let's go. How do I look?" She popped a saucy pose, thrusting out a hip and waggling her eyebrows at her daughter.

Mary smiled, a too-rare occurrence, and two dimples appeared in her cheeks, just like her father's. She tugged at her own outfit—a belly-baring top with shape-hugging pants—and pulled up the hood that disguised her distinctive hair still worn in the dreadlocks Helen had always hated. She might have been a completely different person.

Peering around her mother's shoulder to check her ensemble in the mirror, Mary pressed her mask into place. The simple, gray domino-style mask adhered to her skin through some kind of technology that might as well be magic so far as Helen was concerned. It called attention to her daughter's round cheeks and the spill of freckles across her nose. She seemed both older and younger than her twenty-seven years.

Mary frowned at the mirror. "Honestly, we're both ridiculous, but at least we'll blend in."

Helen examined their reflections. "I don't know. I think we rock it." Mary certainly exuded mystery in her shades of gray and draping hood, like some kind of sexy ninja mystic.

Mary wrinkled her brow at her reflection. "The whole superhero getup is a little weird, but I understand why they do it. Marketing and identity protection all in one."

"Thank you for doing this for me. I know you never wanted to be in the spotlight."

Mary shrugged. "I won't be. Who is going to care about 'The Mentalist' when they've got a man who can pick up a truck and a woman who can make fire?"

"The Mentalist? Is that what they came up with for you? That's the best they can do?"

Mary aped shock, laying a hand on her chest and gasping in fake outrage. "This from a woman they're calling 'Blaze'? What are you? A pothead or a middle-aged stripper?"

Helen twirled an imaginary feather boa and hummed "The Stripper." Mary joined in, shimmying her shoulders and rocking back into her hips. They were both laughing so hard they were almost crying when a knock came on the door. "Are you ready?"

"Ready as we'll ever be," Helen called out, wiping her eyes and putting her red and orange mask back into place.

AN OFFICIOUS-LOOKING young man stood outside the door. He managed to peer down his nose at Helen, despite being only an inch or so taller than her and turned on his heel. "This way, please."

He led the way through a few gleaming white corridors, and directed them into a weird little tram, with egg-shaped cars. As he seated himself at the front, safety belts slid across their bodies.

Helen stiffened, but Mary didn't react, so she forced her shoulders down and reabsorbed the spike of heat that rushed to her hands. This was not the moment to melt something out of jumpiness. Clearly the weird little sci-fi train was how people moved around the facility when they weren't incarcerated here but were free to move at will. Maybe the Director was a fan of *Logan's Run*.

Helen rolled her neck in circles, listening to the rustling popcorn sound of tense muscles and tissues resisting movement. She warmed one of her hands, just to one hundred forty degrees or so and gripped her neck so the hot palm rested on the sorest spot, like a heating pad. After a few moments, the tight spot loosened and Helen found she could turn her head all the way to the side again. Leaning into that movement, she looked out the side windows, but it was like trying to watch the scenery from a rollercoaster—all light and movement and little to discern.

The ride was short. The fastidious man who met them at her quarters tapped something on the outside of the car and the bubble dome rose. Helen pushed herself to her feet, leaving a sweaty palm print on the metal hand railing. The man wrinkled his nose at her and, for a moment, Helen considered steaming up his glasses to watch him trip, but she held herself back. He turned on his heel and walked off without a word to either of them.

Mary followed him and Helen fell into step beside her daughter. "Are they always this hospitable?"

Shaking her head, Mary frowned. "The Director's assistant is out of town and Richard has a stick up his ass about filling in for her."

"Richard, huh? So, he's well named?"

Mary touched a finger to her nose, their old symbol for "Bingo."

A few steps ahead of them, Richard, already re-named "Dick" in Helen's brain, stood holding a narrow door open. He barely waited for Mary to snag the edge with her fingers before disappearing down a white passageway.

"What's with all the white? I feel like I'm walking around in an iPod."

Mary snorted. "I'm sure Steven thinks it makes us look all sci-fi and sleek."

Steven? Interesting that Mary was on a first-name basis with the Director of the Department. She'd been so focused on what this moment meant for her that she hadn't been properly curious about what was going on with her daughter.

The narrow white hallway ended and Dicky-boy stood waiting, not bothering to disguise his annoyance and impatience. As Mary laid a hand in the open door, she turned to him and smiled. "Thanks." Her voice was so sugary Helen's hackles went up.

A quick glance revealed her daughter's boot holding Captain Littledick's shoelace to the floor. When he turned to go, his foot didn't go with him and he was forced to pinwheel to avoid a face-plant. "Careful there, sport," Helen offered, avoiding eye contact with her daughter so they could both keep straight faces.

Sir Dickface didn't so much glance their direction as he marched down the hallway back to wherever they kept him, pulling his jacket back into place and brushing at the sleeves. The two women sputtered as they tried to suppress the bout of hilarity that overtook them. Finally, Mary let out a low "Whooo" sound and began to get herself under control and Helen followed suit.

"Ready?" Mary asked, face sober again.

Helen ran her hands over her tunic and took a deep breath to lower her shoulders. "Let's do this."

The door opened into an ordinary boardroom with a wide table and a big LED display on the wall. No one else was inside yet. Helen walked over to the coffee pot and poured herself a cup. She grimaced when she took a sip—cold. She'd gotten good at warming the liquid without melting the disposable cups. The key was to control the flow of heat into the liquid while avoiding the glued seams of the cup itself. Precision work, but one of the handier, day-to-day uses she'd found for her powers. All these months incarcerated and restricted, she'd learned subtler uses of her abilities, ones that could slip under the radar of her jailers.

She sipped it and grimaced. "All this technology and they can't make a decent cup of coffee."

Mary snorted. "I know, right? You'd think they could spring for something better than the store-brand generic."

"I'll keep that in mind."

Turning too fast toward the voice, Helen sloshed the coffee onto the floor.

Mary crossed her arms and glared at the man who had entered the room so quietly neither of them heard him. He was handsome in a professional sort of way, like an orthodontist or a chiropractor—clean cut, clean shaven, and smartly dressed. "Steven, this is my mother. Mom, this is Steven. Most people call him 'the Director,' because he's weird like that."

"I'm so glad to talk with you in person, Ms. Braeburn."

Helen frowned down at her hand, held snugly in his. She couldn't remember giving it to him. "Helen, please."

The Director's smile expanded, and Helen felt he was a good man, trustworthy and kind.

Mary stepped between them, laid a hand on the Director's arm, and raised an eyebrow at him. To Helen's surprise, the man looked sheepish. He stepped back, and Helen wobbled a little on her feet, as if a support had just been removed.

"Come. Sit down, please." The Director gestured at the chairs around the table. He took one at the center of one side, and Helen and Mary took two opposite him.

"The others will be here soon. Our debriefing ran a little over."

The three of them sat in awkward silence for a moment. Helen took in a breath to speak and swallowed her words three times. Everything she could think of was either brown-nosing or kowtowing. It didn't matter that it was true that she was grateful for the opportunity. Saying so out loud was cringe-inducing.

They were saved from the silence by the arrival of the rest of the team. Helen recognized Patricia, of course, and the handsome Latino who carried her out of a burning house once then flung her against a wall another time. To be fair, she was throwing fireballs at him and the others at the time. She didn't recognize the Black woman in sunglasses.

They entered the room in silence, though it was clear they had been in conversation until the moment they'd opened the door. They all eyeballed Helen in turn as they filed into the room.

The Director stood. "Thank you all for your time today. I'm sure you know Helen Braeburn, codename Blaze." He went around the circle introducing the others. "Patricia, the Lizard Woman of Springfield; Fuerte; and Agent Rogers. I believe you've met most of them."

No one smiled, though Fuerte dipped his head in recognition when his name was called. Helen was surprised he would be the softie of the group, given their history, but she was grateful to have anyone on her side, especially when Patricia was glaring at her with yellowed eyes and seemed to have grown a little larger every time Helen glanced her direction.

Ignoring the tension in the room, the Director rested his hands on the table and leaned nearer to Helen. "The fifth member of our team, Flygirl, is off duty today, so you'll meet her another time." Standing, he spread his hands to encompass the group, and his voice boomed in the small space, as if he'd picked up a microphone. "We're all so pleased you are joining us."

Agent Rogers pushed her sunglasses up to rub the skin between her eyes. "Stop it, Steven. My head hurts enough."

The Director's expression faltered. "Of course. Fuerte, can you dim the lights?"

Helen shot Mary a look, and Mary held her fingers in an "L" for "later". Helen was growing more curious about the Director with each passing moment. She'd hold Mary to that promise to fill her in.

When the lights were dimmed, the Black woman removed her sunglasses. She rolled them around on the table for a few seconds before she noticed Helen was watching her. Giving a little half-smile, she snapped the glasses closed and clipped them to the front of her shirt. "Okay, let's hear what you've got in mind."

The plan the Director laid out was nearly word for word what Helen had been told. Some of the people "under the care" of the UCU would be released, to show the public that rehabilitation was possible. There would be a press conference, and Blaze would be introduced to the public at that event as a new member of the UCU's special talents force.

"Ms. Braeburn is the ideal candidate for bringing this to the public," the Director finished. Helen managed not to laugh out loud about her incarceration being touted as a rehabilitation program—like the catacombs of the UCU were some sort of home for wayward women instead of a prison and experimentation center. Instead, she studied the faces of the rest of the group.

Four skeptical faces regarded the man. Mary's face was neutral, but she looked like she was concentrating hard on something. When Patricia's yellow eyes narrowed in Helen's direction, she fought the urge to shiver. There was something carnivorous in the woman's expression.

Helen cleared her throat and all eyes in the room turned to her. "I know we've had a rough history."

Patricia snorted, and Fuerte elbowed her, then waved for Helen to continue.

She continued speaking, forcing herself to make eye contact with each of them in turn. "I have learned from my mistakes. I understand the danger I became, to myself and to others. I appreciate the chance to turn that around and find a way to use my abilities to help people. I won't throw away the opportunity."

Fuerte rewarded Helen with a hesitant smile, and Mary winked at her. But Agent Rogers and Patricia crossed their arms in almost identical postures of distrust, their faces offering no clue as to what they might be thinking. The Director looked pleased.

Fuerte was the first to speak. "Mary, do you think she is ready?"

Mary remained quiet for long seconds, and Helen's face burned with embarrassment. Would her own daughter fail to stand up for her? She'd thought their relationship was on the mend.

After the pause stretched long enough to grow uncomfortable for everyone, Mary cleared her throat. "You all know Mom and I have had our conflicts, and that she didn't come to the UCU willingly. But she has benefitted from the care she has received here."

She focused her attention on Helen, dipping her chin in a quick nod. "Mom means what she says. She has every intention of making good on this chance and proving she can be trusted. I think we owe her the opportunity to show us."

MARY'S GOT A BAD FEELING

As the others made their way to the door, murmuring to each other and shaking their heads, Mary tapped Leonel's arm. "Fuerte, can I talk to you for a second?"

A flicker of uncertainty crossed Leonel's face before he responded. "Of course."

Mary glared pointedly at the Director, who was still standing there. After a long second's pause, he caught on. "Of course, of course! I'll let you two catch up. Ms. Braeburn, may I see you to your quarters?"

Helen peered over her shoulder as the Director took her arm, and Mary tried to project reassurance. She didn't like letting the Director spend time with her mother without her there to run interference, both to keep her mother's temper under control and to make sure the Director didn't exert undue influence over her mother's perceptions.

She elicited promises from both of them but wasn't entirely reassured by either. She narrowed her eyes at Steven as he closed the door, and he ducked his chin in the slightest of nods. She'd have to hope that was good enough.

Once the door closed, she tried to shelve her worries about her mother and focus. When she turned back to Leonel, he had removed his golden sun mask, and the expression on his face was surprisingly anxious. He didn't say anything, so she sat back down, facing him.

"I wanted to ask you about Jessica," she said.

"Jessica?" His voice lifted in surprise and his gaze drifted to the door the others had exited through. "What about her?"

"She's been a little off lately, don't you think?"

Leonel frowned, considering her words. "I don't know. Off how?"

"It's hard to explain. It's more of a feeling than anything she's said or done." She thought about the last time she'd seen Jessica. The unexpected hug—were they hugging friends? The over-enthusiasm, the false brightness. It hadn't felt sincere. How did one explain these kinds of things?

"Have you seen her recently? I mean, outside of work?"

He shook his head. "Not since summer." His cheeks reddened. "She is a newlywed though, so she's probably, um, busy at home."

Mary considered that. It didn't explain the feeling she was getting. This felt more like Jessica was hiding something. "I don't think it's that." She paused, rolling things over in her mind. "Did you know she's getting a tattoo?"

Leonel's eyebrow shot up. "Really? What's she getting?"

Jessica hadn't told Leonel, her best friend? That *was* interesting, and not in a good way. "She didn't say, but she did ask for a recommendation for a place to go. She told me she wanted to commemorate the anniversary of her cancer remission."

"Did you recommend somewhere?"

"Yes, I sent her to a guy I've worked with before. He's good." She pulled back her hair so Leonel could see her ear. "He did this one for me." She tugged her neckline to one side, revealing some star-shaped stones in a line below her collarbone. "These too."

Leonel's eyes widened. "Is she getting something this elaborate?"

"My guess is probably not."

Leonel flopped back in his chair, and it creaked ominously. He loosened his grip on the armrests and shifted guiltily, petting the armrest like it was a kitten that needed soothing. "I hope you won't take it the wrong way when I say Jessica does not seem the sort of woman to get a tattoo."

"That's what I thought too. She's pretty vanilla."

A gentle laugh lifted the corners of Leonel's mouth. "Vanilla? Is that what you call it?"

"Come on, Leonel, you're not that old." She poked him, a teasing lilt in her voice. She leaned closer and grinned at him. "And you're not that vanilla."

Leonel turned his face away but not before she saw the spots of color that lit his cheeks.

She pulled her jacket back on and tugged the zipper into place. "Will you talk to her? If she'll talk to anyone about what's going on with her, I think it will be you. I have a weird feeling."

If anyone understood about her weird feelings, it was Leonel. They fought The Six together not so very long ago, and her psychic resistance had saved him from falling under the thrall of their leader.

"Of course."

Leonel stood to leave, and Mary turned to the hidden door she entered through, wondering if she could find her way back to her mother's cell that way or if she should follow the standard path. Hand on the hidden latch, she paused.

"Leonel?"

"Yes?"

"What did you think I was going to say? You looked worried when I asked to talk to you, and relieved when I mentioned Jessica."

"Oh." He looked down at his boots. "It's nothing."

She crossed her arms over her chest. "You know you can't lie to me, right? I can tell." She waggled her fingers. "It rolls off of you like a black cloud."

The truth was Leonel was such a bad liar that she didn't need psychic powers to tell when he was dissembling. She was surprised he hadn't spilled the beans and told the whole world who he was by now. But protecting David and his family was strong enough motivation to keep that secret close to his chest.

"I thought you wouldn't want me to work with your mother."

Now it was Mary's turn to be surprised. "Why would you think that?"

"It was me." His soft brown eyes were wet. "On the college campus? It was me who threw her into the wall. I thought I'd killed her."

Mary stepped closer so she could peer up into his face. "Now listen here, Big Guy." She jabbed his chest with a finger. "Don't be ridiculous! My mother was throwing fire, threatening the lives of your friends, not to mention random college students and people driving by in cars."

She poked him again, and he was kind enough to take a step back, as if it were possible for her to shift his stance. She folded her arms and leaned into one hip. "You did the right thing."

"You think so?"

"I *know* so. I'm the idiot who broke her out and almost got myself and half the city burned up in the process, because I hadn't seen it. I didn't understand."

"The Director asked me to show her the ropes. I didn't want to agree, but somehow I did. You know how it is with him."

Mary's lips pressed into a thin pink line. What did the man have in mind, pushing Leonel to work with her mother? She did know how it was with Steven, better than most. Mary was one of the few that could feel and resist his influence.

She still remembered what the Director did to Sally Ann's reporter boyfriend when his ordinary persuasion hit a block too. She'd stayed quiet up till now, figuring it was the price of having her mother kept someplace safe—out of ordinary jail, and with people who might be able to help her.

Maybe it was time to reconsider that stance.

"Mary?"

"Sorry, Leonel." She shook her head. "I've got a lot on my mind." She focused on him again, pushing down her other worries to consider later. No matter what the Director was thinking, Leonel was a good person, a kind person. She couldn't wish for someone better to guide her mother through this transition from villain to hero.

"You're the right person for this, Leonel. If there's anyone who can teach my mother what it means to be a hero, it's you."

SEEDS OF DOUBT IN PATRICIA'S GARDEN

"What the hell is he thinking?" Patricia growled as she and Sally Ann made their way down the hall. Scales rolled up her arms, then settled back in, a sure sign she was agitated.

"You know how he can be," Sally Ann said. "The man does not lack for confidence."

She sounded tired, and Patricia shortened her stride, remembering Sally Ann wasn't supposed to be out of bed and walking around, and that it was her fault the woman had a concussion. Walking more slowly, she asked in a quiet voice, "How are you doing?"

Sally Ann lowered her sunglasses to squint at Patricia for a moment, before sliding them back into place. "Light still hurts, and I have to be careful how I move or I get nauseated. All in all, maybe the second worst concussion I've ever had. Not as bad as the time I tried to jump my motorcycle over a jackknifed semi in the rain, but worse than the time I got flattened by a falling I-beam. It is better than it was yesterday at least."

Patricia stopped. "I'm sorry."

Startled, Sally Ann stopped, leaning a hand on the wall. "Did you just apologize?"

"I did. I seem to be doing that a lot lately." *Because I keep screwing up,* she added silently.

Sally Ann dropped the sunglasses again, studying Patricia's face. "We need to talk. Let's go to my room so I can get out of this light."

Patricia followed Sally Ann through the corridors in silence, anxious about how this conversation was going to go. Sally Ann had every reason to be upset with Patricia. At the museum, she'd deviated from the plan and caused a lot of avoidable damage. If Leonel hadn't been there to catch the damned winged dinosaur, the museum would have lost one of its most valuable tourist attractions.

She'd wanted to feel like a hero, to win a fight. After the argument with Suzie that came out of left field, she'd been shaken to her core. She wasn't used to second-guessing her actions or doubting her decisions, but that's what was happening now. In her desperation to do something, she could have caused a real tragedy.

By the time they arrived at Sally Ann's door, Patricia was so worked up she was having trouble keeping her scales hidden.

But Sally Ann didn't say a word about the fiasco at the museum or Patricia's attempted apology. Instead, she told Patricia to sit down and to fill her in about how it went with Dr. Liu.

"It was weird."

"I bet."

Patricia skipped over all the personal drama and shared the highlights, focusing on the worst part—the potential for a mole. "I'm afraid she's right. There's no way for Daniel Price to have known about the frogs and where we sent the samples unless he's got someone on the inside. But who could it be?"

Sally Ann grabbed a weird little neoprene sleeve off the side table and stretched it over her head, covering her eyes and forehead and pushing her hair into a weird little tuft sticking straight up the middle. It would have been funny if Patricia didn't know it was a treatment for the headaches that came with the concussion.

Fluffing up the pillows into a sort of bolster behind her, Sally Ann lay back. After a long moment of silence, she finally spoke. "Do you think it could be Helen?"

"How would she have communicated with him? I mean, she was under wraps. And she didn't even know Cindy's father. Plus, did she know about the frogs at all?"

Sally Ann breathed out hard, like a rhinoceros preparing to charge. "No. You're right. It can't be her. I guess I wanted it to be so I could use that to change the Director's mind about this whole crazy plan."

"Cindy seems more likely. She's outsmarted our security measures a couple of times already. But if it's her, why would she tell me?"

Shifting position so she lay on her side, Sally Ann grunted. "Could she be pretending to play along? Acting like she's on our side to manipulate you?"

Patricia groaned. "I don't know. Ever since this all started happening, I haven't trusted my instincts anymore when it comes to Cindy. It's why I've stayed away. I can't tell if she's being real, or if she just knows how to push my buttons and is playing me for a fool again."

Sally Ann flopped out an arm, and Patricia offered her hand, grateful when Sally Ann squeezed her fingers before she pulled the arm back and bent it under the pillows.

"Can you grab my water for me? It's nice here in the dark and I don't want to take this thing off."

Patricia grabbed the water bottle on the side table and positioned the straw so Sally Ann could take a drink without moving.

"Listen." Sally Ann's voice had gone raspy. "I'm going to say something. I don't like that I'm even thinking it, but it needs to be considered. Can you check for any surveillance in here and disable it?"

Patricia didn't like the sound of that. Obviously, Sally Ann wanted to tell her something she didn't trust the rest of the facility with. But she also knew it was impossible to make a good decision if you weren't considering all the possibilities. So, she adjusted her eyes to use her infrared vision and examined the room.

Over the years, working with the science team, she'd developed more facility with understanding what she saw this way—when she used what she thought of as her "Lizard Vision." The big bright orange blob was, of course, Sally Ann, but there were plenty of other EMF indications in the room at lower levels. Some of them were the medical monitoring equipment, but there were two odd spots that didn't make sense—one above the window and another on the floor, near the door.

When she examined them both, she found small, subtle holes in the molding and removed a tiny black disk from each. She closed her hand around them, not sure what she should do with them or how to ask Sally Ann without saying what she was doing.

Sally Ann picked up on the problem. "My water tasted a little funny. Maybe you could get me a fresh bottle and drop the garbage into the hall can while you're out?"

Genius. Patricia turned and walked out of the room to the nurse's station, dropping the listening devices onto a table in the waiting area on the way. She didn't know if Sally Ann would want to put them back, so their discovery remained a secret.

A moment later, she re-entered the room with a fresh water bottle, which she offered to Sally Ann. "This should be better."

Sally Ann shifted to a sitting position, then held her neoprene-clad head in her hands for a moment. Patricia stood holding the water bottle and waiting until Sally Ann held out a hand for it. "Thanks."

Sitting back down, Patricia crossed her legs and waited. After a few long pulls on the straw, Sally Ann started talking. "How much do you know about the Director?"

"Not a lot."

"Okay. Humor me. What does he look like?"

Patricia leaned forward, her interest piqued. She flashed to the photograph she'd taken in the Director's office when they'd all been celebrating Cindy Liu's capture. The one where the man in the photograph didn't match the one she saw with her eyes. "He resembles a younger Robert Redford: square jawed, tanned, a little gray at the temples."

Sally Ann huffed. "Huh. To me, he resembles one of the Baldwin brothers, stylishly unshaven, White frat-boy vibes, a little cold around the eyes."

Patricia waited, desperate to understand where this was going.

"To Mary, he looks like Jimmy Stewart around the time he filmed *It's a Wonderful Life*." She paused.

"So, it's not only that he can read minds. He can control them?"

"Not exactly, but he can nudge people in the direction he wants. Some people are more susceptible than others. When we were fighting The Six, he worked with me, helping me build a resistance to his influence in hopes that it would translate to a resistance to their influence. It worked, to some extent. It's exhausting, but I can push through his projections sometimes, and I can feel it when he's trying to alter my perceptions. Mary can always tell."

Patricia suspected something along those lines but hadn't wanted to believe it. She groaned. "So, he's been manipulating us all this time?" She stood, feeling as if lightning had shot down her spine. "Can he change how you feel about something?"

"Sometimes. What do you mean?"

"Yesterday, when I was in here visiting you. I had no intention of volunteering to go talk to Cindy, but the words blurted out of my mouth."

Sally Ann frowned. "Yeah. That's how it works sometimes."

Patricia stalked over to the window, flashes of all her time with the UCU streaking across her memory, making her second-guess so many of her decisions in the past few years. Were they her own ideas? She started to speak several times but swallowed her words, unable to decide what to say, before she flopped back into the guest chair and grunted something incoherent, but definitely impolite.

Sally Ann pushed her headache mask up on her head, squinting at Patricia. "If it makes you feel any better, he's not always doing it on purpose. It's as natural to him as breathing. He has to concentrate on *not* exerting influence on the people around him. And at heart, I still think his intentions are good."

"That doesn't make me feel better." In fact, it made Patricia feel a little worse, like she ought to have been strong enough to stand against him. Like a new weakness had just been revealed.

"Me either." Sally Ann sat the bottle on the side table, put her mask back in place, and lowered herself back on the pillow. "And that's not the worst bit."

Patricia scooted to the front of her chair. "It's not?"

"You remember last spring in Ohio, right?"

Patricia nodded, then realized Sally Ann couldn't see her with the mask on. "Um, yeah. Having my mother kidnapped was sort of memorable."

"What happened to Daniel Price when we left him there?"

Patricia considered. "Some other authorities were going to pick him up. Maybe the FBI or something."

"I've been checking. There's no record of him after that night, not in any database or communication channel I can access. It's like he disappeared from the world."

"Until he showed up in the Natural Sciences Museum." Patricia's stomach gurgled with acid. This wasn't good.

"Yep."

"I think you'd better say it directly, Sally Ann. What's going on here?"

"The Director might be our mole—playing at something bigger than we thought, cutting some kind of deal, using the UCU to get something he wants."

"Like what?"

Sally Ann rolled back onto her back and threw her hands in the air, like she could grab something in the air above her. "I wish I knew."

SATURDAY

JESSICA'S FLIGHT

J ess? Are you all right?"

Jessica blinked. Walter's face was cloudy with concern. How many times had he called her name? She shook her head to clear her mind and turned on her most charming smile.

"I'm sorry. A little preoccupied, I guess."

He laid his hand over hers and gave her fingers a squeeze. "Anything I can help with?"

Should she tell Walter about her appointment to get a tattoo? Obviously, he was going to notice, but she wasn't asking his permission. Even if he objected, she was going through with it, so would it be better to apologize later? She wasn't sure if he and her mother had been talking about the emeralds. He might try to stop her if he bought into Eva's nonsense about the emeralds changing her.

"I'm trying to make up my mind about something," she demurred.

Walter returned to the plate of fluffy pancakes in front of him. "Does this have to do with the governor's wife?"

Jessica had almost forgotten her talk with the First Lady of their state. Was that yesterday? She should have been thinking about it. After all, Mrs. Cafry—Francine—intimated the head of their organization might not be trustworthy at the core. And it was big news that the Director was thinking of expanding their organization, going statewide rather than just citywide in their support of regular law enforcement and rescue services.

But all she'd been able to think about was protecting her access to the emeralds since her confrontation with her mother. She'd been itching to get back to the attic and check on the supply she kept hidden in the trunk with her father's old scuba gear, especially since some of them were out of her hands now, left with Zeph for the jewelry he was making for her.

Walter pulled her back into the moment. "Was I right? Was she trying to recruit you? Was it another good will project, like her 'Love is Love' campaign during her husband's last term?"

"She wanted my opinion about the Director."

Walter knitted his brows. "Really?"

"I think he's planning to take the UCU statewide, expanding our reach."

"That is exciting!"

Jessica nodded, even though she found the idea troubling and exciting at the same time. She supposed the Director of an agency didn't need to vet his ideas with his underlings, but she didn't like the feeling he was keeping secrets from the rest of the team. Something about the whole scenario didn't sit right with her.

But very little did sit right with her these days. She brushed it aside. "It would give us a wider range of cases. It's been too long since I did anything that felt like it mattered."

She'd even missed the attack at the museum, since she'd been out late patrolling on Wednesday and not on the duty roster when the call came. It was her own fault. She'd been pushing everyone away, requesting solo missions and strange hours. She just didn't want to be with the others. They asked nosy questions and made her feel edgy.

"Everything you do matters." Walter laid his hand over hers again.

She turned hers over so they could interlace their fingers. He pulled their joined hands to his face and rubbed them against his cheek, making something in her heart soften.

"Maybe you could switch off night patrol for a while. It's been awfully quiet the last few weeks. The boys and I miss you at home."

She pulled her hand free and grabbed her glass of orange juice, using the drink to disguise her consternation. He didn't say it, but he must have suspected she was using work to avoid time alone. Were they about to have a fight about it now? She'd been avoiding that too.

She glanced at the stairs, knowing the boys would be down for breakfast any moment. They probably woke up when they smelled the pancakes and bacon, even though there was no school today and they could have slept in.

"They're not up there," Walter said.

Jessica blanched. "What?"

"I asked Eva to take them out for breakfast today so we could have a little time for us two."

"That was sweet of her."

Walter shifted his chair, then came around the table to sit beside instead of across from her. He leaned in to give her the tenderest of kisses. "Mmmm. You taste like maple syrup."

She kissed him back. "So do you."

"You know," he said, pressing his lips near her ear to whisper. "I don't have to go in until this afternoon."

Jessica let her face fall, aping disappointment she didn't feel. "But I have a ten o'clock."

Walter stroked her cheek, then let his hand fall to her neck and shoulder. "Actually, you don't. Richard called. Sally Ann isn't cleared for training after her injury Thursday. Your session is canceled."

Jessica didn't know Sally Ann had been injured. She truly *was* out of the loop. She leaned into the warmth of Walter's kneading fingers.

Abruptly, Walter let his hand fall. "Jess, what's going on here? You're so tense I could bounce quarters off your levator scapulae."

"My what?"

"Your neck. I'm surprised you can still turn your head, it's so tight."

"Is it?" A flutter of panic tightened her chest. She wasn't hiding this as well as she'd thought. "I have been working a lot."

"Yeah. Suzie said she'd check into your schedule, but then she left town to see her mother."

Another thing she'd missed. "Oh, is her mother sick or something?"

"I don't know. She hasn't made contact beyond saying she'd be gone for a few days." Walter tilted his head, peering into Jessica's face intently.

She let her gaze slide away, but he tucked a finger under her chin. "Talk to me, Jess. Something is wrong here and I want to fix it, but I don't know what's going on."

Pushing back her chair, she moved past him, taking her plate to the dishwasher. "You wouldn't understand."

His voice went soft, not far above a whisper. "Maybe not." He cleared his throat. "But I want to try. Is it me? Have I done something to upset you?"

Jessica wrapped her hand around her necklace and felt the emeralds' heat against her palm. Almost instantly she calmed. She turned around. Walter sat where she'd left him, hands on his knees, eyes wide with concern.

He was such a good person, such a kind man, and she was lucky to have him. She knew that. All he'd done was save her friends, but she couldn't forgive him for taking her emeralds.

It had been the right thing to do. It saved Leonel! What was wrong with her? Was she so selfish?

Almost as if he could read her thoughts, Walter said, "This started last spring, I think. Before the wedding. I thought it was nerves about the ceremony, or stress about having to work with Dr. Liu during the Power Surge. Even on our honeymoon, it sometimes felt like your mind was somewhere else."

His voice broke. "Jessica, are you sorry you married me?"

She flew to him, landing in a crouch at his feet and burying her face in his chest. "No, no, no. It's not that. I'm the luckiest girl in the world to have found you. It's me. There's something wrong with me."

He rubbed her back in gentle circles, so comforting and warm. His hand moved up to rub the back of her head, and the clasp of the cord to her necklace caught on his watch. He reached around with his other hand and began to fiddle with it, and Jessica saw red.

She leapt back, landing as far away as she could and still be in the same room, the broken necklace cord clasped in her hand. "What are you doing?"

Walter looked confused. "My watch was caught on the clasp, Jess. I was trying to untangle it."

"You were trying to take them."

"Take them?"

"My emeralds."

Walter stood, stretching his hands to the side and moving toward her. "Is that what this is about? The emeralds?"

Tears flowed down her cheeks. "They're mine, Walter. And you didn't even ask when you took them."

Walter stopped moving, standing motionless in the middle of the kitchen, his face gone paper-white and bloodless. "Jess! I was trying to save lives! And you were hundreds of miles away, saving other lives. It wasn't possible to ask you." He laid a hand on the table, like he needed the support. "Are you saying you would have refused?"

She shook her head but inside her head a voice was screaming, "Yes!" She covered her face with her hands, unwilling to look into his eyes and let him see the resentment that must show in hers. What kind of person would let others suffer because she didn't want to part with even the smallest shard of her collection? Did this mean she was evil? As bad as any of the so-called villains she fought—lower than Dr. Liu or Daniel Price or any of them? No. She'd never hurt anyone. Not on purpose. She was better than that.

Walter held out his hand. "Jess, darling. Jess. You've got to give me that necklace. It's done something to you."

Eyes burning, Jessica backed another step away, shaking her head. She squatted and burst into the air. A moment later, she was gone, the top kitchen window rattling in its frame the only sign of her exit.

LEONEL IS TOO LATE

Leonel spun his phone around on the tabletop, as if that could make Jessica respond to his messages. He'd texted three times without receiving a response—yesterday afternoon, this morning, and a few minutes ago.

He was fighting the urge to send another message but didn't want to seem too pushy. He was worried after his conversation with Mary the day before. What was going on with Jessica?

David wandered through the kitchen, pausing to plant a kiss on the top of Leonel's head. "Why don't you call her?"

"I tried that too. She didn't answer."

"Does she have a house phone? Maybe her phone is on silent or something."

It wasn't a bad idea. Leonel thumbed through his contact list and saw he indeed had a house number saved for Jessica. He pressed it and listened to it ring. As the fourth ring was becoming the fifth and Leonel was getting ready to hang up, a breathless voice came on the line. "Hello?"

"Walter?"

"I'm sorry. Who is this?" Walter's voice rasped, like he'd just finished a coughing fit or had been yelling and ruined his voice. Leonel had never heard him sound like that, and his heart lodged in his throat.

He kept his voice calm even though his pulse skyrocketed. "It's Leonel. Is everything okay?"

There was a long pause. Leonel could hear Walter breathing, and the breaths were coming too fast. Everything was definitely not okay.

Speaking more firmly, he tried again. "Walter? Are you there?"

"Can you come over?"

There was a note of panic in the younger man's voice. Leonel was on his feet and running to find his shoes in an instant. "I'll be right there."

JESSICA'S HOUSE was on the other side of the beltway, a drive that should have taken twenty minutes, but Leonel made it in fifteen, drawing the angry glare of the lady next door in her garden as he skidded into the Roark-Peeples driveway. He forgot to put the car in park when he leapt out and had to pull the car back by its bumper to keep it from rolling into the shrubberies.

Brake set, he jogged up to the front door, struggling to keep himself from speculating. He'd know soon enough what was wrong. "*No se necesita comprar problema,*" as his mamá always used to say. No need to borrow trouble. It'll come soon enough on its own.

He rang the doorbell and shifted on his feet, listening for children running to the door or the click of Eva's heels on the hardwood floors, but he didn't hear anything and the silence made his chest feel tight with worry. Unable to wait any longer, he turned the handle and found the door unlocked. He ducked his head inside. "Walter?"

Stepping the rest of the way in, he closed the door behind him. "Eva? Frankie? Max? Is anybody home?" Spinning, he peeked through the window back out at the driveway and saw the minivan was gone, but Walter's electric car was charging in the usual spot. So maybe the kids weren't here, but Walter, at least should be. It hadn't been that long since he'd called.

Leonel drew in a breath for a louder yell, then he heard a creak on the stairs. Walter was standing midway down the stairs, swaying on his feet. Leonel was by his side in a flash, making the man sit down, then running to the kitchen for a glass of water. "What's wrong?" he asked, shoving the glass at the scientist.

Walter's hand shook as he drank the water, and some of it dribbled down his chin and onto his shirt, but he didn't wipe it away. He sat there looking lost, like he had no idea what to do with the glass now that it was empty.

Leonel took it from him and set it in the corner of the stair. He grasped Walter's hands in his and rubbed them. The man's skin was cold and moist, a bad sign. "Walter, I'm here to help. Can you tell me what happened?"

"It's Jessica," he said, sounding as lost as he looked.

Leonel had seen this many times before in the field—people who'd been through something traumatic could have a lot of trouble putting it into words. He tamped down his own rising panic, knowing pushing Walter would not help, even though he wanted to pick him up and shake him until the words fell out.

"Is she hurt?" Images of Jessica lying broken and bleeding somewhere flashed across Leonel's imagination, testing his ability to project calm patience.

Walter pressed the heels of his hands into his eyes and shook his head. "No. It's the damn emeralds."

The emeralds? Leonel peeked down his shirt front, where he wore a thin sliver of emerald on a simple chain. But the emeralds saved him— saved all of them. They were why Jessica alone had not experienced weird fluctuations like the rest of them—she always kept emeralds on her person.

If something happened to Jessica's emeralds, did that mean she'd lost control? Was she floating somewhere unable to direct her movement? Like the day they'd become friends five years ago, when Leonel, new to his strength and taller man's body, tugged her down from her own ceiling?

He looked up at the chandelier and into the parts of the rest of the house he could see from the stairs but didn't find any sign of Jessica. Returning his gaze to Walter, he saw some color was coming back into the man's face.

In a clear effort of will, Walter focused on Leonel's face. "She's not here, and she took them all with her."

"All?" Were the boys in danger? And Eva?

"All the emeralds. I checked—the attic window was hanging open. She must have gone straight there when she flew out of the kitchen."

Leonel hurried up the stairs and rounded the corner, nearly colliding with the stairs lowered from the open attic hatch. In two quick steps, he was up there, searching for signs. Near the window, still hanging unlatched, an old-fashioned steamer chest stood open, with strange equipment littering the floor around it—some weights, a diving mask, swim fins, and other things Leonel didn't recognize.

The window was open, and Leonel leaned out, as if he could find Jessica on the horizon, but it was clear blue sky as far as the eye could see, not even a cloud to break up the view.

When he returned to the stairs, Walter wasn't there. "Walter!" he called, cursing himself for having left the man alone even for a moment in such a state.

"Kitchen!" came a returning call, and Leonel rested his hand on his chest, rubbing it as if he could, by touch, slow the heart within. He drew in three long steadying breaths and forced himself to walk at a normal pace to the kitchen.

Walter was standing at the sink, water dripping off his face and hair. The man must have ducked his head under the tap in an effort to shake off his sluggishness. Leonel opened a drawer in the familiar kitchen where he had cooked for Jessica and her family many times, pulled out a soft dish towel with a picture of a chicken on it, and handed it to Walter.

"Thanks." Walter's voice edged nearer its normal tenor.

"How can I help?"

Walter waved at the coffee pot and collapsed into one of the chairs at the table. Leonel poured two cups of coffee, rewarmed them in the microwave, and added cream and sugar to both. He placed one in front of Walter and sat opposite him, a large hand wrapped around his own mug.

Breakfast dishes still cluttered the space, and Leonel stacked them, wiping the surface with a napkin to give himself something to do while Walter gathered his thoughts. After a couple more minutes, words began to spill out of Walter, a torrent of things that didn't make sense at first, but eventually he understood what happened.

"Have you called the UCU?" he asked.

"Not yet." Walter's eyes widened. "Do you think I have to?"

Leonel frowned. "I do. Where are Eva and the kids?"

"They went out to breakfast. Eva was trying to give us some time alone."

"Okay. You text her. I'm going to call David. I'll get him to take the kids to our house. We'll make it sound like a surprise playdate we arranged. No reason to worry the boys."

"Yes, yes. That's a good idea."

Forty minutes later, Eva, Walter, and Leonel stood on the narrow porch, waving at David and the boys as they drove away, the boys already excited about the promise of a visit to the paletería and an afternoon fishing at the pond with their adopted Abuelo.

As soon as the truck was out of sight, the three turned and went back inside, faces grim with determination and worry. They'd figure this out, together.

PATRICIA: HANGOVERS AND APOLOGIES

Patricia's head was splitting. The third glass of wine had been a serious error. She'd been in the habit of a glass in the evening for a while now, but she'd still felt wound up tight after the second glass. The third one relaxed her to the point that she could sleep, but now the inside of her head was a desert, with nary an oasis in sight.

Stumbling to the shower, she left the lights off but turned on all three shower heads as high and hot as the system allowed, one pelting her lower back, another aimed where her neck met her shoulders, and the giant rain shower head dropping a monsoon from above. By the time she turned off the water, steam filled the room until it looked like a scene from *Dracula*.

With a swipe of her forearm, Patricia cleared a swath of mirror and stood staring into her own eyes for a long moment—the whites were lined with fine red streaks and the under-eye bags would have required extra luggage fees at the airport. "Hey, beautiful," she said, fumbling for the toothbrush.

Normally, she liked to go for a run first thing on Saturday morning, leaving Suzie resting in bed and coming back with coffee and bagels for them both. But today, the thought of sneakers pounding on the running path made her sick to her stomach. She'd better stick to water this morning and give her body time to deal with things.

It made her feel old that something as little as a third glass of wine could spoil her morning, but in her heart, she knew it wasn't the wine or the years or even the mileage. It was the worry. The stress. And the empty side of the bed.

Dressed in stretchy pants and a loose tank top a few minutes later, Patricia stood staring into the refrigerator, lamenting the lack of anything appealing on the shelves. There were eggs and some bacon and cheese. She could whip up an omelet or egg scramble or something, but the thought of cooking for one was depressing. It wasn't much less depressing to consider going out to breakfast alone, but she was considering it. At least she wouldn't have to clean up afterward.

Finally, she yanked open the door, dropping her sunglasses into place and jangling her car keys. As she stepped over the threshold, something caught on her foot. She looked down and found a smooshed bouquet of pink and white lilies.

A very familiar bouquet.

She stooped down and picked them up, then spun around on the stoop, searching for Suzie.

At first, she didn't see her, but then she glanced out toward the lake and spotted her sitting on a bench under a wide-branched magnolia tree, the leaves beginning to lighten to the brownish-yellow they took on in the fall and winter. Without stopping to think, Patricia broke into a run and within a few seconds she was standing in front of the bench, bouquet in hand, breathing hard, with no idea at all what to say.

Suzie didn't say anything either and the two of them stared at one another for a long moment until Suzie patted the bench beside her. Patricia obeyed the implicit request to take a seat, pushing herself into the opposite corner, not wanting to crowd Suzie if that wasn't what she wanted, even though what Patricia wanted was to scoop Suzie into her arms and spin around on the lawn like a couple in a cheesy romance.

Suzie was okay. She was back. There was hope.

When Suzie still didn't say anything, Patricia laid a hand in the space between them. "I'm so glad you're all right. I was worried."

"I needed some space."

Patricia kicked at some small rocks at her feet, sending one skittering out into the pond and startling a duck who quacked at her angrily.

"No need to take it out on the ducks. *I* was the asshole." Suzie huffed a quiet little laugh.

Patricia's heart clenched in her chest. "Pretty sure that was me."

Suzie rested her hand in the no-woman's land between them. Not close enough to touch yet, but nearer. Patricia twisted in her seat, turning to face Suzie.

She looked tired and not as polished as usual. Her hair was pulled back from her face with a headband, and she was wearing a t-shirt that was too big for her with a giant picture of a soccer ball and the words "Lady Griffins" emblazoned on the chest. Gray leggings and clunky white sneakers finished the ensemble. Patricia couldn't remember ever seeing Suzie wear sneakers.

"You look good," she said.

Suzie raised a skeptical eyebrow.

"It's nice to see you looking more relaxed. Casual Suzie."

She tugged at the t-shirt. "This was still in the closet in my old room at Mom and Dad's. There was a time when I lived in these clothes."

"I didn't know you'd played soccer."

"I wasn't any good."

Patricia shifted in her seat. "I doubt that. You're amazing at everything you do."

Suzie turned sideways, so the two women were now face to face. She put her hand over Patricia's. "No. I'm really not. And I need to learn to be okay with that. Everybody messes up sometimes."

"My field hockey coach used to tell us, 'Let your mistakes make you better, not bitter,'" Patricia offered, swinging her elbow in an imitation of her old coach's delivery.

Suzie grunted. "That's awful. Did she get it off a cereal box?"

"He. That's an Ed Parker special, right there."

Suzie's jaw dropped. "Ed as in Shorty's in Bedford, Indiana? That Ed?"

Patricia had taken Suzie to meet Ed the last time they visited Indiana, and he thoroughly charmed her and insisted on giving them their milkshakes for free. Suzie thought he was fabulous and was always chiding Patricia for not showing proper gratitude for all the man had done for her.

"Yep."

"What was he doing coaching field hockey?" Suzie asked.

"Our regular coach was in a car accident, and we weren't going to be allowed to play without a coach—regulations. Ed didn't know a damn thing about field hockey, so he left the strategy to me and my co-captain, and stood on the sidelines cheering for us and calling out folk wisdom phrases he'd stolen from *Reader's Digest* or something."

Suzie smiled, and seeing her smile made something in Patricia's chest light up.

"Did he have any other inspirational gems?" Suzie asked.

"Let's see. There was, 'It's not how big you are, it's how big you play.'"

"Wait, he said that to you?" Suzie gestured at the length of Patricia's legs.

"Well, no. But the rest of the team was a mite shorter than I was."

"What else?" Suzie scooted closer, turning their wrists so she could join their hands.

"I was fond of, 'It takes balls to play hockey!' That one gave some of the field hockey moms the vapors."

"I bet it did."

The two of them fell silent. "Suz—" Patricia began at the same time that Suzie started, "Pat—." They gaped at each other, neither one sure how to move forward.

"We have a lot to talk about and work through," Patricia said. "Would you like breakfast?"

"You buying?"

Patricia smiled. "Anything you want."

Suzie slid to her feet. "Come on, then. You can buy me a crepe and a mimosa, and I'll buy one for you."

"That sounds good, but I think I'll hold off on the mimosa."

JESSICA: ON THE LAM

Landing on the flattest part of the roof over the attic window of her ex-husband's new house, Jessica crouched, staying close to the terracotta tiles. Tall Oaks was the kind of neighborhood where people noticed things and called the police about them, so she needed to be careful not to be seen. She didn't want to have to hurt anyone.

The neighborhood was quiet, and the tiles felt nice and cool beneath her. The stress and exertion of the morning left her sweaty and exhausted. Her light blouse and leggings were damp with perspiration, and she half-expected to put off visible steam as she lay there gazing up into the light gray autumn sky. The wind was picking up, and she scented rain on the breeze. *Damn it.*

Remaining still for a long moment, she stared up at the sliver of sun visible through the darkening clouds and caught her breath. After the fight with Walter, she'd burst into the sky and flown and flown and flown, with no destination in mind. Her mind screamed at her to go, to get away. She'd gone over a hundred miles before she could make herself stop. Then she'd flown in circles, not knowing where to go, unsure of where she was. It took some time for her to work her way here, once she'd decided on a destination.

She hadn't spent this much time in the air in a long time. Was anyone searching for her yet? Did Walter call the UCU? If he did, what had he told them?

Who would they send to bring her in? She hadn't seen any sign of pursuit but knew they'd hardly make it obvious. Would Leonel or Patricia have to do it, or would they send agents who weren't also her friends? She wasn't sure which way she hoped it would go down.

When they came for her, would they try to bring her down quietly? The Director would want to protect their reputation, leaving no one the wiser that one of Springfield's heroes was now one of the city's most wanted. Sally Ann and Suzie probably already had a contingency plan ready, complete with spin for the press.

Luckily, the boys were out with her mother when it all came to a head. She knew, no matter what else might happen, she could trust Eva to make sure the boys were okay.

Her head swam, so many conflicting emotions swirling there. Fear, anger, and exhaustion melded into a brew that left her desperate, wanting to cry, or scream, or punch something, or maybe run back home and let Walter wrap his arms around her and tell her it would all be okay.

She needed some time to figure this out. She gripped her pendant, pressing it into the flesh of her palm, and let out long, slow breaths until there was no longer any shake in the exhale, a process of several minutes.

Distant thunder rumbled. Time to get moving. After another check of her surroundings to make sure she wasn't being observed, Jessica drifted off the roof and hovered outside the attic windows peering into the dark house. It looked like Nathan was out, maybe taking a run or getting brunch somewhere.

She knew her ex-husband had a girlfriend now. The boys told her about it. "She's really tall, Mom, like taller than Dad, and she talks funny." Jessica checked Nathan's social media later and discovered her ex was dating a model from New Zealand, someone he'd met through his charity work.

When they'd gotten divorced, Nathan moved on from cancer-related charities. It hadn't worked as well for him without the show pony of a cancer-surviving wife to use for PR and he didn't want to explain what happened to end their marriage, neither the truth—where his wife developed powers of flight and left him for a life of crime fighting—nor the story they'd agreed to tell if anyone asked—where they'd grown apart after the turmoil of her cancer battle but were still friends.

Now, he preferred the music scene, serving on the board for the local opera house and the performing arts center. His model-girlfriend made a perfect companion for that. Jessica wasn't jealous—she didn't want him back. But it stung a little, seeing him move on without a hitch, even if she'd done the same thing herself.

At least Nathan could be of use to her now—no one would expect her to go to her semi-estranged ex-husband for help. If all went well, he'd never even know she'd been here. She could rest for a bit, maybe get food and water as well as some clothes that better disguised her identity and protected her skin. Her arms were lined with small scratches from tree branches that grazed her when she flew too close to them, and she'd collected a few bruises from bad landings.

She was cold. And a storm was coming.

The blouse and leggings she'd put on for breakfast was too light for the chilly day. It was colder in the sky than on the ground, and she'd been flying high, trying to stay out of view, above the point where most people would notice her, in the clouds. She didn't have her cowl and wig to disguise her. There hadn't been time for that.

Placing her feet against the siding, Jessica gripped the shutters covering the attic window and pulled them open. They resisted—the wood had swelled in the frame—but they bent enough to let her reach the window inside. Jessica hung there for a moment, examining the glass.

Funny that her espionage training with the UCU would be used to break into her ex-husband's house. But her role in fighting crime over the last few years involved gaining access to more than one building from a high window. She knew quite a bit about alarm systems and locks these days.

This window was not alarmed. In fact, despite the sign claiming the house had a security system, it didn't appear to have one. Crime was uncommon in Tall Oaks, after all. It was a well-patrolled neighborhood where most of the calls were complaints about parking and lost pets.

The windows weren't secure either. Not that she blamed Nathan for that. Most homeowners weren't worried about breaking and entering through the attic. This side-sliding window featured a visible lock on the beam where one side slid into the other. Not difficult to work open, for someone who knew what she was doing. The tricky bit was usually being quiet, but no one was home, so even that wasn't as much a problem.

Jessica braced herself against the shutters for leverage and wiggled the window in its frame with a practiced motion. After a few moments of effort, the lock jiggled loose and Jessica slid through the now-open window and dropped to the attic floor.

She had to hand it to Nathan. His new house offered great storage.

And for a woman barely over five feet tall, it wasn't even necessary to walk hunched over. Now, to find the box she wanted.

When they'd divided up the household after their divorce, a few crates of her old clothes had gone missing, and Jessica guessed she'd find them here in Nathan's attic. She pulled the lids off plastic tubs and peeked inside. Camping gear, kid art, college paraphernalia, a few unfamiliar things that must have come from his mother's house. She moved each bin back into place, feeling like she needed to cover her tracks.

She was kneeling on the floor, leaning into a deep trunk, when she heard the floor creak behind her. She was across the room in a flash, flying to the window and ready to flee.

"Jessica? What are you doing here?"

Nathan stood underneath a yellow swaying pull-string light, clinging to a support beam like it might keep him from drowning. She hadn't seen him in person since last Christmas—Eva served as the drop off/pick up person for the kids during his visitations, and he canceled as many of them as he kept. They'd mastered the art of coordinating parenting questions via text, and he left most decisions in her hands.

When they did have to talk in person, he never met her eye. But here they were, face to face again, and she'd flown across the room in front of him.

The last time he'd seen her fly, Nathan ended up unconscious, and she'd let him pretend it never happened ever since. They never talked about her work with the UCU. So far as she could tell, he never spoke of her at all. The Director promised to take care of things if Nathan ever became a risk to her family, but nothing had been necessary.

But he had to know, didn't he? He'd been married to her for ten years, after all. When he saw Flygirl on the news, even with the cowl and wig to disguise her, he must know it was her. Even if the boys never talked to him about her new career, they talked to each other in their beds at night. She'd heard them. Max was still hoping he would inherit some kind of superpowers himself, though Frankie kept explaining Mom was more like Spider-Man, getting her powers by accident, than like the X-Men who just developed them naturally.

Jessica forced a smile onto her face, lowered herself back to the ground, and took a few slow steps toward her ex-husband. "I'm in trouble, Nathan. I've got to hide for a while."

He backed away, and Jessica stopped, worried he'd back himself right down the stairs and into a hospital room again. "I don't want any part of that stuff." He made a flying motion with his hand. His eyes narrowed with anger, and his voice sounded tight. "You leave me out of it."

"I will. All I need is some clothes." She'd hoped for a place to rest, too, but if she were better prepared for the weather it would help.

"Why would you come here?"

"I'm in trouble. I couldn't think of anywhere else to go."

Nathan sneered at her. "Ask your mother, or that new husband of yours."

She couldn't ask Eva or Walter for help, but she wasn't about to tell Nathan that. "It's complicated. It's best I stay away from them right now."

Nathan's eyes widened. "Is someone chasing you? Did you bring your freaky trouble into my house?"

"No, no, it's nothing like that."

He puffed out his chest. "I'm going to need you to leave, Jessica."

"I will." Her voice was soft and placating—she tasted something sour in her throat, hearing the wheedling nasal tone of her words. "Like I said, I need some clothes."

He blinked, cocking his head to one side. "Why would you come here for clothes?"

"It's best I don't go home right now, and I remembered some of my old clothes had gone missing when you moved out. I thought they might be here."

"Maybe over there." He indicated a pile of light blue crates stacked in another corner, behind him and away from the window. "That's where I've put all the stuff I haven't gotten around to donating or throwing away yet."

Of course, he'd just shoved her belongings to the side, rather than reaching out to see if she wanted them back. Jessica moved toward the pile and Nathan backed up again, wincing as if he expected her to attack him.

She set down the camping knife she'd forgotten she was holding and raised her hands to show they were empty. "I'm not here to hurt you, Nathan. I swear it. Let me find something to protect me from the storm and I'll leave. It'll be like I was never here. You won't hear me leave. I'll even close the window when I go."

Nathan glared at her again, then nodded once. He turned and went back down the stairs, closing a door she couldn't see from where she stood.

Moving quickly, Jessica flung herself at the crates Nathan pointed out.

Sure enough, there were three of them full of her old things. She found a hoodie and toboggan and tugged them on over her blouse, then grabbed a backpack out of the camping gear and stuffed it with anything she saw that might be useful. A survival blanket, a water bottle, a flashlight.

Her hand hovered over the ridiculously large knife in a leather holster, intended to clip over a belt. She could remember arguing with Nathan when he bought it, and his insistence they'd need "a real knife" for their little family expedition to an AAA campground twenty minutes off a highway.

He'd cut himself with it on first use, trying to clean the one fish they'd caught, one not much larger than the knife. They'd had to wake the old woman in the trailer who ran the campground to get help cleaning and bandaging the wound.

They'd never gone camping again.

She took the knife, tucking it into the backpack. Maybe it would finally be useful.

After one final glance around, she moved back to the window. Swinging her legs out, she sat braced against the side of the house for a moment, listening and thinking.

She pulled her phone out of her pocket. She'd turned it off, but if the UCU was looking for her, they could still use it to track her. She hated to give it up, but if she wanted to stay ahead of her pursuers, it would be smart to let it go.

She turned it on and tossed it back onto the floor behind her before taking once more to the skies.

If the UCU came knocking, it would serve Nathan right.

SUZIE TO THE RESCUE, PART 1

An hour later, in a café a few blocks away from Patricia's condo, Suzie and Patricia had finished an awkward breakfast. Sipping coffee, each waited for the other to make a move, neither sure what should come next.

Suzie fidgeted in her chair, trying to figure out the best way to broach what she now thought was her overreaction a few days earlier. Patricia, on the other hand, seemed content to avoid the topic entirely, tossing out small talk gambits as if they'd woken in the same bed that morning, like any normal Saturday. That didn't sit well with Suzie either. If they were going to stay together, they'd have to confront these issues, like it or not.

They were both saved from floundering around any longer when Suzie's phone lit up and vibrated across the table, endangering the saltshaker.

With quick reflexes, Patricia caught the phone before it crashed to the floor and returned it to Suzie, eyebrows raised in question. "L.A." flashed across the screen.

Suzie raised a finger and pressed the phone to her ear. "Suzie speaking."

Leonel's voice came through the speaker at a deafening level. Suzie grimaced and turned the volume down, then placed the phone beside her ear again. "I see," she said. "All right. Meet us in my office in ten minutes."

She placed her wallet on the table and tapped it, catching Patricia's eye. Patricia took the cue and waved for the waiter while Suzie stepped outside the café into the breezy late morning sun. Focused on her phone, she stopped in the middle of the walkway, failing to notice the dirty looks shot her direction by passers-by.

After a few seconds, a shadow fell across her screen. Patricia stood there with two travel cups in her hands. "What's going on?"

Suzie grabbed for one of the coffees, a grateful smile flashing across her face. "I'll tell you on the way. Can you drive?"

Patricia held out a hand for Suzie's keys.

"That explains a few things," Patricia said, once Suzie had filled her in with everything Leonel told her about Jessica's sudden flight and Walter's fears about how the emeralds might have affected her. Grimacing, she turned left onto a crowded street and laid on her horn at someone who tried to cut her off.

Suzie murmured agreement. "I should have been paying more attention."

Patricia laughed, shaking her head, as she cut across two lanes of traffic to get to the right turn she needed.

"What?"

"That's the crux of it, isn't it? Whenever a crisis hits, we're all asking ourselves what we could have done to prevent it, what clues we missed, like there was a right answer and we were foolish or blind. But it's impossible to know, out of the thousands of things that happen each and every day, which are the ones that are going to matter, which are the ones that will bring you regret."

"But it's my job," Suzie interjected. Her voice cracked a little, making her wince.

"Your job includes a lot of things, Suz. And even if we reduced it to just the people-management aspect, which is not nearly everything you do, it includes a lot of people. Jessica is only one of them, and on the surface she seemed to be doing fine. I thought so. Leonel thought so. Even her own husband thought so. Trying to figure out what we missed isn't going to help anybody now. The real question is where do we go from here."

Suzie rested her phone on her knee for a moment, letting Patricia's words sink in. She wasn't sure she agreed, but a sore place in her heart soothed a little. Patricia had been paying more attention than she let on.

Pulling into the parking garage and entering the private area behind the security checkpoint, Patricia maneuvered the car into Suzie's favorite spot and threw it into park. She placed a staying hand on Suzie's knee when Suzie turned to exit the car.

"What's the play?" she asked.

Suzie blinked, not sure what Patricia was asking her.

"I mean, how are we doing this? Are we telling the UCU what's going on and bringing in our official channels? Or is this flying under the radar?"

"Nothing has happened officially yet. Walter called Leonel and Leonel called me. That's as far as it's gone." Suzie tilted her head to examine Patricia from a different angle. The woman's face was so carefully expressionless she had to be hiding something. Suzie's heart rate sped in anticipation of another complication. "Why do you ask? What's going on?"

Patricia ran a hand over the top of her head, pushing her short red hair into unruly spikes. "It's the Director. Listen, I know this isn't the right time to bring this up. We've got to find Jessica, and calm Leonel down before he breaks something, but telling the Director what's going on might make things worse."

Suzie's head reeled as Patricia rattled off a summary of her conversation with Sally Ann, and the concerns they both shared about the Director's real motivations and possible complicity in something they didn't yet understand.

How many times had her intuition spiked around the Director during the last couple of years and how many times had she pushed her worries away, telling herself she was being paranoid? And here was Patricia telling her that her inner voice was right. The man was not entirely on the level.

She'd already known—at least at some level—about his manipulative mental powers—they all learned the Director had something special when they were facing The Six—but the more worrisome part was his intentions for the UCU.

This wasn't just her job. She cared about these people, loved making a difference with them. If the Director was putting her friends in danger for some kind of personal gain, cutting secret deals, she'd have to rethink her participation.

"Suz?" Patricia was waving a hand near her face. "You okay?"

She shook her head. It was a lot to take in, especially when she was already at saturation, between her fight and reconciliation with Patricia and Jessica's breakdown and disappearance.

But the team needed her.

Promising herself a few days at the beach once they found and saved Jessica, she closed a mental door and focused on Patricia's blue eyes, ignoring the concern she saw in them.

"All right. Let's handle this without the Director, at least until we know how far we can trust him. The important thing is finding Jessica."

The two women didn't talk in the elevator or as they made their way through the empty halls to Suzie's office, each pursuing her own thoughts. They arrived to find Leonel pacing in front of the door, wrapping his arms around himself to keep from causing any damage.

"You've got to help us find her!" he exclaimed as they arrived.

Patricia rubbed Leonel's back and spoke softly in his ear, exhibiting tenderness she seldom let others see. Suzie scanned her ID to open the door and waved them both inside. Patricia kept talking to Leonel, but Suzie tuned it out while she logged in to her system and pulled up the tracking software. Finally, she got a ping on Jessica's phone.

"What's in Tall Oaks?" she asked.

The murmured conversation between the other two stopped. "Rich people," Patricia offered.

Lifting his head from his hands, Leonel wrinkled his brow in concentration. "Isn't that where Nathan lives now?"

Patricia blinked. "Who's Nathan?"

Leonel's eyes widened, then narrowed in disapproval. "Jessica's exhusband."

Patricia shrugged. "How the hell would I know where he went?"

"If you paid a little attention when your friends talked, you might." Leonel's voice lowered to something like a growl.

An answering rumble came into Patricia's voice. "What is it with everyone saying I don't pay attention?"

"If the shoe fits—" Leonel began.

Suzie cut him off, waving a hand in exasperation. "Would Jessica go to Nathan's house?"

Both of them went silent, thinking. Leonel spoke first. "They are not friends, but they are also not enemies. So maybe she would?"

Suzie spun the monitor around to point at a map. "Her phone is pinging at an address in Tall Oaks."

Leonel stood. "Let's go."

Patricia rested a hand on his shoulder. "Hold on a minute there, cowboy. We need a plan."

"We go to that address, we get Jessica back. What more is there than that?"

"Rich people don't take it well when you go smashing into their houses accusing them of harboring fugitives. Do you want to be the one that gets us on the news again?"

Leonel sat back down, groaning as he did so.

After a pause, Suzie asked, "Do either of you know Nathan?"

"Not really," Leonel admitted. "They were already getting divorced when Jessica and I became friends."

"I do," Patricia said.

When Suzie and Leonel whirled in her direction, she smirked. "You don't have to act so surprised. I am housebroken, you know. I have season tickets to the opera."

"What does that have to do with anything?" Leonel asked.

Patricia rolled her eyes. "So does he. We've served on committees together."

"Why didn't you mention this before?" Leonel was standing again, his face mere inches from Patricia's.

"I didn't know it mattered." Scales were rising on Patricia's neck. Their voices were growing louder. It was always this way with these two. They couldn't stay off of each other's nerves, especially when they were under stress. Suzie tried to tune them out, focusing on her screen and jotting down the address.

The office door swung open and everyone went silent.

"Miss Grayson?"

The Director stood in the doorway, one hand on the doorknob, his cool, even gaze taking in Patricia's reddened face and Leonel's sweaty brow, before focusing on Suzie.

"I didn't know you'd returned. I came to see what the commotion was."

Suzie flicked off the monitor, locked the computer, and picked up her purse, acting as if two superheroes screaming in her office was the most natural thing in the world. "I came to get a couple of things." She tried to replay the last part of the conversation in her head, wondering what exactly the Director overheard.

The Director squinted at Patricia and Leonel but didn't ask what they were doing there. His face, placid as the surface of a lake on a still day, gave no hint of what dangers might lie beneath. "Can we expect you back in the office on Monday?"

Suzie didn't know if any of them would come back. It all depended on how the search for Jessica went. But there was no reason to let him know that. "Definitely. All my personal business is taken care of, and I'm ready to get back to saving the city."

"I'm glad to hear it. Let me know if I can be of any help."

As the Director walked down the hall, Suzie glared at the now-contrite heroes. "How much do you think he heard?"

"I don't know. I didn't hear him coming and then there he was in the doorway." Patricia cocked a thumb at Leonel. "And this one yelling at the top of his lungs."

Suzie wanted to read them both the riot act, but it would have to wait. "We'd better go. I don't know how long we have before the Director gets involved and we're no longer in charge of how this turns out."

BACK IN THE CAR, Leonel whipped out his new, more durable phone and started texting. As he slipped the phone back into his pocket, he said, "Walter is going to go into the office and see if he can keep the Director busy. Eva's going to stay home in case Jessica comes back. The boys are good to stay with David for as long as we need them to, but they are going to have questions."

Suzie frowned. The boys were both too smart to deceive for long, and Jessica's eldest had a nose for falsehoods of any kind. He would be trouble when he got a little older. For now, though, they needed to find Jessica and convince her to let them help. Then she and Walter could figure out how to handle the boys.

She glanced over at Patricia in the passenger seat. She was dressed casually as she'd been when Suzie turned up on her doorstep that morning, and her face had that pinched expression it got when she drank too much and was suffering the consequences the next day. That wouldn't do. They needed her at her best.

Reaching across, Suzie popped the glove box open, fished out a bottle of Tylenol and handed it to Patricia. "Take a couple of these. There's a water bottle in the door pocket."

Patricia obeyed, downing most of the water.

"Here's what we'll do. When you get there, you're going to ring the doorbell, limping like you hurt yourself out jogging and ask to come in and use the phone to call for a ride. Cash in on your acquaintance with Nathan to get inside." Twisting around to look into the backseat, she continued, "Leonel, you're going to watch the house from outside. Remember to keep an eye on the sky in case Jessica is in there and decides to escape that way. If she comes out, do your best to track and follow her. Take the car if you have to."

Leonel grunted his assent.

"What will you do?" Patricia asked.

"I'll wait for you to call, then I'll show up to pick you up. I'll make an excuse to get into the rest of the house and see what I can see."

A few minutes later, Suzie parked the car a half-block away from the address the tracking software led them to. Patricia hadn't been kidding about the wealth of the neighborhood. Everything was so pristine it made her eyes hurt. Leonel took up a spot on a bench in the little green space across the street from Nathan's house.

As Patricia started to walk away, Suzie stopped her, uncapped the water bottle, and flung the contents into her face.

Patricia sputtered. "What the hell was that for?"

"You need to look like you've been out jogging. It's hot for fall."

Patricia squinted. "Uh-huh."

Suzie tiptoed to plant a kiss on her jawline. "And maybe you deserved it, just a little bit."

Grinning, Patricia jogged up the street. A couple of houses down the street, she made such a good show of a stumble that turned her ankle and gave her a need to limp that Suzie had to fight the urge to go assist. "Nice job," she breathed, forcing herself to turn away and trust Patricia to handle it from there.

SALLY ANN IS STALLING, PART 1

Sally Ann finished her third lap of the hospital ward. While grateful she'd been approved for light activity, holding back her frustration with the recovery from her concussion was difficult. The doctors kept reminding her it had only been two days, and that these things take time, but forty-eight hours could feel like a lifetime.

At least it didn't hurt as much to think now. She could still make herself nauseated by moving too fast or forgetting to wear sunglasses when exposed to bright light, but it had improved from what it was a couple of days earlier, and she was trying to be grateful for the progress.

Stopping at the nurse's station, Sally Ann let them know she was heading to the gym. After grimacing through another recitation of the limits on her allowed activities, she escaped.

Pushing through the double doors at the end of the hospital wing felt like bursting into the open street from a smoky saloon. On Saturday, the facility was light on personnel—if there were no crises in process, most of them opted for a so-called "normal" schedule, with Saturday and Sunday spent on rest and relaxation.

The change in scenery did a lot to bolster her mood. Maybe she could convince the staff to let her sleep at her own apartment tonight. If Darrin could get free, they could Netflix and chill, though they'd have to take it easier on the "chill" than usual. She didn't want to explain to the medical team that she hadn't been "exercising" exactly despite the bouncing movement.

She was smiling at the thought when she rounded the corner and almost smacked into the Director. He was moving fast, so focused he moved past her without acknowledgement. "Working weekends, I see," she called after him.

The Director stopped, snapping his head around like he'd been caught at something. With a casualness that looked forced to Sally Ann's practiced eye, he came back to her. "Agent Rogers! What are you doing out of the hospital ward?"

"I got the okay to go to the gym, if I'm a good girl and stick to low-impact things like stationary bikes and walking."

"Stationary, huh? Somehow, I don't think that's your style."

"Where were you in such a hurry to get to? Is there something going on?" Sally Ann knew she wasn't cleared to work yet, but if her team was on a mission today, she wanted to know about it.

The Director's face flickered in and out of focus for a moment, and Sally Ann felt the pressure at the base of her skull she'd come to recognize as a sign of the Director exerting his powers of influence. She gritted her teeth to keep her mind clear. "Something I can help with, maybe?"

He shifted on his feet, focusing on something in the distance before he refocused his gaze on her, having apparently come to a decision. "It's Ms. Roark."

A spike of alarm shot through Sally Ann. "What about her?"

"That's the thing. I'm not quite sure. I heard something this morning, and when I tried to call her, I got her voicemail."

"Is she on call today?"

"No," he admitted.

"So, she might be taking my advice for once, trying to keep a bit of work-life balance. She is still a newlywed after all."

"Of course! Walter! Why didn't I think of that?" The Director pulled out his phone and pressed a couple of buttons. Somewhere behind them in the hall, a phone rang and they both turned.

A rather harried Walter Peeples stopped in the middle of the hallway to juggle the things he was carrying so he could get to the phone in his pocket. The Director hung up the phone and the two of them moved to intercept him.

"Walter, I was trying to call you."

"Steven! I was coming to see you."

Sally Ann blinked at them both. A strange tension rolled between the two men. "Don't mind me," she said. "I was just out for a stroll."

"That's great!" Walter said. "They're letting you off ward so soon." He gestured up at the bright lights. "Come on, let's go to my office to talk, where I can dim the lights for you."

Sally Ann wasn't sure about being included in this little talk, but it seemed Walter wanted her to come along, so she fell into line behind him, following him to his office.

She hadn't visited Walter's office in a while, but not a lot had changed. Depending on where your eye fell, it found some variety of organization and chaos. Walter adjusted the lighting to a mid-level dimness. "How's that?"

Sighing with relief, Sally Ann took off her dark glasses. "Perfect. I didn't realize how much the light was bothering me."

"The light sensitivity is my least favorite part of recovering from a concussion." Walter moved a stack of papers off one of the chairs. "Come, sit down." Plopping the pile into the middle of his desk, he fell into the chair behind it.

The Director settled into one of the chairs, and Sally Ann took the other, crossing her legs and wishing her psychic powers worked differently so she could figure out what was wrong with Walter. Vibrating with agitation, he was trying to hide it. Walter was normally an open book, so Sally Ann knew something serious was happening.

Stretching her neck as if to clear a kink in it, she peeked at the Director. He looked thoughtful, leaning forward in his chair, one arm on each arm rest, and his fingers steepled in front of his face, index fingers tapping against one another. His gaze was focused on Walter, studying him with a cold, analytical expression he didn't usually let others see.

What the hell was going on here? "I didn't know you'd had a concussion, Walter." She gestured at the specimen jars and books lining the shelves around the room. "Wouldn't think that would come up in your line of work."

"Oh, you know, the occasional lab explosion."

Sally Ann's eyes grew wide, remembering Dr. Liu's house lab explosion.

Walter laughed. "Got you! I'm kidding. I've had two concussions, though. One from a car accident when I was in my twenties and one in a taekwondo tournament a couple of years ago when I took a kick to the head. Neither as bad as yours, but both miserable enough to give me an idea how you might be feeling."

She held up an imaginary glass and tipped it in his direction.

The Director still wasn't saying anything, and a strange silence fell over the three of them. Walter said he was looking for the Director, but he didn't seem in any hurry to tell them why. Neither did the Director seem particularly anxious to ask Walter about Jessica, despite the concern he'd expressed a few minutes ago in the hall. The whole thing left Sally Ann feeling like she'd entered during the second act of a play and had missed something important that would make the rest make sense.

"How's Jessica?" Sally Ann finally burst out.

Walter knocked over a pile of files with his elbow and hurried to right it. "She's all right," he said, though he didn't look at her as he spoke, and Sally Ann noticed the way his hand tightened around the file folder in his hand. He forced his fingers to relax and smoothed the pile of paper as if he was petting a dog. "Actually, that's what I wanted to see you about," he said, turning to the Director.

"Do tell."

There was something hard in the Director's tone. Sally Ann couldn't escape the feeling he was angry, but she didn't know what reason he could have to be angry with Walter.

Walter cleared his throat. "I had a brainstorm this morning. About the emeralds."

The Director's eyes narrowed, but he waved a hand inviting Walter to elaborate.

"We haven't done a full study on the longer-term effects of exposure to the emeralds. I mean, we know they afforded Jessica some protection during the power spike crisis last year, and we've seen success in managing power fluctuations for the other Liu-vians by having them wear emerald shards, but we haven't studied the whys and wherefores of that."

Leaning back into his chair, the Director looked the picture of nonchalance, but Sally Ann noted that his fingers kept up a steady tapping on the armrest of the chair. "So, are you asking to fund a study of your wife, Walter?"

Walter turned red. "Not only that. I mean, yes, I am worried about her —worried there is too much we still don't know about the effects of the emeralds—"

The Director cut him off. "I'm teasing, Walter. It makes sense. We should understand the implications for the sake of our agents and the general populace. It will help us be prepared if further intervention is needed."

He lingered over the word "intervention" in a way that prickled Sally Ann's senses. What was the man driving at?

Looking away, the Director continued. "I know you don't trust her, but it makes sense to bring Dr. Liu in on this. Other than Jessica, she's the person with the most prolonged exposure. And if we can gain her cooperation, her insights would be helpful."

Walter pressed his lips together, but he nodded. Sally Ann well knew he didn't think including Dr. Liu was a good idea. It was something the two of them agreed on—keeping her around was asking for trouble. The woman was dangerous. But the Director insisted, and any protests thus far had been ignored.

The Director seemed to forget that Leonel, Jessica, and Patricia had their lives turned upside down by Dr. Liu, and the fact they'd built something good out of the changes thrust upon them didn't change how they'd gotten there. Sally Ann never forgot Dr. Liu was a kidnapper who cared nothing for the rights of others. If she'd had her way, Liu would never see the inside of a lab again, even if she lived to retirement age all over again. The chaos surrounding her was not worth any insight they might glean.

"I'll take that under advisement," Walter said.

Sally Ann suppressed the urge to give him a fist bump. That might be the closest he'd ever come to telling the Director no.

The man didn't like it. Sally Ann saw the tightness in his jaw and felt the change in pressure in her ears, a physical manifestation of the Director's psychic manipulations.

The Director stood. "Schedule some time with Suzie, and we'll talk through your budget allocations and staffing needs."

Walter jerked his head up. "Suzie? Is she back? Is her mother okay?"

The Director looked confused. "Her mother?"

"Wasn't that why she left town? Something to do with her mother?"

"Ah yes, that is what she said, isn't it? Yes, she's back. In fact, I saw her a couple of hours ago in her office with Leonel and Patricia. They were in quite a tizzy over something. I thought I heard something about Jessica. Do you know anything about that?"

As he'd spoken the last line, he'd leaned forward abruptly, focusing on Walter with a laser intensity. Sally Ann's head swam, and she gripped the armrests, feeling as if the chair were spinning.

"Sally Ann?" Walter was on his feet and around the desk in seconds.

The vertigo ceased as suddenly as it started and Sally Ann groaned, gripping her now-throbbing head.

Walter wrapped his fingers around her wrist, checking her pulse. "Steven, you'd better call the hospital wing and have them send someone."

Sally Ann opened her eyes. "I'm okay now. It was just..." She trailed off, uncertain how to finish the sentence. *It was just the Director's psychic powers making me feel sick?* The Director looked at her and shook his head subtly, the warning making the hairs on the back of Sally Ann's neck rise.

She took a deep breath. "You know, I don't know what that was. Maybe you should call the hospital wing."

She didn't want to go back to her room, but taking care of her would keep them distracted, would keep the Director from manipulating Walter. She didn't know what was going on, but that had been no gentle psychic nudge—it was more like an attack, the kind of shit the Director pulled on Darrin, the kind of thing he'd promised never to do again. And here he was trying it on Walter. And it all had something to do with Jessica.

She was in no shape to take him on, but she could at least slow him down until she figured out what he was up to.

SUZIE TO THE RESCUE, PART 2

The ten minutes while Suzie waited for Patricia's call, and then the ten minutes she made herself wait before she made her way to Nathan's house were twenty of the longest minutes in recent memory, but she didn't want to make whoever answered the door suspicious by arriving too quickly.

Leaving the keys in the ignition in case Leonel needed to make a quick getaway, she pulled out her headband and mussed her hair, tugging her t-shirt askew to sell the image of a woman who hurried out the door after getting a worrying phone call. She paused to spray an aerosol concoction Dr. Suggs created up her nose, preparing for her part in the plan. Finally, as she walked to Nathan's house, she texted Leonel, who sent back, "No sign of her yet."

The door was opened by a balding man in his later thirties, dressed in expensive gym clothes. "You must be Suzie." He offered his hand to shake. The palm was a little sweaty, and the fingers might have trembled a little. "I'm Nathan. Come on in."

Stepping across the threshold, Suzie took in the house at a glance. Not a mansion, but on the way, glossy in the impersonal, out-of-the-box sort of way these kinds of neighborhoods favored, decor that shouted, "Money!" but borrowed taste from a bored interior decorator who'd already worked six houses exactly like this one. She could walk into any house in the neighborhood at random and find much the same.

She followed Nathan around the corner to a large living room, where Patricia was stretched out on a sofa, with her foot elevated on a pillow covered in a towel, a medical cold pack pressed against her ankle. She'd really sold her injury, from the look of it.

Suzie went straight to her, remonstrating. She wasn't sure who Patricia claimed was coming to get her—a friend? Her girlfriend? So, she tried to play it cool, and leave her actions open to interpretation. A lift of the eyebrow elicited a shake of the head, so she knew Patricia had seen nothing helpful about Jessica. Suzie bent over Patricia's foot and a drop of blood fell onto the ice pack.

"Suzie! Your nose is bleeding!" Patricia cried out, real alarm in her voice. Suzie maybe should have warned her girlfriend about her intention to use this tactic.

Winking at Patricia to let her know that was no real cause for concern, Suzie flung a hand up to her face and smeared the blood across her cheek. She turned to Nathan, who recoiled. "I'm so sorry. It's a stress thing. Is there a bathroom I could use to get cleaned up?"

Averting his eyes, Nathan directed her up the stairs. He hesitated before letting her go up alone. "Third door on the left."

Suzie kept a hand pressed to her nose while she jogged up the stairs, relieved to see that following his directions would take her out of view of anyone in the living room. Downstairs, she could hear Patricia's voice—something about the nosebleed being nothing to worry about.

Good, Patricia would keep Nathan busy with conversation about her supposed medical malady, giving Suzie a few precious minutes to snoop.

First, she needed to stop the nosebleed. She pulled a small chapstick-like tube from her pocket and held it to her nose. An astringent odor made her eyes sting for a moment, and just like that, the minor blood flow ceased. Dr. Suggs was a genius. That worked like a charm. She wished she'd had something like it to escape some of the awkward dates of her college years.

After a quick dip into the bathroom to run the water and leave a towel mildly soiled with blood to sell her nosebleed yet further, Suzie crept down the hall, searching for any sign that Jessica was or had been there. The house seemed empty. Good news for her purposes but strange.

Did he live in this big place all by himself? Of course, it was Saturday, prime brunching hours, maybe he had a new partner now and she was out having some girl time today.

Stopping in the middle of the hall, Suzie pulled out her phone and connected to the tracking software. No change. Jessica's phone still showed as being inside this house. But where?

Deciding to take a chance, Suzie called the phone. In the quiet of the empty upstairs, she heard the buzz of a phone rattling against something solid. Closing her eyes to listen more carefully and holding her own phone to her chest, volume turned low, she tracked the sound to a spot in the ceiling at the end of the hall.

In front of her was a plain white door, the same as any of the others in the hall, but Suzie knew from studying the layout of the house that this one couldn't lead to a bedroom or much of anything of any size. She'd already been gone a few minutes, but she'd have to take the risk and trust Patricia would keep Nathan down there with her a few minutes more.

After one more check to make sure she was alone, she eased open the door, grateful the new construction meant the door opened smoothly and silently. Peering through the door, she found a set of unfinished stairs leading up a poorly lit stairwell to the attic. Perfect.

Moving quickly now, she vaulted up the stairs trying to marry speed and stealth. But the attic, too, was empty. Several storage boxes were open, with contents flung around, but there was no sign of Jessica. Redialing the number, Suzie moved through the low-ceilinged room, grateful for her short stature for once.

A familiar buzz sounded behind her and, sure enough, there was a cell phone on the floor by the window. The window hung ajar, and when Suzie pushed it open, she found a few strands of blond hair wrapped around the handle.

So, Jessica had been here, but she was gone, leaving her phone behind. She must have realized they'd be able to track her through the device.

Why did she come here in the first place? Was there something here she needed or wanted? Or was it a distraction, a way to get them looking in the wrong place while she went an entirely different direction? Did Nathan know she'd been here? Was he hiding her?

Suzie pocketed Jessica's phone and used her own to take some quick photos of the scene for later study, then scrambled back downstairs, closing the door behind her.

She made it to the top of the main staircase right as Nathan came to check on her. She noted that he seemed agitated—his eyes darting over her shoulder as if to verify what part of the house she was coming from. "So sorry about that!" she chirped, pushing past him to return to Patricia's side.

"I'm parked a couple of houses up," she told Patricia, widening her eyes to indicate that Patricia should follow her lead. "Do you think you can make it, leaning on me?"

Patricia made a show of removing the ice and testing the flexibility of her ankle. "It should be okay." She shifted on the sofa and slipped her foot back into her discarded sneaker. "Thanks so much for the rescue, Nathan."

"Absolutely!" Nathan shoved his hands into the side pockets on his lycra pants, pulling them out and revealing more about the shape of his body beneath the cloth than Suzie wanted to know. Walter was a major step up from this guy.

"You make sure and get checked out," he added. "Ankle injuries can be tricky."

Meekly, Patricia nodded. "Don't I know it. Remind me to tell you about the time I kept kickboxing after I got hurt in a tournament sometime. Not my brightest idea ever."

Nathan laughed. "Yeah. We can't all be superheroes."

Suzie pulled Patricia's arm across her shoulders to make a show of helping her to the car. "Not all the time, anyway."

SALLY ANN IS STALLING, PART 2

S ally Ann groaned as she leaned back in Walter's chair. He'd insisted she take the desk chair, which allowed her to recline while they waited on the medical team. She was already feeling better—the weird vertigo dissipated as soon as the Director backed off on his psychic attack. But she didn't tell the men that. It seemed better to let them believe she needed assistance.

The Director tried to make his exit, but Sally Ann and Walter managed to get him to stay put. Sally Ann didn't know what was going on, but it was clear to her Walter was here to stall the Director in some way. She was only mildly surprised to realize, when it came down to it, she trusted Walter more than the Director. If there was a right side of this to be on, it was with Walter.

Although agitated, the two men continued some attempt at small talk. Sally Ann went quiet, listening with her eyes closed and trying to pick up something that would help her understand what this stand-off was about. Shifting in Walter's chair, adjusted for someone a few inches taller, she rested her hand on the pile of files on the table in front of her and was hit with a panicked spike of anxiety that made her pull it back violently.

Luckily, the Director's attention was focused elsewhere when it happened. Walter noticed, but she shook her head at him, and he looked away. Sally Ann didn't know what kind of conspiracy she'd signed on for, but she was in it for sure now.

Sally Ann's psychic paper-reading trick had come in handy over the past year or so, and she'd been working on honing it. Sometimes, she could slow the barrage of emotions and images that came her way, but her concussion made that more complicated. It required focused concentration.

Bracing herself mentally, she dropped her hand back on the piece of paper. She rode the wave of panic that assailed her and tried to dive deeper, to find the cause. Images flew by in quick succession, and Sally Ann fought the urge to throw up, but then something clicked, the volume turned down, and the images moved in slow motion. She saw Jessica, hand grasping her ever-present necklace, eyes narrow and face reddened with rage. Vision-Jessica backed up two steps, squatted and burst into the air, rattling the dishes in the racks by the door. She felt Walter's anguish as if it were her own heart being squeezed.

"The emeralds!" The two words came through as clearly as if Walter had shouted them into her ear.

Sally Ann pulled her hand back into her lap, rubbing the fingertips against her pants to calm the tingle within them and within her brain. She fought the urge to look at Walter, not trusting herself to keep her feelings under wraps if their eyes met.

What had the Director said when he'd asked her about Jessica earlier? Something about not being able to reach her. But Jessica wasn't on call in the first place. It was her day off. So, if there was an emergency, he shouldn't have called Jessica. This must be about her in particular. She thought about the image again—Jessica clutching the necklace at her chest.

There was a pause in the conversation on the other side of the desk, and Sally Ann opened her eyes a crack to see what was going on. Walter got up and moved to her side. "You okay, there? You're looking a little green around the gills."

Sally Ann sat up straighter, meeting the Director's curious and piercing gaze with her best stonewall expression. "I'm all right. Another wave of vertigo. I must have pushed it too much today."

Walter glared at the door to his lab. "What's taking them so long?"

"I'm terrible at waiting," Sally Ann said. Now that she knew Jessica had gone rogue, she understood Walter's desperation to stall him. If Walter was here, then Sally Ann would lay money that Patricia and Leonel were out there turning the city upside down in the search for their missing friend.

Scrambling for another reason to keep the increasingly restless head of the UCU where they could keep an eye on him, she hit on the idea of getting him rolling on the current big case—the followup to the fight at the museum. After Darrin's bombshell about the disappearance of the gunmen, Sally Ann really wanted to hear what the Director would offer. "How about a debriefing, Steven? Distract me with news on our museum gunmen?"

The Director's face flickered in her view again, which didn't help her headache, so she didn't have to fake not feeling well. After a moment, his visage settled into the narrow, utterly forgettable face Sally Ann knew as his true one.

She glanced at Walter, who was watching the Director and looked faintly troubled, but decided that wasn't what mattered right now. She pushed a little harder. "Did we learn anything about who they are or what Daniel Price was after?"

"Wait," Walter interjected. "Daniel Price? Cindy Liu's father? Isn't he locked up?"

Sally Ann rubbed at her forehead. "Didn't you update the rest of the team, Steven?"

"I didn't. Apologies." He waved a languid hand. "You take care of that for me, or Ms. Grayson does. With you both out, I guess it slipped through the cracks."

A spike of anger drilled up from Sally Ann's already turbulent stomach. Was this grown-ass man waving off his responsibility to the entire team with the excuse that someone else usually does it? She managed to keep her expression placid, despite the deep-seated desire to invite the Director to come to Jesus and remind him she was not his mother and neither was Suzie.

Her mama's voice echoed in her memory. "Never let them see they've gotten under your skin." And Sally Ann closed her eyes and started counting backward, a trick she often used to make herself think before she spoke.

Walter saved her from the struggle of finding something politic to say. "Well, I'm here now. Tell me what's going on."

The Director launched into a description of the attacks on the lab at the museum and on Dr. Reed. Walter's face changed color two or three times, going pale and reddening in turns. When the Director got to the part about sending Patricia in to talk to Dr. Liu, Sally Ann worried Walter might explode.

"Did Patricia get anything useful out of Dr. Liu?" Sally Ann already knew Patricia had walked away with a suspicion that the UCU had a mole problem, but it would be interesting to see what Steven said.

He shrugged. "We haven't debriefed about that yet."

Sally Ann tried to school her face back into controlled lines, but he must have seen the shock and anger in her eyes because his eyes widened and he raised his hands, as if to show he was unarmed. "It's been a busy twenty-four hours, rolling out the rehabilitation plans, especially with Ms. Grayson out of town."

Ah, yes, the rehabilitation plans—his crazy stunt to win over the public by unleashing Helen Braeburn on the streets again. Sally Ann couldn't read Walter's expression. "When's the big reveal?" she asked.

"Monday."

She'd already known that—Darrin told her—but she feigned surprise. "So soon?"

"No time like the present!" He rubbed his palms together, as if he expected to be handed a gift of some kind.

Maybe he did. She hadn't pieced it together yet, but she suspected the handling of Daniel Price and this UCU as a rehabilitation center for powered people were interconnected.

"That seems fast. I mean, Helen hasn't been out on the streets for what, two years?"

Steven raised a finger and waggled it in the air. "No need to be negative. Mary's working with her. And Leonel agreed to mentor her. In fact, they're going out tomorrow, so Leonel can show her the ropes."

Sally Ann crossed her arms over her chest and tilted her head to one side. She was trying to figure out how to tell her boss she thought his lack of caution could get people hurt, when the door burst open and a couple of white-coated members of the medical staff brought in a wheelchair.

They each took one of her elbows and moved her to the wheelchair and Sally Ann let them, even though she felt capable of the movement on her own. The Director stood, rocking back and forth on his heels as he watched the procedure. "Looks like they've got this under control," he finally said. "Rest up, Agent Rogers, we need you at your best. Exciting times ahead!" He swept out the door and was gone.

Walter's entire posture sank, like he'd been held up by adrenaline and determination alone. He looked more like he needed the wheelchair than Sally Ann did.

"Walk me to my room?" Sally Ann asked. "I think we still have more to talk about." She shot a significant glance at the pile of paper she'd picked up so many signals from and willed Walter to follow her lead.

"Yes," he agreed. "I think we do."

LEONEL CRACKS THE CODE

Leonel slid into the backseat when Suzie stopped at the agreed-upon corner and nearly pulled the handle off closing the door. The combination of boredom and anxiety jangled his nerves like a fire alarm. "Did you find anything?"

Suzie tossed him the cell phone she'd found in the attic.

"Jessica's phone! So, she was there."

"Emphasis on *was*." Suzie met Leonel's gaze in the rearview mirror. "She was gone by the time we arrived, and she must have realized we could use the phone to track her, so she left it behind."

Suzie spun toward Patricia. "Did Nathan know? Was he hiding her? I thought he was acting kind of weird, but I don't know what he's normally like."

Patricia shook her head. "I don't think so. He seemed annoyed with me. I don't think he was keeping any secrets." She twisted in the seat to look at Leonel. "I assume you didn't see anything?"

Leonel sucked air between his teeth. "Do you think I would have kept it to myself if I had?" Taking a deep breath, he went on. "No, nothing more exciting than some aggressive ducks and a couple of old ladies gossiping."

"You were the most interesting part of their day. They probably couldn't decide if they should call the police on you or invite you home with them."

Leonel was in no mood for this kind of teasing. He ignored it and turned his attention to Jessica's phone. The lock screen lit with a picture of her boys when he tilted the phone. Leonel remembered when the picture was taken—a day spent at the lake, fishing and barbecuing. It had been a happy day. He could only hope they'd have the chance to experience more like it soon.

He slid a finger up the screen and typed in the passcode. The phone unlocked and he started poking around, though he had no idea what would be useful in tracking Jessica down.

"What should I look for?" he asked.

Suzie swerved, slamming on the brakes. Without checking traffic, she spun the wheel to pull into a parking lot, throwing Leonel and Patricia against each other. Swinging around as she threw the car into park, she gaped at him. "You got it open!"

"She hasn't changed the password. It's her cancer-versary, the day she was declared in remission."

Reaching a hand over the seat to take the phone, Suzie grinned. "Leonel Alvarez, you are a hero! I assumed we'd have to spend hours breaking into this thing. I could kiss you!" The young woman went silent, opening and closing apps and peering at the screen.

Leonel felt guilty about the breach of privacy, but he was desperate to find Jessica before something awful happened. He'd find a way to make it up to her later, after she was safe and well again. The minutes stretched on, and Suzie didn't say anything, though she did pull out her own phone and write down a few things in her notes app.

He raised an eyebrow at Patricia, but she shrugged. Leonel tried to tamp down his impatience, watching cars pull in and out around them, and reining in the dark alleys his imagination insisted on traveling, alleys where Jessica was hurt, alone, and afraid. He kept returning his gaze to the tops of the buildings, hoping he'd see a flash of movement among the clouds.

After a few minutes, he felt Patricia's hand on his arm. He jumped, banging his head on the roof of the car.

"It's not your fault, you know," she said.

"What?"

"I can see it in your face. You're even worse than Suzie, thinking you should have known, should have seen this coming, but this isn't your fault. She pushed us all away."

Leonel tugged the ends of his hair and tucked the strands behind his ears. "Walter says it's the emeralds. His watchband got caught in the clasp of her necklace, and she was like another person, like a cornered animal, enraged."

Patricia grimaced. "I saw something in her face, on the Ohio mission, something strange—possessive and fierce. Have you ever noticed how often she touches the emeralds she wears?" Patricia pulled the necklace cord around her neck, resting the flat disk of emerald in her palm and looking at it. "This tiny shard was enough to give me back control, but Jessica wears a big chunk of it all the time."

She held her fingers in the shape of a large circle, indicating something the size of a shooter marble and frowned at her hand. "She has for years. Almost since the beginning. After all this time, we still don't know enough about what this does, or how it works."

Leonel rested a hand over his chest, feeling the matching necklace around his neck. "Too much of a good thing?"

Suzie gasped and both the heroes turned to her.

"What is it?" Leonel demanded.

"What did you find?" Patricia asked at almost the same time.

Suzie spun the phone around, showing Jessica's calendar app. "Did you know Jessica is getting a tattoo?"

Patricia's "no" and Leonel's "yes" overlapped, and Patricia glared at Leonel. "You didn't think this was worth mentioning?"

Leonel crossed his arms over his chest and returned the glare. "When would it have come up?"

Suzie laid on the horn, silencing both heroes. She extended a hand to Leonel. "Tell us what you know about this tattoo."

"Mary told me. She said Jessica was asking her about tattoos and she'd recommended a friend of hers. That was why I called this morning—to ask her about it, maybe convince her to go out shopping with me like we used to so we could talk, and I could make sure she was okay. But Walter answered the phone instead and here we are."

Scrolling through the messages, Suzie read from the screen. "Instructions for care of micro dermal implants."

"Implants?" Patricia burst in. "I thought we were talking about tattoos."

Leonel shrugged. "People do both together sometimes, a piercing and a tattoo. My youngest daughter was thinking about getting one before her sisters talked her out of it."

Patricia had her own phone in her hand now, looking up images.

"Wait. Like this?" She showed them both a picture of a butterfly tattoo with gemstones embedded in the wings.

"Yes, like that," Leonel agreed.

Suzie groaned. "This isn't good."

Leonel's brows knit in confusion. "I agree it's not like her, but lots of people commemorate special things in their lives with tattoos. It's not that weird."

Suzie growled in frustration. "No, Leonel, it's not that. Don't you see? It's the stones. Jessica wants to have some kind of jewelry permanently embedded in her flesh. She's seeing an artist known for making custom pieces." She held out her phone and scrolled through gallery images of people sporting various kinds of piercings, all with unusual jewelry.

Leonel and Patricia exchanged a look. Leonel was relieved to see Patricia didn't seem to get it either.

Suzie smacked a hand on the steering wheel triggering the horn then waved at the pedestrian walking by to show it had been an accident. She narrowed her eyes at her companions. "Think for a moment, you two. What kind of stone would Jessica want to make a permanent part of her?"

"The emeralds!" Leonel and Patricia said in near-perfect unison.

"We've got to stop her!" Leonel said.

Patricia nodded. "Who knows what that would do to her?"

Suzie put the car in drive and pulled into traffic.

"Where are we going?" Patricia asked, sliding back into her seat and putting on her seatbelt.

"Your place. We need a plan."

SUNDAY

PATRICIA IS TOO OLD FOR BABYSITTING

Patricia lingered at the threshold. She'd never been back here, not since the night of the fire almost five years ago. She'd even avoided meeting Leonel at his house when she could, so as not to have to see the wreckage of Cindy Liu's house and relive the tumultuous night when everything changed.

But she'd promised Sally Ann she would accompany Darrin, keep him safe if she could, so here she was, about to walk into her past mistakes. There seemed to be a lot of that going on.

There was still a giant hole where an explosion destroyed a large portion of the basement lab and the surrounding house. Patricia knew from listening to Leonel complain that the city refused to raze the structure so far because the owner was missing and insurance investigations were ongoing. Neither the insurance company nor the bank nor the city wanted to pay for the demolition, so the house squatted there like a wounded beast.

"What are we looking for?" Patricia asked Darrin.

The man shrugged. "I don't know, but I think I'll know it when I see it." He knelt and poked at some debris on the ground, probably a piece of what had once been the siding for the house.

He glanced over his shoulder. "Homestead Park is back there, right? On the other side of the creek?"

Patricia's eyes narrowed, but she nodded.

"So if I was a lab animal and I survived whatever happened here, it's not that far-fetched to think I might have hippity-hopped my way over there and set up house, maybe with a cute little pond-frog. You know, have a few tadpoles who can shoot lightning from their eyes or jump unusual distances, even though passing on those traits shouldn't be possible since they were lab-created?"

Patricia crossed her arms over her chest, letting thicker layers of scales roll up them, adding size to her already impressive bulk. Darrin's eyes grew wide, and a boyish grin lit up his face. "I knew it!"

Allowing her pupils to change to yellow, Patricia tilted her head at him. "Knew what?"

"That you changed size. You look different in different images—more or fewer spikes, more or less of, well, you. How big are you underneath all that?"

Patricia blinked at him, using both sets of her eyelids, one at a time, then smiled. After all these years, she was well aware of how unsettling most people found it.

But Darrin clapped his hands against his cheeks and bounced a little on his heels, like a little boy who'd spotted the shiny red bicycle he'd been asking for under the Christmas tree.

Patricia shook her head. She couldn't help it. She was starting to like the man. "Maybe that's a question for when we know each other a little better," she said. She pushed past him and into the lab. Metal supports had been added by one of the exploration teams. Patricia was glad to see them. Made it less likely the house would fall down around their ears while they poked around.

"I doubt there's anything of interest still here, after all these years," she said. "I'm sure it's already been picked over."

Darrin was kneeling on the floor, poking at some scraps of paper, lifting them with a pen. "You mean by the 'spacesuit guys'?" He laughed. "That's what the neighborhood kids call the researchers in hazmat suits. I'm not sure we're looking for the same things. Some of what I want to know, they already know."

Patricia blew out a hard breath. This was ridiculous, babysitting Sally Ann's boyfriend, when she should be out there, finding Jessica. Not that she knew where to look. If any of them could track her down, it was Suzie.

Patricia tried playing detective, back when her change was new and she'd been desperate to find Cindy Liu and make her pay. Months of searching, and she'd found nothing. Dead end after dead end, with no idea where else to go. In the end, she only found her quarry because she got kidnapped by Cindy's crazy father.

A wave of guilt shuddered through her guts as she remembered her failure to protect the others. Leonel had gotten shot because he'd come to rescue her. He might have died, and it would have been due to her own foolishness—opening mysterious packages and running full speed into a trap.

Pushing down the useless emotions, she knelt beside Darrin. "So, the frogs?"

"Uh-huh. And anything else that fills in some of my blanks."

Patricia thought about that. "What has Sally Ann told you?"

Darrin pressed his lips together and sucked his teeth. "What she can. It's tricky, her and me. She's in the business of keeping secrets, and I'm in the business of trying to root them out."

He settled more solidly on his heels, looking up at Patricia. "So, I piece it together out of hints, innuendos, and the occasional press release. If Sally Ann hints that I should be in a certain place, I go."

"Did she tell you to come here?" Patricia couldn't imagine why Sally Ann would have sent Darrin here.

He shook his head. "No, we talked about the park. But I know something crucial happened here almost five years ago, something involving Cindy Liu, who's been missing ever since, and it appears that no one's looking for her."

Patricia was glad her scales made her expression hard to read. This man was perceptive, and that could be a problem. "What would you do, if you found her?"

"I'd ask for her side of the story." He grinned again. "Preferably in an exclusive interview aired in primetime."

"I was here, the night of the fire." Patricia was surprised to hear the words come out of her mouth.

"I know."

Patricia whipped her head around.

Darrin stood up, rubbing his hands together to shake any dirt back to the floor. "Relax, Patricia. Everyone knows. I mean, no one knew who you were then, but that's one of the most famous early sightings of the Lizard Woman of Springfield, back when you were a rumor. Enough people saw you that night it became impossible to pretend you didn't exist."

Patricia frowned, reminded of her efforts to scare people away from the house that night. If that's what the public thought about every time they saw her, no wonder they still backed away, despite her more heroic actions since. Once that wouldn't have bothered her, but she found it stung a bit, being feared by the people she wanted to help.

"That's not what I meant. I was in the house, too, before the fire."

Darrin didn't say anything, but his gaze locked onto Patricia.

She took a deep breath. She had no direct orders not to talk about Cindy, but she never spoke of it all the same. Not outside the circle of those already in the know. "Cindy and I were college roommates. We were friends for more than forty years." That "were" stung, but whatever they were to each other now, it could no longer be called friends.

Darrin nodded. Patricia wondered if that meant he already knew. He might. Such information was not hard to track down, especially for a determined journalist. He knew Cindy Liu's name and would have checked into her past. Did colleges keep records of roommates? Would he have thought to do more than a cursory search into that part of Cindy's life?

She kept her voice brisk and breezy. "I assume you already know about her work?"

He spoke quietly, but without hesitation, brushing his hands against one another to shake off any dirt. "She was building quite a name for herself in women's health and aging when she disappeared."

"They forced her out—at the medical research company she'd been working for. Made her retire. Cindy's work was her entire life, and she didn't take it well." That was putting it mildly.

Patricia gestured at the shattered and melted equipment still littered about what had once been a state-of-the-art research lab. "She took everything she'd saved and invested it here, building a lab in the home she inherited from her mother, a place where she could continue her work in peace. She had big dreams for what she might accomplish."

Darrin walked over to the isolation chamber, or what was left of it. "I've only been able to identify some of this equipment. High grade stuff, for sure, some of it custom-made."

Patricia poked at the broken tile in the floor with her taloned foot. Something crinkled. "You're young. I doubt you know what it's like, being shoved aside after devoting years of your life to your work, treated like you are used up and useless just because you have some gray in your hair now."

He didn't answer, and Patricia continued. It felt good to talk about this. "I was excited Cindy was moving to Springfield. After all these years, we'd be able to see each other regularly."

It was true. She'd made a lot of plans for the things they'd do together once Cindy got settled in, and there'd been a nice circularity to it: Patricia knew about Springfield because she'd visited Cindy at her mother's house, she'd built a life here, and then Cindy inherited the house and come back home.

It hadn't all been roses and sunshine though. Even when they were talking on the phone about it, there'd been something in Cindy's voice, a bright false note that spoke of trouble on the horizon. "If I'm honest with myself, I knew something was wrong from the outset."

She turned to the wall. It was blank now, but she remembered it covered with charts and graphs. The lab guys must have packed it up for study long ago. "There was this manic energy about her—obsession, determination to prove something. I'd seen her like that once before— right after her fiancé lost his fight with cancer. She threw herself into the research like it could save him, refusing to admit it was a battle already lost. It nearly killed her."

She paused, peering into Darrin's serious, calm face. "I saved her back then. I found her, helped her find her way out of that dark spiral." She let out a long breath of frustration. "If we'd had more time, maybe I could have helped her again. I like to think I could have."

She turned back to face him and found his dark curious eyes fixed on her. "It all came to a head so fast—she'd barely moved in here when her experiments went sideways, pulling me in. The others too. You always think there's going to be time to talk things through, to work things out. Before you know it, it's too late and the chance is gone."

She paced as she spoke, her spikes growing longer in her agitation. She smacked one of the still-recognizable animal cages and it fell into pieces.

"Maybe her boundaries were always loose, and I didn't know it, but once she started working on her own, without the oversight of companies and grant limitations? She stopped caring about the people affected by her experiments and only cared about the knowledge she could gain."

The words were spilling out in a torrent now. So much she'd needed to tell someone, she wasn't sure she could stop even if she tried. "Do you know how I found out I was bulletproof?"

Darrin shook his head, eyes wide and serious.

"She shot me." She crossed to the desk, remembering where Cindy kept the gun. "I'd come to her for help, and she gave me a cream. I thought

I had extreme eczema or something, but my skin was thickening, and I was scared I was developing cancer or something."

Standing by the wall, she turned to face it. "She asked me to turn my back so she could try something, and I heard a noise. I turned around to find my best friend lowering the gun she'd just fired into my back, this giddy grin on her face, like it never occurred to her she could have been wrong…and I could've ended up dead."

Patricia's voice caught, and she coughed. "I'm not sure she even cared. She just had to know."

She ran a talon along the desktop, leaving a narrow track in the dust and dirt on its surface "By then, she was experimenting on herself, too, getting younger by the day, desperate to stop it before she turned back into a child. In the face of that, little things like laws, ethics, and morality lost all meaning for her."

She turned, taking in the mess of melted metal and charred paper, and then turned back to Darrin. "I guess this is where our friendship died. I just took a long time to realize it."

A CLOSE CALL FOR JESSICA

The door opened and Jessica jerked awake, smacking her head on the ceiling and falling back into the bed beneath her. Sleep-flying always happened when she was in crisis, like it was going to help to wake up disoriented because she'd floated to another part of the house while dreaming.

Gripping the comforter and trying to calm her breathing, Jessica squinted at the window where heavy rain battered against it, trying to remember where she was and what she'd heard. After a moment or two, she remembered the events of the last couple of days and her flight that ended in a stormy landing on the back deck of this rental house.

But what was the noise? The storm had darkened the sky to the point that she didn't even know what time it was. The clock on the nightstand unhelpfully blinked twelve o'clock, victim of a power outage sometime since the house was last rented. Had there even been a noise or was it a nightmare?

No. There were definitely feet moving around downstairs. Wet, booted feet squeaked on the parquet flooring. Someone bumped into a piece of furniture and cursed softly.

Fully awake now, Jessica rolled to the floor silently and edged her nose over the half-wall separating the loft bedroom from the rest of the house so she could peek down at the area below.

Two police officers stood in the living room, the door standing open behind them, shining flashlights around, their rain slickers dripping puddles. The taller one looked young, barely out of training, willowy and lost in the dark blue raincoat. He flung his light around in quick, jerky movements like he thought he might be attacked at any time.

Beside him, a medium-height, stocky woman stood her ground and moved her light around the space in careful, regular sweeps. She kept her back to the door and turned her body rather than spinning herself in a circle like her partner. Of the two, she was clearly the more capable, but Jessica thought the boy's inexperience might mean he was more dangerous.

"Maybe it's a false alarm." The boy's voice was lower than his appearance suggested. "There's no car outside or anything."

"We still need to check it out. The owner says the lockbox was opened, but no one has rented the house this weekend."

The young man let out a frustrated burst of air. "If they'd follow some basic security and change the lock codes between rentals…"

The older officer laughed, a deep chuckle that reminded Jessica of her mother. "I get it, Alex. But you know how Ms. Wiedrich is. Honestly, I'm surprised she's moved near enough to the 21st century to do the electronic lock box that alerts her. Bet her granddaughter gets credit for the innovation. You went to school with her, right?"

Upstairs, Jessica crawled across the floor and located her backpack and her sneakers. She slid the shoes on and slipped her arms through the straps of the bag.

So much for the assumption no one would be checking on rental properties this time of year. It seemed like a good idea, returning to the house she and Walter stayed for some of their weekends away. She'd hoped it would serve as a place she could shelter and slow down for a moment, some place safe, familiar, and isolated.

She'd taken some cash before she disappeared, thinking she could stay off the radar that way, but a fat lot of good it had done her. No one will rent you a place to stay for cash. She'd been refused at three hotels ranging from "quite nice" to "creepy and seedy" before she gave up on that plan. The guy at the nice hotel sniffed as he turned her away—as if he thought she smelled bad—and Jessica worried he'd call the police. The guy at the seedy one had eyed her in a way she didn't like, and she left before he could make her an offer that might necessitate flattening him.

Not knowing whether she was being chased was the most stressful part of all of this. She had no idea if she could walk freely into a coffee shop or if her face had been all over the news as a missing person. Every human interaction felt like a risk. She'd spiraled all day, wavering between going home and accepting the consequences or continuing to run.

She'd decided on running three times, only to circle back when she thought about how Max and Frankie would feel. Her mother and Walter were bad enough. The kids would never understand if she disappeared.

At least she'd managed to get a few hours rest at someplace dry and clean. Now she'd have to get back out without being seen.

She got back to her feet, pulled the comforter across the bed so it would look unused, and thought about how best to escape the room without alerting the police officers. Then, the heavy flashlight she'd grabbed from Nathan's camping gear fell out of her backpack side pocket and hit the floor with an attention-demanding *thunk*.

"You hear that?"

"Yep. Came from upstairs." The officer had spoken softly, but she cleared her throat and called out in an authoritative boom. "This is the police. Come out with your hands up and identify yourself."

Cursing to herself, Jessica knelt and reattached the flashlight to her bag. She didn't want to hurt these people, but she couldn't let them find her here. Footsteps were already on the stairs, so there wasn't time to get away. She thought about the knife she'd hidden in the backpack, but there wasn't time for that either. She'd have to hide.

Snagging the throw off the foot of the bed, she flew to the top of the old-fashioned armoire, thankfully free of knick-knacks. She curled up like a cat in the couple of feet between the top and the ceiling, clutching the backpack to her stomach and pulling the throw over herself just as one of the officer's heads came into view on the stairs.

She watched through the peephole she'd left for herself, gripping her necklace like a talisman. The gem warmed against her palm, comforting.

No one looks up. She remembered all the times Sally Ann told her that during their training sessions and prayed the maxim would hold. How often had she hovered three feet above someone who never tilted their head the few inches it would have taken to spot her? *Be still. Be silent. Be invisible.*

The boy's face came into view, small under the large uniform hat with the plastic bonnet that protected it from the rain. He looked greenish, maybe from the light or maybe from his tension and his jaw flexed like he was grinding his teeth. He already held his gun in his hand.

Jessica's body tensed as she thought through ways she might disarm him if necessary, preferably without hurting him or getting anyone shot, especially not herself. Dust tickled at her nose, and she pinched it closed with her fingers. This was not a good time to sneeze.

Behind him, the other officer said something too quietly for Jessica to hear, then added, "Easy now. Even if there is someone here, it's probably just someone seeking shelter from the storm. No need to be hasty."

The boy didn't put away the gun, but he did remember to breathe again and loosened the death grip he had on it. Without coming the rest of the way up the stairs, he shined his light over the top of the half-wall. This time he went slowly, methodically exploring the room with a bright circle of light.

Jessica closed her eyes when the bright light ran over her face, not wanting a telltale reflection to give her away. She held her breath, counting in Mississippis like she was playing a game of playground hide-and-seek. *One Mississippi, two Mississippi, three…*she was on ten before she dared open her eyes.

The light was focused on the bed. Jessica hoped he wouldn't notice the comforter wasn't perfectly square on the bed or the pillows were skewed to one side of the double bed.

"I don't think anybody's here," he finally said, and Jessica let out a breath. She heard his boots on the stairs as he clomped back down to join his partner below.

"Maybe it was something landing on the roof," she said. "Some of the squirrels are getting chonky on tourist scraps." The door closed with a rattle, and the house fell quiet again.

Jessica stayed in her hiding place, listening. For a while, she couldn't hear anything but the wild beating of her heart, eventually replaced by a sort of windy white noise of panic that might have been her own brain tormenting her.

When her side started to complain about staying curled tightly so long, she pushed the throw blanket off and let herself float into the rafters, bouncing across the ceiling until she could see down into the rest of the house.

Empty.

She sneezed, then laughed, a manic little giggle. She flew for the bathroom, suddenly overtaken with an urgent need.

That had been close. Too close.

LEONEL TEACHES AN OLD DOG NEW TRICKS

Leonel swung his arms back and forth as he paced around the UCU garage. The idea of taking Helen out on a training and orientation mission when he should be helping scour the city for signs of Jessica was almost more than he could take. They'd talked for hours the night before, mostly in circles. They'd talked it through again when Walter was able to join them.

The truth was none of them knew where Jessica was likely to go, at least not until it was time for her tattoo appointment, two days away. Once Suzie found out Jessica had removed five thousand in cash from the Tall Oaks bank branch near Nathan's house, they'd all felt deflated. Cash would let her avoid detection much more easily.

She'd emptied her attic stash of emeralds. All Walter found when he went up there was the empty jewelry chest and an open window. When Eva double-checked, she'd thought a duffel bag was missing, so Jessica might have packed some other things too. They all knew Jessica abandoned her phone after the stop at Nathan's, but no one knew why she stopped there and what she'd taken, if anything, from his attic space.

Suzie latched onto the tattoo appointment. "If all else fails, we can catch her at Zephyr's," she'd said. "She doesn't know we know about the appointment, and she's desperate enough to try and make the emeralds a permanent part of herself." They'd gone round and round about whether they should tell Zeph or show up and catch Jessica by surprise. But that was Tuesday and this was only Sunday. Never had forty-eight hours felt so much like an eternity.

Today, Suzie would talk to Mary, and Patricia would run down any leads. David would distract Jessica's boys and keep them safe. Eva would hold down the home front. That left Walter and Leonel.

Suzie insisted they both should stick to their regular schedules to avoid raising suspicion. So, Walter was in the gym and would continue to the lab, and Leonel was here, at the UCU, getting ready to mentor the woman he'd tried to kill four short years ago.

Whether he liked it or not, Suzie was right. Given the trust situation with the Director, they needed to keep the whole mess under wraps as long as they could. He recognized the suitability of the plan, but Leonel struggled with lying; subterfuge was not his strong point. But for Jessica, he would try. He'd continue to pray the whole thing would be resolved by nightfall.

At long last Helen Braeburn stepped from the elevator, flanked by one of the medical staff and a blue jump-suited agent Leonel didn't recognize. They'd gone flamboyant for her costuming. In comparison to her bright yellow tunic and all the flame-themed details on her pants and mask, his own working clothes—metallic red shirt and black pants with boots—appeared subdued.

His current uniform had been a compromise after what he thought of as the gigolo costume. He'd felt so ridiculous, like some sort of Zorro-pirate combination. The darker shirt he wore now was far less flashy and more practical in its fit. After he'd gotten shot on the Indiana mission, it wasn't hard to convince them he needed real protection, even if he was going on a goodwill mission, like today. Goodwill missions didn't always stay that way.

Maybe Helen felt the same way. Or maybe she liked the flashier stuff. To be safe, he'd keep his opinions to himself for now. Walking up to her, he thrust out a hand. "Hi Blaze. Welcome to the team."

She took his hand hesitantly, tilting her head to the right as she looked up into his face. "Fuerte, right?"

He dipped his head in acknowledgement, wondering if she recognized him. Did she even realize he was the same man she'd fought at Dr. Liu's house four years ago? They were standing there, still holding each other's hands limply, when someone put a hand on Leonel's shoulder. He whipped his head around to find the Director, having appeared in their midst without a sound. Had he been with the others on the elevator and Leonel had failed to notice?

Helen yelped aloud, and Leonel felt a little better. It wasn't only him who hadn't realized the Director was there.

The Director patted both of them on the shoulder as he spoke. "Helen, I can't tell you how excited I am about this. And Fuerte is one of our best —I couldn't put you in better hands."

Leonel tried not to grimace, his stomach a mass of roiling guilt, both at his history with Helen and keeping secrets from the Director. "I'll take good care of her, sir."

"I know you will!"

And just like that, the two of them were alone.

Leonel led the way to the blue sedan parked at the end of the row and opened the door for Helen before moving around to the driver's side. Helen was buckling her seatbelt as he got in.

"So, this is it, huh?" She gestured at the car. "Somehow I expected something fancier."

Leonel patted the dashboard like the car's feeling might have been hurt. "Wait till you see the Dact! And Blue Betty here has some surprises despite her ordinary appearance."

"But we drive ourselves?"

"It depends." Leonel put the car in reverse and easing out of the parking garage. "In this case, there's no expectation of danger or difficult terrain. The worst we'll have to face is crosstown traffic. Plus, it's Sunday, so barring a disaster, lots of agents aren't working today."

Helen pushed her lip out in a quizzical expression. "I hadn't thought of it as nine-to-five work, but I guess I should be glad there is some expectation of limits on working hours."

"Absolutely. There are moments when it's all-hands-on-deck, of course."

"Like when someone is throwing fireballs on the college campus?"

The car swerved and Leonel hurried to get back into his lane. Swallowing hard, he said, "Yes, things like that."

A silence stretched for a few long seconds before Helen broke it. "Listen. I don't hold it against you. You were trying to keep people from getting hurt. I wasn't thinking clearly that day."

"That's kind of you to say, but I should have found a way to stop you without hurting you."

Helen surprised him by laughing. He nearly swerved out of his lane again trying to look at her. "Mary told me you were a complete softie. I thought she had to be exaggerating but maybe not."

"Looks can be deceiving," Leonel said.

"I don't know. You can be intimidating when you need to. I've seen that firsthand. But I also remember you carried me out of the fire at Dr. Liu's house, even though I was immune to the heat and you weren't. Mary says you're one of the good ones, and Mary isn't one to throw around praise lightly."

Leonel was grateful his mask covered the blush that ran up his cheeks. "No, she is not one to blow sunshine."

Another silence fell, but this one felt less awkward and more companionable. When they got caught in a mild traffic backup, Leonel pointed at the radio and Helen shrugged, so he clicked it on. "Bidi Bidi Bom Bom" by Selena filled the car and Leonel started to dance a little in his seat, before he checked himself, shooting a glance to Helen.

To his surprise, she was mouthing the lyrics. "Do you speak Spanish?" he asked.

Helen laughed. "Not in the least, but I know this song all the same. I mean, doesn't everyone who ever went dancing in the 1990s? I don't even know what the lyrics mean, other than I figure it's about love."

"That's pretty much it."

As Selena sang the verses, Leonel called out English translations, and they both joined in singing the chorus. By the time he pulled up at the park where they'd be meeting a group of Boy Scouts for a Q&A, he was feeling energized and far less nervous about getting through his day with Helen.

Helen hung back and watched for the most part, while Leonel fielded questions from the children, handed out signed copies of his comic book, and posed for pictures. She did a small demonstration of fire wielding right before they left and received applause from the adults and the much more satisfying oohs and ahs from the boys.

The sky had been darkening all morning, and now the clouds turned black, so the scoutmasters loaded their charges into minivans and waved goodbye, leaving Leonel and Helen to make their exit. They'd just made it into the car when a cloudburst opened up over them. Leonel turned on the engine so they could enjoy music and air conditioning while they waited for it to clear up.

"That was fun," Helen said.

"Yes, this is definitely the fun part—when you get to interact with the public and no one's life is in danger."

"You're good with kids."

"I ought to be! I raised four daughters and now we've got four grandkids."

Helen turned to stare at him. "You don't look old enough to be anyone's grandpa."

"We started young, and I might be older than you think. People see me as younger ever since—I mean, I'm fifty-three."

"Fifty-three? Why, you're just a baby. I'm on the dark side of sixty now."

The rain let up a little, and Leonel pulled the car out to drive them back to the UCU offices. Leonel's thoughts rambled. The morning with Helen had been so pleasant that a lot of his guilt and anxiety about mentoring her was assuaged, but he still kept an eye on the skies, hoping for a glimpse of Jessica.

It was strange, too, working with someone while keeping his name and identity a secret. He'd almost slipped so many times talking about his family and his history. The worst part of maintaining a secret identity was policing his conversation and connection with other people all the time, but he knew it would be foolish to trust Helen too soon. She needed to prove herself first.

"What are you looking for?"

Leonel settled back into the seat with a guilty wiggle. "Keeping an eye on the skies," he said. True enough, even if it was a friend and not the clouds he was worried about.

As if they'd been waiting for a cue, the skies opened up again and suddenly cars were skidding, horns were honking, and everything came to a standstill. Leonel flipped the windshield wipers up to as fast as they could go but could only catch glimpses of the road ahead of them. Leonel pulled the car to the side of the road and turned on the hazard lights. "It's less stressful just to wait."

Helen was reaching for the radio dial when the screech of squealing tires and crunching metal pulled their attention back to the road. On the bridge ahead of them, an SUV spun sideways across both lanes. A horrible groaning sound filled the air, and Leonel threw open the door of the car. "Stay here!" he yelled, sprinting into the road ahead.

HELEN DIDN'T BURN THIS BRIDGE

Of course, Helen didn't stay in the car. Who the hell was Fuerte to tell her to stay, like she was some kind of child or a misbehaving dog? And after she'd flattered him all day, working to ingratiate herself in a way she hadn't done in years.

Flinging open her door, Helen stepped out into the storm, a tirade at the ready and immediately regretted it when the rain soaked her to the skin in a matter of seconds. She turned up her internal heat and steamed off the excess water while she tried to catch a glimpse of Fuerte so she could follow him and give him a well-deserved piece of her mind.

At first, she couldn't see much, but when the downpour ebbed for a moment, she spotted him, dodging among the stopped cars on the bridge. Where was he going? Horns were honking and people were screaming. Several people were standing in the rain trying to take video with their cell phones, but she couldn't see what they were all so heated up about.

Someone screamed, "They're going to fall!" and she spotted the black sedan teetering on the edge of the bridge, back squashed in, and the mostly-destroyed railing that was the only thing keeping the car from falling. A piece of metal sheared off and fell spinning beyond her sight.

Helen held her breath.

Fuerte did stuff like this every day. Surely, he could save those people. He was almost there—just a few more yards.

But seconds before he would have reached the car, the remainder of the railing gave way and the little car fell, plummeting into the roiling water below.

Helen shrieked in horror, along with everyone else on the bridge. They all gasped when Fuerte climbed up on the railing and hung out over the edge, one hand over his eyes like a pirate gazing out to sea, studying the water below.

"There they are!" People were yelling, pointing and screaming, and Helen rushed to the railing to see for herself. The car bobbed and swung around in the swiftly swirling water, looking even smaller in the wide expanse of the river.

She thought she saw a face pressed up against the glass, but it was hard to tell with the waves and the on-again, off-again rain. Regardless, whoever had been in the car was trapped inside. There'd been no chance for them to escape.

Fuerte was there, down on the shore, diving into the water. How had he even gotten down there? Helen felt as if her heart had stopped beating, frozen in her chest as she watched the churning water, until someone spotted Fuerte's head out among the waves, his golden sun mask a bright spot in the darkness. "There he is!"

Coming back to her senses, Helen stumbled back to the car, digging through her bag and grappling with trembling hands for the emergency phone she'd been given. She did her best to give a coherent statement of events to the young man who answered and hung up while he was still assuring her backup was on the way.

Slamming the car door, she took one deep breath and clambered down the hillside, holding on to pieces of vine to slow her movement as her feet kept sliding in the mud. It was hard going, and, eventually, she gave up all pretense of grace or decorum and sat on her bottom and wriggled her way down.

At the base of the hill, she scrambled for the rocky area at the water's edge, only to stop when she got there. What could she even do to help?

What good was the ability to wield fire when the problem was water? Take away the fire and she was a fat, middle-aged woman who couldn't even swim well. There wasn't a damn thing she could do.

The thick storm clouds regathering in the sky were blocking what limited light they should have had at this time of day. So, Helen raised a column of fire in the palm of her hand and held it out to the water like a lantern, praying she wouldn't find Fuerte unconscious there or reveal the floating dead bodies of the people who'd been in the car.

She nearly cried with relief to see Leonel standing waist-high in the water, fighting the current.

He turned toward her and gave her a thumbs-up and waved both arms up toward the sky. Understanding, Helen raised a matching column of fire in her other hand and projected the fire several feet out in front of her, illuminating the area under the bridge with golden light.

Being a glorified flashlight wasn't glamorous, but it was something she could contribute, making it easier for Fuerte to see what he was doing.

In the newly illuminated area, Helen spotted the fallen car several yards further away, wrapped partway around one of the supports of the bridge. The wake was stronger there, and the car scraped and bumped against the concrete, rending the air with horrific screeches.

The car had already sunk halfway up the windows. Helen could see desperate hands smacking the backseat window, could imagine the terrified people inside the car. How many were in there? Was the driver unconscious or dead? Was water filling the car? How deep was the water here? How long did they have?

She blinked and Fuerte was there, holding onto a maintenance ladder on the bridge with one arm and grappling at the rear of the car, water dripping from his hair and sheeting down his back, turbid water buffeting his broad back. The car had lodged firmly, but each gush of the storm-glutted river rocked the vehicle and threatened to carry it away or finish sinking it.

Thunder rolled and Helen's heart rate sped—another deluge would surely send the car spinning downstream.

While Helen watched, Fuerte grabbed the back bumper and pulled. The car groaned as it shifted. Fuerte lifted higher, freeing a wheel caught in a crevice. The water roared, the current veering toward the car, like the malevolent water wanted to carry the nose forward and pull it beneath the murky surface.

But Fuerte held on. One arm braced around the metal rung of the maintenance ladder, he pulled the car and the vehicle shifted toward him.

His shirt was soaked and clinging to him like a second skin. Helen could watch his muscles work under the wet red fabric. She found herself holding her breath.

It wasn't his concentration that broke in the end, but the bumper.

The plastic cracked and came off in his hand. Helen screamed her frustration. "No!" The fire in her hands flared higher.

Fuerte pinwheeled, knocked off-balance by the shift in momentum and fell backward into the water, a tall splash obscuring him from view. The car spun, and Helen was sure it was over, that the car would spin helplessly downstream. But luck was on their side. The car caught against the pilings of the bridge.

A long moment later, Fuerte resurfaced and swam his way back toward the car. He grabbed at the dented metal but struggled to find a way to hold it.

"Forget the car!" she bellowed. "Get the people out!" The wind was whipping hard enough that Helen had trouble keeping the fire contained to her palm, but Leonel whipped his head toward her. Something dark streaked his yellow mask. Helen could not be sure if it was mud or blood. Distantly, she registered the screams of onlookers from the bridge, but she didn't spare them a glance.

She raised her flame higher providing all the light she could. The orange light shone on the dark windows of the car, reflecting back the fire. She could no longer see if the people inside were moving.

After the briefest pause, Fuerte climbed back onto one of the pilings, then leapt onto the roof of the car, landing with difficulty but managing to keep from sliding off. Clutching at the point where the roof met the windshield he pulled. A horrible metallic shrieking rent the night, audible even over the thunder and the traffic and the roar of the river. The roof pulled back like the top of a can of cat food.

Lying across the destroyed roof, Fuerte reached into the car. A moment later, he had a person in his arms. He jumped into the water and started swimming, a one-armed sideways motion. The progress was agonizingly slow, but finally he made it to the broad rocks at the edge of the water and laid down his burden.

Helen rushed to his side. He screamed, "Do what you can to help her! I've got to get the others!" He dove back into the water.

The person sputtered, and Helen let out a breath. They were still alive! Grabbing the survivor under the arms, she pulled them further into shore. It was a girl, no more than seventeen years old, shivering and crying.

Helen laid a hand on her arm. "This is going to feel weird," she said, "but I promise you, it's okay." Closing her eyes, she concentrated on letting her heat out slowly, not enough to scald the kid, but enough to make her stop shivering. Resting her other hand on a nearby rock, she heated it until it almost glowed. "Stay close to this rock. It will help keep you warm." The girl stared at Helen, eyes wide.

Without giving the girl another glance, Helen turned and ran. By the time she got back to the water's edge, Fuerte was back at the car.

She raised her column of fire, a beacon to help him navigate. He'd jumped on top of the car and was stretching his body inside, but he didn't come out with anyone in his arms. He crouched there for a moment, head bowed, before he took a deep breath, jumped back into the water, and disappeared under the waves again.

She didn't see it when he came back up, but suddenly the car jerked away from the piling where it was wedged and shot forward a few feet. Helen cried out, sure the river had succeeded at last in wresting its treasure, the car and the lives it contained, from the bridge support.

Casting her light about to see what was going on, she saw Fuerte's head break the surface by the passenger door, his mouth open wide to suck in air, and then he disappeared under the water once more, and the car shot forward a few more feet.

Helen kept her head on a swivel, trying to keep an eye on Fuerte's progress and check on the survivor she'd left back on shore at the same time. The young woman was huddled beside the rock Helen had warmed, still sitting upright, so she remained conscious. Helen could only hope the other passengers would fare as well.

She scanned the shore and saw a few people making their way to the banks of the river, but none of them looked like rescue workers. No one carried ropes or gear or anything more helpful than flashlights in their hands.

When Helen cast her gaze back to the water, the car jerked, wobbling in a strange manner that made Helen afraid Fuerte had lost his grip and the angry river had stolen back control of the car. But instead of spinning or sinking, the car rose into the air, emerging as if it were on a hydraulic lift.

At first, Helen couldn't fathom what was happening. After a minute or so, it became clear—Fuerte was under the car and near enough to shore that he could walk instead of swim. She could make out the shadowy shape of him in the small gap between the bottom of the car and the surface of the river.

The car continued to rise, an inch or two at the time, the wheels now clear of the surface of the river, and water flooding out the seals of the doors. Only when the car cleared the water completely did Helen see Fuerte supporting the entire chassis across his neck and shoulders. He began to walk. Impossibly, he took one step, and another, four thousand pounds of automobile supported on his back and arms.

He moved slowly, fighting his way through the currents that tugged at his limbs. He had to find purchase for one foot before moving the other, and every second Helen was sure would be one second too long and the man would be swept downstream and dashed against one of the stone supports or rocky outcroppings. So far as she knew, Fuerte was not indestructible, just strong. If he fell, he could break his neck and die like anyone else.

Down the bank, a flat rock jutted out of the rapid flowing water and Fuerte made for it. Shouts and whistles of encouragement echoed through the valley and hope rose in Helen's chest. He was going to make it!

Before she knew what she was doing, Helen lowered herself down the short slippery bank and crossed the wobbling stones, her legs and feet instantly going numb in the frigid water. Fuerte rested the car on the stone, but it was too large to fit—only two wheels rested on the slab. "I'll have to hold it," he shouted, voice hoarse. "Get the kids out!"

Meeting Fuerte's eye across the back of the car, Helen grabbed the front passenger door handle and pulled. A girl fell out. Helen lunged and caught her. She took a second to feel the girl's throat and yelled to Fuerte. "She's still breathing!"

Moving as fast as she dared, she lowered the girl to the ground and opened the back passenger door. She found a pale boy, dark hair plastered across his blue-tinted face. He couldn't be more than twelve or thirteen, and his stillness was chilling.

"No. No. No. No. No." Helen chanted to herself like the refusal was an incantation, pulling the boy free and laying him on his side on the ground beside the girl.

Another child sprawled in the backseat. Helen grabbed for him but was too short to reach the other side of the car. "I can't reach him!"

The car shifted. Fuerte was lifting it at an angle, and the boy edged toward her but got caught by the seatbelt. Stretching, Helen pushed the button, releasing the belt, and the boy slid rapidly across the seat. Helen barely had time to brace before the boy collided into her. They fell to the ground together, and Helen rolled him off of her to safety. Tears of relief ran down her face when he sputtered and coughed.

That left only the driver. Helen got back on her feet, shouting to Fuerte she was going for the last one. Peering into the car from the front passenger side, Helen couldn't tell if the driver was a male or female, but she could tell the slender arm was bent against the steering wheel the wrong way. She reached up and over for the seatbelt but jabbing her finger into the button had no effect. "The seatbelt's jammed!"

The car shifted and Helen slid back out, backing away. On the rocky shore behind her, the kids moaned and coughed. Helen spared a glance for the trio. Two of them were sitting up now, but the blue-faced boy lay on his side, unmoving.

The car rocked on its perch and Helen stood frozen for a long moment, not sure if she should try to help the kids who were already free of the car, or the driver, still trapped inside.

"Lady! Help! I don't think he's breathing." It was the girl who had fallen into her arms. The terror in her rasping voice snapped Helen out of her indecision, and she hurried to the kids. All three of them glowed bluish under the storm clouds, and the conscious ones shivered in their wet clothes. There wasn't much she could do for them, but she could at least warm them up.

Kneeling on the ground, she spoke soothing nonsense, promising help was on the way, though she didn't have any idea if it was true. Surely it was true. She'd called the UCU and someone else must have called 911. Reaching into the center of the group of kids, she rested her palms flat on another boulder along the rocky shore, willing heat into her hands. Within a few seconds, the rock began to steam. A few more seconds and it was radiating heat.

The two fully conscious kids huddled up to its warmth and Helen turned to the boy who lay motionless on the ground. She checked for a pulse, his wrist limp and clammy as a fish in her hands. At first, she couldn't feel anything, but then she thought she detected the lightest feathery flicker under her fingertips. She moved her hand to the boy's throat. There was a pulse.

Behind her, back in the water, came a horrible metallic creaking, but Helen ignored it, keeping her focus on the boy on the ground. Fuerte would manage or he wouldn't and there was nothing she could do to help.

But this kid? Maybe she couldn't save him. But maybe she could.

It had been years since she'd taken a CPR class, and she'd never used it on anything besides a practice dummy. She remembered she was supposed to check his airway first—or was that for choking? Resting a warm hand on his back, she tugged gently on the boy's chin with her other hand. A trickle of water dripped out of his slack mouth. The pulse she'd found just a moment before disappeared.

With no idea whether it was the right thing to do, but determined to try something, she tilted him forward over her arm and thumped him on the middle of his back. Nothing. The world seemed to fall away around her until it consisted of only herself and the boy.

She lowered him to the ground on his back and dug her knees into the rocky river beside him, trying to find purchase so she wouldn't slip or have a jagged rock pressed against her skin. In her head, she sang "Staying Alive" remembering the Red Cross trainer said the song gave the right rhythm for compressions.

Pinching the boy's nose and tilting his head back, she sucked in a breath and blew into his slack mouth. She moved her hands to his chest and pushed, brain scrambling to remember how many times you were supposed to do compressions before giving another breath.

Her fire power flickered under the meat of her palms, stress seeking release, but she held it back. After a moment, the boy's soaked clothes steamed under the touch of her hand. She got to the end of the chorus and pushed another breath into the boy's mouth, cursing her past self for not learning something that would help now. When she moved to compressions, water sputtered out of the boy's mouth, so she moved him to his side, supporting him over her arm, hoping gravity would help pull the water from his lungs.

The boy coughed and Helen almost whooped with joy. He gagged and she held him tightly, patting him on the back and telling him it would be okay. She hoped she wasn't lying. She spared a glance for the other two kids and saw they were now four.

Fuerte squatted beside the heated rock, the driver's seat to the car propped up next to him, the driver still strapped to it. He must have yanked the entire apparatus from the car. The first child rescued had joined the others, and they were all bundled together in a group hug with the driver.

Fuerte sat watching her, propped against the warming rock. She tried to smile at him, but her face tightened, and she cried instead, a big ugly sob. Her body slackened, and she let herself slip to the ground, cradling the lanky teenage boy in her arms.

They'd done it.

SUZIE TAKES A STAND

When the lights flickered for the third time then stayed dark, Suzie slammed her hands on the table, making her coffee jiggle in the cup. Reaching for it, she knocked it over and scrambled to grab all her papers and her laptop and ferry them out of the way.

This was how the whole day had gone, and Suzie felt jagged and useless. After plopping a dish towel on top of the spill, she took a sip of the coffee remaining in the mug and found it had gone cold hours earlier when she'd been absorbed in her futile research. It was all she could do to make herself swallow it rather than spitting it out on the rug.

Patricia left early, sent by Sally Ann to assist Darrin. Suzie suspected it was just a way of keeping Patricia busy, but she wasn't going to complain. Computer research was tedious work and Patricia looming over her or pacing around wouldn't have helped. Better to keep the Lizard Woman busy and distracted, leaving Suzie free to read endless police reports and social media posts searching for keywords that could mean Jessica had been seen somewhere.

She'd stayed at Patricia's the night before, crashing on the sofa. Neither of them was ready to share a bed again so soon, but neither of them wanted to be alone last night either, not with the feeling of crisis hanging over them all.

Leonel had his family, and Walter had his mother-in-law and the boys, but Suzie and Patricia only had each other.

When Patricia went out, Suzie stayed, and she hadn't bothered to change out of Patricia's shirt, one soft from years of wear and faded so that the university logo on the chest could no longer be read.

Patricia's condo was a better place to work than Suzie's own apartment: a bigger table, better wifi. It felt more like home than her own place did, too, a discomfiting realization. She'd never been much of a nester, and her apartment, since she and Patricia had gotten more serious, became little more than a glorified locker where she dropped things off and picked things up when she needed them.

A spat of rain splattered against the large windows with a sound almost like knocking and Suzie walked over to watch the rivulets streak down the glass. It was the kind of day that called for cozy pants and a good book, but Suzie's mind was spinning in twenty different directions. Where was Jessica? Was she all right? Was she doing the right thing by not reporting her disappearance?

She took another sip from the mug before she remembered the coffee had gone tepid and beyond. She hurried to the sink to spit the mouthful out, then turned on the faucet, washed out the cup, and hung it back on the hook next to Patricia's matching one. Suzie's was black with white letters and Patricia's was white with black letters. They both read "Hers."

One might think all this worry about Jessica would flatten out her relationship woes, but they still nibbled like small fish at the back of her brain, adding to her agitation. Suzie shook her head vigorously, as if she could shake the worry and restless energy out. It would work out, or it wouldn't, but there wasn't much she could do about right now.

The lead they'd gotten from Jessica's phone was a good one, and they'd stake out the tattoo parlor on Tuesday. But that was two days away, and it didn't help them find her now. The struggle of trying to go about life as normal was wearing on them all.

It's only been one day, she told herself. But finding a woman trained by the same organization that trained you—a woman who could fly—was a whole different level of challenge.

Suzie was normally up for any challenge and revelled in this kind of work. But right now, with thunder rumbling in the sky and the electricity and wifi flickering in and out as it wished, she felt like she was spinning her wheels uselessly.

Enough.

Sliding on her sock-clad foot, Suzie returned to the living room to gather the clothes she'd arrived in yesterday. She'd go into the office.

There would be power there, and maybe the change of setting would jostle something useful out of her brain.

⁓

THIRTY MINUTES LATER, she was in her office, fresh coffee in hand, staring at her whiteboard and trying to organize her thoughts. Turning instead to her computer, she brought up the records on Sally Ann to see if she was still in the hospital wing or if she'd been sent home. The medical note said the patient complained of a return of headaches the night before, so would be kept under observation a little longer.

Suzie was stabbed with another jolt of guilt. She'd hardly spared a thought for Sally Ann since she'd been knocked out of commission by the fight at the museum. Had that only been Thursday? It felt like a lifetime ago already. After all, four days ago she stormed out on Patricia. She hadn't even been in Springfield when the attack on the museum came—she'd spent most of the last few days in her car, driving back and forth, trying to drive faster than her anger and confusion.

She scanned the reports. She hadn't read them yet, relying on what she'd picked up from Leonel and Patricia's bickering to ascertain what had happened. It was a juicy one, all right.

Hostage situation, suspected goal of theft of artifacts, but none actually taken. No civilians injured, beyond one man who had taken a minor blow to the head from one of the gunmen.

Strange weapons, including some kind of sound-wave gun that caused serious damage. Patricia destroyed it, and the explosion threw Sally Ann across the room and concussed her. Leonel made the news for saving the pteranodon skeleton, which is probably why the two had been arguing so much—Leonel always came out smelling like a rose, while the press didn't know what to do with Patricia, even when things went right.

Suzie turned back to the report. There was no information about the gunmen. No names, mug shots, arrest records, not even mention of where they were being held.

That was strange.

Then the followup—the discovery that the lab in the lower level had been broken into, the samples and test results on the strange frogs taken and Dr. Reed knocked unconscious.

Suzie gasped, refocusing her eyes on the report.

Daniel Price? Dr. Liu's father? Leaning back in her chair, Suzie groaned. Nothing good could come of his presence here. She dug through the work orders and calendars, resource allocation spreadsheets, and emails. She couldn't find evidence anyone had even been assigned to investigate further, let alone any progress or discoveries.

Something was more than fishy in this whole thing—like any investigation was being suppressed, or at least not being pursued in a way that might yield results. Suzie had been out of town when it happened, but the Director should still have assigned a team. Suzie's stomach sank.

Patricia said she doubted the motivations of their boss, and Suzie had questions herself, but this was worse than some self-aggrandizement or power grabbing. This was corruption, choosing which crimes would and wouldn't be pursued. It stunk of power-mongering, trading of favors, and backroom deals. Suzie didn't like it.

In fact, she wouldn't stand for it.

SALLY ANN AND SUZIE MAKE A PLAN

Sally Ann had been watching light move across the ceiling for the past hour. The psychic attack by the Director the day before, whether or not it was intentional, set her recovery back to that frustrating stage where even rolling over too quickly in bed made her feel like throwing up.

Being stuck in bed alone with her thoughts hadn't been the best medicine, though. Jessica was missing. The gunmen from the museum had disappeared. Darrin was poking into things that might bring trouble his way. And worse than any of that, Sally Ann wasn't sure she could trust her boss. The whole thing would have made her sick if she wasn't already there. She clenched her fists, wishing with all her might she could just punch something.

Gentle fingers rapped at the door. Assuming the duty nurse was checking on her again, Sally Ann groaned. "Do we have to?"

"Do we have to what?" Suzie's voice gave Sally Ann a jolt.

Catching herself before she turned her head too quick, Sally Ann raised a hand into the air and flexed her fingers in a Bruce Lee beckoning motion. "Where have you been? You missed everything!"

As Suzie entered the room and took a seat in the bedside chair, Sally Ann rolled over slowly, propping the pillow under her neck so she could meet Suzie's eye. Worry wrinkled Suzie's brow, so Sally Ann figured she must look as bad as she felt.

"You should see the other guy," she quipped.

Suzie threw up her hands. "I'd like to, but no one knows where he is. What the hell is going on around here? I go out of town for a couple of days and everything falls apart."

Lowering her voice to just above a whisper, Sally Ann asked, "Have they found her yet?"

A quick shake of the head. "No new leads today."

Acid swirled in Sally Ann's stomach. She'd been hoping for better news about her missing team member. "Well, shit."

There was a pause. Sally Ann's eyes were closed, but she could hear Suzie shifting around in the plastic-covered hospital room chair.

Finally, Suzie blurted out, "Why did no one tell me Daniel Price was involved in this?"

Sally Ann's eyes flew open at the accusatory tone, and the room blurred and shifted around her for a moment. She groaned a little and laid a hand against her head as if it were actually spinning and she could hold it in place. "Well, you weren't exactly here to be told."

Sally Ann softened her tone, regretting the misplaced blame. Suzie didn't deserve her ire. In a more conciliatory mode, she explained. "We all rely on you to keep information flowing in the right directions, and with you out of town, the Director…"

At the mention of the man, Suzie's smile dropped off her face, replaced with something tight and agitated. Apparently, Patricia told her girlfriend about their concerns.

"So, let me get this straight." Suzie held up a hand, counting off points on her fingers. "Last spring, we had Daniel Price in custody in Ohio, and we were ordered to leave him there, with intervention by other parties implied."

Sally Ann raised her thumb. "Correct."

"Three days ago, there's an attack at the museum that turns out to be a smokescreen for data theft from the herpetology lab, and Daniel Price was captured on camera at the scene."

"Correct."

"And, since then, both the gunmen and Daniel seem to have disappeared, with nothing in our records to say where they've gone."

"Three for three."

Suzie stood up, walked over to the window and pulled up the blinds. Sally Ann stayed where she was, not wanting to put herself through the disorientation of rolling over again.

"There's more," Sally Ann said.

"Tell me."

"Yesterday, you sent Walter to the office to stall any official action regarding Jessica, right?"

Hesitation crept into her voice, but Suzie murmured acknowledgement.

"So, I got pulled into that situation, which is why I'm back in bed today." Sally Ann described the Director's strange behavior in the meeting with Walter, and the signals she picked up from the paperwork, as well as his lack of concern about the unsolved museum case and his focus on the rehabilitation press conference for Monday. "So Darrin is out there poking around this morning."

"I know. I was there when Patricia took the call."

Sally Ann widened her eyes. No one had said, but she'd gotten the distinct impression Suzie and Patricia were on the outs, that the real reason for Suzie's sudden trip up east had more to do with that than any concern for her mother's health. But maybe that wasn't the case.

Suzie must have picked up on the unasked questions because she waved her hand at Sally Ann, like she was shooing away a pestering insect. "I don't want to talk about it right now. Yes, I went out of town, but I got back yesterday morning. I was at breakfast with Patricia when I got the call from Leonel. I've been trying to help locate Jessica ever since, for all the good it's done any of us."

She stalked back over to the chair and flopped down into it, hard. "Remind me never to go out of town again—it's too complicated trying to figure it all out when I get back." She sat for a moment, bouncing her foot in nervous agitation. Then she leaned forward, looking Sally Ann directly in the face.

"The way I see it, there's one question we need answered before all the others: can we trust the Director?"

Sally Ann rolled over on her back and used the bed controls to raise herself to an incline. "That is the million-dollar question, isn't it?"

"Has anyone asked it?"

Sally Ann opened her mouth then smacked it closed again.

She hadn't asked.

In fact, there were a lot of questions she hadn't asked in the last couple of years, things she'd told herself must be happening for a good reason. But knowing about the Director's powers of mental manipulation, she found she had questions about why she hadn't asked her questions. Had she, too, fallen sway to his persuasion?

"We need Mary," she said.

"Mary? Helen's daughter?"

Sally Ann had to keep reminding herself not to nod. Would Dr. Suggs consider letting her have another dose of her healing formula? She raised her thumb in agreement.

"Why?" Suzie's voice betrayed her confusion, and Sally Ann pondered how compartmentalized some knowledge was within their organization. That couldn't be good. Bad decisions came out of incomplete information, and they all relied on Suzie to organize resources and keep them on track. If there was anyone in the entire organization who needed to know everything, it was her.

"You remember when we were dealing with The Six, right?"

Suzie wrinkled her brow. "Of course. That was the first big case after I joined the Department. The group of psychic thieves that came out of Bethesda. Those experimental surgeries Dr. Harvey was doing."

"Right. Mary did some consulting for us on that case."

"Doing what, exactly?" Suzie crossed her arms over her chest, but her expression was curious.

"Mary's special."

Suzie's eyebrows rose. "Like, Liu-vian special?"

"Dr. Liu doesn't have anything to do with it, but yes. She can feel and resist mental manipulation."

If Suzie's eyebrows rose any higher, she'd be wearing them as a headband. "Even the Director's?"

"She's one of the few he can't influence."

"None of this is in her file." Stridency spiked in Suzie's voice.

Sally Ann coughed a little and winced, angry again at the cause of her current pain. "I wouldn't think Steven would want too many people to know."

"That he uses mental powers to get what he wants or that Mary can resist him?"

"Yes."

Suzie stood. "That's not going to fly."

Sally Ann lifted her head, regretted the movement, and let it fall back onto her pillow, then regretted that too. "What are you going to do?"

"It's time we talked with the Director. I'll set something up with Mary."

Suzie bent and turned off the bedside lamp. "You get some rest. We're going to need you tomorrow."

MONDAY

MARY STEPS UP

Ladies! How can I be of assistance?" The Director swept into the conference room with a theatrical air. Though dressed in a plain gray suit, he gave the impression of wearing an opera cape. Mary squinted at him and waited for him to sit down. The man was putting it on full force this morning, excited about his damned dog and pony show, where her mother would be the dog, or maybe the pony.

In the two executive chairs to her sides, Sally Ann and Suzie sat in silence. They'd agreed Mary would drive this conversation, at least at the outset, and Mary felt a righteous indignation rising within her. This intervention had been a long time coming, and part of her thrilled at being the one to bring this particular hammer down. After everything she'd just been told, he more than deserved it.

The Director tilted his head, puzzled at the cold reception, and seated himself on the opposite side of the table, folding his hands in front of him. "To what do I owe the pleasure?" he asked, his enthusiasm reined in.

He turned a radiant smile on Mary, "Does this have to do with your mother? What a debut! Her first training mission and she and Fuerte save a carload of kids from drowning!"

Mary was proud of her mother for her part in things the day before, but she wouldn't let herself be sidetracked by congratulations. They needed to know what he was up to, and better to get that settled before the big press conference. She nodded once, a tight little dip of the head. "I'm sure that'll make for some good press."

"All press is good press, but good press is even better!"

Suzie nudged her foot under the table. Mary took the hint. "It's time to come clean, Steven."

The Director spread his hands in a classic gesture of surrender. "I've got nothing to hide. What do you want to know?"

His visage flickered and a warm, friendly feeling blossomed in Mary's guts. Mary checked on her companions. Suzie's gaze had gone unfocused and dreamy, and Sally Ann held her hands on the sides of her head, her skin taking on a greenish pallor beneath its golden brown.

Mary smacked the table, startling all of them. "Cut out that Jedi shit! You're going to put Sally Ann back in the hospital."

The Director froze, closed his eyes to concentrate, and the bubble popped—the unnatural warmth dissipated. The chronic buzzing, so constant you stopped noticing it, finally ceased, and Mary's ears blessed the silence.

Sally Ann groaned aloud in relief.

Suzie shook her head, like someone trying to wake up, then looked at each of them in turn. "What just happened?"

Mary held a hand out to each woman. When Suzie called her and asked for her help, she'd explained that with direct physical contact, she'd been able to share her resistance with Leonel when they were fighting the Six, so each of them slipped a hand into hers without question. They sat for a moment, hands joined in a line like a seance, staring across the table at the Director.

His brows came together, and the wave of disapproval rolling off of him made Mary's teeth hurt. "Should someone say grace?" His quip fell flat, no humor in his voice now.

Sally Ann used her free hand to turn over the photograph of Daniel Price, in the herpetology lab and pushed it toward the middle of the table. Cindy Liu's father's latest skin suit stared straight into the camera, a smug expression on his placid face.

The Director's expression tightened yet further. The glad-handing smile frozen in place now and turning into something more akin to a grimace.

Without his glamor, he resembled a ferret more than young Jimmy Stewart—the visage he often wore for Mary. She knew Sally Ann saw someone who could be another Baldwin brother. Suzie said he'd always reminded her of her father.

The Director once confessed to her he encouraged people to see him how they wanted to, so it wasn't that he projected any particular image. Instead, he used his mental persuasion to push people to see him as a strong, trustworthy leader, and their own brains concocted that image.

"What the hell is going on here?" Suzie demanded. "You ordered us to leave Daniel Price on the ground in Ohio last year, even though he kidnapped Patricia's mother. You told us he'd be taken care of through other channels, but here he is turning up like a bad penny—no record of the gunmen or where they're being held, no evidence of any kind of investigation opened into his reappearance."

"This is sketchy, Steven." Sally Ann's voice sounded so sad. Mary turned to look at her. She'd expected Sally Ann to share her outrage and anger, but Sally Ann seemed...tired. Her expression reminded Mary of her father's face, when she'd been caught shoplifting as a teenager. Disappointed, deflated, depressed.

Mary could see where Sally Ann was coming from. She'd joined the Department as a believer, unlike Mary, who came to it unwillingly, as a way to get some help dealing with her suddenly fire-wielding mother. Believing in something and finding out it wasn't all it promised hurt more than learning the details about something you were skeptical about in the first place.

Steven sat across the table, his face so impassive it had to be an act. She found she resented his calmness, when there was so much to be riled up about. Part of her wanted to review her taekwondo lessons, using Steven as the practice dummy.

Mary relied on this man to help her mother. She'd even begun to trust him, a little. Had he been using them all the whole time? She could protect herself from his powers, but there were other ways to manipulate a person. Had she fallen for garden variety flattery and gaslighting? Believing him when he told her she was important to their mission?

Squeezing the hands of the other two women, she leaned forward in her seat, bringing her face nearer the Director's. "They deserve better," she said. "They deserve a leader they can trust, not a man cutting shady deals for his own purposes."

"It's not like that," he protested, and the bubble of his influence poked at the edges of Mary's resistance. She took in a sharp breath and let it out in an angry hiss. The probing feeling backed off. She felt Sally Ann and Suzie looking at her, and she squeezed their hands to signal she was fine.

"What, exactly, is it like?" asked Suzie, tilting her head to one side. Her tone was perfectly flat yet still threatening, and Mary was reminded of Hal from *2001: A Space Odyssey*.

Steven must have heard the underlying challenge too. His face paled. "I can't tell you."

"You expect us to accept that?" Sally Ann didn't bother to try to pretend to be civil or professional. Her anger was on full display. Mary could feel the wobble in the woman's limbs, but Sally Ann kept any sign of weakness off her face.

That little bubble tried to rise again, but Mary caught the Director's eye and shook her head.

He settled back in his seat and focused on Sally Ann. "You used to trust me." The hurt in his voice sounded genuine.

Sally Ann huffed out a noisy puff of air. "That was before I found out you've been using your mental influence, not only on our enemies, but on all of us. Now I'm left wondering if I signed with the Department of my own free will in the first place. How can I tell what's real?"

She smacked her hand on the photograph, leaving a damp palm print across Daniel Price's face. "Trust is a two-way street, and you're not giving me a reason to believe in you."

The Director pushed back his chair, his mouth drawn into a tight line. "Can we talk about this later? The press conference is in a couple of hours, and I've got preparations to make."

Suzie stood, without letting go of Mary's hand. "If you leave this conference room without explaining what is going on here, I'm holding a press conference of my own."

For a second, young Jimmy Stewart flickered in and out of focus. Mary concentrated until he looked like Steven again.

He shrugged. "I can't. Secrecy is part of the deal."

Suzie barked a harsh one syllable laugh. "So, there is a deal."

His mouth twisted in a childish expression of misery. Mary didn't feel sorry for him. He'd brought this on himself.

"And this deal protects Daniel Price." Suzie turned to Sally Ann. "Who do we know who our dear Director would want to cut a deal with, who would also want to protect that scumbag?"

Sally Ann locked eyes with the Director, making sure he was focused on her. "Bertrand Dietrich."

"I know that name..." Mary fought to pull the details from her memory.

"He funded Daniel's research," Suzie filled in, not breaking her eye contact with the Director.

Sally Ann cleared her throat and pushed up to her feet, giving the impression of a cat coiling to spring. "Here's the thing, Steven."

Something in the way Sally Ann said his first name sounded like she had said something else entirely, something more along the lines of an expletive. Mary pushed her chair back and stood arm and arm with Sally Ann and Suzie—like a three-woman line of Red Rover, daring the Director to break through their line.

Sally Ann growled. "When we found Daniel Price in Ohio, you ordered me to leave him there. You told me he'd get his punishment through other channels. I *believed* you."

She narrowed her eyes until they were mere slits in her face. "But, lo and behold, here he is, on my doorstep, stealing research and threatening violence in my city. So, I guess those other channels saw fit to give him back his freedom, if they ever even impinged on it in the first place."

The Director opened his mouth to speak, but Sally Ann held up one hand, and he closed it.

She went on. "Not only is he still walking free, there's also no record of the gunmen from the museum ever having been arrested. We don't have them in custody, and neither, it seems, does anyone else. The weapon that gave me this concussion is not in our lock-up or in any of our labs for analysis. There's no transfer to another agency either. So, this looks a lot like my boss is taking orders from someone and protecting an enemy who directly attacked our people."

"I can explain that—"

"You told us it was a matter of jurisdiction, that Daniel was Bertrand's to handle," Suzie broke in. "And I trusted you."

The Director sputtered. "I never said—"

Sally Ann cut him off. "You can lie and manipulate by what you don't say, too, Steven. Don't pretend you didn't know we would assume Daniel would be picked up and face justice with some other group. You're not that stupid, and neither are we."

Mary's head was on a swivel, trying to watch all of them at the same time.

Steven slumped down into his chair bonelessly, like he wished he could ooze out onto the floor and hide under the table. His voice shrank. "Bertrand said he'd take care of it."

"And you accepted that at face value? You didn't demand details?" Incredulity or maybe rage had Sally Ann's voice rising in pitch.

Suzie burst in. "Daniel Price kidnapped his own daughter, drugged and kidnapped Patricia, tried to take over Leonel's body, and imprisoned Patricia's mother, all in the last two years."

"Not to mention the string of murders that landed Cindy's father in Daniel Price's body in the first place," Sally Ann added.

Mary let out a low whistle. It was an impressive rap sheet, especially for a man who supposedly died some fifty years ago.

A sad laugh escaped the Director's throat. "Well, when you put it like that…"

All three women stared at him, and a cold silence filled the room for a long moment. Mary found her voice first. "What do you intend to do about it?"

Something very much like panic shone in the Director's face, and waves of persuasion hit Mary full force, taking the wind out of her. She stumbled a little, the effort of resistance making her dizzy. Then she felt Suzie and Sally Ann at her sides, each wrapping an arm around her waist, and holding her hands in theirs. The faith and solidarity bolstered her, and she shoved back with her mind.

The Director's head jerked to one side as if he'd been smacked by an invisible hand. He gulped in several large breaths, leaning forward to support himself on the table's edge. Then, he folded himself into the chair. "What would you have me do? These are dangerous people. I can't back out now."

The three women sat down again.

Suzie let go of Mary's hand and reached into her bag. She tossed an old-fashioned steno pad on the table and uncapped a pen, holding it poised over the paper, like this was an ordinary brainstorming session, the kind they might have at the beginning of any mission. "What exactly are the terms of this deal you've made?"

JESSICA ON THE OUTSIDE
LOOKING IN

Jessica lay on the roof of the Springfield Art Museum, staring at City Hall across the street, wondering what the hell she was doing there. The smart thing to do would be to leave town and keep going, putting some distance between herself and the UCU before they moved against her. But here she was, a few yards away from some of the only people in the world that could stop her, waiting for a press conference to begin.

Walter must've turned her in by now.

The thought made her stomach churn. A year ago, she'd been so full of hope for a new life and a new love, and here she was now, floundering.

Sliding her necklace over her head, Jessica held the emeralds in the palm of her hand, turning her fingers until the gems caught the sunlight and glittered. They were beautiful, and even better than that, they were *powerful*. The energy that thrummed through her every time she held them was like nothing else she'd ever had in her life, and she wouldn't let that go.

Not even for Walter.

Still, she found herself scanning the crowd, hoping for a glimpse of him or her mother. Seeing the boys on a school day would be a bonus. She'd been shoving down thoughts of her children since she took flight after Walter's attempt to snatch her emeralds. Max and Frankie were two more things she'd have to figure out, alongside what to do about her marriage, her career, and her life.

She'd considered so many options in the past two days—everything from walking back in and pretending nothing was wrong to flying west until she fell out of the sky from exhaustion and starting a whole new life wherever she landed. But she'd been pulled back here—back to Springfield, back to the UCU, back to her family.

Back to her emeralds.

She'd left a stash with Zeph at the tattoo shop, to have her jewelry made, and there were more shards and samples in the UCU in the laboratories. The thought of leaving them behind made it hard to breathe.

She'd take them all back, and then she'd disappear. Once she'd settled somewhere, she'd find a way to get her boys back, she promised herself. She couldn't take them with her, after all. They couldn't fly and she couldn't stay here on the ground.

Lying back, she stared into the sky, blessedly clear and cloudless overhead, which was a relief after she'd spent much of the last couple of days cold and damp. In fact, it was so clear the tile was growing uncomfortably warm beneath her, and she worried she might get a sunburn. That was autumn in the South for you, unable to make up its mind.

The press conference was scheduled for 11:00 a.m. and the clock in the City Hall tower read 10:45, so Jessica counseled herself to stay put. It would be worth a little discomfort and even a sunburn to find out what was going on with the UCU, and this public event was an opportunity to see where she stood. What had Walter told them? What would the UCU tell the public, her fans?

Besides, if she moved now, she'd attract unwanted attention. People would be watching the sky, expecting Flygirl to arrive in style, and they'd spot the suspicious-looking woman in a ball cap and hoodie for certain.

Jessica held the set of pocket binoculars she'd taken from Nathan's camping gear to her eyes and scanned the scene. A dais was placed at the top of the stairs, draped with red velvet and the city seal and with the state and national flags set behind, fancier than the setup the mayor generally used. Fifteen minutes ahead of showtime, a few reporters already sat in chairs at the bottom of the stairs talking amongst themselves, and a small crowd gathered behind the rope on the sidewalk and spilled out into the road, which was blocked off for the event.

From her perch on the roof, Jessica thought the crowd sounded like bees. Focusing her binoculars on the people below, she spotted a few familiar faces among the spectators, including Leonel's husband, David, with two of their granddaughters, the twins, dressed in clashing outfits, one in a pink frothy dress with a flower in her hair and the other in ripped jeans and a baggy sweatshirt. Behind them stood a couple of agents Jessica recognized, even though they were dressed in civilian clothing.

So, Leonel would be here as Fuerte.

A twinge twisted her gut at the thought of Leonel. He'd been a friend to her through some of the roughest patches in her life. He'd kept her sane through her divorce, kept vigil by her bedside when she'd been burned in the campus fight, cheered her on as she learned to control her erratic flight. He'd been a listening ear, a shoulder to cry on, and her most ardent cheerleader, outside of her mother. Heck, he'd been her "hombre de honor" on her wedding day.

And how had she returned that kindness?

When Leonel was shot, she had run away, leapt into the sky and flown toward the horizon. When he'd gone through a rough patch with his husband, she'd been too busy with her own wedding plans to offer real support. When he lost control of his strength, she'd resented his cure because it meant he took some of her emeralds. And now, she had disappeared again. Knowing Leonel, he was worried sick.

She was a terrible friend.

A TAP at the microphone drew her attention. Suzie, dressed in a pale blue dress, laid a folder on the dais and waved at the crowd before disappearing back into the building. The show must be about to start.

Sure enough, a few seconds later, a whoop ran through the crowd as Leonel burst out the front doors of City Hall and took a place to one side of the podium. He smiled and waved at the crowd, hamming it up a little with muscle-man poses. Patricia followed quickly behind, to more measured cheering and some mutterings that were hard to interpret, but she waved to the crowd as she moved into place on the other side of the podium.

An ache spread in Jessica's chest, and she found she was teary. She should be up there with them, waving at the crowd and helping people in need, and she had ruined that forever. Her friends would be sent to apprehend her now. She'd have to fight them, to take back what was hers.

Through her tears, Jessica missed the entrance of the mayor, a tall, slender woman with silver gray hair perfectly coiffed in an old-fashioned roll, sleek and serene as her designer suit. She walked to the podium and greeted the gathered crowd. "Thank you for coming out this afternoon. Looks like we'll get a break from the rains after all!"

She waited for a beat until the murmuring settled, then continued. "Springfield has been fortunate in our partnership with the heroes of the Unusual Cases Unit, which has been instrumental in protecting the people of Springfield from people with strange abilities. I know I feel safer knowing they're here."

Someone shouted something Jessica couldn't make out, but the mayor apparently heard the heckler, because she frowned out at the crowd, shielding her eyes with one hand. She opened her mouth to speak but must have decided it was better to ignore the comment than spoil the moment with argument. She cleared her throat.

"We've got some big news for the community today. Without further ado, let me bring to the dais our own Dr. Kent Lawson, the Director of the Unusual Cases Unit."

A slender man in a well-cut suit stepped briskly through the door and walked with purpose to the microphone. Jessica noticed again how much the Director resembled her father when he'd been young and healthy, with the square jaw and forthright gaze she remembered from her childhood. A kind of pride and desire to please blossomed in her chest, and she wondered if he was disappointed in her for not being there today for this big announcement.

A banner unfurled behind them, covering the space from the clock tower to the top of the staircase with the logo for the UCU at the top and "Champions of Springfield" in calligraphy at the bottom. The middle was blank.

The Director leaned into one elbow, all casual ease at the microphone. "Friends, our heroes have worked hard to keep Springfield safe for her citizens."

A series of still images projected on the banner. Sort of a best-of-UCU montage of the stories that ended well or made the news in a positive light. Rapid-fire juxtapositions between scenes of destruction, tearful and grateful citizens, and anguished faces of people taken into custody—the earthquake woman from the hospital, the lightning woman from the park, the telekinetic boy, Agatha and the other members of the psychic gang they'd called "The Six."

Jessica recognized several shots of herself, including some she'd never seen, as well as staged publicity stills. Her best work would never make the news, of course, as stealth was the key element. Going where no one else could go and getting back out unseen.

But this answered one question—they weren't telling the public anything about her yet.

The Director paused, letting the crowd take in the stream of images. "Rescuing people and fighting threats to our security and livelihoods is only part of our work. Behind the scenes, we've been working to rehabilitate some of these formerly troubled citizens of Springfield into productive members of society."

Jessica knew about this plan, of course. Walter told her. The Director planned to build a reputation for care and support of Springfield's more unusual citizens, a rehabilitation center for wayward mutants.

The Director stretched over the podium toward his audience, compassion softening the lines of his face. Jessica felt an urge to declare her loyalty as she listened.

"So many of these citizens were not truly to blame for the havoc they wrought on our fair city. They were victims as much as perpetrators, unable to control the sudden change in their bodies. But we've been able to help them."

The images changed, showing a still Jessica hadn't seen before. Leonel, outfitted as Fuerte, sat next to the river with a group of kids, all of them soaking wet. Behind them lay an upended car, dented and missing part of the roof. All of them were looking at a woman kneeling nearby, dressed in a bright yellow tunic and flame-red pants, holding out her hand, palm upraised. A small fire rose from her flesh.

Helen Braeburn.

Jessica fell back, a swirl of conflicting emotions running through her. She'd known they were planning to introduce Helen as the poster child of this new venture, but she hadn't been prepared for it to happen so soon. She'd honestly expected Mary would be able to talk the Director out of it. But Helen had already been part of a rescue mission.

When did that happen? Jessica had only been out of the loop a couple of days, but she'd missed a lot.

A squeak emitted from the speakers, followed by a murmur of a woman's husky voice. Jessica pulled her gaze away from the images on the screen to center her binoculars on the dais again.

A short, stocky woman with strawberry blond hair joined the Director at the podium. He adjusted the microphone down to her height, both of them laughing chummily at the number of inches difference between her stature and his. Everything adjusted, the woman gripped the podium and looked out at the crowd, which went silent in anticipation.

"You might know me as Flamethrower," she said. "That's what I was calling myself when I laid siege to the college campus almost five years ago."

Jessica gripped her Franken-arm, which still bore scars from the multiple skin grafts she'd undergone, recovering from that so-called siege. Her body rose involuntarily a few inches into the air, and she forced herself back down into contact with the roof. Anger washed over until it roared in her ears like rush-hour traffic. She missed some of the next bit, focusing on remembering to breathe and rubbing the chunk of emerald around her neck to soothe herself.

Helen kept talking, her voice a little teary. "I will always be grateful to the UCU and the city of Springfield for helping me find myself again. I will do my best to prove myself worthy of the support I've been given. Second chances are hard to come by, and I owe all of you for mine. Thank you!"

Acid boiled in Jessica's guts at the thought of the woman who had once gleefully tried to kill her serving alongside her in service of the city. Part of her knew she was being unfair—she believed in second chances and rehabilitation, didn't she?

But she'd taken a great deal of comfort in knowing Helen was locked away, but it appeared the key had been in the lock all along. What was next? Setting Dr. Liu loose on the city again? What did the law even mean? Where was the justice?

The Director led a round of applause for the inspirational story of recovery and rehabilitation. "Thank you, Blaze!"

Helen moved to join Leonel, who greeted her with a one-armed shoulder squeeze, a charming gesture that had every camera in the press section clicking away. Jessica's chest tightened, and she found she was clenching her jaw.

Had Leonel come to peace with this so easily?

A few months ago, over a late-night ice cream and sad movie date, he'd admitted he was still haunted by the thought he might have killed Helen during that fight. Jessica told him he'd done the right thing, stopping her before she could hurt more people. But maybe he believed he needed to make amends. The man had the softest heart.

The Director smiled benignly at the crowd, pulling the microphone back up to his comfortable height before continuing. "Blaze is one of our success stories. Of course, they won't all be as public as hers. Some of the cases we've taken on never made it into the press, nor the people we have been able to help return to their regular lives, with the resources they need to control and make positive use of their unusual abilities. We look forward to continuing our partnerships with law enforcement and expanding our cooperation with medical and mental health services in Springfield."

The mayor returned to the microphone. "Thank you, Director. I'm excited for this new development in our city's good fortune. We'll now have a few minutes for questions from the press."

As the press jostled, as antsy as kindergarten students to be called on, Jessica turned her binoculars back on the crowd. No Walter. No mom. No kids. Even though they'd had no reason to expect her to be here, she was hurt they hadn't shown up. Maybe it was for the best. She knew what she had to do.

SALLY ANN SETS THE TRAP

In a small meeting room in the city building, Sally Ann listened to the press conference on her phone. Thanks to another round of Dr. Sugg's healing formula, she was feeling a lot better, but too much bright light, especially blue phone or computer light, still made her nauseated, so she'd settled for sitting in a darkened room listening to the audio, rather than live observation under the afternoon sun or watching the video.

On the other side of the table, Suzie scrolled through messages on her phone, occasionally making a grunt or sigh. The Director stuck to the script, which made Sally Ann feel a little better about their decision to let him go on with this press conference as scheduled. When the applause died down and the press questions began, Sally Ann picked up her phone, turning it so she could see the video. The light hurt, so she turned it down, but she didn't stop watching. She liked watching Darrin work, and she knew he'd be out there in the press corps.

She was rewarded in short order when the Director called on him. "Mr. Berger?"

"Darrin Berger, *Springfield City News*. I noticed Flygirl isn't present today. Can you tell us where she is?"

Sally Ann held her breath. She hadn't told Darrin a thing about Jessica having gone missing, but the man could smell a secret like a bloodhound could track an escaped convict. He'd landed on exactly the question the Director hoped no one would ask.

"She's off duty today, resting up." The Director deflected.

Before he could move on to another question, Darrin pressed. "We haven't seen much of Flygirl in the skies of Springfield lately—"

The Director cut him off. "I'm sure you understand I can't share full details about the whereabouts and doings of our agents, Mr. Berger. It's a matter—"

A gasp went up from the crowd, and Suzie scrambled around the table to check Sally Ann's phone over her shoulder. The camera panned across clouds for a few seconds, a dizzying change of perspective that had Sally Ann groaning and fighting nausea.

Then the camera operator found what they were looking for and zoomed in on a woman, hanging in space. She wore sweatpants, a ball cap, and sunglasses rather than her usual blue spandex costume and cowl, but there was no doubt it was Jessica.

She was disguised enough under the hat and sunglasses to protect her identity, but the crowd knew her all the same. After all, there was only the one flying hero in the city of Springfield, even if she wasn't wearing her flashy unitard. She raised an arm in salute, then fell backward and flew out of view, the crowd cheering below her and shouting "Flygirl!" amid whoops and hollers.

When the camera view returned to the dais, the Director spread his hands. "I guess that answers your question." No one would have known Jessica's appearance surprised him.

"I knew we should have had people watching the perimeter." Sally Ann banged a fist against the table. Damn her concussion. Between that and the Director's manipulations, she felt like her brain was running at fifty percent. Her instincts were off, and she'd missed an opportunity to bring Flygirl back into the fold because of it. The best they could do was use traffic and security cameras around town to track where she went from here.

"It's okay." Suzie glanced up from the screen long enough to lock eyes with Sally Ann. Suzie's pale blue eyes were steady and sure and serene. "This is good. Now we know she's all right. Better yet, we know for sure she's back in the city, and we can be ready for her at the tattoo shop tomorrow. This is the break we needed."

She waved her phone as she walked to the door. "I've got to call Walter."

Sally Ann felt like shit again. She hadn't even considered how Walter must be feeling, not knowing if his wife is alive or dead. "Get your head out of your ass," she hissed at herself. "The team needs you."

She turned her attention back to the video and watched the Director deflect another round of criticism about the damage done to the city in defending it. In the background, Patricia's face was so carefully still that she might have been a statue of Lizard Woman instead of the real thing.

Leonel broke a few walls himself, and Jessica had broken a lot of glass in the past few years, but somehow it was always Patricia the press focused on when they wanted to complain about the UCU. You had to know her well to see it, but Sally Ann knew it stung.

When the camera swung back to the press corps, Sally Ann searched for Darrin but didn't find him. Knowing him, he'd tried to chase down Jessica. Hell, he might even have found her. Maybe the UCU should hire him as a bloodhound.

Whatever you didn't want him to know, the man would be right there, microphone in hand and an uncomfortable question at the ready. She didn't really wish he wasn't good at his job, but it was still a strange position to be in—on the other side of the table, trying to control the story while her own boyfriend tried to pull at any edges and find the secrets beneath.

"Come on, Steven," Sally Ann hissed, rubbing at her temples. "Plant the seed." The press conference was about to come to an end, and he hadn't yet laid the trap for Daniel Price and Bertrand Dietrich.

As if he'd heard her prompting, he smiled into the camera for the next bit. "I'm proud to announce we're opening a new research facility next week, one focused on studying the underlying causes of these strange mutations in Springfield's citizens and developing treatments."

"That's our boy." Sally Ann grinned.

The mayor stepped forward, sharing the podium with the Director. "We are pleased to partner with the UCU while repurposing some of the vacant industrial space on the eastern side of Springfield, making it useful again and helping our citizens at the same time. Recycling in the truest sense!"

Sally Ann was waving her hands over her head in celebration, twinge in her head be damned, when Suzie came back in.

The pensive expression on Suzie's face lightened. "I take it our fearless leader played his part."

Sally Ann did a fist pump in the air. "So smooth. The mayor played along so well it was like you'd written her lines."

Suzie ducked her head.

"Wait, did you write her lines?"

"Not exactly." Suzie shrugged, raised her voice into something higher and more breathy, and waved her hands while opening her eyes widely. "I might have praised her genius in making such an ecologically conscious choice, gushing about how much less wasteful it is to reuse old facilities than to clear land to make new ones."

Sally Ann shook her head, careful to do so slowly. "How does Patricia keep up with you?"

Suzie dropped into a sort of curtsey, then spun around and picked her bag from the chair, gesturing for Sally Ann to follow her. "She does the best she can."

"Don't we all?"

HELEN WANTS TO HELP

Helen stood in the hallway of the City Building, peeking between the blinds at the crowd as it dispersed. Her heart still beat a million miles a second, but she felt lighter than she'd felt in quite some time. That went better than she'd expected. No one threw over-ripe fruit at her or even yelled insults, and honestly, she might not have blamed them if they had.

Smiles, handshakes, and applause. More than she'd dared hope for.

Someone behind her cleared their throat and Helen spun around, expecting to find her daughter Mary, ready to congratulate her on how well she'd done at the press conference. After all, Mary stayed up late into the night practicing with her, helping her hit all the right notes for the crowd to receive her well, despite her history.

But it wasn't Mary.

Instead, she found herself face to face, or rather face to chest, with Fuerte.

"Congratulations, Blaze!" His voice brimmed with supportive enthusiasm, enthusiasm he clearly felt and wasn't putting on for her benefit. He was that kind of person. "You were on fire!" He waggled his fingers in the air in some awkward gesture meant to suggest flames.

Helen laughed. "Maybe not this time."

Confusion clouded Fuerte's face, then he shook his head. "Sorry. I didn't even think about that. I could have picked a better metaphor."

"It's okay. I'm teasing. And thank you!" It was nice to hear someone else tell her it had gone well.

Helen peered past Fuerte down the hall. "Have you seen Mary? I kind of thought she'd be here."

Fuerte dropped his gaze to his boots and tried to shove his hands into the front pockets, even though his uniform pants didn't have any. Helen was already beginning to realize Fuerte did these things when he was uncomfortable or nervous. She guessed life as a super-strong superhero didn't require much subterfuge, which was good since Fuerte was terrible at keeping any kind of poker face. He knew something he wasn't going to tell her.

"She's nearby but can't come talk to you right now."

That was oddly evasive, considering this was her daughter they were talking about, but Helen pushed any worry away. After all, she'd see Mary soon enough herself and could ask what's going on and he hadn't sounded worried.

"Well." Her voice trailed off. Changing tactics, she punched Fuerte lightly on the shoulder. "Speaking of fans, the crowd loves you, don't they?"

"You are kind to say so, but I think it's the uniform."

Helen took a step back so she could examine Fuerte better. He wore the usual yellow half-sun mask, his long, lightly curling, dark brown hair flowing around it and down to his broad shoulders. Beneath the mask, his mouth and chin were bare, as was the upper part of his chest, golden-brown skin visible where the close-fitting red jacket had been left partially unzipped—a choice she knew the wardrobe woman made at the last minute when she checked them all over before sending them through the door. The jacket tapered to his tight waist, and he wore looser but still attractively form-fitting black pants tucked into tall boots.

"It is a good uniform," she said, "but it's all about how you fill it out, Fuerte."

Fuerte ran a hand over his hair, a gesture that called attention to the impressive size of his biceps. "It's better than the pirate gigolo outfit they tried to make me wear at first. This is the worst part of this whole thing for me—the PR team trying to make me into some kind of sex symbol."

Helen looked down at her own figure, artfully covered in a tunic, loose in the right places to disguise her belly a bit, but wasn't fooling anyone, and shook her head. "I'd take it while you can get it. Time is not always kind in that regard."

Fuerte moved back to the window, though the angle of his head suggested he was keeping his eye on the sky rather than the dispersing crowd. He didn't react to what she'd said and was obviously both agitated and distracted.

Helen studied him. He'd been keeping his eyes on the skies a lot on Sunday, too, when they'd been at the park and even during the chaos at the bridge. Now that Flygirl had flown by during the press conference, she was sure she knew what he was watching for.

"Why wasn't she on the dais today?" Helen asked, deciding to set a lighted match to the kindling

Fuerte startled, then rolled his shoulders down. "Who?"

Was there something between the two of them? She thought she'd understood Fuerte was married, but she supposed the one didn't rule out the other.

"Flygirl," she said, watching him carefully.

Fuerte's mouth popped open like he was going to protest or argue, but he snapped it shut again without saying anything.

Helen went on like she hadn't noticed. "I know she's usually a big hit at these events. I used to watch all the television appearances with my keeper, while I was in custody."

She remained in custody, but the restrictions were looser, and she slept in something more like a room than a cell now, even if she couldn't leave the facility whenever she wanted, so she wouldn't bring that up right now. Complaining about her lot in life to the man who stopped her from burning innocent people a few years ago didn't seem like the right play.

She let a little question into her voice, a curious uplift that stopped short of asking directly. "Strange she wasn't part of the shindig today. Just a fly-by and a wave?"

Fuerte's shoulders sagged, and he pulled back his fingers, letting the blinds flap closed again. Hesitancy made his soft voice into something even more tender. "She's been dealing with…some personal things."

The man was a terrible liar. He wasn't even lying, exactly, just not telling all he knew. Something strange was going on with Flygirl. What kind of media darling skipped out on a chance to shine in front of a crowd? Helen had seen her type before and Flygirl wasn't one to shy away when there were cameras and adoring fans around.

Maybe it really was "something personal" but Helen was sure there was more to it than that. Something a little shady maybe. That would explain Fuerte's reticence. Curiosity lit up her brain, but she knew one mission together didn't rate her that kind of trust, so she bit back her questions.

"I hope everything's okay," she said, and found she meant it. She didn't know Flygirl, and what she'd seen didn't fill her with warm fuzzies, but she was getting to know Fuerte and anything that made that kind and gentle man fret like this couldn't be good. If only for his sake, she hoped Flygirl got it all figured out soon.

"Me too."

DON'T SEND A GIRL TO DO A
LIZARD'S JOB

When Patricia came in from the press conference, Suzie was standing in the hall, waiting for her. "We've got to talk." She handed Patricia a water bottle, voice all business.

A chill ran down Patricia's spine—that was never a good sentence to hear from your lover, even when it was true. Especially if it was true. They had plenty to talk about—they'd yet to talk about either Suzie's sudden flight or her return—but Patricia had been relieved to put off any of that talk. She still didn't understand what went wrong.

True, she hadn't been listening carefully, but no matter how many times she ran over the conversation in the Italian restaurant in her mind, she couldn't find what line she had crossed to elicit such a dramatic reaction from Suzie.

Suzie was usually so reasonable, and Patricia had been floored. Part of her didn't want to ask, because she might get the "You should already know" line, and she'd never taken that well. People should just say what they mean instead of assuming it's obvious, especially if the person they're making assumptions about is her.

It probably meant she was a shitty human being, but Patricia had been grateful Jessica provided a distraction, even if it came in the form of falling apart and possibly ruining her life and Walter's.

If they were busy dealing with Jessica's crisis, she could put off dealing with her own, if that's what this was. Emergencies brought out the best in

Suzie—she shone when she had a problem to solve. Sure enough, as soon as Leonel called, Suzie jumped to the rescue, coming up with plans and putting them into action.

Spending hours searching the city for someone who might or might not want to be found was preferable to a long heart-to-heart about all the ways she'd failed the woman she loved.

This was different from every other relationship in her sixty-odd years...and she'd had some very odd years. Like it or not, her heart was well and truly engaged this time, and when—*if*—it ended, she already knew she wouldn't take it well. So, yeah, she'd been happy to put off the entire conversation as long as possible.

But the check always comes due, and her extension had just been revoked. Telling herself to grow a pair, she pushed her shoulders back, downed the proffered bottle of water, and met Suzie's forthright gaze, doing her best to hide any worry that might reveal itself there. "All right. Let's talk."

She followed Suzie down the hall, up some stairs, and down another hall, and up some more stairs, hardly paying attention to where she was going, until Suzie pushed open a door and the two of them emerged on the roof of the city building, a gust of wind whipping Suzie's skirt tight against her thighs.

Even more surprising than Suzie's selection of location was the discovery they weren't the only people up there. Sally Ann shoved off the wall where she'd been leaning when the door opened, and Mary Braeburn picked herself up from where she'd been sitting on the ground.

Patricia's spikes expanded and she forced them to retract, pulling in her armored scales until she appeared once more like the red-haired former businesswoman most people knew her as. Her gaze bounced between the three women, all their faces grim and serious. "What's going on here?"

For a long moment, all three of the other women remained silent, shooting looks at one another Patricia couldn't decipher. Finally, Sally Ann pushed her sunglasses down and peered up at Patricia over the top of them. "It's the Director."

Another gust of wind smacked into them, and Patricia lifted her chin, appreciating the cooling effect. It was hard to tell if the heat was internal or external, but the wind was almost as bracing as the words. "Tell me," she said.

~

A FEW MINUTES LATER, the other women fell silent, and Patricia knelt on the rooftop, her head resting in her hands and her mind spinning. It all made sense, but that didn't mean she liked it. Some of it she'd known or at least suspected.

There'd been something fishy about the whole situation in Ohio, but she'd been too worried about getting her mother out of there and dealing with her transformation control to question it at the time. She never gone back to check and see what happened to Daniel Price, trusting that the man would be handled through other channels, and she could go back to deflecting bullets and smashing things with the UCU.

That lack of curiosity wasn't like her. Just like it hadn't been like her to volunteer to talk to Cindy on Friday. She'd thought she was getting soft, maybe, or tired. But now she wondered how many of her decisions of the past few years were truly her own and how many had come about from mental manipulation.

It didn't surprise her to learn the Director had cut a deal to expand the reach of the UCU. That's what people in power did, and the best you could hope for was limiting the corruption and the end trajectory leading to some greater good. She'd always thought she was a realist about how politics worked, that she could see the line between outright self-service and compromise to serve a greater good. But this didn't feel like business as usual.

This felt like betrayal.

Damn it—she'd let herself *believe* in the Director and the mission of the UCU. She'd thought she was serving on the side of right, helping keep people safe from the things ordinary law enforcement couldn't handle. Had that all been a mistake? Had she been a tool in a larger game the whole time?

Anger coiled through her, to the point she was having trouble keeping her scales under wraps, and she felt Suzie pull her hand back from her shoulder as spikes began to protrude.

The list of the Director's sins grew in her mind. Daniel Price, not only left unpunished for what he'd already done, but given resources that put her and the other agents at risk again and again. The man shot Leonel! Drugged Patricia! Kidnapped her mother! And they'd let him go?

And now they told her the gunmen who'd held Springfield's citizens hostage at the museum had been turned over to Bertrand Dietrich and erased from UCU records as if they'd never existed. Like they'd never fought at all.

"I'll tear his arms off." Patricia rolled to her feet and stomped toward the stairs.

"Wait!" Suzie called after her.

Patricia wouldn't have stopped for many people, but Suzie was a special case. She turned around to face her girlfriend, struggling to pull her scales in and look at her with human eyes.

"It's not going to be enough to stop the Director. We have to get our agency out from under the influence of Bertrand."

Patricia growled, impatience roiling in her guts.

"We have a plan." Suzie's eyes sparkled, almost singing the next bit. "You're going to like it. You'll get to smash things."

A slow grin spread over Patricia's face. "You know me well."

TUESDAY

INTERVENTION TIME FOR JESSICA

Jessica circled the building three times, once from the clouds, once from the trees, and finally, once from the ground. No signs of trouble were in evidence. The street was quiet this early in the day, with only a couple walking a dog and a woman sitting alone outside a coffee shop in view. Jessica herself was probably the most suspicious thing in sight.

But Jessica's senses were still on high alert, something akin to panic bubbling within her. She told herself it was paranoia, ignoring the mocking voice in her head that finished the quote, "Just because you're paranoid, doesn't mean they aren't coming to get you."

No one was coming to get her. Why would they? She hadn't told anyone about the appointment. Not even Walter.

The one person who knew anything at all was Mary, who suggested Zeph in the first place, and Mary didn't know when her appointment was or even that she made one.

Jessica sucked in a deep breath and blew it out slowly, then did it three more times, trying to still her jangled nerves.

She'd feel better once the procedure was done. Once the emeralds were embedded in her skin, a part of her forever, she could stop worrying. She'd figure out how to get back to her old life once this was over.

She took one final deep breath, laid a hand on the door, and pushed it open. It smacked the wall, jiggling the displays. A nervous giggle escaped her throat. "Sorry. I guess I don't know my own strength."

She looked around, expecting to see Callah, the tattoo artist she'd consulted with a few days earlier, or Zeph, the shop owner and artist, but she didn't see anyone at all.

That was odd.

Maybe they were in the back? She wasn't early. She'd made herself wait until her appointment time, not wanting to come off as too eager.

"Hello? Callah? Zeph? It's Jessica." Her call echoed in the quiet and the hairs on the back of her neck rose, along with her body which lifted a couple of inches off the floor with a familiar tickling feeling in her guts.

"Be right there!" A bright voice called out.

Jessica relaxed, her heels coming back in contact with the floor. Probably, Callah was in the bathroom or something and Zeph had not seemed like a morning person, so he might be nursing a cup of coffee still. *Calm down*, she counseled herself again. *You're acting crazy.*

The door at the other end of the waiting room bumped open and the silhouette of a large man appeared, his details hard to see since the morning light shining through the windows had him backlit. "Zeph?"

The man stepped forward but didn't say anything. Three slow steps and he was standing in the light. It was Leonel, looking supremely uncomfortable. He shoved his hands into the front pockets of his jeans and scuffed one boot against the floor. When he gazed back at her, his eyes were full of tears.

"Leonel?" Jessica's voice cracked. She cleared her throat and fought to keep any tremor out of her voice. "What are you doing here?" She backed up a step, the foot behind already moving up onto the toe for quick push-off if needed.

He held out his hands. "We came to help you."

"We?" Jessica whipped her head around, realizing there were more figures in the other doorways, blocking her path. In a second, she was on the ceiling. She didn't even remember deciding to flee, but there she was, poised against the ceiling tiles.

"Let us help you, Jessica." Leonel kept walking toward her, his gait and voice steady and calm.

Jessica scuttled backward like a crab, scooting toward the door. "I don't need any help."

"You do. Look at what you're doing!"

"I was getting a tattoo."

Leonel opened his hand, revealing the emeralds he'd kept hidden in his palm. "We both know it was more than that, Jessica."

"Those are mine!" She screamed and dove for Leonel, not even sure what she intended to do. She rammed into him at full speed, knocking him to the floor, but as he fell, he wrapped his arms around her, pulling her against his chest and holding her there.

She struggled, but his arms were like steel bands, affixing her. He was saying something, but she couldn't hear it over the roaring in her ears. Leonel had been her friend through so much, but in the end, he was siding with the people who wanted to separate her from the emeralds.

"Why are you doing this to me?" she cried out.

"I'm trying to help you. Can't you see that?"

All Jessica could see was red. Unable to break Leonel's grasp, her arms pinned to her sides, Jessica felt hot tears of rage pool in her eyes. The tears might as well have been gasoline for the way they fueled her anger. Luckily for Leonel, she didn't have Helen's fire powers, or he'd have been a pile of ash on the carpet.

All she needed was a little leverage.

If Leonel would loosen his grip even a couple of inches, she could slip out and fly away, but each time she tried to wriggle away, he pulled her in.

Straining, she stretched out a hand, fumbling for the knife strapped to her thigh, but Leonel kept her pinned too tightly. The futility of the struggle both exhausted and enraged her.

"Please!" She cried out. "Let me go!"

"I can't do that," he said, but in drawing in the breath to speak, he shifted just enough.

Jessica propelled herself up his torso, colliding with his chin with all the force she could muster.

It worked! His grip loosened for a second and she slipped out, dropping to the floor beside him. Behind her, she heard footsteps but kept her focus on Leonel. He spat blood on the floor before he got back to his feet.

Three blue jump-suited agents leapt to his side. He waved them off, keeping his eyes locked on Jessica. "It's nothing. I bit my tongue." Leonel spread his hands placatingly, but strengthened his stance, preparing for another tussle. He met Jessica's gaze and spoke softly. "It's all right."

On the floor between his boots, the emeralds sparkled in a shaft of sunlight. The roaring sensation in Jessica's ears grew louder, and she pulled the knife from its leather holster, spinning once in place to make sure everyone in the room could see. The two agents nearest her stepped back.

It wasn't the same quality as the weapons the UCU provided, but it was a nasty-looking thing, and it would do the job if she used it on one of them. The room crackled with watchful energy, but no one moved.

"I'm going to need you to give me those emeralds back, Leonel." Jessica spoke as evenly as he had, willing him to cooperate and not make her hurt him. She'd taken the same de-escalation trainings, after all. She recognized "the voice" they'd all practiced together, calm, steady, slow, projecting empathy and acceptance.

Leonel knelt and scooped the scattered gems back into his palm. "These are the problem, Jessica. You've had too much exposure and they've—"

Jessica never found out what he was going to say.

Before he could get back to his feet, she flew over and behind him and positioned the smooth edge of her ridiculous hunting knife mere centimeters from the skin of his throat. Her elbow forced his chin to the side and against her hip, making sure the most vulnerable part was accessible.

She tapped his shoulder with the other hand. "Slowly."

He didn't move and she pressed the knife in gently, drawing a thin bead of blood on her friend's exposed neck.

Leonel twisted to drop his fistful of emeralds into the palm of her hand. The movement pushed him even closer and the familiar smell of his aftershave tickled her nose. A wave of doubt wobbled within her. It wasn't too late. She could drop the knife, let them take her back to the UCU.

She closed her fingers around the emeralds, and a surge of something wonderful and terrible thrummed up her arm. She wanted both to laugh and to cry. Her heart sailed with exultation and triumph while something else in her brain screamed warnings.

"On the floor." She moved her knife arm, releasing her grip on his head, and shoved his lower back with one upraised foot.

As he slid forward into all fours, Leonel slipped a foot between hers, but Jessica anticipated him, and her feet were no longer on the ground. His foot slid sideways in empty space, the intended leg sweep merely toppling him onto his side.

Jessica rolled through the air in a back somersault and ended up pressed against the ceiling again, braced for a push off in whatever direction would serve her best. A quick scan of the room found five agents, four of them between her and the door, and one still standing in the other doorway, the one that led back into the office and consultation rooms.

Spinning as she flew, Jessica hurled toward the lone man, focused on his left shoulder. When she clipped him, she was moving at full speed and the man rotated to the side and clattered into the wall, his head clunking the concrete block. Something fell out of his hand and skittered across the floor.

Momentum beats size, Jessica murmured to herself, one of the mantras of her training with Sally Ann.

Darting through the doorway and around the corner, Jessica searched for another way out. The place must have another door, a window she could slip out, something.

The skylight! Zeph's office had a lovely skylight above his desk.

Booted footsteps and shouts echoed in the hall behind her, and she jackknifed her body to take the corner fast. Just as she rounded the corner, something hit the back of her thigh, but she didn't slow down.

Two more seconds and she was in Zeph's office, hovering to undo the latch on the skylight. Her vision clouded, but she fought off the sudden drowsy feeling and made her way through the now-open hatch, scratching her arm on the frame. Her flight was irregular, and she knew she was drugged. A tranquilizing dart must have clipped her thigh a few moments before.

Below her, voices were shouting and something else brushed her calf. Her vision blurring and doubling, Jessica could see two of the building across the street. The one on the right looked more solid so she veered toward it, laughing out loud when her feet skittered on broken rooftop tiles. She'd picked right!

She ran across the roof and plummeted down the other side, landing in an alley. A quick glance around revealed no one, but she knew she didn't have much time before whatever she'd been hit with would knock her out. She needed a hiding place and fast!

The empty alley lacked helpful objects she might hide behind. Where was an abandoned car or a giant pile of garbage bags when you needed one? A lone dumpster filled the space by the far wall, where three buildings met and made a dead end. She leapt toward it, covering half the distance in a long bound, and landing off kilter, scraping her elbow on the gravel-strewn ground.

There was a slender gap between the dumpster and the wall. Refusing to let herself think about germs, filth, rodents, and tetanus, Jessica wriggled her way in, wedging her body against the rough metal. She closed her eyes, listening with all her focus for sounds of pursuit and hearing nothing. Her head swam again, and she fought off a wave of sleepiness as long as she could.

In the end, she lost the fight. The world blacked out.

PATRICIA AND CINDY, GIRL TALK

Patricia slammed the door open hard enough it bounced off the wall and swung back at her. She caught it neatly in one taloned hand, only denting the door a little, and shoved her way into Cindy Liu's tiny cell of a room, her fully transformed bulk barely clearing the frame. Since she had not bothered to pull back her spikes, they screeched as they scraped along the metal frame. When she slammed the door shut behind her again, everything in the room shook.

Cindy had been lying on the bed—as Patricia well knew since she checked the room monitor before making her entrance. But now, the seemingly-teenaged septuagenarian leapt to her feet and perched atop her pillow, pressed against the shelf that served as the headboard, eyes wide with shock.

Once she saw it was Patricia, she lowered herself to a seated position and settled her face into something more like its usual impassive lines, but Patricia saw the fear in her former best friend's eyes and knew she'd made her point.

"What did you do to her?" Patricia growled the words, making no effort to soften the rasp that came with her transformation.

Cocking her head like a curious dog, Cindy looked up at her. "Do to whom?"

The affected disinterest in her tone was a dead giveaway. Cindy never sounded as cold as when she was avidly interested in or excited about something. Patricia glanced at the fingers gripping the blue coverlet into clumps and Cindy loosened her hold, smoothing the bedding out with her palms. In her heat-sensitive lizard vision, Patricia could see Cindy's whole body now registered in reds and oranges.

Good. She should be afraid.

"Jessica."

Cindy's mouth fell open, slack-jawed surprise briefly on show. "Jessica? I haven't even seen her since the Ohio mission. What could I have done to her?"

Reaching to her throat, Patricia grabbed at the necklace around it, tugging it loose without opening the clasp and throwing the offending jewelry on the bed.

Cindy picked it up. A slender, almost translucent slice of emerald strung on a simple, stretchy black cord. She raised it to the light to examine it and, for a moment, something within the surface seemed to writhe. Cindy touched it with her finger, and a curious expression flitted across her face, something akin to the face a caffeine addict makes when they get their first whiff of a cup of coffee. Anticipation of relief intermixed with annoyance at the need.

Tightening her hand around the gem, Cindy climbed down from the bed to stand in front of Patricia, glaring up at her with her hands on her hips. "What are you trying to tell me? What's happened?"

"Is this what's going to happen to all of us?"

Cindy let out a sort of exasperated hiss. "Is WHAT going to happen to all of us? You're not making any sense."

Patricia slammed her arm against the wall above the wall frame, leaving a satisfying dent in the drywall. "Thanks to you, Jessica has blown up her life. Run away from her husband, her kids. She's so wrapped up in these damn emeralds, she was trying to get them embedded into her skin. If you even talk about taking them away from her, she loses her mind."

"Ah," she said. "I wondered about that."

"Wait—you knew?" Patricia's voice went deeper and more gravelly as the spikes on her shoulders expanded.

Cindy managed to keep her face impassive, though she did take a step backward before she could stop herself. "More like, I suspected. She's always doing this." Cindy touched a hand to her chest, rubbing a thumb where her ribcage met her breasts. "I figured that was where she was keeping her emerald."

Patricia grunted. She and Leonel discussed this a couple of days earlier and came to the same conclusion. Jessica's habit of touching the emeralds was more than a harmless nervous habit or way of reassuring herself. If only it had been that innocuous.

"Did you know?"

Cindy threw her hands in the air and yelled inarticulately, then forced her words out through clenched teeth. "Did. I. Know. What?" She jabbed a finger into the air between them. "You keep talking like I should know what you're talking about, but I've been locked in this room for more than two years now. What do you think I know?"

Patricia ignored the verbal assault. "That the emeralds were addictive."

"I didn't."

When Patricia grunted, Cindy glared up at her. "I did not know. In fact, I'm not even sure they are addictive, or at least not for everyone. I only began to suspect a few months ago."

Cindy flopped down onto the bed, laying on her back and spreading her arms out to the sides to grip the two edges of the mattress. She spoke to the ceiling. "My own relationship with the emerald formula can be a little irrational, but it's hard to know the root causes of something like that when you're busy turning back into a child and you're incarcerated by the people you went to for help. Maybe it's the emeralds, maybe it's my fucking life." She pulled the bedding free from the narrow mattress, wrapping her fists in it, then letting the elastic snap back away.

Patricia spoke more gently this time. "What do you mean, irrational?"

Cindy rolled up on one elbow and counted off on her fingers. "Feelings of panic if I don't have enough supply on hand to make my next dose of formula. Willingness to take crazy risks to ensure access—remember the whole chameleon invisibility thing? Hyperawareness when emeralds are nearby."

She pulled Patricia's necklace out of her pocket and laid the flat gem on her palm, strings dangling down her arm. "I find myself hoping you'll forget you threw this at me, and I can hide it away somewhere so I'll have it, just in case."

"In case of what?"

"I don't know. That's the irrational part." She flung a hand through her hair, sweeping it back out of her eyes. "So far as I can tell, I'm stable now. I've appeared the same age for more than a year, with the exception of the return of some gray hair last year, when everyone was having those power spikes." She closed her fist around the gem. "There's no evidence I need this gem in any way, but I want it."

She tilted her head to one side and squinted at Patricia. "I take it you don't feel the same?"

Patricia shook her head. "No. I wear the shard because Walter said I should, and because it helped me regain control over my transformations. Sometimes I forget to put it on at all."

Cindy rolled the gem around in her hand, flipping it across her knuckles. After a long silence, she said, "Do you remember that time in Bay Village, after Michael died?" She almost whispered the words, pain still making her voice catch after all these years.

"Of course, I do." It had been thirty years ago, but Patricia remembered all too clearly.

Cindy nearly died, throwing herself into research like something she could discover in her experiments would bring her fiancé back. Depriving herself of sleep in the name of progress. Hardly remembering to eat.

Patricia flew out there to check on her when she'd stopped communicating. She'd arrived in time to intervene, but the two seldom mentioned it after that day. The moment hung between them now, thick with love, embarrassment, gratitude, and discomfort.

"After you went home, I nearly fell right back in the same hole. The formula I developed to keep myself awake wasn't all that different from methamphetamines, no matter what I told myself about natural ingredients and non-Western ideologies." She glared sharply at Patricia, and the sudden eye contact felt almost like a challenge. "Your insistence that I call you every day and my belief you would be able to tell if I was using was the only thing that held me back."

"I didn't know that." Patricia pulled in some of her bulk, letting her body return to something more like her natural human form, if still armored and taloned. The fire that sent her roaring in to tear information out of Cindy extinguished, leaving an ashy smell in her nose and a suspiciously salty feeling in her throat.

"It's like that sometimes. Some people are susceptible and some aren't. Some people can smoke a little on occasion to take the edge off and shrug it off if it's not available. Other people..."

"Blow up their lives if their supply is threatened?" Patricia offered.

"Just so," Cindy said.

Patricia leaned against the door, letting her gaze bounce over the spartan room. "But Jessica's supply wasn't threatened. Walter says she has more samples than he does."

Cindy pulled a notebook and pen out from somewhere. "Let's start at the beginning."

"You know the beginning. You were there. You poisoned her—all of us, if we're being honest—with your untested products, kidnapped her and ran tests on her without her permission and then Li, um, Fuerte rescued her, breaking her out of your lab."

Cindy rolled her eyes. "You're never going to let that go, are you?"

Patricia raised one eyebrow and transformed her eyes. "Would you?"

Without answering, Cindy returned her attention to her notebook. "When did Jessica's strange behavior start?"

Patricia thought. Walter said Jessica had been distant sometimes, even in the weeks right before they got married. He'd thought she was just preoccupied with the ceremony and party arrangements, and things seemed fine on their honeymoon, but once they got back, they'd hardly seen one another. He'd blamed it on work, but Suzie said Jessica chose the night hours that kept her away from her new husband and her boys herself. It sure looked like she was avoiding spending time with her brand-new husband.

"It's hard to say. You know how it is. Someone behaves a little strangely and you think you know why, so you write it off at the time and it's only later you wonder if it was a sign of something else."

Cindy tapped her pencil on the pad but didn't say anything. When Patricia stayed silent, she began toying with the emerald shard Patricia had thrown at her.

Patricia snatched at the cord, tugging it out of Cindy's hands. She held it up, shaking it. "It started with these. When we got back from Ohio. Walter used emerald shards to help your victims get their conditions under control again."

Cindy clucked her tongue. "But Jessica never experienced a surge or change like the rest of you did."

"We thought it was because she always kept emeralds on her, that they'd stabilized her. Walter's theory was something about a half-life to the effects and that was why all of us who'd stopped using your products flared, but Jessica didn't."

Cindy paused, tapping her pen against the pad, slowly, then faster until it was a drumbeat. Finally, she dropped the pen and looked up, her eyes bright and almost feverish. "Where did Walter get the emeralds he used?"

Patricia shrugged. "I don't know. I assume they have samples, collected from your lab and storage unit."

Cindy shook her head. "Jessica stole the samples from my lab, before you all blew it up."

Rankled by another accusation, Patricia turned away from her former friend's piercing gaze. "Excuse me, I believe your pet flamethrower set that fire."

Cindy groaned in exasperation. "All right, all right, it's all my fault. Happy now? Assigning blame isn't going to get us anywhere."

"Maybe not," Patricia agreed. "But it does make me feel better."

She held out a hand and pushed her talons out and pulled them back in rhythmically, thinking. "So, you're saying Walter might have taken the emeralds he used from Jessica's collection, and she was upset about it?"

"Exactly. Jessica believes she needs the emeralds to control her flight, doesn't she?"

Patricia grunted, folding her arms over her chest. "They've run tests. She can control her flight without them. It doesn't even slow her down."

"It doesn't matter if it's true that she needs them. Does she *believe* she needs them?"

Images of Jessica wearing diving weights on her ankles, dark circles of stress and worry making her look ten years older, flashed across Patricia's memory. The manic joy on her face when she darted through the air at the college campus. The emeralds made all the difference in that moment —gave her control and confidence and speed. In the same position, wouldn't anyone believe they needed the gems?

"Fuerte would know better. They're closer. But if I had to guess, yes, she does."

Cindy was absorbed in her notebook, drawing diagrams Patricia didn't understand and arrows all over the page. Patricia watched her in silence for a long moment, a deep sorrow making her heart heavy in her chest.

Despite the pain and suffering that sent her barreling into Cindy Liu's room, this had been genuinely wonderful—almost like it had once been between them when they were young. Two women plotting together, solving problems, laying plans. Moments of confession and trust Patricia had shared with very few people in her life. Really just two people: Cindy and Suzie.

She had missed Cindy. Still did. But the woman couldn't be trusted, and she'd been sent to lay a trap. It was time to make good on her promise, even if she longed to trust Cindy again, to rely on her without second-guessing every interaction.

Patricia cleared her throat. "So, you think Jessica would come for the emeralds?"

Dark eyes snapped up from the notebook, a shrewd gaze examining Patricia long enough that she started to feel squirmy. "So, I take it she's gone right now. Your buddies here at the mutant zoo don't know where she is?"

Patricia nodded, hoping her scales disguised the troubled expression and doubts on her face.

"Yes. If you can find a way to let her know where the emeralds are being kept, she'll come for them. I know I would."

Patricia blurted it out, speaking quickly. "We're opening a new research facility, out in the old industrial park, for study of the emeralds and their effects. They will be moving the supplies and equipment out there tomorrow." Patricia tried to sound matter-of-fact, like she wasn't revealing anything that mattered, or setting a test for her former best friend.

She couldn't even be sure if she hoped Cindy would spring the trap or not. It didn't feel like winning either way.

A thoughtful expression spread across Cindy's face. "I suggest you get ready."

SALLY ANN EASES BACK IN

Sally Ann sat in an empty cargo truck with Agent Gabe Driver watching blue jump-suited people move crates, barrels, and equipment into the warehouse. Gabe was sure they hadn't been followed in their uneventful ride, so everything was going smoothly.

Smooth could be dull, but it beat laying around in her hospital room by miles. The medical team agreed she could be here today, so long as she promised not to exert herself more than necessary. "Ease back in," Dr. Suggs advised. "Something unlikely to require combat or too much decision-making."

Sally Ann was doing her best to abide by that. She'd learned the hard way that you can't rush healing from a concussion, no matter how difficult rest and recuperation was. She also knew too much time without a problem to solve left her irritable and restless.

Today, she didn't have a significant headache so far, and if she could keep her distance from the Director so he didn't send her reeling with more psychic manipulations, she was hopeful she could resume something more like her normal activities soon.

Gabe was the perfect partner for this. Of course, there was no danger that he'd talk too loud—he was mute. He wasn't going to ask too many questions either. He wouldn't have pried even if he did speak. Their relationship had always been one of mutual respect and consideration. She was grateful for his quiet companionship now and knew that if any kind of shit did hit the fan, she could rely on him.

Not that they were expecting trouble. All the information they had released through the press and internal channels indicated this move would happen tomorrow. Even the agents moving equipment and cargo only learned their day's duty a couple of hours ago. Leaks should have been near impossible.

If the trap they laid was successful, Daniel Price would show up tomorrow, having either heard the announcement during the press conference, or heard from his daughter and their likely mole, Cindy Liu. He'd expect to take advantage of the chaos of setting up, but he'd find full security already in place. They'd take him in, publicly enough to keep Bertrand and his secret organization from being able to sweep this one under the rug.

"Hit me," Sally Ann said. It was Gabe's turn to be the dealer and she could see that he had a King on his knee. Maybe she had a shot at beating him this hand.

He cocked an eyebrow at her, his eyes asking if she was sure. Sally Ann squinted at the man, looking for any hint as to what was in his hand, but Gabe was a closed book. She'd never been one to play it safe, though. "Hit me." She smacked a fist against her chest.

Gabe passed her a card. She made a show of keeping it hidden as she peeked under the corner. A two. With the eight and six already in her hand, she was still under twenty-one. She smirked at Gabe. "All right, then. Let's see what you got."

He flipped his hidden card. Nine. Lucky nineteen.

"Damn it." She spread out her losing hand for him to see.

Ignoring his silent laughter, Sally Ann had just reached for the deck to shuffle it for another hand when the truck parked next to theirs flipped end over end, rising high into the air and landing with a screeching thud. Flinging the cards into the air, Sally Ann gripped the dashboard as their own truck swayed in the movement. "What the hell?"

Gabe was already in motion, snapping his fingers at her to put on her seatbelt. Sally Ann hastened to obey, clicking the harness into place. In a matter of seconds, Gabe turned the truck completely around and raced toward a military-style jeep with a large gun affixed to the bed and an equally large and somewhat familiar man wielding it.

Blue lights lit up in coils around the barrel of the gun and, recognizing the weapon as something like what they'd seen at the museum, Sally Ann managed to yell: "Dodge!"

With impossibly quick reflexes, Gabe spun their cargo truck left and pulled into a wide turn that circled the jeep. A whoosh of air swept by where they'd just been, the window at the back of the truck shattering.

This wasn't good. "Get us out of here, Gabe."

Gabe tightened his grip on the steering wheel and continued his circle wide, going around the back of the warehouse to the maze of connecting roads behind. The radio was going nuts with reports of damage. Sally Ann lunged for the handset and pressed the button. "Code orange, code orange," she announced. "Withdraw. Do not engage."

A string of acknowledgements followed, and the radio fell silent. Sally Ann trusted the agents would follow their orders, but they might not all be able to disengage. "Get us back to headquarters," Sally Ann told Gabe.

Sally Ann pulled her phone from her pocket and dialed Suzie's direct line.

Suzie picked up before the first ring finished. "Tell me." She already knew it would be bad news.

"We need backup." Sally Ann laid out the situation. "I didn't get a look at the shooter, but the gun he was using was just like what we saw at the museum, only bigger."

"On it," Suzie said.

After she hung up, Sally Ann sat there for a long moment with the phone in her hand. She itched to tell Gabe to turn the truck around, to go back and fight, but she knew firsthand what kind of damage that weird sonic gun could do. Either their agents had made it to safety, or they were already beyond her help.

Gabe seemed to sense her distress and the truck accelerated, hitting speeds it should not have been able to accomplish. Sally Ann gripped the safety handle and flashed a grateful smile to Gabe. She owed him again, for more than her blackjack losses.

A SCANT FIVE MINUTES LATER, Gabe had completed the normally fifteen-minute drive, and the truck came to a stop in the private section of the garage under the bank that housed the UCU offices, steam billowing from the tires and gaskets. "Get the Dact ready." Sally Ann slid out of the truck.

Gabe grinned like she'd promised him a million dollars and offered a tiny half-salute. She returned it before she ran for the elevator. He did love getting to fly the Dact, she thought as the doors slid shut.

When the doors opened, Sally Ann almost collided with Patricia. The two women fell into step but didn't talk as they worked their ways through the corridors to the main conference room. Sally Ann didn't know what she would have said—but the fact that the new facility was attacked at nearly the same time Patricia was laying their trap with Cindy Liu had her feeling conflicted.

On the one hand, that meant Cindy wasn't the mole—how could she have gotten information outside that fast? On the other hand, that meant there was another mole, or worse yet, a security breach in the form of surveillance or infiltration they had not discovered. She didn't have time or the mental space to work her way through layers of suspicion, not when there were lives to save.

She burst into the conference room, flinging the door hard. Patricia caught it to keep Sally Ann from taking a hard rebound to the face. She spared a tight smile for Patricia, then dropped into one of the office chairs. After the briefest of pauses, Suzie came in through the connecting door that led to the Director's office carrying a tablet and folders, Steven trailing behind her, pale and pensive.

"Where's Fuerte?" Sally Ann asked.

Suzie shook her head. "Not back yet." The hangdog expression on Suzie's face was enough to answer what Sally Ann had really been asking. The morning operation, recapturing Flygirl at her tattoo appointment, was a failure. Flygirl was still in the wind.

"Well, shit." Sally Ann stuffed down the spike of worry. They'd have to figure out what to do about Jessica later. They had more immediate problems.

In the few moments in which Sally Ann let her mind swirl around the confluence of events, Suzie hooked her tablet into the system. The projecting wall now showed drone footage of the new research facility. They all watched as a truck flipped end over end, and another truck—the one Sally Ann and Gabe had been inside—made an escape. Even though she'd been there, Sally Ann found it difficult to believe what she was seeing. The drone captured a view of the jeep with the strange weapon before the screen turned to white fuzz.

Patricia took in a sharp breath. "Was that—?"

"The same type of weapon we saw at the museum." Sally Ann glared at the Director. "But bigger."

The Director remained quiet, which was for the best. Suzie pulled up an audio recording of a phone call next and all three of them listened to a man with a slight German accent stating that the UCU had three hours to deliver Cindy Liu or the facility would be destroyed, along with everyone in it.

"How many?" Sally Ann asked.

Suzie kept emotion out of her voice. "Of the fifty agents onsite this morning, thirty-five have reported in. We assume the two in the flipped truck are at least injured. We don't yet know if there are more casualties. Hostages were not mentioned."

"The call?" Sally Ann thought she already knew, but she had to ask.

"Daniel Price. I'd know his voice anywhere," Patricia growled.

Suzie nodded. "She's right. We only saw the one gunman, but we assume Price has more firepower and men at his disposal."

"Gabe is preparing the Dact," Sally Ann offered.

"Are we gonna do it? Just hand her over?" Patricia asked. When all the eyes in the room turned to her, she held up her hands. "I'm only trying to understand the play here."

The Director cleared his throat. "I'm not sure we have a choice."

"There's always a choice," Suzie snapped. More calmly, she said, "But sending Liu in might be our best one." Suzie's eyes held her gaze for a long moment, waiting until Patricia looked away first.

Whether or not she agreed, Sally Ann was confident she'd go along with the plan.

Suzie clicked her keyboard a couple of times, and the screen showed a schematic of the new research facility. She pointed out a few places on the map, marked with red squares. "Besides the loss of resources we'd incur if this facility is destroyed, some of these hazardous materials would have serious fallout for the surrounding area. We'd have an environmental containment quagmire at best, and a humanitarian disaster at worst."

Sally Ann leaned both elbows on the table. "And you think sending Liu in will prevent this? That they'll just say 'thanks,' pack up their mad scientist, and go?"

"No," Suzie admitted. "But I do think it will buy us a little time."

The door from the hallway swung open again and a red-faced and breathless Mary Braeburn stumbled through, followed by a wheezing Helen, face still poofy with sleep.

Sally Ann widened her eyes at Patricia who shrugged one shoulder. "So, we're fighting sound with fire?"

"We need every option at our disposal." Suzie checked her phone while picking up the folders she had brought in earlier. "Fuerte should be onsite in five more minutes. I'll send him straight to the Dact, and you all can fill him in in flight." She dropped a folder in front of each of them, a piece of pale blue paper inside.

Sally Ann almost ripped the paper in her eagerness to read the plan.

JESSICA'S NEW PLAN

Jessica woke when a fire truck blared its sirens, rattling through the streets. Her head felt like it was lined with cotton and her eyes ran. Where was she? It smelled terrible.

She tried to fly but found she was stuck. Her body jolted up a couple of inches before her back scraped painfully and something hard and metal pushed into her ribs.

Breathing out through her nose and in through her mouth, she pulled an arm free from where it was wedged and wiped at her face. A woozy, swimming sensation made her groan, but she fought through it to work her way free of whatever was holding her pressed down. Metal, something else heavy and industrial pinned her against something rough, like stone or brick.

It wasn't completely dark, but it was dim, and it was hard to know which direction was up and where she might find her escape. She forced herself to stop struggling and focus. This disconnected feeling coupled with drowsiness meant she'd been drugged. If she could remain calm, she'd remember more about how she'd ended up here.

A breeze wafted from her right side and Jessica turned her face toward it, only to gag at the putrid smell it carried. Something rotten and kind of sweet. Sewage? No. Garbage. A dumpster.

A streak of memory like lightning jolted her. Jessica had been flying, pursued, and she'd hidden behind the dumpster, squeezing herself into the narrow opening in hopes of going unnoticed.

It must have worked because she was still here.

Leonel!

His sad eyes floated in her memory, and she wanted to comfort him, to tell him it would be all right. But it wasn't all right. He'd tried to take her in.

She remembered now—she'd gone to get her tattoo and, instead, ended up in a fight for her freedom. She stretched the hand she'd freed down to feel the back of her thigh. She didn't find a dart sticking out of her flesh, so she guessed it fell out during her flight, but the area was bruised and sore. It could have been much worse.

Wriggling a little at a time, Jessica worked her way slowly and painfully to one side of the dumpster, sucked in her belly to squeeze through the final narrow gap, and fell out onto the ground, scraping her ribs and landing on her knees. She stayed there on all fours for a long moment, light flashing behind her eyes, before she could get herself back on her feet. Leaning against the wall for support, she scanned the alley for threats.

She was alone.

Sagging in relief, she slid to the ground and examined herself for wounds. Nothing too serious. The back of her thigh was bruised and sore, and she had a few minor abrasions, but she didn't seem to have any broken bones, oozing lacerations, or even movement-limiting sprains.

What happened to her pursuers? Surely, they hadn't just let her go. How long was she unconscious?

She looked up at the sky, tinted a shade of orange that suggested sunset. It had been early morning when she arrived. She burst into the air, then stopped and lowered herself back to her feet. Bad idea. If they'd left anyone to watch for her, they'd be watching the sky, expecting her to fly. She'd have a better shot at escaping unseen on foot.

Smoothing her hair and clothes, Jessica leapt to the end of the alley in a short bound, landing lightly on her toes. She pressed herself against the wall and leaned out, peering down the street. The street wasn't crowded, but it wasn't empty either. To the left, a group of young people were standing outside a bar, laughing and talking.

Moving to the other wall so she could see down the right, Jessica spotted a couple of moms with jogging strollers and a young man with a big dog on a leash. She didn't see an obvious agent watching for her, but if they were good at their job, she wouldn't see them, would she?

She waited for a long time, listening and watching. After fifteen minutes or so, the group of young people who lingered in front of the bar started walking in her direction. When they passed her, she slipped out and joined in the edges of the small crowd they formed, her head down and hands in her pockets. The group pointedly ignored her, probably taking her for a homeless person or a junkie. She moved with them for two blocks, before taking a quick turn off to the right and circling around behind a sporting goods store.

After checking to make sure she was not observed, Jessica flew upward, staying close to the wall and in the shadows until she was even with the third-floor windows, left partially open. A quick peek inside showed a dark room, piled with boxes. Perfect. She shoved the window a little further open and slid inside.

The boxes were helpfully labeled with brand names, colors, and styles, so it was the work of a few minutes to find black pants, a clean shirt, a dark hoodie, and some sneakers in the proper sizes. She peeled off her stinking clothes, rolled them into a tight wad, and dropped them out the window by which she had entered.

Pulling the new clothes on caused some pain as her bruises and scrapes made themselves known in the process, but in short order, she was dressed in black head to toe, and smelled a great deal better. The whole process left her a little woozy, so she laid down on the cool, tile floor to rest. After a few minutes, her stomach growled.

Jessica lost her purse in the tussle at the tattoo place, and all the cash inside. That meant her options were limited, but she knew she needed to get some food and drink if she was going to keep going. She decided to risk venturing into the rest of the store. Floating across the room to avoid making the floor creak, she opened the door and hovered there, listening for a long moment. She could hear music and some voices, but they were muted and distant, so she floated to the top of the doorframe, nudged the door open, and slipped out, keeping her body near the ceiling.

She found herself in a narrow hallway with the storage room behind her, a set of stairs to her left, and another room opposite. A paper sign on the door reminded employees no smoking or vaping was allowed in the employee lounge and that violators of the policy would be fired.

After a peek down the empty stairs, Jessica made for the other door. The handle turned in her hand. Unlocked. Easy!

The tiny, airless room stank with forbidden tobacco products and was crowded with a table and chairs, a mini fridge, and several lockers. The garbage overflowed with takeout wrappers and drink cups.

Locking the door behind her, Jessica made short work of searching the lockers. In the pockets of the jackets and purses she found about forty dollars in crumpled small bills. It wasn't much, but it would get her dinner, and once she'd had some food and water, she could decide what to do next.

She unlocked the door, slipped back across the hall, out the window and into the night. She flitted from rooftop to rooftop for a few blocks, nervous to take to the open sky, especially while it was still daylight. She dropped down near the university and made her way to a crowded sports bar. The place was hopping. Exactly the kind of chaotic environment where she could go unnoticed.

A few minutes later she was seated at the bar, eating greasy fries and a burger. The television on the wall played a football game, and an announcer was yelling. Shouts filled the bar, so the local favorite must have won. Jessica glanced at the television screen right as it moved to commercials and spotted the familiar visage of Darrin Berger, Sally Ann's reporter boyfriend.

She couldn't hear him over the boisterous celebration surrounding her, but the scrolling text at the bottom of the screen told her Flygirl had been sighted at the press conference yesterday and the local news at six would have full details.

Intrigued, Jessica lingered over her fries and water the extra ten minutes so she could see what the news said about it all. Meanwhile, she indulged in some people watching.

It had been a long time since she'd been in a crowd like this, and the happy energy lightened her pensive mood. She told herself things weren't as bad as they seemed. The UCU had come for her, and she'd made it out only a little worse for the wear. She could and would handle this.

As the news came on, a breathless young woman stumbled up to the bar and flopped onto the empty stool next to Jessica. "He's such a hottie, isn't he?"

Darrin was a handsome man, if a little slick and over-styled for Jessica's taste. "I've got a friend who thinks so," she responded. "I'm not sure he's my type though."

The girl blinked at her, surprised, then grinned broadly, raising her beer glass in a toast. "That's alright! More for me!"

After the girl danced back off into the crowd, Jessica returned her attention to the screen. "Flygirl under cover?" flashed in gold letters at the top of the screen and Darrin showed footage from the press conference. He didn't know anything—that much was obvious—but he managed to make her unannounced flyby in street clothes sound intriguing.

"The other big news to come out of the UCU press conference was the opening of a new research facility, designed to investigate the proliferation of strange powers in Springfield, as well as probable causes and potential cures." The background changed again, showing one of the old warehouses on the edge of town.

Darrin continued. "The facility, which will be housed in the abandoned buildings in Springfield's former industrial park, is expected to open later this week."

A video clip of the mayor touted their forward-thinking green policies in making use of already developed land, but Jessica tuned out. Dropping her stolen cash next to the plate, she slipped through the crowd and out to the street.

She knew where she needed to go next. The emeralds the UCU held would be studied at the new facility. She could slip in during the chaos of opening, reclaim them, and get away before anyone knew what was happening. The night was already looking up.

HELEN TAKES THE WHEEL

Helen gripped the armrests of her assigned seat in what she'd just learned was called "The Dact, short for Pterodactyl," and tried to look like she wasn't terrified as the ship or plane or whatever-the-hell-it-was lifted into the air.

This was unreal. Despite its enormous size, the Dact was nearly silent. Mary told her about the camouflaging technology that kept it from being seen by electronic surveillance, radar, and the like. It wasn't completely invisible to the naked eye, but it was likely to escape casual observation. Inside, the walls were lined with racks of equipment, and tables and seats were grouped together.

Helen expected a bit of a ramp-up before she was thrust into the thick of life with the UCU, but here she was, already part of a team, facing danger, on her way to save the day if it could be saved.

She should've guessed, given that her low-key mentoring and training mission evolved into rescuing a carload of teenagers from a bridge accident within hours. The universe had no intention of easing her into her new life. This would be a baptism by fire, and she needed to adapt fast, or the journey would be short.

Forcing herself to loosen her hold on the armrests, Helen turned her attention to the other passengers. It was better than watching the landscape blur past in the windows.

Fuerte was seated near the cockpit, deep in serious conversation with

Sally Ann. No one told her where he had been during the briefing meeting, but whatever it was left him agitated and anxious. He looked somewhere between rumpled and harried when he'd leapt onto the Dact moments before it took to the sky.

Helen would lay money Fuerte's absence had something to do with Flygirl. The popular hero was notably absent from the Dact, and this seemed like the kind of mission where having someone along who wasn't bound by the laws of gravity would come in handy.

Across from Helen's seat, Patricia lay sprawled across a row of seats, taloned feet on the floor. To all appearances, she was asleep, but Helen observed the silent interplay between the Lizard Woman and Dr. Cindy Liu when the scientist came aboard, so she suspected Patricia was avoiding eye contact. The tension between the two of them was thick as day-old pea soup and about as aromatic.

Seeing Dr. Liu again had been kind of anticlimactic for Helen. She'd worried her years of anger and resentment at having been manipulated and abandoned might have proved more than she could manage. She'd built it up as a major dramatic confrontation. In her imagination, the rest of the team goggled at her after she let loose her fire and left a small woman-sized pile of ashes steaming on the floor.

In reality, though, Liu didn't even glance Helen's direction as she took her seat and allowed Sally Ann to cuff her to it without resistance. Helen wondered if the good doctor even recognized her, sitting there dressed in the plain blue jumpsuit favored by the agents of the UCU, at least the ones without flashy powers and skills. She hadn't reacted with anger, fear, or guilt.

Helen's first emotion, confronted with the woman she'd spent so many hours plotting the death of, was something more akin to pity than rage. The skinny, pathetic figure with bird's nest hair and ill-fitting scrub-pajamas, seemed nervous, maybe even scared.

That last bit made acid swirl in Helen's guts. In her experience, the good doctor was hard to frighten, or even to intimidate. So, if Cindy Liu was scared, there was reason. Her own anxiety ratcheted, and Helen released steam from her fingertips in an attempt to tamp it down.

Helen glanced over at Mary, seated across from her, but her daughter's attention was focused on the man by her side, the Director, or "Steven" as Mary encouraged her to call him. "Don't play into his attempts to make himself seem mysterious."

Steven didn't appear powerful or mysterious now. He was curled in on himself, his body language broadcasting the misery of a man who would prefer to be anywhere else in the world.

Helen had thought him handsome the other times she'd met him, but Mary explained about his mental manipulation, controlling how others saw him.

Apparently, he wasn't projecting anything now, sitting mere inches from her daughter. He was an ordinary-looking White man, between thirty and forty years old by her estimation, thin in a nerdy-spindly way rather than a runner-athlete way.

Steven slumped against the armrest, leaning as far away from Mary as he could get while remaining in his chair, fist shoved against his cheek. His skin showed the pockmarks of a bad bout of acne in his youth, patchy stubble spread across his jawline, and his hair lay flat on his head and needed washing. Nope, not handsome at all.

Helen already knew from Mary that the man had been handed an ultimatum by the rest of the group: cooperate or leave. He agreed to participate in their plan, but he didn't like it. That explained the expression of misery. No one liked being knocked off a pedestal, especially if they'd worked hard to put themselves on it, and the Director had put a lot of effort into building this little empire, only to find himself dethroned. Helen's pride for her daughter swelled in her chest. Suzie said they couldn't do this without Mary, and Helen saw that was true. No one else could handle Steven.

The ride wasn't long, and all too soon, the Dact was dropping into a small meadow surrounded by woods. Helen unfastened her harness and stood, making a show of stretching to disguise the bout of nervous nausea oozing through her guts. This next bit was all her, which was exciting and terrifying all at the same time.

The driver, a man she had yet to meet, hopped down to the ground first. He fiddled with some buttons and opened a compartment, then slipped inside. As Helen watched out the window, a small armored vehicle nosed out, a little black thing like a miniature Humvee and the same stocky man stepped out of the driver's seat and waved up at the window.

A hand fell on Helen's shoulder, and she jumped, fingertips bursting into flame. Spinning, she found Fuerte smiling at her. "You can do this." He turned her so they faced each other squarely and rested one large, warm hand on each of her shoulders. "I believe in you."

Helen swallowed and let out a nervous giggle. "No pressure, right?"

Fuerte twisted his mouth in something between a smile and a grimace. "Well, maybe a little. But pressure is how we make diamonds."

Helen caught Mary's eye and gave her a thumbs-up, then made her way down to the ground to receive a quick driving lesson. The team agreed it made the most sense to send Helen in with Cindy.

Out of all of them, only she had not encountered Daniel Price directly. That made her the least likely to be recognized, and he would probably assume she was an ordinary agent of the UCU with no special abilities, which made her a stealth weapon.

That was all well and good, but unlike Patricia, she wasn't bulletproof, and though she'd been assured that her specially treated fireproof blue jumpsuit was made of a proprietary fabric similar to Kevlar, it didn't cover her head, which is where she kept all her best parts.

So, Helen was more than a little bit nervous. But this was what she signed on for—a hero's life came with danger. She could and would do this, for Mary. For herself.

The agent on the ground—she'd been told he was called Gabe Driver—waved her into the Humvee, then hopped into the passenger seat and started pointing out controls. It took her a minute to realize the man wasn't merely taciturn, but actually mute; but he was a good communicator all the same, and soon she was maneuvering the little armored car around with ease. Not very different from driving a regular car, except for the onboard weapons and special abilities she wouldn't be allowed to use anyway. She was only the Girl Scout leader driving the van to deliver the cookies. If all went well, she wouldn't even have to light a campfire. If it didn't, well, she'd burn that bridge when she got to it.

When she pulled the little vehicle back around, Sally Ann was waiting for her, one arm draped over the shoulder of a sullen-looking Cindy Liu. "You ready?" Sally Ann asked, stepping to her side

"Probably not," Helen said.

"None of us ever is." Sally Ann pulled a capped syringe out of a box. "They told you about this, right?"

Helen nodded. She didn't like the idea, but she couldn't think of a way out of it. Given her history, she understood the UCU's desire to be able to track her, but it still gave her the willies to think about. Sometimes the twenty-first century was a terrifying place. Helen pulled her jumpsuit to the side, exposing her left shoulder and submitted to the injection. It didn't hurt much, and she didn't feel any different afterward, but it was strange to imagine she could now be tracked like a lost cell phone or identified like a runaway puppy.

"What about her?" she asked, hooking a thumb at Cindy Liu.

"Already done. She tried to escape a couple of years ago and she's been chipped ever since."

That was interesting. Maybe Cindy wasn't as cowed as she appeared, if she'd tried to escape. A quiver of concern spread up the back of Helen's head. She hoped the show of cooperation wasn't just a show. The UCU wouldn't take it well if she burned their most valuable prisoner, even if she was trying to escape.

Sally Ann put the syringe back in the box. "Yours is a little more advanced. We might be able to pick up limited audio, depending on what part of the facility you're in and the level of shielding." She held out a hand for Helen to shake. "Break a leg."

"Not again." Helen shook her head.

"It doesn't have to be your own leg," Sally Ann called back over her shoulder.

WITH THAT, Helen was alone in the car with Cindy Liu. The two women stared at each for a moment before Helen hit the gas and they were off. Gabe had parked the Dact at some distance, to keep it hidden until needed. Helen was supposed to follow the construction road out and drive up the access roads into the research facility, making it harder to trace where she was coming from.

Cindy sat in silence until they hit the first significant pothole, when she pressed her hands against the dashboard and glared at Helen. "I see you still drive like a crazy person."

Ah, so Cindy did recognize her.

"Well, you would know." Helen hadn't forgotten the time she'd gotten into Dr. Liu's car, with its broken seatbelts and semi-functional doors. In comparison, Helen was a model driver, sedate and restrained.

The dust of the construction road dispersed when the car bumped up onto the graveled access road. "Why are you going along with this?" Helen asked.

"I could ask the same of you."

"A shot at redemption. I have a few things to make up for," Helen said.

"You don't think that's how it is for me?"

Helen swallowed. "Honestly?"

"Yes, honestly."

"No. You've never struck me as a woman who apologizes. And this could get you killed."

Cindy snorted. "Daniel's not going to kill me."

"Why not?" Cindy's confidence was surprising. From what she'd learned so far, this man didn't have any compunction about taking life.

"Did they not tell you?"

Helen shrugged. "Tell me what?"

"Daniel Price is my father."

The car swerved into the grassy shoulder, and Helen pulled it back onto the road. Her *father*? But Cindy was older than Helen. Over seventy at this point, despite all outward appearances. Helen had seen the surveillance photos of Daniel Price. He didn't look much over forty. The math didn't add up.

"How can that be?"

"It's complicated. Let's just say my father and I have at least one thing in common: an interest in longevity. The body he's in now is not the one he was born with."

That was a horrifying thought. If Helen lived through this, she'd have to get the full details of Cindy and her father. But for now, she wanted to understand what side Cindy was on.

"So, this is a rescue mission? He's breaking you out?"

"Hardly. This is another kidnapping. It's not me he wants—it's my work. Our shared bloodline is merely the universe's dark sense of humor manifesting in my life again."

"But you're going willingly?"

"How else could I get close enough?"

A shiver ran down Helen's spine. "Close enough for what?"

"Vengeance."

Cindy's icy voice chilled Helen's heart. There was the woman she'd known.

PATRICIA PLAYS A WAITING GAME

Patricia watched the armored car drive away, a swirl of complicated emotions twisting her guts. She bore neither Cindy nor Helen any especial love, but it didn't feel heroic, sending them off into enemy territory unprotected. She told herself it was all according to plan, but it wasn't helping.

Over the past few years, she'd learned to trust Sally Ann to develop a cogent plan, and to do her best to follow it. It wasn't always easy—today for instance, she'd rather just storm the castle, confident her bulletproof flesh would see her through. But the museum had handed her direct evidence that sometimes it was better to take things slower and gather more data before attacking. Less collateral damage that way.

That said, the plan they were operating under allowed for collateral damage in the form of two women in a car, if that's what it took. Patricia wasn't sure she was okay with that anymore. She wasn't done with Cindy, and the jury was still out on Helen. Sending in two physically vulnerable people as the first party didn't sit well with her.

Compounding that, her role was to wait. Tom Petty had been right in that song—the waiting truly was the hardest part. Patricia needed something to do. She was starting to overthink things, diving into that ugly cycle of doubt and bluster which always got her in trouble.

She'd already extracted the update out of Leonel about how the morning went, how Jessica escaped the intervention team and they hadn't located her again. Agents were searching for her, but Jessica was a tiny, flexible woman who could fly. There were so many places she could hide. Even if one of the tranquilizer darts caught her like they thought, she may have curled up on a rooftop to sleep it off. Their best chance at bringing her in unharmed was blown. She was onto them now.

Patricia could tell Leonel was a mess of worry, but the past few years had taught him how to compartmentalize, at least a little. She could remember the time she told him to find his inner Scarlett O'Hara and "think about that tomorrow" and he had blinked at her, uncomprehendingly. That led to a very uncomfortable movie night for the two of them and their partners, where Patricia learned that some movies she remembered fondly from her childhood don't hold up as well as others. She really felt like a dinosaur then. They promised to do it again sometime but let someone else choose the film. They hadn't done it yet.

Restless and anxious, Patricia longed to reach out to Suzie, but she knew better than to waste Suzie's time, making her provide updates when she already had so much on her plate. This was not the time to be needy or clingy. If there was news, Suzie would share it. She knew how much they could all use a win right now. Patricia would have to find a way to soothe and calm herself.

Sally Ann and Gabe huddled together over a tablet, pointing and gesticulating. The two of them would be staying with the ship, so Patricia was sure they were talking through backup plans and contingencies, as well as monitoring the chips in Cindy and Helen. Patricia wondered what kind of data those things sent back. Would they know if harm befell one of them? Or would it be more like a homing signal, showing location even if Helen set them all ablaze or they took a hit from that sonic weapon?

The Director slumped in his chair, head in his hands, elbows on his knees, staring at the space between his shoes. Patricia didn't want to talk to him anyway. If she let her thoughts linger on him too long, they turned a murderous shade of red, and she needed a cool head or she'd be no use to anyone. He could stew in his own juices.

Leonel and Mary sat on the floor a short distance away from the Director. Patricia couldn't hear them talking, but she could tell from the body language that Leonel was reassuring Mary, presumably about her mother's role in the plan. Mary had been a ball of tension from the moment she boarded the Dact, but Leonel got her laughing.

He was so good at this part of things—calming the victim, getting cooperation from onlookers, winning over combative politicians. Diplomatic and kind to his core. And absolutely sincere on top of it—it wasn't an act; he truly cared. It was maddening.

Pacing around the Dact again, Patricia peered out all the windows in turn. Trees. Trees. More trees. Oh, look. Trees. This wasn't helping.

She eventually lay down on the floor, slowing her breathing. The hum of the engines against her back was soothing, and she found herself trying to match the pitch with her voice as she lay there. After a few minutes, she sensed a presence next to her, but she didn't open her eyes or move and whoever it was moved away.

The feet came back a minute or two later and Patricia opened her eyes because someone laid down beside her. She turned her head to find Leonel resting on his back.

"This is nice." He laid a hand on his chest. "I like how it rumbles."

"There was a bridge we used to drive across when I was a kid, visiting relatives in Kentucky. It hummed like this, and if you opened your mouth and made a droning noise as you went across, it would vibrate in your chest and throat."

"That's a nice memory," Leonel said. "The thing I remember about riding in the car when I was little were the blurry trees streaking by the windows. I could let my vision lose focus, and it was like we were driving through an impressionistic painting."

"Do you think they're all right?" Patricia asked.

"I do. Helen is resourceful and Cindy is…well, you would know better than me."

"Stubborn? Arrogant? Challenging?"

Leonel chuffed softly. "Well, I was thinking self-assured, intelligent, and determined, but sure, those work too."

Patricia laughed. "Well, you are ever the optimist."

"It must be hard for you, being forced into interacting with her again."

"That's one word for it."

Leonel sighed. "It can get so complicated sometimes."

"What can?"

"People. Love. Relationships." Leonel thrust a finger into the air with each word, like he was popping balloons. "It's hard to know what's worth working to repair and what is better discarded."

Patricia leaned up on her elbows so she could see the rest of the inside of the Dact. Mary still sat where she'd last seen her with Leonel, turned so she faced the Director, but pointedly looking at her phone instead of at him. "How's Mary?"

"She's mostly worried about her endurance. Monitoring the Director and keeping him from exerting undue influence is tiring."

"I meant about her mother."

Leonel sat up and spun around so they were sitting hip to hip and could see one another's faces. "She doesn't seem worried about that. She told me her mother could take care of herself."

"Is she right about that?"

"Helen can defend herself if the need arises, but I worry she won't have the control in the heat of a fight to protect the innocents at the same time. But she did okay in the rain."

Patricia sat up straighter, rolling her shoulders down. "It sounds like you've come around on her—on her joining the team, I mean."

"She performed a great service at the bridge. I could not have saved all those kids alone."

Patricia doubted that. Leonel would push himself up to and beyond his limits if lives were on the line. If he'd been there alone, he'd still have found a way to get those teenagers to safety. But his generosity of spirit insisted on sharing credit, even if the contributions of others were dubious.

He continued. "I believe in Helen. She wants to make amends for her past madness. Our Director may not have the purest of motives in developing this rehabilitation program, but it doesn't mean there won't be some good to come of it."

"Mixed blessings," Patricia said.

"What?"

"It's what my mother calls moments like this: mixed blessings. When something bad happens but good comes out of it, or something good happens but there are unexpected trade-offs."

"I like it."

"We should get t-shirts." Patricia smirked, slapping her knee against Leonel's side.

Just then, Sally Ann's voice came across the speakers. "It's game time."

Leonel was on his feet in an instant, extending a hand to Patricia. She took it and let him pull her up. They stood for a moment, looking into each other's eyes, grasping one another's forearms. Leonel squeezed her arm once more, let go, and slipped away. "Let's do this!" he called, shooting a fist into the air. *"¡Sí se puede!"*

MARY SUSSES IT OUT

Mary parked the second armored car inside the tree line. After she and Steven climbed out, she hit the camouflage button and watched the car become reflective. If she hadn't known it was there, she wouldn't be able to find it at all. "That never gets old," she said. "This job comes with the best toys."

Steven didn't say anything. He'd been like that all day, sulky and silent. "You good?" she asked.

He gave Mary a wan smile. "What do you think?"

Mary folded her arms over her chest. "You brought this on yourself, Steven. Now you're going to help us fix this. We'll deal with the rest afterward." She took a step closer. "Right now, I need to know if I can rely on you doing your part, so I'll ask you again. Are you good?"

Steven blinked. A different, slow smile spread across his face. "Have you always been this frightening?"

"It runs in the family," Mary said. "Let's go."

The two stepped into the open and walked around the building. From what Sally Ann and Gabe picked up on surveillance, they knew they weren't facing an army. The two men from the museum were in there with Daniel Price. The team watched the video again and talked about the capability of the strange weapons they'd face and the level of damage to expect. The best outcome would be to avoid a firefight all together.

Mekai, the former Secret Service operative they'd faced before, was in there too. Cindy recognized him and used his name when he had escorted them in, so there was no doubt about that part. Gabe rubbed his jaw when Sally Ann told them about the man's presence. They'd tussled before and it hadn't ended well for Gabe. Mary sparred with Gabe on her gym days and he was no lightweight, so Mekai must be dangerous, if he'd come out on top in a fight with Gabe.

Even so, Mekai was the one they weren't supposed to hurt if they could help it. Sally Ann thought they could bring him in, recruit him to their side once they'd defeated his mysterious boss, Bertrand Dietrich.

Mary wished she knew more about Dietrich. She should have been pumping Steven for information while they'd been waiting, but she'd been preoccupied with worrying about her mother, the probability one of them would get shot or otherwise killed today, and her role in keeping Steven under control.

She'd never signed on for this kind of life but had been sucked in because of Helen. It was not her fault she'd been born with a natural resistance to psychic manipulation. Sometimes she wished she'd never realized it, even though she was trading on that very ability to get her mother the help she needed.

As they moved across the exposed asphalt parking area toward the door, Mary spotted the armored vehicle her mother had driven. She noted with relief that it appeared undamaged. Still sitting on all four wheels, no bullet holes or dents. At least Helen and Cindy made it this far in one piece. She knew that already, from the surveillance, but having the evidence of her own eyes was comforting.

The front door slid open as they approached, and a hulking man filled the doorway, an automatic weapon in his arms. "Bill," the Director said. Mary felt the waves of persuasion rolling off the Director and gritted her teeth against the onslaught.

The man dipped his head in recognition. "Director."

"I want to see Bertrand," Steven said. More waves of pressure to cooperate washed over them.

Bill stepped back from the door as though letting them in, then he hesitated, pointing the gun at Mary. "What about her?"

"She's with me." The Director's honeyed voice oozed into Mary's ears. "You don't have to worry about her."

Bill squinted, but he was no match for Steven's persuasion. "I guess that'll be all right." He stepped aside, motioning them to enter ahead of him. "Down the hall." As they walked, she heard him radio ahead that he was bringing the Director and his assistant in. Assistant, huh? It would do.

Mary hadn't been inside the new research facility yet and was a little let down by an ordinary warehouse, a little too dark, with concrete floors and steel walls. Compared to the sleek, science-fiction construction in the underground offices under the bank, this looked awfully boring.

That all changed when she stepped through the door at the end of the hallway. The three of them entered a large room full of impressive equipment Mary couldn't identify, some of it still in boxes or half-assembled. She let out a low whistle of appreciation. Now she could see why the science guys were so heated up about this new facility. Tons of space to work with and a lot of new toys.

Bill, the gunman, nudged Mary in the ribs with his elbow and pointed her toward the rear quadrant of the room. "Back there."

A murmur of voices could be heard even at this distance, angry ones, in the middle of an argument. A young woman and an older man by the sound of it, and the man was growing louder and more bombastic by the moment. "Of course you're coming with us! You're the whole reason we're here."

"Bullshit." Mary recognized the woman's voice now. It was Cindy. She listened, but she didn't hear her mother.

Cindy's voice went on, "We both know you couldn't care less about me. You'd have let me rot there for the rest of my life if you'd been able to replicate my research. I'm here because you need me. You're not good enough to figure it out without me."

"I came to rescue you!"

"I didn't need to be saved!"

When they got close enough to see what was going on, Mary spotted Cindy Liu and Daniel Price standing a scant few inches apart, in identical postures of rage, fists clenched by their sides and faces red and distorted with vitriol. A man in camo stood nearby, gaze flicking between the two fighting scientists before he turned and stalked away. No one glanced their direction, and Mary took a moment to assess her surroundings.

Her mother was there, unharmed to all appearances. She was cuffed to an ordinary office chair. When Helen caught Mary's eye, she lifted one wrist to show she'd already melted the links. Good thinking. Get free, but let the enemy think she was still restrained. Mary's heart swelled with pride. Her mother wouldn't be very useful in hand-to-hand combat, if it came to that, not unless they wanted to kill their opponents. But at least now Mary knew her mother could get up and get out of the way if that was required; or burn it all down if that was what they needed.

She didn't see Mekai or Bertrand. But she knew they would be nearby. Bill the gunman didn't seem smart enough to think of taking them anywhere other than where they'd asked to go, especially with the Director offering a good, hard mental push.

Bill cleared his throat. "We've got company."

Daniel Price glared at his daughter one more time before he spun on his heel, turning his back on her. He lurched toward Mary and Steven, his awkward gait making Mary wonder if he might fall down in the process.

Thrusting out a hand, he greeted the Director with enthusiasm. "Steven! What a great facility you've built here!"

The Director shook his hand, exuding good will, as if Daniel were here at his invitation rather than part of a hostile takeover intended to extort cooperation out of the UCU. "Thanks. We're proud of it. I know we'll accomplish great things here."

"I know you will. I know you will." Daniel turned his attention to Mary, offering her his hand. "And you are?"

"Mary." Mary clasped the offered hand and suppressed a shudder of revulsion. She'd heard the story of how Cindy's father had spent the past century or so murdering other men and taking over their bodies to prolong his own longevity. It wasn't that she hadn't believed it. Sally Ann wouldn't lie to her. But hearing about it was different than shaking hands with a walking, talking corpse.

"My assistant," the Director offered.

"Oh? Did you fire the cute little blonde?" Daniel released Mary's hand and Mary fought the urge to rub her palm against her pants. "Was she… uncooperative?"

Daniel winked at the Director, at least that's what Mary thought he was doing. It looked more like he'd lost control of the left side of his face. Mary wanted to vomit for at least three reasons now.

Steven laughed chummily. "You could say that."

Mary caught Helen's eye again. She saw her disgust mirrored on Helen's face and admired her mother's self-control. Part of her hoped there would be a reason to immolate the man before the day was out, but the moment had not yet arrived.

Steven cleared his throat. "It's always good to see you, Daniel, but I'm here to talk to Bertrand."

A strange expression crossed Daniel's face. Anger? Resentment?

Wounded pride? Whatever it was, Mary perked up at the sight of it. That was good. There was already some kind of wedge between their enemies. They could exploit that. She hoped Steven noticed too.

"By all means, let's talk." The voice came from the shadows beyond Helen's office chair. Mary instantly tensed and tried to catch Steven's eye. Had he felt it? Gentle, but unmistakable—a push at the edges of her consciousness, an attempt to pry into her thoughts.

She slammed down a mental wall. Dear Lord, was Bertrand like Steven? What was Steven thinking, keeping this from her?

The man behind the voice stepped forward into the circle of light with two other men. The White man to Dietrich's left—the same one who left the area when they'd arrived—was dressed in camo like Bill and held one of the sci-fi weapons like they'd seen at the museum. His gaze slid over Mary but lingered on her breasts and hips instead of taking stock of her threat potential. Good. He'd underestimate her and she could use that, if necessary.

The Black man's face was much harder to read. This must be Mekai Davis. He was large and solid. A brick wall of a man, but he didn't hold himself stiffly. He, too, held a gun, but Mary didn't think disarming him would be enough to neutralize him as a threat. She swallowed, hoping Sally Ann was right about the potential to turn him to their side. He'd make a formidable ally, though, right now, she was worried about him as an opponent.

The old man between them looked frail, but his eyes were sharp. Too sharp. Mary noticed the probing sensation again and allowed her mental gate to flex a little. She didn't want him to know she could keep him out if she wanted to. At least not yet. She let a bit of nervous anxiety slide through the crack in her mental wall, and she saw when Bertrand perceived it. His stance relaxed, and he smiled at her before turning his attention to Steven.

The elderly man lowered himself into the chair Mekai pulled out for him. "I don't think we had an appointment today."

"True." Steven grabbed another chair and pushed it over to the small table where Bertrand sat, settling himself into as if he'd been invited. "But, then again, you didn't let me know you'd be in town."

Bertrand's mouth tightened into a displeased little line. "I don't report to you, Sonny."

Steven leaned forward, a bubble of intimidation flowing into the air between them. "No, but this," he gestured at the three men with guns, "is not part of the deal we made."

Bertrand tilted his head and held Steven's gaze for a long moment. He showed no sign he could feel Steven's attempted manipulation.

Mary's stomach dropped and new understanding dawned on her. Steven didn't know about Bertrand. He probably thought he had been manipulating the old man all this time. Dietrich played the Director so well he didn't even know it had happened.

They were in so much trouble.

THE STRONGMAN AND THE
LIZARD

Leonel stopped at the edge of the woods, bending over to rest his hand on his knees. Beside him, Patricia panted softly.

"Figures we're the ones who didn't get a car," he said.

Patricia poked him in the ribs. "You're getting soft, old man. We'll have to work on your cardio."

Having caught his breath, Leonel didn't waste any time defending himself against Patricia's teasing. "What do you see?" he asked, drawing a circle around his face with his finger to signal that she should look with her Lizard vision as well as her human eyes.

Patricia blinked, then leaned out past the tree and scanned the lot in front of them. After a few seconds, she stepped back into the shadows. "Nothing. No heat signatures. No movement. Not even any electrical signals. I don't think they're watching the perimeter."

"All right." Leonel straightened up and zipped his uniform shirt fully up to the neck. It restricted his movement a little, but it was worth it for the protection of the layers of Kevlar and other anti-ballistic materials. Taking a bullet was not an experience Leonel cared to repeat.

"Ladies first." He bowed to Patricia.

Patricia pulled at the edges of her yoga pants like they were a skirt and dropped something that was probably meant to be a curtsey. She strode off, taking a direct path toward the door they'd chosen for their entry point.

Leonel waited a moment before he followed, watching for any sign of detection or attack. He signaled Sally Ann that they had arrived and were going inside, three quick taps on the headset as agreed, avoiding chatter but keeping her updated.

As he took his first step, something rustled in the dry leaves of the tree above him. He peered up into the dark branches but didn't see anything. After a couple of seconds, a squirrel bounded out and leapt to another tree, and feeling foolish, Leonel hurried to follow Patricia.

He caught up with her standing at the door Sally Ann selected for their entrance. Leonel noted the mangled video camera above their heads and pointed at it. Patricia shrugged and dropped a chunk of wire and metal out of her taloned hand.

Shaking his head in mock disappointment, Leonel punched in the door code he'd been given but nothing happened. Maybe they changed the access code or cut the power. Either way, they weren't getting in that way.

With a sheepish grin at Patricia, he grabbed the handle and, with one good jerk, yanked the reinforced door off the hinges. He held the slab of metal for a long moment, waiting for alarms or the sound of running feet, Patricia tense and quiet beside him. When a few seconds passed and neither thing happened, he leaned the thick, steel door against the wall like it was a bomb that might explode, and gestured for Patricia to once again lead the way.

They'd studied the map together back at the Dact, and Patricia followed the route they'd agreed to try, one that would take them upstairs and around to an observation deck above the main floor. Helen had dropped a few clues suggesting that they'd find the interlopers in that main area, but they'd need to verify that.

When the stairs creaked with Patricia's first step onto them, she held a claw in the air to signal Leonel to wait, closed her eyes, and exhaled a long, slow stream of air.

Even though he'd seen it many times now, Leonel gawked as Patricia's spikes and bony protuberances withdrew and scales melted back into pale, freckled, human flesh. Patricia cracked her neck, set one bare foot on the stairwell, and bounded up, almost soundlessly.

Leonel did his best to step lightly, too, but he couldn't drop a hundred pounds at a moment's notice like Patricia. He winced each time the stairs creaked or shifted with his movement. Still, they arrived at the top without attracting any undue attention.

They squatted there together for a moment, listening. Distantly, Leonel could hear raised voices. It sounded like two arguments were going on at the same time.

Rolling back up to his feet, Leonel offered Patricia a hand. She waved it away and stood, stretching her arms above her head. When she moved them back to her sides, they were once again covered in green and golden scales, though she had not brought out her full armor and spikes.

Moving stealthily, the two heroes made their way toward the voices. Leonel caught snippets as they neared their destination.

"This isn't what we discussed—"

"Why should I—"

"You arrogant child, did you really think—"

"Calm down—"

When they arrived at the door to the observation deck, Leonel turned wide eyes on Patricia, wondering what they were about to walk in on. She spread her hands and shrugged, then pushed the door open and stepped through.

Leonel rolled through behind her, keeping low and dodging to the side in case of any gunfire or other attack. He needn't have bothered. The room below them was in chaos and no one so much as glanced their way.

He and Patricia watched for a long moment.

Cindy Liu and Daniel Price stood toe to toe, yelling at each other, while the Director and Bertrand Dietrich scowled at each other across a small table. Mary stood watching, open-mouthed. Three all-too-familiar armed men twitched nervously, changing the aim of their weapons every few seconds.

Then Mary moved. She crossed to the Director and took his hand in hers, a look of supreme concentration on her face. Leonel recognized the expression, remembering the way Mary extended her resistance to him when they fought the Six. He didn't understand what that meant right now—Mary was there to rein in the Director—but he trusted the young woman knew what she was doing.

The Director's face went pale then turned bright purple as he stood up so suddenly he flipped his chair over and sent it skittering across the floor. He lunged at the old man still seated across from him, screaming. "How dare you try to control me!"

A few yards away, Cindy Liu and her father circled one another, their yelling making a wave of incoherent words Leonel couldn't parse.

The armed men started moving, each in a different direction and a wall of fire rose, blocking the way. Leonel scanned the area for Helen and found her sitting in a desk chair off to the side, staring at the fire. It didn't look like she was doing anything, but he knew she must be responsible for the fire out of nowhere. He cheered her on in his mind, praying she'd keep control of the conflagration.

Out of the corner of his eye, Leonel spotted a flash of movement, but there wasn't time to investigate that now. Their team needed them down there. Leonel nudged Patricia and pointed at Mekai. She nodded her agreement, raising her armor and spikes to full intimidation levels.

"Now!" Leonel yelled as he leapt from the observation deck at Mekai Davis, landing just to the man's left and sweeping his legs to take the threat to the floor then moved to pin him there. Unfortunately, Mekai was on his back, which limited Leonel's options if he didn't want to suffocate or injure the man. Somewhere to the side, he heard Patricia let out a growl worthy of her dinosaurian kin followed by a bone-crunching collision.

He had to trust she could handle the other two gunmen though, because at that moment, Mekai reversed Leonel's hold and was trying to pin him on his back. Leonel didn't have time to check to see what she was doing.

Leonel didn't want to hurt Mekai, but he couldn't afford to let him hurt the others either. He thrust his leg out and swept Mekai's out from under him again, rolling at the same time. The two tumbled across the floor bumping into chairs and pieces of heavy equipment as they struggled together.

Separating, the two men got to their feet, circling one another. "I don't want to hurt you, Mekai," Leonel called out. "We don't have to do this."

"I'm afraid we do, actually." Mekai hadn't spoken—it was Bertrand.

The old man sat at the table alone now, the Director crumpled at his feet, blood dripping from the young man's ears, nose, and eyes.

Without warning, Leonel fell to his knees, as if he'd lost control of his limbs. He saw Patricia make a move in his direction, jumping over the large inert form at her feet, but then, she too, fell to her knees, crying out in pain or frustration. Behind her, the wall of fire still blazed, but Leonel couldn't see Helen.

Mekai lumbered toward Leonel, but his movement was awkward. He moved like a puppet who fought the strings meant to guide him, wobbling to the side and having to catch himself to remain upright.

Leonel's cranium roared with pain, and he gripped the sides of his head.

"That's about enough out of you." The voice was soft, but the tone was pure iron.

Leonel forced his streaming eyes open. Mary was on her feet, moving toward Bertrand. Righteous anger seemed to make her eyes glow.

Bertrand squared off against her. As his focus shifted, the pressure on Leonel's head lessened. He pushed himself up on one knee, ready to throw himself into the fray if Mary needed backup.

Mary jumped. She grabbed Bertrand by the head and held him, staring into his face like she might bend in and kiss him.

For a long moment, it was as if Leonel had gone deaf. All sound disappeared, and his ears howled from the strange pressure of the silence. The pressure built, and the pain intensified. Mary seemed almost to grow in size, and the old man's body started to tremble. Blood streamed from his nose, and then his ears, the brackish brown-red liquid running over Mary's hands and dripping on the floor.

All of them were frozen in place. Leonel couldn't tell if he was still being held by the psychic force that had pinned him there or if the scene in front of him made it impossible to look away. Beside him Mekai groaned, pressing his hands over his ears.

Then Mary let go. Bertrand fell backward. As the man's head bounced on the concrete floor, a psychic wave blew out from him with palpable force.

Then it was like a dome lifted. Leonel's head swam from the change in pressure, and he braced himself against the floor, groaning.

Mekai stopped mid-stride, his raised hand falling to his side. "Where am I?" he said, then dropped to the floor like a sandbag. Leonel reached a hand for Mary, who was wiping her bloody hands down her pants. Then she went out of focus and he collapsed face-first into darkness.

JESSICA'S MIXED MOTIVATIONS

Jessica crouched in the tree, transfixed as Leonel and Patricia slipped along the side of the warehouse. What the hell was going on? This was a UCU facility. What reason could Leonel and Patricia have to sneak into it? It didn't make sense. She'd picked the wrong night to reclaim her emeralds.

The darkening sky stretched overhead, beckoning. Jessica's muscles tensed. Her instincts screamed at her to go. Make her escape, find another place to hole up for the night, and come back when no one was here. This might be another trap.

A moment later, a loud wrenching noise broke the silence of the night, frightening a small flock of birds out of a nearby tree. Jessica couldn't help herself. She had to know.

Keeping close to the treetops, she flew along the perimeter until she could see the door. Now she understood the wrenching sound. The metal slab, torn from its hinges, leaned against the external wall. This was getting stranger by the minute. Not only were Leonel and Patricia sneaking around in the twilight, they had broken into a building owned by their own organization. Jessica's heart beat faster.

She darted through the doorway. This was foolish and she knew it. It couldn't lead anywhere good, but her emeralds were in there. Whatever was going on might be just the cover she needed to take them back and fly off into the night unnoticed. She would never get an opportunity this good again.

Shouts came from somewhere far away, near the center of the cavernous building by the sound of it. Jessica picked up speed. The hallways were maze-like and she didn't know how the building was laid out, so she was flying blind. More shouting and noises of heavy things shifting. Was there a fight going on?

Finding a staircase, she flew to the top, hoping to get to a vantage point where she could see the facility in its entirety. A few seconds later, she reached the roof. The building was set up, she could now see, with a wide, open section in the middle, with wrapping tiers surrounding it. She bolted for the middle then let herself sink.

The scene below her was hard to understand. A brawl had erupted. Smoke billowed, obscuring her view, and sparks flew off some of the equipment with terrifying pops and crackles. She stared at the chaos for a while, trying to figure out who was fighting with who and if anyone was winning.

There!— Leonel scrambled with someone on the floor, a muscular man in a dark suit. Nearby, another man, this one dressed in camo, rolled on the floor shrieking and flailing to put out the flames engulfing his jacket. Patricia punched a man holding a gun and he dropped bonelessly to the ground, his weapon skittering away, disappearing into a wall of fire, and exploding.

Inexplicably, the resulting fireball collapsed and extinguished. Jessica twirled—not so inexplicable after all: Helen Braeburn stood at the periphery, wiping sweat out of her eyes.

Was that the Director at the table, struggling with an old man? Who the heck was that? The Director seemed suspended — held back from making contact with the old man despite his flailing attempts to attack, his shoes slipping out from under him as he howled in frustration. The old man smiled, holding up a finger like he was scolding a small child. The Director's face darkened, and he clutched at his throat.

Jessica hovered, watching, her heart pulling her in eight directions at once. How would she even *find* her emeralds in all this chaos? Could Leonel and Patricia handle this fight alone? She owed them her life, she knew, yet they would lock her away given the chance and take her emeralds from her. Jessica darted around, trying to get a better view while her mind spun.

One voice echoed in the rafters, audible above the cacophony of all the others. "My work is mine!" Jessica zeroed in on the source just in time to see Cindy Liu rush at a man in a lab coat and drive a long sharp object through his eye. She flew toward them but not fast enough to stop Cindy. She pulled her dive at the last moment, hovering above the scene, aghast.

The man—she now recognized Daniel Price—fell to the ground, twitching while a puddle of blood gathered under him and soaked the shoulders of his white lab coat. Cindy pulled the spike out of his eye and stood holding it in front of her, drops of blood falling onto the floor and oozing down the spike toward her hands.

The world spiraled in, until all the other chaos in the room fell away and all Jessica could see was Cindy Liu, standing over the dead man, frozen. They both watched Price twitch until he stopped, still at long last. They stared transfixed a long moment beyond that.

Then Cindy seemed to come back into herself. She swung her head wildly as she took in the scene, dropped her weapon, grabbed a box that looked like a small metal cooler, turned on her heel, and ran for the entrance. No one pursued her. Cindy Liu was going to get away.

Before she knew she had decided to do it, Jessica was in motion, picking up speed and hurtling toward the slender woman's back as she fled.

HELEN PICKS HER MOMENT

Helen had never been so glad for middle-aged invisibility in her life. The square-headed asshole hadn't even bothered to search her for weapons. Not that he'd have found any. Helen was her own weapon.

"Okay, Grandma," he'd said, shoving her down so hard the office chair almost rolled out from under her. "You wait here." He cuffed her wrist to the armrest. She made a little whimpering sound, channeling her best imitation of a helpless old woman frightened by an idiot who thought strapping a woman to a chair with wheels would keep her in place.

He stood beside her, holding his big gun like it might make up for the size of his intellect and his other likely shortcomings. If this is all they were up against, the fight would be short. She might not even get to set anything on fire. Honestly, she was disappointed.

Then a man in a lab coat entered the area, set a small metal box to one side, and lurched across the room, arms outspread. "Cindy, liebchen. You're here!"

When everyone's attention focused on him, Helen took the opportunity to melt the links that held her cuffed wrist to the chair. She didn't know what she might need to do, but whatever it was, it would be easier if she didn't have to lug office furniture around with her. Best to keep her options open.

At the sound of the man's voice, Cindy Liu's entire body went rigid. If anger were electricity, the entire room would have been engulfed in lightning. "Vengeance," she'd said, back in the car. This scarecrow must be Cindy's father aka Daniel Price, the object of her ire.

He certainly didn't look intimidating. Maybe five foot six or seven, average build, wire-rimmed glasses, a lab coat, and an unsteady gait that reminded Helen of someone recovering from a stroke. But looks were never the whole story. She herself was evidence of that. Cindy even moreso.

As the man hobbled toward her, Cindy rolled her neck and bounced on her feet like a boxer preparing for a fight. *Oh my, this was going to be good.* When he got within reach, the diminutive scientist pulled back her arm and struck him hard across the face, a good, resounding smack that rocked his head to the side.

Beside her, the square-headed oaf with his emotional support gun gasped. Helen suppressed a grin, watching Daniel scramble to keep his feet. Clearly, all of Cindy's time incarcerated had not taken the fire out of her.

A radio crackled and Helen's guard pulled it from his pocket and held it to his ear. Helen couldn't hear what was said, but she knew that the man was annoyed by the way he shoved the radio back into his pants and backed slowly away from the scene. He would much rather have stayed there watching this confrontation unfold than go deal with whatever he'd been called to manage.

To Helen's surprise, Daniel waved off help from the other gunman and yelled at him when he tried to intervene with Cindy. "Keep your hands off my daughter, you misbegotten moron!"

The gunman raised his hands in the air and took a step back, shaking his head as he did so. Helen turned her chair to watch the fight unfold, wondering how much of this Sally Ann and the rest of the crew back on the Dact were able to pick up. Cindy and Daniel circled each other now, Cindy waving her hands to emphasize her points while Daniel slowly revolved, struggling to get a word in edgewise.

"You don't understand," he managed.

"No. You're the one who doesn't understand." Cindy stalked toward him, fists clenched at her sides. Was she going to hit him again?

Movement pulled Helen's eye away from the argument. Mary had just entered the room alongside the Director, following Helen's favorite guard. With the one guard returned, the other stormed out. Someone didn't like being told no. He was about to miss the good part.

The next phase was beginning.

While everyone was focused on the argument, Helen held up her wrist with the dangling chain to show Mary that she had freed herself, then slipped her hand back into position so she still appeared restrained.

Stopping a few feet away from the bickering father and daughter, the guard cleared his throat. "We've got company."

That broke up the argument for now, and Daniel staggered toward the pair. Helen kept her eyes on Cindy, trusting her daughter Mary to manage the next bit. Abandoned mid-tirade, Cindy's sweaty face burned a deep purplish red and her eyes blazed like hot coals in her unlined face. She spun away from the scene and stomped toward Helen, kicking at the cabinets and crates in her path.

Something fell off the top of one of them, and Cindy picked it up. A long metal pole extended from a plastic stand, like a miniature flagpole. Helen thought she'd seen something like it in Cindy's basement laboratory, with test tubes clamped to it. A sense of foreboding filled Helen as she watched Cindy examine it.

Beyond Cindy, Helen could see Mary. She, the Director, and Daniel were joined by three other men: one so old that he looked like a stiff breeze might take him out, the square-head who didn't like "no" seemed to have picked up a fancier gun while having his snit, and the tall, broad gorgeous mountain of a man dressed in a suit that showed off his physique who had met Cindy and her at the door. He was Mekai Davis, the one Sally Ann wanted to recruit. Helen wouldn't mind having a chance to work with him. He could give Fuerte a run for his money when it came to well-muscled beauty.

This new trio moved to a table, ignoring Daniel Price and leaving him standing alone in the center of the room. Mary remained at a distance, edging closer to her mother. Helen tensed, not sure where she should focus her attention—on the trio at the table or on Cindy and her father.

Daniel Price purpled with rage when the others walked away from him, but he didn't do or say anything. He glared at the old man, his whole chest heaving and his hands clenched in front of him. Helen watched as he lurched toward the table only to stop after a couple of steps. He groped at his head like it pained him.

The conversation at the table began amiably enough, but Price spun away right as it grew heated, his eyes searching the room. Helen wasn't sure what he was looking for, but his path was blocked by Cindy Liu, who still held the strange lab implement she'd picked up, twirling it in her hands, testing its weight. Helen put both her feet on the floor, ready to spring into action.

All at once, everyone was yelling. Dietrich and the Director leaned across the table now, faces near enough that they could bite one another, and Cindy Liu closed the distance between herself and her father while he stumbled away from her. A strange look came over Mary's face, and then she was at the table, too, her hand on the Director's.

The guards got antsy, and Helen made her move, raising a wall of fire separating the guards from everyone else. And that's when Fuerte and Patricia leapt into the fray from somewhere above.

MARY'S SPHERE OF INFLUENCE

Mary tried to watch everything all at once, but there was too much happening. Once Bertrand Dietrich arrived, the Director had unleashed the full force of his persuasive powers and for a moment, the vertigo of both psychic men exerting their skill threatened to knock Mary over. It was like riding the tilt-a-whirl with your head in the foot space while a couple of giants pulled on your legs like the two sides of a wishbone.

Luckily, Dietrich had dismissed her almost immediately and wasn't treating her as a threat. She slammed down protective gates in her mind, and her equilibrium came back into balance. After a moment, Mary could think again.

Steven doesn't know. The realization still glowed in her brain in dangerous orange neon. If she intervened, Bertrand would notice her and then her day would get a whole lot worse very quickly. If she didn't, the Director's arrogance might get them all killed anyway.

Bertrand's power dwarfed the Director's. She didn't know if she was strong enough to keep him out of her brain if he focused the full force of his influence in her direction.

Mary glanced over to make sure her mother was okay and found her focused on Daniel Price and Cindy Liu. Before she could talk herself out of it, Mary crossed the few steps to the table where the two men sat talking. Ignoring the armed guards, she stepped to Steven's side and took his hand.

Closing her eyes, she imagined her awareness like a bubble and stretched it wider until it encompassed them both. The Director's eyes went wide in sudden comprehension, and Mary felt a wave of fear and anger erupt from him like a tongue of fire. She snatched her hand back, breaking the connection.

Steven leapt from his chair, flipping the chair over so it clattered across the floor. Bertrand's eyes snapped to Mary for a moment, and her blood ran cold before he refocused on Steven. She distinctly heard, "I'll deal with you next," even though the old man had not opened his mouth.

"How dare you try to control me!" The Director's face had drained of color, but as he screamed his outrage, it darkened to a dangerous shade. He lunged at the old man, hands outstretched. At the same time, a wall of fire arose and two loud thumps resounded.

Mary spun. Her mother stood, her face tense with concentration, her focus on the flaming barrier now blazing between the gunmen and the group at the table. Through the flames, Mary could make out the silhouettes of Patricia and Leonel.

She froze, trying to figure out which way to turn. Should she protect her mother? Join the fight with the guards? None of this was in the plan. She had been sent to hold the Director to his word, not take down armed men or put out literal fires.

As she waffled, Cindy Liu hurtled past, knocking Mary with her shoulder as she raced toward the door. Right behind her, Jessica flew, gaining on the mad scientist with each second. Dodging the speeding woman, Mary landed on her ass with a solid thump.

Jessica was there? That was definitely not part of the plan. Did Sally Ann know?

A wet gurgling pulled Mary's attention back to the scene at the table. The Director hung suspended, the toes of his fancy shoes scraping the floor but not really making contact. His eyes were wild with panic. He clutched at his throat, but there was nothing for him to grab. Tears streamed down his cheeks, blending with the blood pouring from his nose and ears and leaving his face a messy torment.

Bertrand shook one finger at him, almost casually, like he was indulgently admonishing a wayward child. A strange light filled his eyes— something gleeful and at the same time cold. He was enjoying this! *The bastard.*

Back on her feet, Mary lunged for Steven's hand, but with a flick of his wrist, Bertrand swept the man several feet to one side as easily as tossing a handkerchief. Mary grabbed at empty air. Glaring at her, Dietrich squeezed his hand closed and a horrid cracking sound let her know that the Director was beyond all help now. Bertrand opened his fist, and Steven collapsed at the old man's feet in a heap of inarticulate limbs, staring vacantly from now-empty eyes.

Mary threw up.

Somewhere behind her, Leonel shouted. "We don't have to do this!"

Bertrand sat back down in his chair, crossing his legs and tugging his trousers into a perfect line. His gaze didn't waver from Mary's face, nor did he open his mouth, but his voice emanated from Leonel's direction. "I'm afraid we do, actually."

Pressure built, and Mary heard a high-pitched whine. She tore her gaze from Bertrand's and saw it as one by one, everyone else fell to their knees or dropped entirely to the floor. The gunmen, her mother, Patricia, and finally Leonel all succumbed. Only the man in the suit kept moving and his gait was awkward and off-balance. When Leonel howled in agony, Mary's anger spiked through her with the clarity of a gunshot.

"That's about enough out of you," she said, squeezing the words through her gritted teeth. She took a step toward the man. Instantly an invisible wall arose between them, but Mary took another step forward, and yet one more, pushing past the resistance.

Surprise lit Bertrand's gaunt face, then something else. Delight? "Interesting. I thought something was off about you." He stood, wobbling only a little as he got to his feet. He tilted his head and waved her on. "Let's see what you've got, little girl."

Mary closed the remaining space between them in a single jump. She reached for Bertrand's head, pressing one hand against each ear. He waited, seeming to study her.

She ignored the scrutiny, closing her eyes and concentrating fully on her power. Stretching the bubble of her influence again, like she did when she wanted to protect someone, she imagined her power as a physical sphere surrounding the elderly man's head, something like an astronaut's helmet.

The man trembled, the shake barely perceptible, but undeniably there. Mary peeked—peering at the old bastard through slitted lids.

Bertrand's eyes narrowed, and she began to feel his pushback, like the force of someone else's forearm in an arm-wrestling match. He increased the pressure, trying to inch her backward, but Mary kept her focus on the bubble, thickening the layers.

Anger shrieked so loudly in her mind that Mary's vision went white for a moment, but she persisted through the pain, eyes clamped shut. Bertrand's bony fingers clasped her wrists, and it was hard to tell if he was holding them to keep himself upright or trying to make her let go. There was no strength in his fingers.

It didn't matter. With each mental push, the addition of each new layer of the sphere, the force of Bertrand's influence dampened. His mental shouting diminished in intensity until it was like overhearing an argument in another apartment through the wall, muffled and ill-defined. Only then did she dare reopen her eyes.

Bertrand's pale gray eyes were wide now, and watery as busted capillaries made the whites red. Blood flowed from his nose, but he made no attempt to wipe it away. All the remaining color leached from his pasty flesh until he looked more a ghost than a flesh and blood man. Mary's palms grew wet, and she realized the asshole was bleeding from the ears as well. Disgusted, she released her grip, letting him slide to the ground.

He fell back into the chair then slid out of it and onto the floor. His head bounced on the concrete floor with a clonk like a fallen coconut, and he twitched a couple of times, and then the world tilted and righted itself.

"That's what I've got, old man," Mary said, wiping her bloody hands down the legs of her pants.

JESSICA'S CROSSROADS

By the time Jessica caught up, Cindy had nearly reached the door at the other end of the facility. Jessica gripped Cindy by one arm and swung her around.

Cindy screamed as she spun. "Let me go!"

"As you wish." Jessica let go.

Momentum forced Cindy Liu to one side, and despite all her struggles to slow herself or change her trajectory, she collided hard with a row of metal cabinets and crumpled to the floor. The case she'd carried broke free of her fingers and bounced a few feet away. The impact must have dazed her because she sat there, making no attempt to get up and get away.

Jessica flew to her side and lowered herself to the ground. "What the hell is going on here?" she demanded. She grabbed the woman by her clothing, pulling her up hard and fighting the urge to shake her. "Where are my emeralds?"

Cindy raised a hand to her head, a couple fingers bent wrong, and wiped blood across her brow as she stared up at Jessica, her pupils black pinpoints. "It's my father." Her voice was shaky and thick. "I think... I think I killed him for real this time."

Jessica let Cindy slide from her grip and squinted back at the other side of the room, taking a couple steps until she knocked against the metal box, but it was too far away for her to tell what was happening. She crouched down to pick up the container before returning to the woman who changed her life, surprised to find something like concern welling up within her. "Yeah," she said. "I think maybe you did."

She grabbed Cindy's arms and tugged her to her feet. "Come on. Let's go."

Cindy's movements were clumsy and slow, but she didn't try to pull away and Jessica half-guided, half-carried her back across the facility, the movement made even more awkward by the metal case Jessica lugged in her other hand. If Cindy thought the case worth stealing, it must house the UCU collection of emeralds. Jessica wasn't going to give up the chance to reclaim them for herself.

When they drew near, she gasped. The scene was littered with bodies —Jessica identified them as she scanned the area, feelings of relief and dismay swirling through her with each discovery.

Helen lay on her side, and Mary squatted beside her. Flame flickered in the palm of one hand each time Mary jostled her mother, so she was alive at least, if unconscious. Most of the fire was out, too, so Flamethrower had controlled that better than Jessica would have guessed.

A few feet away, Patricia lay on her stomach, working to push herself up onto all fours. Her transformation moved back and forth at random as she struggled to regain control. She locked eyes with Cindy, and Jessica would have sworn that she saw relief on the Lizard Woman's face.

Daniel Price lay where they'd left him, the pool of blood around his head continuing to spread. The old man now lay on his back, unmoving, one skeletal hand stretched toward an overturned table. All three of the gunmen, including Mekai, were holding their heads and groaning. The closest things to bystanders in the group were still alive then.

Beside Mekai, a large man in a red shirt lay face down on the floor, unmoving. Dropping Cindy unceremoniously next to her father's corpse, Jessica flew to Leonel's side and rolled him over. "No-no-no-no-no-no!" She chanted it like an incantation, willing truth into her words. He couldn't be dead. He couldn't!

She felt for a pulse in his wrist and his throat, where the cut she had inflicted that morning when she had held a knife to it accused her of her failure, all her failures, but her own heart was beating so fast she couldn't tell what was her and what might be him. She thrust her head against his chest, listening. Gripping the material of his jacket, she closed her eyes and tried to focus, tears rolling down her cheeks. After a few seconds, a hand landed on her shoulder. Jessica jumped, scooting away from Leonel on her backside.

"Let me." Mary dropped to her knees beside the inert man and repeated everything Jessica had just tried, minus the panic.

Jessica curled her legs against her chest and rolled into a ball. She held her breath, her brain frozen in a white fog of panic. She couldn't make herself watch what Mary was doing, but she assumed she was administering CPR based on the fast-paced counting.

At long last, Mary fell back and let out a sigh. "He's breathing."

The two women had time to share a weary stare of mutual understanding before the sounds of running feet made them look away. Sally Ann burst into the room, followed by several blue-suited agents. Jessica stood, wavering between a desire to fly away and wanting to stay. While she waffled, Sally Ann drew a weapon out of her belt, aimed it at Jessica, and pulled the trigger. Whirling, Jessica stumbled into a table, knocking it over, and revealing the Director lying beneath, the light in his eyes gone cold and blood streaming down his face. She yelped.

Jessica leapt for the sky, only to feel the tug of something wrapped around her ankle, an anchor tethering her to the earth. Her head whirled and she landed on her bottom, feet kicking at the hand holding her. The grip was fierce, and Jessica forced her eyes to focus, folding the multiple blurry images into one man in a red shirt who wouldn't let go. She kicked at Leonel's chest, but it was a weak feint. It wouldn't have worked on a man with half Leonel's strength, and it definitely wouldn't work on Fuerte. Tears blurred her vision as she struggled.

"Jessica," he said, his voice rough with pain and sadness. "Jessica, you've got to stay. We need you. Your boys need you. I need you. We can get you help. Please let us help you."

Jessica's head swam. What had Sally Ann shot her with? It was hard to think. Her eyes sought Cindy and the metal case. The emeralds. Why else would Cindy have taken it? Rage overtook her and she raised her free leg, preparing to bring it down on Leonel's skull with all the strength left in her.

But before she could, another needle pricked her neck, and she was falling into darkness, someone's arms wrapping around her and lowering her to the floor. "Not again," she groaned before she collapsed into a heap.

SALLY ANN ON THE SCENE

The aftermath of a battle was always a logistical nightmare, even when you're on the winning side, and Sally Ann's head throbbed. Gabe kept circling around and trying to make her sit down, but Sally Ann was fed up with resting and sitting on the sidelines. Her team had been forced to fight in the field without her, and the results were horrific. It was up to her to take over now.

She scanned the building again, cataloging the damage and casualties.

Half the UCU medical staff were on site, working alongside Springfield's regular EMTs to minister the wounded while agents freed their coworkers, most of whom had been injured when the facility had been taken, and secured the prisoners, all of whom also needed medical care. They'd sent back for more stretchers.

One of the gunmen suffered serious burns, another had a broken arm and damaged jaw. Dr. Liu was catatonic. They strapped Jessica, still unconscious, to the gurney so she didn't float away.

Mekai Davis, former henchman to Dietrich, broke his hand punching one of the supporting pillars when the full range of mental manipulation he'd suffered the past few years came into focus. When someone told him that Bertrand Dietrich was already dead, he dropped to his knees, deflated. He sat on the ground just out of range of the pool of blood surrounding Daniel Price's dead-again body, running one hand over his head, clutching the other to his body, and contemplating his shoes.

Agent Lucas Austin sat by his side talking quietly with him. Sally Ann relaxed. Austin was their best talent recruiter. He was the man who'd brought in Patricia. He'd helped recruit Sally Ann herself. Mekai was in good hands.

Sally Ann was piecing together the full story of what happened, connecting the dots based on what they'd heard in surveillance, what she saw now, and what the survivors reported. There were a lot of contradictions, and a chaotic scene sprawled across the facility. It would take time to understand the full story and all the ramifications.

She stood looking down at the three corpses. Bertrand Dietrich lay on his back, eyes staring sightlessly at the rafters, expression frozen in something like surprise. Daniel Price or Anton Lorre or whatever Cindy Liu's father had become, was dead again, permanently this time to judge by the congealing pool of blood surrounding his head and soaking the shoulders of his lab coat.

And Steven. The Director. Their boss, their betrayer, one of their team. A whirl of emotions washed over her, anger, relief, worry, and fear, cycling over each other until she thought she might vomit. Someone stepped up next to her and squeezed her hand. Sally Ann spun in surprise to find herself face to face with Suzie Grayson, phone at the ready.

"How can I help? What do you need that we don't have yet?"

"A plan to move forward." Sally Ann gestured at the body at her feet. "We seem to be an organization with no one at the helm at the moment."

Suzie snorted. "He wasn't much of a leader in the first place. We don't need him. We've got you and we've got me, and we're more than a match for this. I say good riddance to bad rubbish." She paused, her expression inscrutable and cold in a way that made Sally Ann glad she couldn't read minds more directly.

The phone in Suzie's hand chimed and she took a step away, answering questions and giving orders in rapid succession. "Of course they'll have to be guarded. Yes, I'll approve the overtime. Just make sure none of them are left unguarded."

Sally Ann realized she hadn't even thought about security for the prisoners. She'd been too focused on care for the fallen and understanding what happened. Leave it to Suzie to notice the things that might have fallen through the cracks otherwise.

Suzie hung up and turned back to Sally Ann. "All right. Walk me through it. Let's start with the dead. What happened to the Director?"

Sally Ann pointed at the old man lying on the floor a few feet away. "Bertrand Dietrich."

Suzie wrinkled her brow. "This old guy? He's got to be eighty if he's a day." She squatted down to peer at the corpse on the ground as if it were a particularly interesting bug. "I know Steven was hardly Leonel, but this guy looks like he'd have trouble fighting his way out of a wet paper bag. What the hell happened?"

Mary walked up. Her pants were stained with bloody handprints, vomit streaked her shirt front, and she still looked a little green under the gills, but she was at least upright. She'd been able to walk out on her own power and see her mother into the ambulance. "Mom's all right. She's dehydrated and has a hell of a headache, but Doc Suggs isn't worried. She's already trying to flirt with Leonel."

Sally Ann squeezed Mary's shoulder. "That's great news. Could you tell Suzie what you told me, about Bertrand and what happened to Steven?"

Mary grabbed a chair and straddled it. Sally Ann squelched her desire to tell the woman not to move anything because it was evidence. Old habits from her police days died hard. Mary downed a bottle of water that a passing medical tech thrust into her hand, then took a deep breath, and launched into her tale, recounting how she'd detected Bertrand's manipulations and how Steven lost his shit and threw himself at the old man when she revealed it to him. "Bertrand never even touched him. He did this with his mind."

"That's disturbing," Suzie said, not sounding the least bit disturbed, or even ruffled. She gestured at the corpse at her feet with one pointy-toed shoe. "So what happened to Bertrand then?"

There was a long pause during which Mary played with the empty water bottle in her hands. Finally, she lifted her chin and looked them both in the eyes before she spoke, a defiant flame lighting her gaze. "I did." Mary's chin wobbled, and she clamped her mouth shut with a determination Sally Ann recognized for an attempt to hold in emotions.

Sally Ann nodded, widening her eyes at Suzie to stifle further questions. "You can tell us about it after you get some rest. We'll take things from here. Go get cleaned up."

Suzie opened her mouth but closed it again when Sally Ann shook her head at her. This wasn't the time.

Mary stood, took a few steps away, then called back to Suzie. "Oh yeah, Patricia's arguing with the med techs about the fluids. I was supposed to ask you if you could come talk her down. She keeps breaking their IV needles by transforming her arm at the last second."

A strained note crept into Suzie's voice. "All right. Tell them I'll be right there."

Sally Ann arched an eyebrow. "You okay?"

"Me? Oh yeah, I'm fine." Suzie sighed. "It's just that Patricia can be…a bit much sometimes, you know."

"Preaching to the choir, Sister Suzie." As Suzie turned to walk out, Sally Ann grabbed her arm. "You know she's a grown-ass woman, right? You know you don't have to put up with her shit."

Suzie's eyes glimmered with something that might have been tears for a second. "I know. I haven't decided what I want yet."

"Fair enough. But if you need backup, you know I've got you."

Suzie nodded, then made her way to the exit, her heels clicking on the concrete and echoing in the high ceiling.

Another agent came up to her, saluting. Must have been one of their military recruits, a young man whose face she didn't recognize. "What do we do with them, ma'am?"

"Bag 'em. Take them to Walter Peeples at HQ. His team will want to examine all three of them, I'm sure."

"Yes, ma'am."

Sally Ann didn't linger to watch her former boss take up his new residence in a zippered bag. She had the living to worry about.

TUESDAY, ONE WEEK LATER

PATRICIA, ENDINGS AND BEGINNINGS

Patricia closed the door behind her and stood leaning against it for a moment. It had been another fraught visit with Cindy Liu. She was healing from her physical wounds, already down to a few bandages, but the psychic wounds were going to take longer.

In her heart, Patricia believed Daniel deserved to die. Or rather, Anton Lorre did. Daniel Price, she reminded herself, died many years before, when he got too close to Anton's nasty secret. The poor man's body had been taken over by Cindy Liu's father, the last in a string of stolen lives. So, from that perspective it wasn't murder. It was more like beheading a zombie, wasn't it? Putting down something that shouldn't have been alive in the first place. Not that Cindy could see it that way.

Yes, Anton Lorre deserved to die, but Patricia understood that killing him herself had been a whole new order of magnitude for her former best friend. In spite of all the damage Cindy wrought in the world, she never intended to harm anyone. Her goal had always been to help, but it was her hand wielding this weapon, skewering Daniel's—Anton's—brain.

Cindy grew up thinking her father had died in her early childhood, then got him back a few years ago, only to eventually orphan herself all over again. It would take time. At least time was something Cindy had plenty of, having reset her body's clock. If all went well, she'd have another six or seven decades ahead of her.

It might be enough.

~

FOOTSTEPS SOUNDED in the hallway behind her, and Patricia turned around to see who approached. Leonel came barreling around the corner, Suzie by his side. Suzie was briefing him for his next meeting, the one where they informed the mayor of Springfield about the unfortunate loss of the former Director in the line of duty and Leonel's assumption of the mantle of leadership for the UCU.

It took them the bulk of the past few days to convince Leonel to accept the position. Sally Ann talked to him about the importance of calm rationality in the face of impossible situations. Suzie presented him with statistics about his popularity with the citizens of Springfield and what a difference he could make in the role. Mary and Helen told him there was no one they'd trust more to help the organization find its heart again. David supported them, as it would pull Leonel out of the field.

Patricia herself had been the deciding factor. She'd sat him down and told him to stop being a baby. He was the only person for the job, and if he didn't accept it, she would take him out back and thrash him until some sense got knocked into him.

"You really think so?" he'd asked, all sad puppy dog eyes.

"Absolutely," she'd said. And she'd meant it. "The fact you don't want the job is a good sign. You'll make sure we stay on the right side of things."

"That's a lot of pressure," Leonel said.

"It is," Patricia agreed. "But your strength has never been about your muscles, Leonel. It's about your heart. Listen to your heart and let it steer you."

Now, she fell into step with Suzie and Leonel and elbowed him in the ribs. "Just smile at her and flex your muscles, Big Guy. She'll fall at your feet."

"*Dios mío*, I hope not."

Suzie glared at Patricia. "You're not helping. Go bug someone else."

Patricia shoved down the spike of irritation at Suzie's rough words. She was trying hard to follow Suzie's lead and figure out what their relationship would be now. She held up her hands in surrender. "Alright, alright. You don't have to worry, Leonel. The press already loves you—and Sally Ann will take it out of Darrin's hide personally if he says anything unflattering about you."

Stealing a quick squeeze of Suzie's shoulder, Patricia spun on her heel to turn left at the intersection, making for the medical wing, leaving Leonel sputtering in Suzie's capable hands.

Two armed guards stood outside Jessica's hospital room. Gaining admittance required a radio call to Leonel, and the scanning of Patricia's identification badge. They were taking security seriously. Jessica was the epitome of "flight risk." They confiscated Patricia's shard of emerald, promising to return it when she left the room. Patricia's heart sank at the thought of the long road ahead of them all and was reconsidering this visit when one of the guards opened the door and gestured her in.

Taking a deep breath, Patricia crossed the threshold. She stopped one step inside the door when she found Walter and Sally Ann were already there. "Excuse me." She moved to duck back out.

"Come in," Jessica said. "Please," she added, when Patricia hesitated.

Patricia complied, though she felt awkward about it. Sally Ann patted the seat next to her and Patricia perched there, legs folded in tightly to try to take up less space. Walter was seated on Jessica's bed, stroking her forehead.

Jessica looked terrible. So pale that it was hard to tell where she ended and the bedsheets began. The room was cool, but her short blond hair was dark with sweat, plastered to her skull, matted and ratty. A smell of panic and antiseptic wafted from her. Her cheeks were wet with recently shed tears.

The scene made Patricia jittery, so she cleared her throat. "How's our patient doing today?"

All three sets of eyes turned on Patricia, and she wished she'd kept her damned trap shut. She'd always been horrible at this part. What possessed her to even come there today? Jessica had her mother, her husband, and the rest of the team. All of them were better suited to providing care and distraction. She didn't need Patricia bursting in like the proverbial bull. There was nothing here to punch on her behalf.

Jessica cleared her throat. "Walter, Sally Ann, could you give me a moment with Patricia?"

Both of them were startled at the request, but they agreed and made their way out the door. Walter squeezed her arm as he walked by, and Sally Ann widened her eyes in a way that Patricia understood as a warning to behave herself. Patricia froze in place at Jessica's bedside, fighting the urge to run after them and make them stay.

As soon as the door was closed, Jessica said, "I need to ask you a favor."

Patricia swallowed. "All right. What do you have in mind?"

"I need you to be my accountability partner."

Patricia was sure she'd misheard her. "What?"

Jessica bunched the sheets in her hands, the motion revealing the straps that kept her tethered to the bed. Patricia already knew Jessica sometimes sleep-flew, so she was a flight risk in more than one way as she struggled to find her balance and break the hold the emeralds had over her.

Patricia sighed. "Why me?"

Jessica waved a hand at the door Sally Ann and Walter had passed through. "Walter is too soft. He's so happy I'm back that he's ready to forgive me everything and welcome me with open arms. Sally Ann blames herself for not noticing what was going on sooner and intervening."

Patricia opened her mouth to confess she felt the same way but snapped it shut when Jessica's voice broke into a sob. "And Leonel—oh, Patricia, I hurt him so much."

Before she knew she was going to, Patricia reached out and took Jessica's hand. "He isn't going to hold a grudge."

Jessica cried harder. "No, he isn't. And that makes it worse. He should hate me for the horrible things I said and did to him when he was trying to help. But he won't." She squeezed Patricia's hand. "I'll always know I don't deserve his forgiveness, even if he thinks I do."

Pulling her fingers free, Jessica wiped at her eyes. Patricia grabbed the tissues off the table and handed her the box, counting the tiles in the floor while Jessica hiccupped, blew her nose, and calmed herself down.

"So, why me?" she finally asked again.

"Because you'll keep a clear head and call me on it when I falter," she said. "Because you don't love me, at least not like they do, and you won't let affection cloud your judgment when it matters." She turned her puffy, tear-reddened fact to Patricia. "Please. I need you."

Patricia stood up, crossed to the door and opened it, staring into the hallway. The long, white walls stretched as far as she could see, and part of her longed to flee—just take off running and never come back. But she couldn't do that, wouldn't do that, not to Jessica. Not to any of them. Speaking over her shoulder, she said. "Okay, I will."

She paused, palm against the door. Before she slipped through, she added, "You're wrong about one thing though." She stepped through, not daring to make eye contact with the woman strapped to the hospital bed. "I do love you."

The door fell closed behind her, and Patricia leaned against it for a long moment before she squared her shoulders and strode down the hall.

END

ACKNOWLEDGMENTS

It's been the journey of ten years and two publishers to see this little idea of mine to completion. Who knew that a silly comment to my husband about hormones causing superpowers would eventually manifest as five novels, two novellas, and a collection of short stories? The Menopausal Superheroes series is complete!

I'm grateful to a LOT of people, but my family gets top billing for their support and encouragement. I'm fortunate to have people in my life who will let me rant, help me get back on the horse I fell from, brainstorm with me, will let me ignore them and my other responsibilities for long hours at a stretch while I actually write the suckers, then celebrate with me when we've made it to the end. We're going to need a really great cake for this one, multiple layers. Ice cream, too.

My critique partners struggled through all of this with me, multiple versions, long conversations, and pushes to do the hard stuff when I didn't want to. So, my thanks to WIP and Dulce, my two creative collectives. It's scary out there and no one wants to go alone. My professional organizations also offered me support and advice when I needed it most. Thank you to the Women's Fiction Writers Association and the NC Chapter of the Horror Writers Association. You were great companions for this journey, and I look forward to taking on the next one with you.

My wider writing community of other writers, publishers, bloggers, and friends helped me keep my head up when I thought I'd never get to "the end." The real reward really is the friends I made along the way... though I wouldn't turn down some actual cash dollars or an invitation to Hollywood either.

Most importantly, I have to thank the readers! Writing books is lonely work by its nature, but the connection with readers is what it's all about. It'll never cease to thrill me that complete strangers are read my work and find an expression of themselves in it, too. Thanks so much for coming on this ride with me. I hope you love where it ended.

ABOUT THE AUTHOR

If you're looking for Samantha Bryant, check the woods first. She likes to get lost there in order to find herself, and she's probably near the water. She's a fan of the small beauties of life, especially the ones Mother Nature made and enjoys taking macro photographs of the things she finds on her walks. Her rescue dogs think this is a great idea because it means they get lots of time to romp in the sunshine.

In her writing life, Samantha mostly writes superhero and horror stories, which one depends on whether she wants to save the world today, or burn it down. She also likes to play in other genres from time to time, including science fiction, literary fiction, and poetry. Her influences have been mostly complex, complicated, and problematic women, full of passion and willing to make trouble to make a difference.

Check out her full catalog on her website http://samanthabryant.com or find her wasting time on several social media platforms as @samanthabwriter.

ALSO BY SAMANTHA BRYANT

<u>Menopausal SuperHeroes</u>

Book 1: Going Through the Change

Book 1.5: Friend or Foe (novella)

Book 2: Change of Life

Book 3: Face the Change

Book 3.5: The Good Will Tour (novella)

Book 4: Be the Change

Book 5: Change for the Better

Through Thick and Thin (collection of short stories)

Agents of Change (the novellas and short stories in one volume)

Menopausal Superheroes Omnibus edition Vol 1

Coming soon! Menopausal Superheroes Omnibus edition Vol 2

FRIENDS OF FALSTAFF

Thank You to All our Falstaff Books Patrons, who get extra digital content each month! To be featured here and see what other great rewards we offer, go to www.patreon.com/falstaffbooks.

PATRONS

Dino Hicks
John Hooks
John Kilgallon
Larissa Lichty
Travis & Casey Schilling
Staci-Leigh Santore
Sheryl R. Hayes
Scott Norris
Samuel Montgomery-Blinn
Junkle

Thank You for Supporting Independent Publishing!

We believe that you should be able
to read your books, your way.
That's why this Falstaff Books
print edition includes a digital copy
at no additional cost!

Just scan the QR code with your device,
follow the directions on Prolific Works,
and enjoy!
You can also join our newsletter when prompted,
and never miss an awesome Falstaff Release!